D0434779

ANOTHER FAUST

DANIEL & DINA NAYERI

CANDLEWICK PRESS

Copyright © 2009 by Daniel Nayeri and Dina Nayeri Viergutz

First edition 2009

Library of Congress Cataloging-in-Publication Data is available.

Library of Congress Catalog Card Number 2008940873

ISBN 978-0-7636-3707-1

2   4   6   8   10   9   7   5   3   1

Printed in the United States of America

This book was typeset in Slimbach.

Candlewick Press
99 Dover Street
Somerville, Massachusetts 02144

visit us at www.candlewick.com

"So, who do you think we should dedicate it to?"

"I don't know. Let's just get this over with."

"What? What's the problem?"

"Nothing. I just think we should move it along."

"Well, we can't move it along until you say what's wrong."

"There's nothing wrong!"

"You're all pensive."

"What, now you're trying to police my moods?"

"Are you kidding?"

"All right, I've had enough of this. Let's just dedicate it to Oprah and get it over with."

"This is ridiculous. If you're going to be so angry, we can do this later."

"No! Let's just do it now."

"Fine! Who do you want to dedicate it to?"

"This is stupid. I'm sick of *you* dictating everything."

"You're *so* stupid, sometimes."

"*You're* stupid."

"Moooom!"

"Moooom!"

This book is dedicated to our mom.

Prologue

Five Years Previously

London

Victoria didn't have time to play. She didn't have time for friends or laughing or jumping or any other thing little kids do. Victoria was ten, but she didn't like ten-year-olds. At all the London dinner parties, her job was to shut up and look well-behaved for the adults. She would sit in a big plush armchair, her feet barely touching the floor, and she would pick the petals off a bouquet of blue hydrangeas in a nearby vase. She would quietly brood as she watched the adults circle the room, drink tea or cocktails, and comment on the sculptures in the foyer.

Her little brother, Charlie, loved parties. He let old ladies pinch his cheeks and performed Mozart concertos on his toy piano, a Steinway baby grand. He was just five, but most of his babblings were in Spanish or Greek. Victoria was not amused by him. She wanted him gone. She watched her mother hold Charlie in her arms, while he laughed a happy, oblivious laugh. Charlie was the good-looking one. Victoria straightened her thick glasses in a mirror and turned away, disgusted. She hated those unhappy parties. She hated her graphing calculator and her schoolbooks, her tutors and instruments, her frizzy hair, her packed calendar, her father's glasses, and her little brother's genius IQ.

But that hatred was exactly what drove her to try to win — like a moth to a burning lamp. Because for Victoria, only one thing in life was valuable: winning — at any cost — and *that* she knew how to do. She spent her days in a blaze of activities, never fully enjoying any of them, just concentrating on her duty to win — bringing home prizes and certificates and good grades like a starved cat bringing a dead bird to its owner.

"In this life, you have winners and losers," Victoria once announced to her startled algebra teacher. "The more you win, the higher you go. Professor at Oxford and a Nobel Prize — *that's* winning in your field. Last I checked, private tutoring is not."

Of course, she came back to the room a little later with her hands behind her back. She smiled for the nervous old lady and apologized. She had to. The hag would be grading Victoria's exams whether she was a loser or not.

Victoria hated her schoolbooks and activities because they were her best friends, and like her mother, she had learned to choose friends she didn't like. Riding, chess, piano, tennis, painting — she had tutors for each one, each unhappy like her. *You're slouching on the horse. Your moves are clumsy. Your fingers are fat. Your fingers are fat. Your fingers are fat. . . .*

Victoria's fingers *were* fat. Another imperfection to add to her father's long list. Luckily, the list wasn't all that long when it came to debate, her favorite activity, the one that let her vent her anger. "I suppose our daughter isn't all that bad," her father said once, when Victoria brought home a national trophy. No, Victoria wasn't that bad at all. During her debate rounds, Victoria could humiliate her opponents (she always did) and pretend that she was finally older, away from her parents, and powerful.

Considering they were never around much, Victoria's parents managed an enormous volume of criticism. As for family time, Victoria got their e-mails. And their occasional update meetings at breakfast were enough. Her father leafed through calendar pages and ate toast and jam as though food didn't have a taste. It could have been butter on cardboard. Her mother stirred her tea and read the *Times*.

Her father: "Vic, it says in my calendar that you had some event. . . ."

"Yeah, I had a debate."

Her mother: "Don't say *yeah*, Victoria; it's so common."

Her father: "Did you win?"

"Almost. I came second to Liddy."

Her mother: "Speaking of common . . ."

Her father: "And why would you let Liddy beat you?"

"She had a great rebuttal. I didn't anticipate —"

Her father: "Didn't anticipate? Then it stands to reason that you should lose."

"Daddy, I've won the last four —"

Her mother: "You're only as good as your last performance."

It didn't matter what they said. So what if Victoria stormed out when she lost at anything? So what if she obsessed over the paint on the ceiling, stood in front of the mirror, and tried to pluck every stray hair? So what? Victoria knew what was important. Her new debate tutor said as much; and Victoria believed. Because her new debate tutor was tall and regal, honey blond, and even prettier than Victoria's mother.

Glasgow

A few hundred kilometers away, in a less-educated part of the island, a boy named Christian was running down an alley with a bag of hamburger buns and a package of hot dogs flapping behind him. He stopped by a moldy brick wall to catch his breath. The grocer hadn't kept up, but he was hopping mad. Tomorrow the police would be looking all over Glasgow for Christian. He'd broken two of the shop's windows. He looked down at his loot. He'd grabbed the wrong buns. He took a bite of one of them. Stale as the bricks behind him. Christian didn't notice. He had eaten almost nothing for the last three days. That morning, he'd felt so faint, he got caught trying to steal a man's wallet. Christian took another bite. The day had ended better than it started. "Happy birthday to me," he said, and began to walk home.

Home was a shanty made of three sheets of corrugated metal and a mud floor. Spare tires and car parts lay discarded all around the shanty, which was settled in the hollow near a bridge. Sometimes volunteers dropped food or old coats from the overpass onto their roof; sometimes drivers tossed burnt cigarettes and dead batteries. Once someone gave a butane space heater. That was a good day. No one in the nearby town spoke to Christian, but they knew what had happened to his mom, the way his father had shut down and stopped working. They gave food, but they didn't talk to him. It made them feel good, he thought, like they really took care of their own.

His last birthday had been different. They had had a house then, and Christian had had a mother. Everything had been better. Christian's dad was a burly, red-bearded man, with a laugh as thick as the bogs. That was before his "bonnie girl" died, before his eyes went dark and he checked out of this world altogether.

Christian bent back the metal sheet and stooped down and into the hut. His dad was still asleep, wrapped in discarded coats, his beard gray and matted — a home for parasites. Christian's last birthday had fallen on the day of the Ceres Highland Games. Back then, his uncles had been around. On any given night, as recently as a year ago, the town could hear his uncles and his dad at the local tavern, singing songs, telling stories of loch dragons, or just causing a ruckus arm wrestling one another to the ground. His last birthday, Christian had won the Junior Kilted Mile and the Junior Sheaf Toss events. Like his uncles, Christian was a strong athlete. But lately, he had given up the Scottish games, preferring to listen to football games on a handheld radio he had found outside the hut. He listened with hunger, dreaming of comforts that the players might have. He wondered if he could have that someday. When he played outside with the neighborhood boys, he imagined himself signing the next big football contract, the one that would get him out of this life.

Christian gently shook his dad. "Dad, Dad, I got some food."

Christian's dad groaned and tried to open his eyes. It was still tough for him; the nights were hardest. Christian could remember the nights not long after his last birthday: the lights would be off in the one room where they both slept. Christian would lie awake and listen to the faint sound of his father, the giant, whimpering to his dreams. Christian had had to take care of things from then on. He'd been caught stealing a few times. The landlord had finally kicked them out in the middle of an evening when the rain just wouldn't stop. Christian thought to grab a few things, a picture of his mum, some coins from a coffee can, and his only prized possession, his journal — the one his mother had given him two birthdays ago, when he had asked for a series of adventure books and his mother had said, "Write your own, lad. Why rely on other people's imagination?" The truth was, they couldn't afford novels just then. On the night of the eviction, it had taken them only ten minutes to pack their belongings. His father didn't have anything he wanted to remember or keep. As a parting shot, Christian had stolen the landlord's pen.

The camping stove in their hut had run out of butane, so Christian couldn't cook the hot dogs. He cut them up and arranged them on the hamburger buns. Christian hated hot dogs. He didn't just hate them. They made him angry. They made him want to scream. For weeks, he had eaten practically nothing else. Hot dogs for breakfast. Hot dogs for lunch. Hot dogs for supper. Always in a different bun, whatever he could grab first. Of course, he hadn't told his dad how much he hated it all. He never told anyone anything — except that pretty blond lady in the park, the one with the stylish hat and long black coat, who had sat down next to him and asked all the right questions. He had told her a lot of things. Even the disturbing things, like the fact that the smell of hot dogs now made him want to hurt someone and the fact that, if he had one wish, he would no longer use it to bring his mother back.

Christian reached under his bedding — more old coats — and got out his journal. As he sat on the dirt floor, he tried to think of something beautiful to write. There was nothing beautiful in his world anymore. He wrote anyway. It was his escape, his mother's one legacy. But Christian hadn't seriously considered being a writer for a while now, because for the past few months, all he could think about was being rich and free. It was a louder desperation, and it was growing at a heart-stopping pace until it was too big and unwieldy for Christian to control. It was gargantuan now, a longing far more urgent than any other desire. *If you're poor, you can't afford to sit around dreaming up stories for your life. You follow the money.* First he would be a sports star, then he would write. First he would be rich, then he would have time for everything else.

Christian felt a sudden, searing pain across his chest. With every pump, his heart felt clenched. He put his hand inside his shirt and tried to ignore the pain. It would be better in the morning. As he squeezed his eyes closed, Christian wished for anything but this. He'd give anything not to be hungry all the time. But he didn't have anything to give, and so it was useless to wish.

A few kilometers outside Rome

Belle ran into the bedroom and plopped on the bed so that Bicé couldn't possibly ignore her. "Hey, Bicé. Would you rather be disgustingly fat all your life and go to heaven or thin and gorgeous and then go to hell?"

"What?" Bicé snorted with laughter.

"C'mon, c'mon, which would you choose? Seriously!" Belle nudged her twin sister and gave her a mischievous look.

"Belle, there is nothing serious about that question."

Belle rolled her eyes at her sister's righteous attitude. She wished Bicé would play along.

"You'd pick hell, wouldn't you?" said Bicé, her head still in a book.

"You could wear a red dress!" said Belle, determined to distract her sister.

"I'm busy, Belle. Anyway, who cares what you look like in heaven?"

"It would be forever. And I could be gorgeous," Belle said breathlessly, posing like one of the starlets she had seen on magazine covers.

"I think you're gorgeous," said Bicé with a smile.

"You think *you're* gorgeous."

"Same thing."

Bicé and Belle were identical twins — two raven-haired little girls who had an entire Italian town mesmerized. A few paces outside the big city of Rome, Belle and Bicé lived in a pretty little town with hills and tree-lined trails and old-fashioned gelato shops — the kind of town where ancient ladies, the village *madres,* still wore vintage nylon stockings and talked about handsome soldiers sweeping through the town square.

"Do you realize that you've been reading for six hours?" said Belle.

"What else am I going to do? Sit around and think about fat

people?" said Bicé without looking up. *"Ihr naht euch wieder, schwank-ende Gestalten,"* she practiced out loud. Apparently, she had moved on to German. The girls' parents were linguistic scholars and travelers. They spoke seven languages. Belle only spoke two — barely.

"You don't have to be such a show-off," said Belle as she walked to the mirror. She picked up some tweezers and looked at herself in the mirror. "They already like you best."

Belle thought about the lady from church, the one who had spoken to her mother for half an hour on Sunday. She was tall, blond, and the kind of beautiful that made Belle squirm with jealousy. "What a brilliant little girl!" she had said of Bicé. "I've never met one who speaks five languages."

"Yes, well, she enjoys it, and we like to let our daughters do what they enjoy," their mother had said. "Belle will find her niche soon too."

"And so pious," the lady had continued. "Is it true that she reads the Bible in Greek?"

Belle mumbled, "I hate being a twin," and continued inspecting the curve of her brows.

"If it would make you feel better, I'll dye my hair blue," offered Bicé. Belle laughed, despite the pain she felt in her chest. It might not be so bad sharing a face if at least it was beautiful. If she were fantastically beautiful, no one would mind that she couldn't blather out a few pleasantries in Mandarin. But Bicé had talent; there was no denying that. That was how she set herself apart from her twin. But what did Belle have?

Lost in thought, Belle stared at herself and then at her twin, her mirror image except for the tiny mole above Bicé's lip.

9 ⟨∞⟩

"You know it's not my fault," said Belle.

"I know it's not—wait—what are we talking about?"

"That you speak more languages than me."

"Maybe if you didn't spend so much time thinking about your cheekbones—"

"What's wrong with my cheekbones?" Belle's hand flew to her face.

"Don't pout," said Bicé. "It makes your face look swollen."

"You mean it makes *your* face look swollen," said Belle, pouting.

"Maybe if you didn't try so hard to be the bad one, people would give you a break."

Belle glared at Bicé for a second. Then she turned back around to the mirror. "No, they wouldn't," she said. "They'd never let me be different." Belle looked at her sister in the mirror and saw that she was hurt. Deciding to drop the topic, she plopped herself onto the bed and rested her head on her sister's lap. "Brush my hair, sis?" she said with a sweet pout. Belle could tell that Bicé wanted to say something, but for all her languages, Bicé just couldn't communicate that well. Instead Bicé just grabbed the brush and began to stroke Belle's hair, black and glossy, just like her own. It was Belle's habit to let Bicé play the mother, pretending not to notice as she struggled to say the right thing. But even Bicé couldn't give Belle what she wanted most. No one could.

Montmartre, Paris

Someone once said that "French is the language that turns dirt into romance." Valentin knew this to be true because he lived in Paris, and when he wasn't feeling romantic, he was feeling like dirt. Valentin's parents were poets in Montmartre. They sat in cafés discussing love and the "tragedy of being" with other writers, sipping on deep red wine at all hours of the day. Somehow, they managed to make a good living, selling their work to journals and luring rich benefactors to their circle.

Valentin spent his time on his own. He was free to roam around the city, "learning from life," as his father liked to say. He would walk through the streets of Paris, running errands for local shop owners, writing little poems for waitresses in exchange for cups of *chocolat*, and eavesdropping on conversations of cheery tourist families. As a result, he came to know something that most children should not have to realize until much later: that he was small and insignificant in this big world.

But as his father said, "Suffering is such sweet, stinging inspiration."

"I'm going out," said Valentin one afternoon. His father, who was already on his second bottle of wine, nodded and began to drift off to sleep. Valentin wondered why he had bothered to say anything. He walked out and thought that it was the perfect day to wheedle a few croissants out of Monsieur Genet's barmaid or to read in the bookshops until they kicked him out or to visit the beautiful lady. The beautiful lady would never ask him to leave. She would only say the most reassuring things—that he was talented and bound for greatness. Valentin wanted to be a famous poet—not because he loved poetry but because he loved fame.

As he was getting up from an evening nap on the steps of the Sacré Coeur cathedral, something grabbed Valentin's attention. In front of the massive church, in the crowd of tourists and worshippers, sat his own mother. *What's Maman doing there?* thought Valentin. *She's supposed to be meeting with her publisher.* It didn't make sense. But that was definitely his mother, and the man with her was definitely not the priggish Monsieur Brottiere. This young man was wearing paint-covered jeans, with bits of paint in his wavy hair. Valentin's first instinct was to approach them. But then he thought of his father, sitting alone, drinking himself into a stupor. He'd lost all hope in anything but the fact that his brilliant wife was going to "turn the brutish head of the world with the delicate yoke of her pen." He was an awful poet but never stopped being proud of his wife.

Valentin crept a bit closer to listen. The pair began to walk. Valentin followed them. He crept among the crowds, close behind, all the way to a neighborhood in a wealthy district of Paris. He noticed the way his mother laughed; it was different from any laugh Valentin had ever heard from her.

"Have a good afternoon?" the man asked her.

"Boring. Nothing ever happens. I got no work done."

"Well, everyone has dry spells," he said, glancing at his paint-stained shoes. "Do you want to come up?" They were standing in front of a doorway. Valentin had ducked into an alcove just a few feet away.

"All right," said Valentin's mother with a smile. "Do I get first pick of your new paintings?"

"Only if you dedicate your next poem to me," said the man playfully. He was childish, thought Valentin, not like a grown man.

"Don't be silly! Everyone would know," said his mother.

They went inside. Valentin ran dizzily into the street and waited for a light to turn on in one of the windows of the apartment building. From the dark street, he could see the walls inside. They were covered with beautiful landscape paintings of the French countryside. Valentin noticed that they were exactly like the ones his mother had given him and his father for Christmas. Night was falling over the city. Street lamps burst to life. Valentin stood there too long, watching their backlit silhouettes. Finally he picked up a rock from the gutter and sent it flying through the glass. He heard his mother scream from inside as shards fell to the ground. By the time the man's naked torso appeared at the broken window to see who'd done it, Valentin was already down the street.

At home, he found his father asleep at the table. *I would teach her a lesson*, thought Valentin angrily, *instead of cowering at the kitchen table, hugging a bottle.*

That night, when Valentin got into his bath, there was an unfamiliar spot on his chest. He tried to rub it off. But as his wet hand touched the small black dot, it only grew bigger. He lowered himself farther into the bath to wash it off. As the mark entered the water, it grew even darker and more pronounced. *What's this?* Valentin thought. *What's happening to me?* The mark was ugly, a black spot over his heart — as if his heart had exploded and spewed a black bile onto his skin. And no matter how hard he rubbed, it wouldn't go away.

 Something in Common

Victoria, Christian, Belle, and Valentin live far from each other and have never met. In fact, they are as different as four children can be . . . except for one thing.

Panic. Wherever they were, they all sat up in their beds. It was the middle of the night. *What was that?* Their nightclothes clung to their backs. When they moved, the cold sweat made their spines shake. *Just a tree branch outside.* But it didn't look like a tree branch. It looked like hair — wild, snaky hair slithering in the wind. It could be hair. It could be hallucinations. Or it could be shadows from the clouds. It could be suffering fingers, scaling the walls of their unhappy homes. It could just be the storm . . . or it could be someone outside.

No, it would seem that these children have nothing in common. But by the next morning, they all had disappeared.

Chapter 1
Our Little Game

A country house somewhere in Europe

From the outside, the house was a picture of serenity, like something out of a painting. It looked like the kind of hideaway that some pretty young family would use as a refuge from the day-to-day rush of modern life. It was tucked away in the middle of a wooded patch far from the nearest town. Surrounding the wood sat acres and acres of green meadows and rolling hills. Within the wood, there was a clearing, with patches of fragrant flowers, a few tree stumps where the little forest had been cleared, and the lonely country house.

Beyond the big wooden door, however, there were no scenes of a happy family vacation. The carefree charm of the exterior was only an illusion, because the inside of the house was shadowy, covered by patches of dark. Sometimes voices echoed, and it seemed that there were many hallways protruding this way and that. But then, after a while, the room would fill with silence once more. In a corner, partially hidden by a shadow, sat a lady. She was blond and covered from head to toe in a flowing black overcoat, as if she were afraid that a single drop of sunlight would enter the house and burn her up. She sat in the corner, reading, rocking, keeping an eye on something.

"Bicé, Bicé, wake up! Wake up right now!" Belle tried to scream in a whisper. "What's wrong with you?" But Bicé didn't move. She just lay there in the dark, breathing softly.

Belle ran out of the room, feeling her way around, to find the lady. "What did you do to my sister?" she said when she found her. Belle's voice cracked as she spoke, and she did not dare get too close. Under the gaze of the lady's mesmerizing eyes, Belle shivered and shrank away. Shrouded in the loveliness of the rest of her face, the lady's strange left eye might at first go unnoticed. Who would take the time to stare at just one eye? As subtle as a freckle or a gap in a starlet's teeth, it sat demurely on her face. The serpentine beauty of that eye was at once inviting and challenging. It pierced the shadows, an eye in league with darkness. It crept undetected into whoever dared look closely — lightless, loveless, like a kind of venom. For if you happened to catch the gaze of that eye, you might notice that unlike its quite ordinary partner, it was split into four barely distinguishable pieces, each a different shade of heaven's blue. It was as though a tiny crucifix had burned and branded it, preserving its own image while shattering the eye forever. The eye flickered, daring Belle to look.

Without a glance at Bicé's fallen form, the lady said, "She's fine, my dear. She'll be much happier now."

"What are you talking about? She's practically dead. You hurt my sister, and you promised—"

"She's not dead, dear. She just needs to rest. When she wakes up, she'll be happy, and she'll love you again, because she won't remember."

Belle ran a nervous hand through her thick black hair. "Do you promise? You promise she'll be totally normal and won't remember anything?"

"Well, dear . . . I didn't say 'totally normal.' Neither one of you was 'totally normal' when we met."

"Bicé was."

There was a moment of silence, while Belle tried to get a better look at the lady. Since the day they had met, outside her church back in Italy, Belle had found her ravishing — the most beautiful woman she had ever seen. More beautiful than her own mother. It was so easy to forget about the eye.

"You have a pretty face," Belle said, squinting to get a better look.

"You certainly do spend a lot of time thinking about pretty faces."

Belle smiled. "I'm going back to my sister." She turned to leave, but then she stopped and turned back to the lady. "I don't like the other kids very much."

"You'll grow to like them, and tonight you'll meet someone new."

"Is that where you're going?" asked Belle. "I thought it was just the four of us."

"No, dear. There's one more I need to pick up."

Belle felt a surge of excitement, and then she caught the lady's eye and felt a twinge of fear. She glanced down and ran out of the room. After fumbling around for a while, Belle managed to find the room where her sister had been sleeping. She went over to the bed and noticed that at last Bicé was stirring, and that her eyes were open.

"Good morning," Bicé said sweetly. For the first time since their last hour in Rome, she was calm, and for the first time, she was nice to Belle. Belle smiled back at her twin sister. Even in the thick darkness of this room, she could somehow see her sister's face, a perfect reflection of her own. She wondered what Bicé was thinking.

Belle waited, but Bicé didn't speak. After a while, Belle sighed. "I miss Mom," she said.

To Belle's surprise, Bicé laughed. "What are you talking about?"

Belle didn't say anything. She just waited.

"You say the weirdest things sometimes, Belle."

"Why is it so weird to miss Mom?"

"Uh, maybe because we haven't seen our natural mother since we were babies!"

Belle's heart jumped into her throat. "Riiiight." Belle couldn't believe it, but it was true. Just as the lady had said, Bicé had forgotten. She had forgotten everything. She thought they were adopted. She thought they had always been here, living with the lady since they were babies. And most important, she loved Belle again.

"Don't be scared, Bicé. At least we're together," said Belle, putting her head on her sister's shoulder. But Bicé just laughed. "Silly," she said, stroking Belle's raven hair the way she used to.

That night, the girls hid in the dark room and waited for the beautiful lady to come back. Belle watched her sister, who seemed to have returned to her happy, energetic self—despite a head full of the wrong memories—and decided that she would tell her nothing, not even later, not even when they were grown up. She would keep all of her secrets hidden. And she would wait for it all to pay off.

After a few hours of waiting, Belle and Bicé fell asleep. It was hard to tell the time, since everything was so dark and they weren't allowed to go outside. A few times, Belle was woken by Bicé mumbling in her sleep. She would moan and shout things like "I'm not supposed to be here" and "Belle, help me!" The lady had said it would be like this for a while. Belle was still groggy when she heard a long, slow creak, and two sets of footsteps growing louder. She could hear someone taking quick, shallow breaths. She ran out of the room to see for herself.

"Meet your new family, Christian," said the lady to the red-headed boy who was with her. He looked around nervously, squinting to see better. Just then, another pair of feet shuffled past Belle, who was hovering in the hall. It was that horrible girl, Victoria, whom Belle had just met and whom Bicé assumed she had known since they were babies.

"What is this, an orphanage?" the boy asked the lady.

"No, dear, you're not orphans. I'm your mother now."

"I'm Victoria. I got here first."

Belle took a few steps toward Christian. He was wearing a pair of torn jeans and a tattered shirt that said Celtic 31. "Why are you so dirty?" she asked.

Christian mumbled some excuse about playing football outside and a broken tub.

"In my house, Christian, you'll have anything in the world," said the lady in a cold, soothing tone. That was when Christian noticed someone moaning in another room, begging for help.

"I . . . I don't think I belong here," he said as he looked around.

"Of course you do, darling. You all do."

Just then, Bicé screamed again and Christian jumped. "Who was that?"

"Oh, that's nothing, dear."

"I . . . I don't know who you are, or what this is. But I don't want to be here."

"But you do, Christian."

"No, I don't. I'm sorry I ever took up with you." Christian was panting loudly and began to slowly back away.

"It's a pity," said the lady.

"No, it's not! Now let me go! I want to leave—"

Belle looked away for only a moment. In the next instant, a cold wind blew through the house, causing the lady's black robes to flutter all around her. The lady stepped out of her corner, into the speck of light coming through the window. From the constant dark of the room, Belle thought she saw a horrible look pass over the lady's face, like a gargoyle or a gorgon. *Is she some kind of monster?* Belle asked herself.

With a beastly surge, the lady overtook Christian, her robes floating hungrily over them both, stifling the terrified yelp Belle thought she heard. Then Christian was lying motionless on the floor, an anguished look frozen on his face. The lady stepped away from the speck of light and withdrew to her corner, like a satisfied predator. She sank back into her chair, smiling again, lovely as ever.

For a few seconds, Belle was too stunned to move. Then she crept closer to the lady, to the chair in the corner where the light didn't dare go. Even now, Belle couldn't help but think about this strange woman's incredible beauty. She spotted a letter on a decrepit side table, discarded next to the lady, who was sitting in her chair, her back turned to Belle. She was running her long, elegant fingers over the yellowing paper like a toy. Carelessly she picked at the edges with her manicured fingers. Belle didn't want to get any closer, but she didn't have to in order to read the letter. It was written in a big childish hand.

> To: *Phineas the Fence, Celtic 31*
> From: *Christian W.*

Dear Mr. The Fence,

You were dead brilliant in yesterday's match! How do you do that spin kick where the ball goes off to one side like that? Did you always have those wicked uniforms? What d'you do with the ones you outgrow?

Just writing because I'm needing to work out some important grown-up bussiness. I got responsibleties now, and I'm bigger, so I got a serious sort of question for ye, which is how do I get brilliant enough to be a salary player and where do I sign up? You can tell me because I'm not just a kid. I've got someone to care for now and all that. He's gone a bit mental, and he needs me. So I'm gonna handle things. For the sake of him and me.

So what's the worst thing you've ever done? What's the worst thing you'd do? If someone offered, and considering you probably have people to watch over too? I reckon I'd do just about anything.

> *Your mate,*
> *Christian*

P.S. If you're tossing your old uniforms, maybe I could have one?

Belle felt her face flush. She ran back toward the red-haired boy in the Celtic shirt.

"What'd you do to him?" she demanded of the lady as she knelt by the boy and felt his cold face. She put her cheek against his and held his hand as Victoria poked him with her foot. Belle pushed Victoria away and looked up at the lady for an answer.

The lady didn't turn around. She just sat there, stroking the stolen letter.

"Girls, it seems that, like Bicé, Christian won't be joining our little game."

Chapter 2
A Christmas Dinner

By the light of burning beeswax and the flicker of several enflamed bees madly flying about her chamber, she read the Book of Human History and wondered if they (humans, not bees) were entirely made of Pride and Fear. She would study this further in the next millennium. The shadows of the room fled from her, shaking like terrified prisoners. She turned the pages; they crackled at the edges like dead skin. Caesars, warlords, queens, and generals, politicians, popes, and celebrities—she smiled. A few bees gave up and sputtered to the floor. Human history is full of great men, great women, individuals with the will for power—all of them with governesses like her. Chambermaids, midwives, wet nurses, babysitters, stepmothers, different faces throughout the ages, to mask an ugliness dark and deep. She turned to the last page; the book groaned. A charred black hive screeched above her, fell like a ruined city. She laughed at the thought of her children. She would surpass all of the others, the most celebrated of angels, because none of them had ever had five.

New York

Where would you find five lost children after so many years gone by? In that little country house in the wooded patch? On a street in Copenhagen? An orphanage in Madrid? Some far-flung part of the world? Perhaps each of them would have found their own way in some corner of society, getting by on whatever wits or talents they managed to develop. Did Victoria still rage? Did Bicé still study? Had Christian grown into a thief? No one knew, and in any case, no one looked for them; no one ever shed a tear. In an instant, their teachers, friends — even their parents — had forgotten that the children ever existed. They never even felt the void. And so the world went on as it should, with no mention of strange disappearances or midnight kidnappings. Mothers didn't clutch their children tighter in the streets. Governesses didn't watch their kids any closer. Except, of course, for one.

Nicola Vileroy called herself a governess, though she looked anything but. She was tall and beautiful, with a hive of blond hair tied neatly into a bun, a face as radiant as a morning star, and a figure as smooth and willowy as a champagne flute. She was French, with a thick captivating accent, and the face and manner of a fifty-year-old woman who was used to good things. If you believed she was a governess, you would think she governed a prince.

On Christmas Eve, Madame Vileroy stood, looking very satisfied, in a big luxurious ballroom in New York City. This was the moment she, and her children, would step into the Upper East Side scene and would become its focus. Now that her children were well prepared, now that she had taught them enough, she could finally give them everything she had promised, everything that they had bargained for — here in this city where life is lived in the present, where today's moguls are yesterday's nobodies, and where no one cares to delve too far into the past — a city that asks no questions.

At the annual Wirth family Christmas Eve dinner, three hundred overdressed partygoers were mingling in a room decorated with fresh flowers and a forest of candles. Around the room stood several Christmas trees hung with decorations and banked by heavy presents.

Adorned in lush shades of green and gold and illuminated by sparkling tables covered with winter flowers, the ballroom was one of New York's finest. On one side of the room, windows reached from floor to ceiling, and through a rich layer of silk, the partygoers could gaze at the New York skyline, almost obscured by a soft, thick dusting of snow. New in town but already on every guest list, Nicola Vileroy slid across the room, seemingly everywhere at once.

She had arrived at the party with her pack of five teenagers — all striking and strange. When they stood at the entrance, every conversation had halted, replaced by craning necks and fascinated whispers. Mrs. Wirth, the hostess, and Mrs. Spencer, her best friend, stared from across several tables. Mrs. Spencer, the taller of the two, had to lean down to whisper to her friend, the slightly portly, bottle-blond maven of New York society. Though she was several years younger (and far prettier), Mrs. Spencer instructed Mrs. Wirth like a child. Once directed toward the newcomers, the hostess squinted her over-lined eyes until her pupils disappeared behind a curtain of green eye shadow. Mrs. Spencer tucked a shiny brown curl into her elegant twist and grabbed Mrs. Wirth's pudgy arm. The five teenagers stood around Madame Vileroy, surveying the room.

"Who's that?" asked Mrs. Spencer, eyeing the beautiful governess.

"Oh, that's Madame Vileroy," Mrs. Wirth replied. "I met her last week. She's French." Mrs. Wirth was impressed with all things French.

"And the kids?" Particularly interesting was the tall, gorgeous blonde, standing by Vileroy's side, wearing a shimmery red dress that changed shades in every light. She was the most beautiful girl in the room, even among the adults — and the semi-adult trophy wives of certain bankers.

"They're hers," Mrs. Wirth replied. "All fifteen years old. I assume they're adopted."

"And you met her last week?"

"She was with her daughter. The tall, blond one." Mrs. Wirth took another sip of her champagne.

Lurking behind the beautiful one was another young girl, with raven hair and a mole on her upper lip. She was much shorter, which seemed fitting, since she seemed to be looking for a place to hide. She wore a tiny old-fashioned clip in her hair but looked younger than the others. The only bit of resemblance between any of the children was the way this girl's blue-green eyes matched those of the blonde. Despite their other differences in appearance, their eyes were identical.

"But you finalized your invitation list months ago," objected Mrs. Spencer.

"Oh, yes, it was the strangest thing."

Mrs. Spencer squinted at her friend. "You never give out last-minute invitations. Last year you wouldn't give an invitation to that woman who donated a wing to Marlowe."

"Yes, well, I was out to lunch with a few friends, and we sort of collided with her, I suppose. I felt . . . compelled to invite her."

"But you refused to invite my sister when she was visiting for cancer treatment."

"I know," Mrs. Wirth mused. "I just like her."

"And you didn't invite your sister-in-law."

"I thought I made it clear that I happen to *like* this person."

Mrs. Spencer laughed, and then abruptly stopped laughing.

"Well, she must be their nanny or something. It can't be adoption. Who adopts five teenagers?"

"Honestly, does it really matter?"

"You *must* be curious. They *are* your friends now," said Mrs. Spencer with a hint of sarcasm. Mrs. Wirth decided to ignore her jealous friend.

"I do know one thing. They're going to Marlowe."

"What?"

"Is that important?" Mrs. Wirth asked with that ever-clueless expression that annoyed Mrs. Spencer so much.

"Yes! Five kids moving here with their nanny in the middle of the year, suddenly gaining spots at the most selective school in the city — they must be special, or astronomically wealthy, or prodigies. They're competition, Genevieve. I swear, you're so naive."

"You're so paranoid."

"Well, I'm going to find out more," said Mrs. Spencer.

"Nicola! Welcome," said Mrs. Wirth as she held out her hands to Madame Vileroy, who nodded as she removed her gloves. Mrs. Spencer glanced curiously over Madame Vileroy's shoulder toward the children but was afraid to speak since the governess had not yet made a sound. Vileroy's quartered eye, though smiling and a tranquilizing blue, made them shrink back and squint, then lean in to look closer, wondering if this was some new trend in contact lenses.

"Would you like to meet my children?" offered Madame Vileroy. The two ladies nodded like pups. Mrs. Spencer made a motion to move toward the blonde, but something kept her back. It was a sickly sweet smell, like vomit and honeysuckle. When she looked up, Madame Vileroy was introducing a muscular boy with a thick jaw and reddish hair. He looked shy and stood with his head down. He had a dull, melancholy look on his face, and he stayed close to his nervous sister, the shorter one with the mole and raven hair, as if he were her protector and she were his pet.

"This is Christian," said Madame Vileroy, waving the athletic redhead forward.

"Pleased to meet you," said the boy. Without smiling, he extended his hand.

"Christian Vileroy," said Mrs. Spencer as she took his hand after Mrs. Wirth.

"Faust, actually," said Christian blankly, never really making eye contact. "Christian Faust." He repeated his new name, the name Madame Vileroy had given them.

Mrs. Wirth and Mrs. Spencer glanced at each other. *Nanny, then. She must be the nanny.*

Madame Vileroy then looked over at a serious-looking brunette with a head full of tidy, brown waves and a calculating face. The girl stepped forward enthusiastically. She was wearing a long-sleeved velvety dress, glasses, and a gold necklace with the letter *V* at the center. Somehow, she gave the impression that she was vying to position herself close to Madame Vileroy.

"Victoria Faust," said the girl while scanning everything and everyone in sight. Mrs. Spencer was about to make a comment when another one of the children stepped forward. He was thin with high cheekbones and long eyelashes as black as ink and feathered like a quill. His blond hair was curled in tight couplets, and he had deep dimples in both cheeks. He had a smile on his face that was both sweet and probing, the kind of smile that would have been disconcerting if he were older, or less handsome.

"I'm Valentin. Thank you for inviting us," he said, smiling his charming, dimpled smile.

Mrs. Wirth suddenly felt guilty for gossiping about them. Then, as Valentin's smile changed, becoming more intense and less childlike, she felt a bit exposed. He cast a glance at her dress, with the confidence of a fully grown man, and suddenly she felt a little naked.

"You're very welcome, dear . . . and your . . . um . . . sister?" She figured that this was a safe assumption at this point. Valentin grabbed the hand of his raven-haired sister, who was still hiding behind Christian, and said, "This is Bicé."

When he saw that his sister's eyes seemed to be glazing over, he gave her a small nudge in the ribs. She gave an eerie nervous laugh and extended her hand.

"And of course, the lovely Belle," said Mrs. Wirth, eyeing the tall blonde she had met at the restaurant.

The girl stepped forward, nodded at Mrs. Wirth, and shook Mrs. Spencer's hand. Mrs. Spencer suddenly felt the contents of her stomach rising in her throat. She swallowed hard.

"H-hello," she said with a short smile before taking an unnaturally large step backward. Feeling rather dizzy and revolted, she glanced back at Belle, who was now staring at the floor and had taken a step back too. Was that smell coming from her? Mrs. Spencer was curious, but not curious enough to step any closer. It was the strangest smell, like something dirty bathed in citrus air freshener. Meanwhile, Mrs. Wirth seemed not to notice at all. She was chatting with Madame Vileroy and trying to get more information about the family. As they moved farther inside and gave their coats to one of the doormen, Mrs. Spencer regained her composure and brought up the subject of school.

"I understand the children are starting at Marlowe after the holidays."

"Yes," answered Madame Vileroy.

"I've never heard of anyone being admitted midyear. . . ."

"These children are quite exceptional."

"*Really?* Well, I'm sure you know that most students at Marlowe are exceptional."

"I'm sure," said Madame Vileroy.

"Then how are yours different?"

"To start, Bicé speaks twenty-three languages."

"I beg your pardon?"

"Would you like a demonstration?"

Bicé emerged from nowhere and opened her mouth to speak when Mrs. Wirth, shaking off her stunned silence, jumped in.

"Oh, let's not get into school discussions now, ladies. We'd all rather enjoy the party."

She grabbed a glass of champagne from a passing waiter and gave it to Madame Vileroy.

"*Merci*," said Madame Vileroy with a satisfied smile.

After Mrs. Wirth and Mrs. Spencer had gone to greet more guests, Madame Vileroy pulled her children close to her. They gathered around as she looked at them proudly. "My precious children," she said, "I want you to have fun tonight. I have a surprise for you when we get home."

She gave each of them an unnerving saccharine smile. From across the room, she looked the very picture of innocence, a loving mother. In fact, Madame Vileroy wasn't so unlike other mothers. Like them, she had big plans for her children. She wanted to give them the things they desired. She wanted them to be successful and to remain heedful of the lessons she had taught them. But she wanted so much more from these five children. She had chosen them for their potential, for their willingness, and most of all, for their weaknesses. In this, she was very unlike most mothers, who love their children even for their flaws and frailties, because Madame Vileroy loved only the weaknesses themselves. She loved Belle's hatred of her own true self. She loved Victoria's blind hunger for power and Valentin's quest for importance. She even loved Christian's dual nature, with ever-competing desires that left him always fighting with himself. And Bicé, well . . . perhaps with time, the governess would uncover some frailty to love. After all, Madame Vileroy was an extremely skilled governess, and she specialized in these very weaknesses.

The kids turned and dispersed into the party. Christian and Valentin trotted up to a table of food, cracking jokes with each other. Belle, who already had a few admirers staring at her from various corners of the room, sauntered casually to the bar. Victoria glanced at the mingling circles of young people, wondering which ones would be the most useful. As they scattered, Bicé's eyes followed them, though her feet didn't move. She stood alone in the entranceway, like a turtle without its shell, avoiding the eyes of any of the teenagers looking her way. Gone was the confident Bicé of Rome, even the happy Bicé in the cabin. This Bicé was only scared — and mad at Belle for leaving her here. She fidgeted a bit, chewing her nails and glancing at her feet. More than anything, this Bicé was scared of new people — so unlike the way she had been only five years before. As more and more groups took notice of her, her hands folded in front, her shoulders drooping, Bicé began to sway back and forth, as if she were trying to create enough momentum to run out of there.

A group of trendy-looking sixteen-year-olds stood close by, whispering to one another in hushed tones and glancing over their shoulders. Once in a while, one would say something to make them all laugh out loud. Bicé shrank into herself. The entranceway felt like a stadium, a huge open space, with no protection in sight. She turned to leave, only to run straight into a coat checker, who dropped an armful of coats and hangers. The teenagers cackled as Bicé tried to apologize and help the young man, who brushed her away. She stood there, on the verge of tears, when a confident-looking brunette shushed her friends, broke from the crowd, and walked over, all the while trying to stifle her laughter.

"Here, take this." The girl handed Bicé a champagne glass filled with sparkling cider. Bicé turned around just in time to grab the glass.

"I'm Lucy Spencer," the girl said while casting backward glances to her friends.

"Hi, Lucy," said Bicé, confused and thankful. Her eyes darted back to the group of teenagers, afraid that this was some kind of prank. Meanwhile, Lucy was already walking toward the center of the room, almost expecting Bicé to follow.

"Bicé, is it? Wanna go sample the sushi bar? It's from Nobu."

Bicé nodded. "What's Nobu?" she asked, and Lucy thought how naive and uncultured this poor girl must be, while Bicé tried to pinpoint Nobu among the dozen Japanese cities she had visited. *It must be near Hakone,* she thought.

"I'll introduce you to my best friend, Charlotte," Lucy said almost distractedly, and then she moved on to the main point: wheedling information. "Do you go to Marlowe?"

Bicé nodded again. She didn't quite remember.

"Are you going to the school play?"

Bicé shrugged. "I guess so. . . ."

"Then you might meet her," said Lucy. "She wrote it, you know."

Just then, Victoria came pouncing toward them, both eyes strictly fixed on Lucy.

Bicé blanched. Victoria could always be counted on to say something embarrassing.

"So *you're* that girl that's been top of the class for three years?" said Victoria with her arms crossed. When a confused look appeared on Lucy's face, Victoria added, "There was a list on the Internet."

Bicé sighed.

"Yeah, so?" Lucy said, almost defensively. Bicé stood by, trying the sushi and not saying a word. Unlike Victoria, Bicé hated conflict, and it wasn't as if she wanted a new friend all that much. She just wanted to get through the party.

"And what does it take? To be the best at Marlowe," asked Victoria.

"Just the best GPA, I guess. Same as everywhere else," said Lucy.

"What's *your* GPA?"

"What?" Lucy almost choked on her drink.

"Victoria! Don't start, OK?" Bicé begged. It was hard to remember the last time anyone outside the family had shown any interest in her — and now Vic was wrecking it.

"That's OK. You don't have to tell me. I just want to know how it all works," said Victoria.

"Oh, well, it's just the standard five-point system. You can get up to five points for advanced classes and up to four points for regular."

"Right . . . OK, then . . . we know how it works," said Bicé, hoping Victoria would go away.

"I bet there're a lot of people with a solid five, then," said Victoria.

Lucy took another sip of her drink. "Oh, no. It's not possible to get a five on average. Even people who win the Marlowe Prize never get that high. Everyone has to take a health class and phys. ed., and both of those are only worth four."

"Tragic . . ." Bicé mumbled.

"Huh," Victoria said, pretending she found it all to be very much beneath her. "What about college?"

"What *about* college?" Lucy was obviously starting to get annoyed with all the questions.

"At my last school," said Victoria, "most of the kids went to Harvard, except for the ones that went abroad."

"Marlowe is the best school in the country," Lucy said. "The kids go wherever they want."

"See, Vic? People go wherever . . ." Bicé jumped in. "Lucy, I'm sure Vic appreciates all this help. Now, moving on . . ."

"Hush, Bicé." Victoria didn't even bother to look at Bicé as she spoke. She gave Lucy a challenging look. "I bet *I* can get a perfect 5.0."

"Then I hope you have lupus, because otherwise you're not getting out of gym," said Lucy. "And even Michael Jordan wouldn't get more than 4.0 in gym."

"At my last school," said Victoria, "there was this one adviser that you had to know to have any kind of a shot at the best colleges."

"It's not like that here," said Lucy, growing a bit hostile. "Everyone gets a good counselor. They're assigned. Look, if you'll excuse me . . ."

"Excuse you? I don't care where you go. I was just making conversation," Victoria said, her arms still crossed.

Victoria was never very good at keeping people in a conversation. She could be sweet when she tried. But when she wanted information, she had a way of making people feel more guarded, violated — and not just because she asked the most prying questions. She didn't mind if they thought her rude and didn't answer. It was enough for her just to ask. She kept Lucy talking for five minutes more, and she found out a lot more than Lucy suspected. She found out that Lucy was a very unhappy girl, pushing herself almost as hard as Victoria, not because she wanted to but because her mother, Mrs. Spencer, didn't think her daughter was worth much without a name-brand résumé. Lucy and Victoria were a lot alike. She found out that Lucy was running for class president and that she was working on a big paper to impress Ms. LeMieux, one of the college counselors at Marlowe—because at Marlowe, it really *was* like that.

Ms. LeMieux had gone to Yale and had been in the Yale admissions office. Everyone thought a letter from her was a ticket into the Ivy League. Ms. LeMieux knew this and used it to her advantage. She was a boastful and unkind woman who showed blatant favoritism and used her students to boost her social position. Most of the students at Marlowe hated her, but everyone pretended they were close to her. For that reason, this unfashionable, unlikable woman's favor had become a must-have for the over-achieving kids at Marlowe.

Victoria knew all this not because Lucy had told her any of it. In fact, Lucy had gone out of her way to hide most of it. But that didn't matter, because Victoria knew how to cheat. Or that's what Madame Vileroy called it. *Cheating.* Whenever Lucy would look away or into her drink, wondering how to answer, Victoria would peer deeper, boring into Lucy's mind for her inner dialogue—one that Victoria could hear just as well as any spoken exchange.

~☞☜~

Christian and Valentin were stuffing éclairs in their mouths at a table across the room when a girl in a light green dress and long curly red hair approached. She stood several feet away from them, casually looking away, until Christian and Valentin could do nothing but introduce themselves. Charlotte Hill was never at a loss for boyfriends, but for some reason, she was ignoring them all in favor of meeting the new kids. She was always dramatic like that. Maybe that's why she was such a good writer at such a young age. After a few minutes, she fell into comfortable conversation with Christian, even though he was the less handsome of the two. Valentin's debonair quips weren't making much of an impression on Charlotte, not as much as Christian's clumsy attempts at humor, which she'd decided after ten minutes was not an act. She kept giggling into her hand and touching his arm as he turned a deeper and deeper shade of crimson and Valentin rolled his eyes for the thousandth time. She seemed to be having a wonderful time, until all of a sudden from behind her, a door flung open as a troupe of waiters walked out with fresh canapés. The door slammed into the small of Charlotte's back, sending her splaying forward. Just before she fell into the table, Christian caught her in his arms, so that she spilled only a few drops of her drink.

"Thanks," said Charlotte with a laugh, and then, since they were already so close, gave him a little kiss on the cheek. Christian was fifteen and handsome, but he had never been this close to a girl before. Something inside him gave a lurch, and for a second, he didn't know what to do next — and then it was too late. Charlotte's body suddenly went limp in Christian's arms. Like a rag doll, she collapsed to the ground. The music stopped. Everyone turned to see a stunned Christian standing over an unconscious Charlotte — and Valentin, chuckling nearby.

"Way to sweep her off her feet," said Valentin as a group of women came rushing up to help Charlotte.

Christian was appalled at himself. "I didn't mean to . . . she just . . . I was nervous and —"

"You put her in a coma," said Valentin, not minding as people pushed past him to make a crowd. Christian had gotten so tense with Charlotte in his arms that for a second, he lost control. He had never done that before, lost control of his gift. A gift — that's what Vileroy called it, because Christian was the most gifted of thieves. With the smallest touch, Christian could *steal* whatever he needed from anyone. He could take anything, and no one would know. Christian felt a rush of energy. *Charlotte's* energy.

Mrs. Wirth made her way through the crowd. "I think she hit her head," she shouted. "The door must have hit her head."

"Help me!" said Christian, gritting his teeth at Valentin. "Just shut up and help."

"You seem to be doing a fine job," said Valentin.

Meanwhile, next to them, ladies were kneeling beside Charlotte, fanning her face. A man was frantically calling an ambulance on his phone.

"Just fix this, Val," said Christian.

"But then you won't remember that enchanted moment."

"Do it."

"Fine," said Valentin, "but you owe me. Not that you'll remember." He closed his eyes and slipped a hand into his pocket. From Christian's perspective, Valentin's face froze, a quick nothingness fell over him, a blink, then he was standing again with Charlotte prattling on about her last short story. Christian blinked a few times. He remembered nothing. No one remembered anything. The crowd had never rushed over. Charlotte had never collapsed in Christian's arms. The waiters had never slammed open the door. Valentin opened his eyes and smiled. Only he remembered.

To Charlotte and Christian, it was no more than a hiccup. Valentin was saying something, and then his speech jumped and he continued on. He quoted something from literature, and when Charlotte looked impressed he added, "It's a fa-famous quote." Just like that. He landed in the middle of his own sentence. Nothing unusual. Just a boy with a speech impediment. Valentin's speech had skipped several times in this conversation. His face had twitched, like someone with Tourette's syndrome. Usually, it happened just before he said something funny or witty or flirtatious. Just before he delivered his best lines. *It must be nerves,* thought Charlotte, her attention turning from Christian to Valentin.

Valentin listened to Charlotte talk about her play for a while, the one that would be held at Marlowe the day after Christmas. "Basically, it's an ancient conspiracy story that Christopher Marlowe — that's our school namesake — actually faked his own death and wrote under the assumed name 'William Shakespeare,' " she said, her eyes widening. "And there're a few musical numbers . . ."

But before Charlotte could finish her description, Valentin reached over and grabbed her hand. He pulled her away from Christian, just as the door swung open and the army of waiters filed out.

"Thanks," Charlotte said, sidling closer to Valentin to let another waiter pass.

"My pleasure." He winked at her. Charlotte pecked *Valentin* on the cheek this time.

"Nice save," said Christian. He went back to the éclairs, hardly realizing what Valentin had done or that for a split second Charlotte had seemed to be someone he might like.

~☙☙☙~

"Having fun?" said Madame Vileroy, suddenly appearing over Victoria's shoulder as she watched Bicé surprise Lucy by getting them some off-menu treats with her perfect Japanese requests to the sushi chef.

"That Lucy girl is a liar." Victoria sneered, remembering all the things Lucy hadn't said.

"We should introduce her to Valentin," said Madame Vileroy.

"There's a counselor that plays favorites."

"Oh? Is Lucy her favorite?"

"Not for long."

"Why, Victoria, my dear, didn't you know that cheaters never prosper?"

Victoria looked amused. She pulled aside a waiter holding a tray of crab puffs to whisper in his ear.

"You!" Victoria said to the waiter. "Do you know who Mrs. Spencer is?"

"No, miss," said the waiter.

"She's that crow in the peacock dress."

The waiter looked uncomfortable, not knowing what to say.

"I'll give you"—Victoria looked him in the eyes, listening to the excited numbers in his head, assessing his price—"a hundred dollars if you go over there and introduce yourself as Ethan—from the Devonshire Club." She put the bills in his breast pocket without waiting for him to accept.

As the waiter nodded and walked away, Victoria said to Madame Vileroy, "Ethan's the guy Lucy dated last year. Spencer never saw him in person, but Lucy told her that he was a trust-fund baby. And now she'll think he's really a waiter. That should make for"— Victoria looked at her watch—"a good five minutes of entertainment."

Madame Vileroy gave a soft laugh.

Victoria turned and walked back toward Lucy and Bicé, to revel in what Lucy didn't know was coming. Madame Vileroy kept pace, holding her position just over Victoria's shoulder. Victoria approached

Lucy and spoke without waiting for either girl to turn around.

"So you have a boyfriend?" she asked Lucy abruptly.

"What?" Lucy turned, shocked that Victoria was back, and still so graceless.

"Oh, Vic, please . . ." Bicé whispered, shocked at Victoria's behavior. "There's no need to do that . . ."

"Shut it, Bicé. I'm just getting to know our new friend." Victoria smiled, listening to Lucy's personal thoughts of Thomas Goodman-Brown, whom she called *the smartest, nicest, hottest guy . . . ever.* And then, as Victoria waited, Lucy thought, *Is she after Thomas? Where is he?* Lucy whipped around to scan the room for Thomas. She found him, and Victoria followed her eyes to see a young man with deep-set smiling eyes talking to his friend. Victoria noticed Belle hovering nearby, watching him closely. Lucy may have noticed as well. She turned back to Victoria.

"What?" she said again.

"Nothing," said Victoria.

Lucy just shook her head and turned back to Bicé. "So you were telling me what comes after *arigato.*"

Bicé was excited to talk about something she knew and was just about to answer when Victoria blurted out, *"Gozaimasu."* She gave Bicé an unfriendly smile, as if she expected her to be amazed, but Bicé knew that Victoria spoke no Japanese. She just couldn't stop cheating. Lucy was still looking at Bicé. She rolled her eyes, ignored Victoria, and started to ask Bicé another question.

Before she could, Victoria interrupted again. "Taking lessons from Bicé? I thought you were the smartest girl in school?"

Lucy forgot all about Bicé and turned to Victoria. Bicé sighed, finally giving up, and grabbed another cider from a passing waiter. *So much for that,* she said to herself.

"What are you, like, the *Princeton Review*?" Lucy said, warning Victoria with her eyes.

Victoria loved to make people angry, but she was too much of a coward to rise to most overt challenges. "No, I'm, *like*, not impressed," she mumbled with arms crossed and eyes averted.

"Look, I don't know what your problem is, but—"

Just then, Lucy noticed her mother storming toward her, holding a crab puff as though it were evidence in a murder trial.

"Lucy!" she said, almost turning her ankle in her high heels.

Lucy spied a malicious grin on Victoria's face. Victoria heard her think, *Oh, please don't let her do this here.*

Waving the puff in her face, Mrs. Spencer repeated, "A waiter? A *waiter*?" over and over again, as if it were an unforgivable crime. She grabbed her daughter by the elbow and pulled her away. As Lucy followed, she turned back to glare at Victoria. She just knew Victoria had something to do with this—and maybe Bicé did too.

Bicé caught the look and tried to say something, anything, to distance herself from what was going on, to tell Lucy how much she appreciated the little friendliness she had shown, but no words came. And then Lucy was gone.

"Well, that worked," said Victoria with a satisfied sigh. "Now, about that counselor woman."

Victoria marched off, leaving Bicé friendless again, and alone with Madame Vileroy.

"There, there, Bicé, I'll be your friend," said Madame Vileroy.

Belle watched a group of kids her age from a distance. She was watching one boy in particular, her heart pounding hard, as she observed how nice he looked, the way he moved, the way he held his drink. She recited to herself all that Vileroy had told her about Thomas. He was the only son of Charles Goodman-Brown, an important banker, whose wife, Thomas's mother, had died only a few years before. She smoothed her red dress as she remembered Thomas's favorite color. Thomas was Belle's prize, because being the most beautiful wasn't anything without the most popular boy. And in Belle's world, being desired was everything. But in that moment, as she watched Thomas with his friends, she forgot that for five years, she had been obsessed with this one thing—and that he was just a part of a larger scheme. In that moment, Belle only felt scared. She was not used to being so beautiful, and she had to remind herself not to feel so embarrassed, so inadequate.

Belle put down her glass, smoothed her dress for the fiftieth time, and headed toward the bar. She looked at the group of teenagers just in time to catch the eye of the tall, brown-haired boy named Thomas Goodman-Brown. She held his gaze for a second and smiled, her heart jumping into her throat when he smiled back. She turned back toward the bartender, who was moving away from her. She grew more nervous. Next to her, a tall crystal vase held a bouquet of winter flowers. She touched one of the flowers with the tip of her finger, watching as the water beneath it yellowed. She sighed. Everywhere she went, people ran. Those who stayed past the first few minutes were like addicts under her spell. And now she was steps away from the first person she would ever actually try to hold on to—the first addict she wouldn't let break free. A few paces away, a young couple whispered to each other. As they walked past, the woman placed a pack of breath mints inches from Belle's hand. Looking at the mints, Belle wanted to cry. Things like this happened all the time, and each time, she felt completely alone. This was Belle's curse. She had given up all she had to be beautiful, to be loved, and in gaining beauty, she had become repugnant. Madame Vileroy said that it built character, because before anyone could fall under her spell, she had to hold them through this repulsive phase — the lonely phase.

~◦◦◦◦◦

Dinner was announced, and everyone began to work their way toward their assigned tables. Christian walked over to Bicé.

"How's it going?" he asked her as they sat down at their table. Christian was the only person that made Bicé feel comfortable. She sighed. "Where do I start? Belle wants Thomas, but she makes everyone sick. And earlier, Victoria practically gave Lucy a nosebleed she cheated so much."

"No way. She cheated, right in front of everyone?"

"Yeah. She's probably going to start all that crap about needing special treatment again. . . ."

Christian waited for Bicé to say something more, but she remained silent.

"You were talking to that girl for a while," said Christian.

"Lucy? She was nice to me."

"Made friends?"

"Victoria ruined it . . . again."

Bicé was folding and unfolding her napkin, trying not to look up.

Christian mumbled, "I'm sorry."

"Hey, did you meet Connor Wirth?" Bicé asked.

"Yeah, we talked about sports. He's cool."

"You know you're probably going to want to steal from him."

"Maybe not."

"Sorry to break it to you, but he's one of the best athletes, and you don't like to lose."

Christian groaned and plopped his head on Bicé's shoulder. She patted him like a good mother.

They sat silently for a minute. A waiter came by to take their empty glasses.

"This is kinda nice," said Christian.

"What's nice?"

"Christmas. We've never had one before." Madame Vileroy didn't allow Christmas. It was one of her only rules.

"We've watched them."

"It's not the same."

"We should be grateful," said Bicé. "Who else would have taken in five abandoned babies?"

"Yeah, but she turned us into freaks," said Christian.

"She was trying to protect us. And don't tell me you don't like it, Mr. Junior Olympics."

"It has its moments." He shrugged. "She kept you and Belle together."

"And helped Belle become totally different from me."

Christian knew that was a sore subject, so he didn't push it. Bicé had watched Belle's transformation over the past five years quietly. But Christian knew how it made her feel. For the first ten years of their lives, Belle and Bicé had been inseparable. Christian remembered that. He had foggy memories of living with the twins and Victoria and Valentin ever since they were toddlers. Belle and Bicé had been closer than any of the five. And then suddenly, five years ago, Belle decided that she had to be beautiful. And so she began to change. Christian couldn't figure out why Madame Vileroy had just given her what she wanted—so easily, with no bargains or consequences. But she had—like so many of the gifts she gave—and Christian had never been very good at figuring out why Madame Vileroy did anything.

"Speak of the devil," said Bicé. Christian looked up.

Madame Vileroy took a seat across the table and picked up a fork. Belle arrived and took a seat next to Madame Vileroy. Belle always sat next to Madame Vileroy. Belle's other side was usually empty, except for the occasional poor soul who had spent *too* much time lurking around her—at first enduring out of politeness or curiosity, then forgetting and sucking in the tainted air, then following her everywhere to feed an addiction. Across the room, people were still staring at Belle. Staring and talking. And so Belle was content.

The table eventually filled with all five kids, Madame Vileroy, a couple, each of whom was at least seventy years old, and a few others. For the lack of anyone else to talk to, Bicé had turned to the older couple next to her. They seemed to be able to amuse her, and they didn't notice her awkwardness. The old man liked how this little girl laughed at his jokes, and so he kept talking about wars and droughts and everything that's wrong with kids today. Once, Madame Vileroy said something to the old man—something benign, like "I remember that." And he bristled and turned white, as if he knew her and she wanted something from him. Madame Vileroy just smiled her honey-sweet, molasses smile and whispered something to Belle.

Throughout, Christian concentrated on his meal while Valentin tried to pull him into conversation. "Did you meet anyone you liked? Did you see Victoria handle things with Lucy? Do you want my dinner roll?"

The only response Valentin got was when Christian snapped up the bread. Christian's indifference was fine with Valentin. He was a self-amuser.

A pretty girl passed by the table.

"Wanna see something cool?" Valentin asked Christian.

"Sure," he said. Then he waited a minute. Valentin had a massive grin on his face. A waiter tripped and fell. The girl gave the fallen waiter a strange look as she passed.

"Well? Show me something cool."

"I just did. Trust me — you loved it."

"You come to Rimini for Cornello the box maker, eh? I see it. Many people come, from the mountains, from Africa, from all over, to beg Cornello, but he say no. What can he do, eh? It take him forty—how you say?—anni, anni, years, forty years to make one. A little box like this, fit right in my hand, like this. But bellissimo e perfetto. Nothing more beautiful than Cornello's box. The emperor come to see. He carves so delicate. But now he is old. He no make another. Of course, you want it, no? A pretty lady like you is looking for a pretty prize . . . but he no give. You have to kill him, he say. And you know . . . they say he make it with magic. Forty years, one magic box more beautiful than the world. He always say he will die with it in his hands. But you go see him, eh?"

"He made two, actually. And I've already seen him."

After the party, Madame Vileroy took the children to their new home in Manhattan for the first time. For a large, expensive apartment on the Upper East Side, the place was dark and dingy, probably the only apartment in the neighborhood with windows so small that it was impossible to see the street. As they stepped inside, the children could feel their breathing grow shorter, their skin grow paler, and their bodies grow fatigued, as if starving for fresh, unspoiled air. Even Belle, who was used to foul air, was uncomfortable in the house. The governess switched on a light, and the children looked at one another, confused. It was completely empty. There wasn't a scrap of furniture in the entire house. There were two bedrooms off to one side and a large kitchen on the other. All these rooms too were empty — if you didn't count the dust and the moths.

"Where's our stuff? Why is it empty?" Valentin asked, stepping into the bare room.

"That's the surprise," said Madame Vileroy. "I've packed away our home so I could show you something new."

Bicé spotted three moths on the ceiling. She had a habit of looking for living things in every room. Moving things. Beings whose presence gave her a sense for the passage of time. *Time* — that was the gift Vileroy had given her. She watched the moths zigzag across the room and settle in a corner of the wall.

"I told you that I would show you something tonight," Madame Vileroy said with a mischievous tone as she snaked between Bicé and Christian and made her way to Valentin. She rested her hand on his shoulder.

"Now that you've made some friends, you will need what I'm about to give you."

49

"Bicé didn't make any friends," said Victoria.

"Only because of *you*," said Belle, instinctively shielding Bicé from Victoria. "Don't listen to her, Bicé."

"You should try to project a bit less jealousy, Belle," said Victoria. "It's not attractive."

Bicé snorted. "How do *you* know what's attractive?" she said under her breath. "You'd probably tattoo your GPA on your forehead."

Valentin threw an arm around Bicé. "Good one, sis." Bicé shrank a bit more. She gave Valentin a look that was alarmed, fatigued, and charmed all at once. She wondered why Valentin never called Victoria or Belle "sis."

Madame Vileroy reached into her pocket and took out two wooden boxes, small enough to fit in her hand. Valentin's jaw dropped. *She has two of them.* He looked at Christian, who had the same look. One box was a deep crimson, and the other was a bright baby blue. "This, my dears, is where you'll entertain all your new friends," said Madame Vileroy as she lifted the blue one and tossed it in the middle of the empty apartment. It hit the floor with a faint echo. As soon as it hit the ground, the box began to glow. It was an eerie glow, not beautiful, but mesmerizing, and painful to the eyes. At first, it was just a faint light circling the box, as if there were a candle inside. But then, the circle of light grew bigger; it became more pronounced, slowly filling the room to the point that nothing else was visible. Still, the children could not stop staring. Within seconds, the entire apartment was gone from view. They could see only the light, even when they closed their eyes or looked away. It was as if they had stared at the bright sun for hours and suddenly tried to look away. The light had gone deeper into them than their eyes.

And then, in an instant, it was gone. The painful light, the empty apartment, the stale air — all gone. Valentin rubbed his eyes. Bicé's were still closed. When their eyes adjusted, they saw that they were standing in an entirely new apartment — a beautifully decorated home that looked like it should be on the cover of a magazine.

"Wow," said Belle. "It's so much nicer than —"

"That's what they respect here. Affluence. Pretty things," said Vileroy in a silky tone.

"Then why don't we live here all the time?" asked Belle eagerly.

"Money is easy." The governess shrugged. "What you have in the crimson house is rare, and more precious."

The living room of the blue-box apartment was decorated almost entirely in shades of white and cream, with just a hint of blue in the walls. In the corner stood a small table with a reading lamp and bookcases filled with leather-bound volumes. Three lush white couches surrounded a large glass coffee table, and the walls were covered with French impressionist paintings. Valentin felt a painful pang when he looked at them. He hated landscapes. Belle began to walk around, feeling the soft fabric of the couch, running her fingers down the spines of the books, turning the lamp off and on.

The children scattered, exploring every inch of the living room and dining room. The floor plan didn't fit the original apartment, with its prisonlike windows and lack of light. This apartment had floor-to-ceiling windows leading to a balcony.

"Is it real?" Victoria asked Madame Vileroy when the others were off exploring. "Or is it just my eyes?"

"That depends."

"On what?"

"On what you want to believe. Do you believe that *I'm* real? Is everything you've done real?"

"I think that stuff is real," Victoria said.

"Well, this is as real as the other house," Madame Vileroy answered.

"It feels like it could just be a mirage or something. But I can feel it," Victoria tapped a bookcase with her knuckle.

"If it looks real and feels real, do you think it matters if it's real?"

"Well . . ." Victoria thought that it did matter.

"Of course it doesn't, because the appearance of greatness is enough for you."

"It is not!"

"Sure it is. Accolades rather than accomplishments. That's what you asked for."

It was true.

One by one, Madame Vileroy showed the children their rooms. Great pains had obviously been taken to make the rooms seem typical, but they seemed like caricatures instead. There was the room Belle and Bicé would pretend to share when visitors arrived. It was pink and far too girly. Inside were pictures of Belle winning various beauty pageants and Bicé standing in front of famous monuments all over the world. The shelves were covered with books in every language imaginable, and next to the door was an antique vanity table and mirror.

"Wow, it's like travel-guide Barbie in here," said Bicé. "Do we really expect people to buy this?"

Victoria's room too was a tribute to her talents. Latin trophies, academic team medals, and debate certificates adorned every surface and shelf. Though they were all fake, Victoria seemed happy enough, leafing through her supposed triumphs. Next, they visited Valentin and Christian's room. Sports equipment spilled out of every nook and cranny. Valentin's desk was off to the side and contained several volumes of poetry and prose. There was an ergonomic keyboard and a stack of ancient first-person shooters like *Doom* and *Wolfenstein 3D* next to his computer. Valentin shook his head and moved on.

Christian wondered why the hockey sticks in his closet didn't have tape wrapped around the handles. He would have done that first thing. And there were no dog-eared pages in Valentin's books. It was as if real kids didn't live in the house, only kids from a television show. Every prop was in place, but nothing was lived in.

"It's fitting that you should live here," said Madame Vileroy to Victoria, who was still unsure. "These houses are just like the five of you. They may be genuine. They may be a trick. But they *are* impressive. They give the illusion of grandeur, and that's all that matters. Were they built out of nothing through hard work and sacrifice? Or are they just surface coating to cover up something ordinary? That doesn't matter at all, Victoria."

After a bit of exploring, Madame Vileroy gathered the children back in the living room. "Remember, you will have to quickly revert to this house if there are any visitors. It's important that you know your way around."

They all nodded.

"All right, let's go home."

Bicé began to mumble nervously. She always mumbled when she was anxious, each time in a different language. This time, though, Belle could understand her native Italian.

With another quick flick of her wrist, Madame Vileroy threw the crimson box onto the floor. As the light grew larger and brighter, the entire apartment changed to a bloodlike hue. The light grew painful again, boring deep past the eyes. It was like an eclipse. Belle turned her head. Christian looked down. Nothing worked. In a few moments the entire space was nothing more than an intense, probing light. Then the light disappeared. But everyone's eyes were still filled with red until they were able to open them again.

Inside this house was a scene far different than the peaceful family home of a few minutes ago. At the center was a large round room that took up most of the space. Attached to this room were almost a dozen tiny hallways, like arms extending out to the corners of the apartment. At the end of each hallway were tiny rooms, deliberately separated from the others. A much narrower hallway led from the living room to the east wing, which contained Madame Vileroy's private quarters.

The deep color of the walls, combined with the unsettling light of candles, painted the apartment in hellish hues and patches of shadow. Clusters of candles were jutting from the walls at every height, in every direction, as though they had been stabbed into the sides of the room. And pouring from the hilt of each weapon was wax and fire, like the Water and the Blood. Extending throughout the main room and into each of the hallways, they were like fiery thorns, keeping the children alert and away from the narrowest halls leading to Madame Vileroy's rooms. At the center of the circular living room were six chairs surrounding a big round wooden table. Around the room, openings to each of the hallways were visible every few feet. Between them, ancient bookshelves and mirrors decorated the living-room walls.

Despite all this, the most palpable difference in the room was the air. The stale, rotten air of the empty apartment was back, but stronger. It was as if this house were the very source of the stifling atmosphere they had walked into earlier in the evening, as if the empty apartment still carried the dregs of the poison emanating from that little crimson box.

Bicé mumbled, *"Lasciate ogni speranza voi ch'entrate."*

Belle shuddered. "Bicé, stop that."

They had lived in this house for years, long before New York, since the day they had first arrived at the cottage in the country; yet each time they entered it, it was as uncomfortable as the first time.

Madame Vileroy looked around with satisfaction. "It's nice to be home, isn't it, children?" she said. "I have a few more surprises. If you behave, I'll show them to you tomorrow."

"For Christmas . . ." said Bicé.

"Let's not make a spectacle of Christmas," said the governess. Madame Vileroy hated that day. Without saying good night, she swept out of the room through the narrow corridor leading to the east wing, her luxurious black coat floating behind her.

Victoria looked around, still unnerved by what Madame Vileroy had said. *The results will be real enough,* Victoria assured herself. *And if the rest of it isn't, no one can find out.* She looked up at the ceiling. The room was hot and dark. The air was so thick, it almost moved. Victoria was getting a headache, but something kept her gaze fixed on the chandelier overhead. It was made of glass and filled with little dim candles. She'd seen it a thousand times, but this time it looked as if it saw her back. Victoria was getting dizzy, and the air around her was becoming thicker, harder to breathe. It rolled and undulated all around her. *Is it real?* For a moment, Victoria thought that she could no longer see the chandelier, only the little lights. They were still there — vaguely — hanging in midair above her. Now, as Victoria stared at it, all she could see were tongues of flame, floating alone. They hovered overhead, ready to baptize her with a torrent of fire. Victoria rubbed her eyes. "Vic," called Valentin. Victoria whipped around.

"What?" she snapped. "You scared me."

"What are you looking at?"

"Nothing," she said. She looked back up. The chandelier was there now, glass, candles, and all — as real as anything else in the room.

~~⊗⊗⊗~~

At midnight, Valentin, Victoria, and Belle were sitting around the center table. Valentin leaned back in a chair, his feet up on the table, practicing sleight of hand with a coin. Belle filed away at her nails, while Victoria checked and rechecked and rechecked a stack of lists.

"What a bunch of poseurs," mused Valentin.

"Some of them seemed nice," said Belle, thinking of Thomas and not looking up from her nails.

"You're just thinking of Thomas," said Valentin.

"No, I'm not!" said Belle.

"Yes, you are," said Victoria as she crossed three things off her list.

"Stop cheating," said Belle.

"Ugh, gross!" said Victoria. "You have a dirty little mind, Belle."

Belle turned red and lunged at Victoria. "Stop!"

"OK! OK! Speaking of cheating," said Victoria, "I heard an interesting conversation at the party."

"Yeah, thanks, Vic, but mind reading some girl's SAT score isn't so riveting for the rest of us," said Valentin. "But I wouldn't mind hearing what filthy secrets our little Belle is hiding. . . ." Belle rolled her eyes.

"Actually," said Victoria, "I *overheard* Bicé and Christian talking about how we all got here. About being adopted as babies, and when you started to change, Belle . . ."

Belle put down her nail file and perked up. "What did they say?"

"Bicé was upset about what you've done to her," Victoria said to Belle.

"What? She doesn't know anything. . . . I didn't *do* anything!"

"She doesn't know everything, but she knows that you think she's ugly."

"I never *said* that. I don't think that at all!" said Belle.

"You sold your soul to the devil for a different face," said Valentin. "That might tip her off," he mused out loud while staring at the coin in his hand. "Sold your soul . . . sounds so Middle-earth."

"She doesn't *know,* Valentin. Neither one of them knows what we did. And I know it's hard, but we have to keep our mouths shut."

"It's not hard," said Valentin casually.

"Well, I've never kept anything other than this from Bicé. It wouldn't do any of us any good if they knew. Remember what Vileroy said — those two are not in on this!"

57

Victoria sneered at Belle. "Don't you feel like total scum for treating your own twin like this?"

"I love Bicé!" Belle shot back. "I'm just trying to protect her. You know how she is. This would kill her."

"Oh, right. You're doing it for *her* sake."

"Vic, please! As if you know what it's like to love anyone other than yourself!"

"Whatever, but they'll find out what we did sooner or later," said Victoria. "Christian is starting to feel guilty about stealing."

"I know. And those false memories of 'abandoned children' and childhood traveling are so full of holes," said Belle. "But we have to stay quiet. If Bicé found out, it would break her heart, and she would hate me forever."

"I don't know why Vileroy keeps those two around, anyway," said Victoria. "I mean, I get why we don't tell them. They'd probably screw things up. But why keep them here? Why give them gifts?"

"She probably likes the challenge. Trying to get them to make the deal," said Valentin.

"Christian already has," Victoria said confidently.

"I'm not so sure about that," said Valentin, leaning back a little.

"He did, and then he changed his mind, remember?" said Victoria, remembering that day in the cottage five years ago.

"Then why keep him around?"

"Because there's so much more she wants. I don't think it's just about that one deal," said Belle. "She wants more from us."

Belle bowed her head sadly, and Valentin changed the subject, trying to lighten the mood. "I'll tell you one thing: Christian and Bicé have some crazy ideas about where we got our gifts," he said, laughing. "They think Vileroy's some sort of magic godmother, or a witch or something." He stared at his hand again. "Yeah . . . a really hot witch."

"Gross, Valentin," said Victoria, reading his thoughts.

~∞∞∞

On Christmas morning, Victoria and Madame Vileroy went out to have a look around their new city. Most of the streets were freshly plowed, and the sidewalks were covered with a yellow layer of snow. Despite the holiday, there were plenty of people on the street, chatting, walking their dogs, and shopping at the handful of stores that were open. Madame Vileroy loved to people-watch. She did it constantly — always peering and commenting on people's behavior. If she spotted an argument, she would stop and listen.

Madame Vileroy was wearing her long black flowing coat and a stylish black hat. She was always elegantly dressed, always impressive. Victoria wondered to herself if her clothes were like the blue house, an illusion. In the end, she just didn't care.

"We'll go by subway," Madame Vileroy said as she headed toward Lexington Avenue. The subway never failed to satisfy her desire to eavesdrop.

Victoria, on the other hand, despised traveling by subway. She hated everything that made her seem ordinary. She bought a single-ride pass and walked to the turnstiles. But instead of inserting her ticket and going through, Victoria went to the handicap entrance and pulled it open. The security guard shot her a look.

"I put my ticket there," she pointed to the turnstile, "and it didn't read it." Then she smiled sweetly. The guard smiled back at the sprightly little girl and nodded. Madame Vileroy was already waiting on the platform.

"Strapped for cash?" Madame Vileroy raised an eyebrow.

"Their systems are so stupid. It's just fun to outsmart them."

Victoria tossed her unused ticket onto the tracks. A rat scampered out of the way.

"I'm glad that you know how smart you are, Victoria." Madame Vileroy put her hand on Victoria's shoulder. Her icy fingertips penetrated Victoria's clothes and cooled her bones.

"You don't think I'm being too proud?" Victoria said sarcastically.

"Nothing wrong with self-awareness, my dear."

"They say pride is one of the seven deadly sins," Victoria tested.

"The world is full of stupid people, Victoria. That's why we have rules. But with enough intelligence, a person can be above the rules. She can *make* the rules."

Victoria smiled. Sometimes Madame Vileroy made a lot of sense.

❧☙

Half an hour later, they were in SoHo. Madame Vileroy kept a quick pace, the heels of her boots clicking as she walked. She didn't seem to notice the pretty cobbled streets, the shops decorated in bright holiday colors, or the yellow glow of café windows, half covered in frost, barely revealing the animated scenes within. She just walked, and Victoria followed, taking big steps and concentrating hard. Madame Vileroy's words comforted Victoria, but somehow, she always went back to worrying. The governess was the only person in the world that Victoria couldn't cheat. And so reassurances never lasted long. Victoria kept thinking about the house. *What if someone finds out?* This was what worried her most about the idea that her successes might be illusions. If they were illusions, what's to keep them from vanishing in an instant?

"Victoria?"

"Yes?"

"I have a bargain for you."

Victoria perked up a little. She wished she could take just a little peek into Vileroy's mind. Still, she was eager to listen, because unlike the others, she loved Madame Vileroy's bargains. She always felt like she had won.

"I'm listening."

"I know you've been wondering about how things will turn out for you."

"I guess. . . ."

"You know there have been others, lots of others, over so many years."

Victoria knew what Madame Vileroy was talking about. But she was stunned into silence. Was Vileroy going to tell her more than she ever had before?

"I can tell you more about them. I can show you the kind of success I've had before. And then you can judge for yourself . . ."

"You're going to tell me who?"

"Yes."

"What will you want from me?" Victoria tried to mask it with skepticism, but her voice cracked and gave away the fact that she was ready to give almost anything.

"It's something very small." Madame Vileroy put a long finger under Victoria's chin and turned her face from side to side. "You, my dear, are my favorite. You're the one that will go the furthest. And so, for you, my price is always low."

Victoria swallowed hard. Her eyes shone with greed.

"I want you to be mine only," said Madame Vileroy.

"But we already made that deal. . . ."

"No, my dear. I mean, I want you to be entirely in my service. I want you to promise me that you will never help the others — if they ever ask you."

Victoria's face grew dark. "They would never ask for my help. They don't even like me."

"That's true. They don't like you. But they might pretend. And you might be fooled."

Victoria grew angry. "I'm smarter than they are!"

"Yes, and so you promise?"

"Yes. It's a deal."

"Good. And if you're ever in the position to know something about them . . ."

"You want me to spy for you?"

"Victoria, you don't know this now, but someday soon, you're going to be in a position to know so much more than you know now."

"But I already know how to cheat. I can know anything."

"There are limits to that. People can feel it. Anyway, just promise me, Victoria. If I give you more powerful tools, you'll be entirely mine."

"Yes, I promise."

Madame Vileroy smiled. They entered a pricey boutique that was open on one of the trendy streets of SoHo. The walls and floors were shiny and black, and the large space was wastefully devoted to only two mannequins and four tables holding a few neatly folded pieces.

"So?" asked Victoria.

"So, what?"

"You're supposed to tell me how real this is. Who else has done it?"

Madame Vileroy picked up a black blouse from a nearby table and examined it. She played with the stitching, counting one by one like a rosary.

"I've been with some of the best. People who are famous, people who've gone down in history."

Victoria stepped closer.

"But you, my dear, are the best one. The one with the most potential."

Victoria's eyes shone. "Like who? Who else have you helped?"

"I started with a girl in Egypt. I was with her since birth. She had more ambition than anyone in her time. She wanted to be pharaoh. And she was willing to give anything."

"What was her name?"

Madame Vileroy ignored Victoria's question. "There were so many others. There were years when I had several. There were years when I had none. Some years, they were all killed — in inquisitions and witch hunts. And then I lay low. There was a little girl who had a father who didn't love her."

Victoria's heart skipped. Madame Vileroy went on, glancing at Victoria from the side of her eyes. "Her father had her sent away."

"Where did she live?"

"London." Madame Vileroy smiled. Victoria was confused. *Is she talking about me? But my father didn't send me away. He doesn't even know I'm gone.*

"This little girl was very talented. She impressed all of her tutors. Everyone thought she was brilliant. But still, her father didn't care about anyone but her little brother."

Victoria felt herself overcome with anger and sadness.

"He thought that all the hopes of the family lay with her little brother. So he lavished him with attention and love and presents. Meanwhile, the little girl was shut away, out of sight and mind."

"Did she wish more than anything to be successful?"

"Not just successful, my dear. She wanted to be queen."

"Queen?"

"Yes, Victoria. She wanted more than anything to be the most powerful woman of her age. And she was willing to do anything to get it. She hid a deep blackness under the layers of velvet that covered her heart. And all the while, I was there."

Victoria's mouth went dry. "I think I know who you're talking about . . ."

"I was her closest companion—different name, of course. But otherwise the same."

"I can't believe it. . . ."

"The greatest queen England ever had. The whole world vying for her attention. Worth the price, wouldn't you say?"

Victoria nodded.

"There were others. There are others now. Others you would recognize."

"Really? Who? Where?" Victoria was almost jumping up and down.

"There are many. And I'm not going to tell you about all of them. Just remember that, Victoria. Remember that this is real. And if you ever meet someone for whom life seems too easy, remember that there are others."

"How can there be so many, if there's just one of you?"

"There isn't just one of me. *We are many.* There are *legions* of governesses out there," Madame Vileroy said with a wink.

"Why so many of you?"

Madame Vileroy put down the shirt and leaned closer to Victoria, to whisper in her ear. "Because there are so many whose hearts call for us. And we answer every call. But this is a good time, since they're not burning children anymore."

Victoria's head was spinning when the pretty young salesgirl approached them. "May I put this in a fitting room for you?" She eyed the shirt that Victoria was unknowingly clutching in her hand.

"Oh, no, actually, I'll take it," she said.

"All right. Let me ring that up for you," the girl said cheerfully — too cheerfully for this boutique; Victoria could tell that she was new. Obviously hired for her beauty, she would develop a cold indifferent eye within a month. As the girl was completing the transaction, anger filled Victoria from head to toe. She wasn't quite sure why she was so mad, but she was. Maybe it was the memory of her father.

Maybe it was the idea that there could be people out there who were better than her. Or the reminder that there were so many before who were more successful. She snatched the shopping bag from the girl and stormed out of the store, with Madame Vileroy calmly strolling behind her. When she was out of the store, she grabbed the shirt from the bag.

"This is ugly," she said.

"Hm." Madame Vileroy seemed to agree.

With a swift yank, Victoria ripped one of the sleeves half off. She then marched back into the store, with Madame Vileroy following closely behind.

"This is damaged," she yelled at the salesgirl.

"Oh . . . I'm sorry. . . . Are you sure?"

"Am I sure? Am I sure? Take a look! The sleeve is practically off."

"But it wasn't like that when . . ."

The salesgirl didn't know what to do. It was her first day, and Victoria scared her.

"Are you calling me a liar?"

"Of course not."

"I have never seen such terrible customer service! First you sell me a torn shirt. Then you call me a liar. And now you're just wasting my time!"

"I'm sorry. If you'll just give me a moment, I can give you a refund."

"A refund? Well, that's a given. That hardly makes up for this horrible service."

"Uh, of course not. Let me just see my manager."

As the girl ran to the back office, Victoria took a deep breath. This was satisfying. Rejuvenating. A few moments later, the girl returned.

"OK, let me process that refund for you. And as a Christmas gift from us, we're going to offer you a two-hundred-dollar gift certificate. I hope you'll come again."

"Christmas gift?" Victoria snapped. "Let's be clear that if you're giving me anything, it's not a gift. It's restitution for my wasted time and energy."

With that, she ripped the gift certificate in two and marched out of the store.

A few moments later, as they walked silently along a street, Victoria gave Madame Vileroy a sidelong glance. "Do you think I was too harsh?" she asked, testing her limits with the governess.

"You have to stand up for your rights, my dear. Remember what I said? The world is filled with stupid people. They have to learn to do their job."

"Yeah. Those people make me so angry."

"Anger can be soothing."

"They say it's one of the seven deadly sins," Victoria joked, and Madame Vileroy smiled indulgently.

"You're such a clever girl, Victoria." *No wonder your father sent you to me. . . .*

~∽⌾⌾⌾∽

Sometimes, Bicé would just ride the subway for hours, from one end of the track to the other, from Coney Island to Yankee Stadium, huddled in her seat, listening to all the languages around her. If you saw her, you wouldn't notice anything abnormal, just a girl on the train, sometimes by herself, sometimes squashed in between commuters. Back and forth, she'd ride the rails, practicing her Russian on the R train to Bayridge, her Greek on the W to Astoria. If she wanted Afghani, there was a group of ladies on the 5 line who would get on in the South Bronx and go down to Atlantic Avenue, where all the Middle Eastern markets were. On the way, under their black coverings, they'd gab about everything from their favorite recipes to how difficult racquetball seemed to be. Bicé would position herself next to them, pretend to read a book, and soak in all the slang they could never teach in a textbook. She would find ways to repay the universe, of course, in her own way. Like the time an old, decrepit man stepped onto the train and seemed completely lost and unable to communicate with anyone. She grabbed his arm and began going through her roster.

"*Parlez-vous français?*"

"*Español?*"

"*Deutsch?*"

The man just smiled and nodded.

"*Italiano?*"

"*Dansk?*"

More smiling and nodding.

"*Nederlands?*"

"*Malayalam?*"

"*Gwong-dong-wa?*"

By the time she was down to the West African languages, someone pointed out that he was deaf.

On Christmas Day on the F train, brushing up on her Yiddish,

Bicé tried to keep herself from squealing with excitement when she heard a couple speaking Udmurt. *An endangered language. A real endangered language, right here in the New York subway.*

"Oy!" she said, unable to help herself.

The couple looked at her, then went back to murmuring — about what, Bicé could not quite make out. She looked them up and down. Their clothes were old, patched together, in a rural style. The woman had long hair, and the man's face was covered with a mustache and beard. They seemed out of place, here in New York, as if they were here to act as subjects in a cultural study or a documentary. She had read a bit about Udmurt before. She had made sure to read something about all the endangered languages. She knew where they came from. She knew why they were endangered (because children no longer spoke them), but she only knew how to speak a few words of this particular dialect. It seemed to function on the Slovak syntactical structures. . . . Bicé leaned in closer. The woman gave her a sidelong glance. *Their cadence is eastern,* thought Bicé. Then the train lurched, and Bicé went directly into the man's lap.

"Sorry!" she said, pushing herself away.

Before the couple could reclaim their personal space, Bicé leaned in and stumbled in her own Udmurt, "I am forever apologies, but do you speak of moving picture show?"

The couple could only stare, half startled by the statement, half by the fact that a random girl was semicoherently speaking their semidead language.

Bicé switched to English: "I mean, excuse me, but are you talking about the film festival? Is that what you were talking about? I mean, the subject of what — I wasn't eavesdropping — I just mean, if that *is* what you're talking about, then — I'm sort of practicing Udmurt, you see, and — so, what're you talking about?"

The woman, wide-eyed, stammered, "Y-yes, we're speaking about the film festival."

"Oh, good!" said Bicé, clapping her hands. "Can I join you?"

Before the woman could respond, the train doors opened and the man said, "This is our stop." As the two of them stepped out of the car, Bicé called after them.

"OK, well, we could maybe talk later? Do you have e-mail? We could do a book club."

The doors closed on Bicé's requests. She slowly sat back down and noticed that she was all the way to Jamaica Avenue. It would take an hour to get home, where she could hide herself away in a book. Till then, she sat in her seat, as lonely as you could ever be in a train full of people.

Bicé looked down, a bit embarrassed. When she looked up, she thought she caught a glimpse of Madame Vileroy, sitting in the seat in a far corner. She was wearing her black coat, her blond bun resting neatly on top of her head, casting Bicé a knowing and disapproving smile. Bicé whipped around to get a better look, but Vileroy was gone. Had the governess really been there? Had Bicé imagined it? Was she always watching? The thought sent a shudder down Bicé's spine, and for a moment Bicé was deaf to all the sounds around her. She felt regret at having accosted that couple.

She didn't notice the look on the Udmurt woman's face as she was pulled out of the train. The woman lingered outside for a minute, watching the train take Bicé away. Even though it had all happened so fast, and even though her husband had pulled her

away too quickly, she was in awe of this miracle she had witnessed —
their language, the precious tongue that was fated to die with their
generation, being spoken by a young girl in New York. For her, the
exchange with Bicé wasn't awkward. It was something hopeful — a
moment that changed her perception of this city, a moment that
might cause her to speak well of her visit here.

Without knowing it, Bicé left a trail of memories like this, when
people came away from her feeling better somehow, cared for — the
kind of sensations that were the very opposite of all those little evils
that Madame Vileroy left in her wake.

Chapter 4
Marlowe's Play

Snaky hair. Shadows from clouds. Suffering fingers. Guilty souls are capable of imagining anything, especially through stormy windows on dark, unforgiving nights. She has stood outside many unhappy homes. Through the glass, she has watched them for centuries — though her hair is far from snaky and her fingers do not suffer.

She watches. Simply watches and waits. There is a moment. Always a single moment.

The instant when they first see the mark.

For that moment, she is always there. Unseen. Unheard. Watching.

She observes one of them now. A man. He is tall and slender, rich yet unsatisfied. He hugs the edge of the bath as if scared of what he might see. He pours the water over himself, keeping in the corner, scraping himself clean, facing the wall, scraping himself too much. When he is finished, he looks around again and makes a swift move toward his robe, turning for a moment to show himself to the unknown presence at the window.

The image swims through the foggy haze. The mark, black as death, covers half the man's chest. A vile devilish darkness. She smiles. Soon he will call to her, and the light will never see him again.

~⦿⦿~

On the day after yet another Christmas left uncelebrated, the children and Madame Vileroy went to the Marlowe Christmas play, to visit the school and to scope out more families. Valentin, who was keenly aware that Charlotte had written this play to unprecedented accolades, spent the entire ride to the school brooding. Once in a while, Madame Vileroy would whisper in his ear, telling him that, if he wanted, *he* could be the one at center stage.

"I've never heard of a play performance on December twenty-sixth," Valentin huffed, arms crossed.

"I thought it'd be a good distraction from this tiresome season," said Madame Vileroy.

"You did this?" said Valentin.

"Well," said the governess. "I didn't *not* do it."

~⦿⦿~

The Marlowe School was a tightly packed, gothic-style masterpiece of architecture, each building more opulent than the next. Behind the main building, past a short tree-lined walk, was an auditorium as lush and spacious as Lincoln Center. Each year, the vaulted ceilings of the theater would dazzle with holiday lights, as the various plays, musicals, and concerts of the Christmas season were performed. The wealthy parents, politicians, and power couples of New York would appear in full regalia, entering the hall with as many paparazzi as at the Oscars. Inside, the intermission hall looked like a masque royale. The mayor's wife attended, dressed like a parade float. The mayor spent the intermission swooning over Madame Vileroy. The mayor's girlfriend ran out abruptly when she looked into Vileroy's branded eye.

Whenever they got the chance, the Faust children peeked into the various corners of the school, venturing outside the theater and onto the grounds. They had seen it before. They had spent weeks observing their future school, studying their future friends and rivals. Still, it felt newer, more exciting, tonight than it ever had before. Christian ran over to the athletics building and peered in at the pool through the windows. Bicé snuck off to the library and came back with heavy-lidded eyes.

Valentin spent most of the intermission looking at the plush carpets, glittering chandeliers, and decadent artwork that hung on the walls. This couldn't be a school. Peering closely at the audience, now mingling in the lobby, he could pick out the faces he had seen at the Wirths' party — smug faces, sitting atop tuxedos and ball gowns, wrapped in shawls and covered in jewels, as if they thought that their children were indeed opening on Broadway.

What tools, he thought, and looked over at the governess with a sneer that said, *Wanna have a little fun?* She just nodded as they approached a nearby group. Valentin's heart skipped. At times like this, when Vileroy was feeling generous with her attention, he could have all the fun in the world. He could spend what seemed like hours playing and replaying scenes, conversations. He could have her to himself for hours and hours without losing a second. She could teach him what to do and say, how to trap people and when to let them go.

She was the only one who could accompany him on his trips back and forth. Sometimes the two of them relived a scene fifty times. Sometimes just once. But she was always there. Always willing. Because how else would he learn? How else would he grow into a manipulator of great men, if not for these harmless games, these insignificant party tricks? Everyone has to start somewhere. Every great person needs a great teacher willing to tinker with the small stuff. Thanks to these journeys through time, Valentin might grow up to be a world-famous writer, a powerful politician, a modern-day Caesar. But for now, he needed to get rid of that pesky tic.

Valentin stood in the background, listening, waiting for the right moment to enter each conversation. Next to him stood the governess, undetected by anyone else, whispering things in his ear.

"Do it now," she would say each time one of the Ivy-League dads made a witty comment. Then Valentin would rewind and snatch the comment right from under his nose.

"Go on," she would goad as he said and resaid each line until it was perfect.

He was nervous, which was a change for Valentin, who was usually so confident you'd think he could walk over hot coals without a sweat. Vileroy never responded to his doubtful comments.

"You know," Valentin said with a sigh, "a lot of famous writers weren't that witty in public." She raised an eyebrow, so he added with a smirk, "*You* could just tell me what to say."

"Yes, I could," said the ravishing governess with a playful wink that made Valentin catch his breath, "but this is *such* fun, isn't it?"

And it was. In what seemed like fifteen minutes to the other party-goers, Valentin escorted the unsuspecting Charlotte Hill from mildly interested to desperately in love. Even though everyone wanted to talk to the girl who had written this play, she remained arm in arm with Valentin from the moment he looked into her eyes, with just the right expression of awe and melancholy, and told her that her play was "majestic." Madame Vileroy stood behind them, watching.

Across the room, Belle had been trying to gather enough courage to approach Thomas Goodman-Brown, whom she had been seducing from a distance for twenty minutes now.

Belle turned and tilted her head toward him, and he smiled again. She looked away, her mouth going dry. *No,* she thought, *I don't think I can do this.* Thomas said something to his friend. A few minutes later, the two boys were approaching Belle.

"Hi. I'm Thomas," he said, extending his hand to Belle. "And this is Connor Wirth. Did you just move here?"

"Who's that?" said Connor. He was craning his neck and looking past Belle, at Bicé, who was loitering near a plant and mumbling to herself. Belle made a face. Bicé looked skittish, as if she had done something wrong. She slowly walked over to her sister.

"I'm Bicé," she said in a very soft voice.

Thomas took her hand graciously and smiled. "Are you two together?"

"We're sisters," said Bicé.

"You look nothing alike," said Connor.

"Then I guess you won't believe that we're twins," said Bicé, thinking back to a time when Belle had looked exactly like her.

"No way," said Connor, thinking she was joking.

"And what's your name?" Thomas turned back to the hot girl he had been eyeing all night.

"Belle," she said, her stomach turning, knowing what was coming next.

For a painful moment, Thomas looked revolted. The air around them seemed to have grown heavy and putrid.

"What's that smell?" Connor said before he could help it.

"What smell?" Thomas said politely, though he himself had gone white and was taking a step away from Belle. It was like lilacs and sulfur, he thought.

"It's like something nasty covered with cheap perfume," said Connor, oblivious that it might have been the beautiful girl in front of him.

"Oh, is your mom around?" Thomas joked.

Belle bit her lip.

"Shut up, Tom," said Connor, punching him on the arm.

"I saw you at Connor's party. Did you just move here?" Thomas spoke with slightly less enthusiasm, a change that made Belle's stomach tie itself into a million little knots.

"We arrived last week," said Belle, adding hopefully, "We're going to Marlowe." Despite her own instincts, she kept her answers short and stood a few paces back, afraid of driving him away. It was as if there were a line between them that she couldn't cross — not yet.

"Oh, that's right," said Connor. "Your mom told my mom about you guys."

"You mean Madame Vileroy?" Belle said vaguely.

"She's not your mother?" said Connor.

"She's our governess," Belle responded, working hard to seem sexy and confident.

"Oh," said Thomas, pretending to rub his eye, but really shielding his nose. *What a weird girl.* He didn't know what to say. Part of him was disgusted by Belle — not just the smell but by her words too. She was socially repulsive, slowly tainting the air around her. And her sister did nothing to redeem her. Bicé seemed like a pariah, backing away when he looked at her, inching closer to the corner space between the plant and the wall. *Why is she so afraid? She looks normal. Cute, well dressed, nice eyes.* Another part of him, though, the part that saw how beautiful Belle was, felt intrigued and wanted to stay. Then Thomas spotted his friend Lucy Spencer practically running toward him.

"Hey, Luce. What's up?"

Lucy, who had been grounded by her mother for a full week for her supposed taste in unsuitable boys ("Waiters are the *help*, dear. It's like falling in love with a blender!" her mother had screamed), was more than happy to promise Mrs. Spencer that tonight she would talk to no boy other than "that adorable young Goodman-Brown." "Thomas, I've been looking all over for you," she said in her most dramatic voice. Then she spotted Belle and hooked her arm with Thomas's, while he introduced her. Lucy cast Bicé a cursory smile, and Bicé looked down, ashamed and disappointed.

"What's that *smell?*" said Lucy.

"Connor, tell them about the sports teams," said Thomas, changing the subject. The air felt thick. It felt like the time last summer when he'd drunk too much with Lucy and sampled some random pills at a party. It felt cloudy and warm. *But still really gross.* Belle saw the intoxicated look on his face and moved closer. He backed away. *Too soon,* she thought. Connor, who loved to talk about sports and had spent way too much time in locker rooms to care about unpleasant smells, jumped right in.

"Well, let's see. We have pretty much everything at Marlowe. Are you two into sports? The girls' field hockey team is short this year. Wait. What about your brothers?"

"Christian plays a bunch of sports," said Bicé. "Tennis, swimming, golf—"

Connor didn't let her finish. "Thomas and I play golf on the varsity team! Marlowe's the best. Does he have a handicap?"

"He's competitive and moody sometimes," said Bicé almost to herself, "but I wouldn't call either of those—"

"He meant a handicap in golf," said Lucy. "Where did you say you're from? Turkmenistan?"

"They have golf in Turkmenistan," said Bicé casually.

"How do you know?"

"I went . . . once," said Bicé.

Bicé was pretty sure she had been there. She remembered traveling to so many places with Madame Vileroy. Maybe she had gone there when she was eight or nine. She wasn't sure. It must have been around that time, because Belle looked just like her then. Bicé grouped her whole life into two periods: before Belle changed and after—when Bicé had a best friend and when that friend was gone. Within those two chunks of time, she didn't keep track of days or months. It didn't matter. Bicé cleared her throat and kept looking at the floor.

"Whatever," said Lucy.

"What kind of music do you listen to?" asked Connor, trying to lighten the mood.

"Gregorian," said Bicé lazily.

"Right." Connor scratched his head. "I think I heard them play at the Elbow Room last week."

~⚬⚬⚬

A few minutes later, Thomas excused himself, casting only a sideways glance at Belle, who did her best to hide her disappointment. Lucy grabbed his hand. "I'll go with you," she said in a most girl-friendly tone. She looked triumphantly at Belle and said, "But let's go somewhere more private. Something here smells rotten." Belle seethed, hating Lucy and wanting to pull Thomas away from her.

As the pair walked away, Bicé immediately relaxed. "Well, sis, I think it's safe to say that she won't be inviting us to sit with her at lunch," she said, popping a miniquiche from a passing tray into her mouth. Belle stood apart from the group. Everyone else had moved away from her. But everyone outside a certain distance was staring at her with jealousy. She pulled herself to her full height and caught a glance of herself in a window. She *was* beautiful, she reassured herself. But Thomas obviously hadn't thought so. He'd jumped at the chance to take off. *Sometimes it takes more than one try,* she thought. *Next time.*

~⚬⚬⚬

Through the backstage area where the teenage actors were rushing to get ready for act 3, out the service entrance, across the outdoor pathway connecting the theater to the main building of Marlowe School, walked Victoria, by herself, brushing her fingers along the lockers lining the walls of the dark hallway. She was bored of them all already, bored of the little kids they called her peers. Victoria couldn't wait for the semester to start: hour after hour of answering every question, finishing all her quizzes first. It was as easy as hearing her teacher's thoughts. She couldn't wait to see all her classmates' faces. As she walked down the stately hall of the prestigious school, she knew this would be the staging ground for her own unveiling.

After five years of living in the crimson house, Victoria wasn't afraid of the dark. Her heels clicked and echoed through the hall and ended in a ghostly *ping* at the other end, at a point far beyond her line of vision. Not far behind her, moving at the speed of her own steps, followed a cluster of moths. They were tightly packed together, about the size of a fist, and they remained always the same distance behind, above her left shoulder, as if pulled by a string. They made no sound. They were barely visible, their tiny black bodies merely specks against the dark backdrop of the sleeping school. Why were they there? What were they planning to do, hovering behind Victoria? But Victoria did not ask these things, because she, slowly creeping through the darkened halls of her new school, was busy hatching her own plans.

She had already identified her first move. She would beat out Lucy for the top spot in the class. She would get out of all those stupid class requirements and score a perfect 5.0. Yes, Lucy had said it was impossible, but who was Lucy to tell her what she could or couldn't do? She was better than Lucy. She had more talents. She was a *winner*. She didn't need to take retard classes like the others, so it was only fair that she should get something that was inaccessible to them. She'd sweep the school of every prize, every accolade, everything they had to give. She'd be class president. She'd cheat her way to the top of this ridiculous school, and then she'd be Vileroy's favorite. From there, it was only a matter of time. She'd go to Harvard. Run for Senate. Maybe even be president of a small country. Vileroy would *have* to help. After all, wasn't that just exactly the kind of thing the governess had always wanted for them? Wasn't that what the *other* girl from London had asked for and received? *Think big, Victoria.* Behind her, the swarm of moths silently scattered as she turned and walked back to the theater.

~◦◉◦~

Belle sat silently in the dark theater next to Madame Vileroy. Occasionally she looked across the aisle at Thomas and his father, both engrossed in the final act of the play. The woman sitting next to Belle pulled her body away, as far from Belle as it would go. Despite the play, Madame Vileroy hadn't missed a thing. Without turning to Belle, she leaned in and said in a conspiratorial whisper, "Wouldn't it be nice if you could control that?"

Belle's head snapped around. Madame Vileroy only said things like that when she was making a deal. "What do you mean?" Belle whispered a bit too loudly.

"Shh," a long-necked woman behind them hissed.

Madame Vileroy calmly turned her head to look at the woman. She slowly winked her normal eye, leaving only the branded one, which flashed just slightly. The woman let out a little yelp and cowered back in her seat. Madame Vileroy smiled and turned back to Belle. "I mean, you're the most beautiful girl in the room. You could have anyone you want — anyone who'll wait long enough."

"But I can't force them to stay."

"I have something that will help you to control the air around you."

"I can change it?"

"No, you can change how people react to it. They can react any way *you* want them to — stay as long as you want them to."

Belle was silent. She didn't want Madame Vileroy to read on her face how much this was worth to her. But it was too late. She was turning white. Beads of sweat were appearing on her forehead and shoulders, dripping down into her low-cut camisole. Belle could feel her chest growing wet with perspiration. Instinctively, her hand flew to her chest to hide the black mark growing visible over her heart. Madame Vileroy leaned closer, and like a skilled governess, slipped a napkin into her charge's trembling fist, which Belle held tightly over her heart. Belle dried the sweat and listened with anticipation.

"How many times have you tried to wash it off?"

"Three times today."

Belle hung her head. She remembered those hours spent in the shower, watching her own chest turning black as the water penetrated her skin, a reminder of her own true nature.

"Well, dear, I'm happy to help. But you have to do something for me."

"What's that?" asked Belle, sounding scared.

The governess reassured her. "Don't worry, dear, nothing's as big as what you've already given up."

"What do I have to do?"

"Small things. Nothing any regular girl your age wouldn't do. See that man over there?" she said, pointing to a distinguished-looking man with a gray beard three rows down. "First, I'd like you to find a way to get him to come for a visit. Do you think you can do that?"

Belle nodded but raised an eyebrow. This sounded like a rather strange errand. Why couldn't Vileroy do it herself? But then again, Belle already knew the answer to that. Madame Vileroy liked it when her children were *involved* in the things she did. It was as if she wanted collaborators — in everything. As if she wanted to implicate them in her crimes, since she herself could never be punished. This was Madame Vileroy's own weakness, for all her years of expertise.

"Then I'd like you to take Christian an evening snack."

"A snack?" Belle repeated the odd request slowly. "When?"

"Yes," Madame Vileroy said casually. "I'll let you know when."

"What should I bring him?"

Madame Vileroy cocked her head and put a long finger against her cheek, as if she were thinking. Then she said, "Oh, I don't know — hot dogs? It's very easy. On hamburger buns . . ."

"That's weird."

"Some people have weird habits, dear. Just do what I ask."

Belle had to admit, the deal *was* an easy one to take. Much easier than it had at first seemed it would be. Then again, that's how Madame Vileroy made deals. Dangle something, make it seem impossible to have, then ask for what she wanted, which seemed easy in the face of all the possibilities.

"OK," said Belle, repeating to make sure. "Invite that man, a snack for Christian. Got it." It seemed too easy. Belle didn't understand why Madame Vileroy hadn't given this gift to her in the first place. The chores seemed harmless enough. She wondered if she should give it more thought, given what she knew of her governess.

She looked up and caught the bearded man craning to look at her. Across the aisle, she caught a glimpse of Thomas, with Lucy on his other side, stroking his hand. For a second, Belle's gaze caught his, and he quickly looked away. She looked down and coughed, and the woman next to her left her seat to find another. An usher tripped on a tear in the carpet and sent a stack of programs scattering to the floor.

"OK, deal."

Chapter 5
Hide

Ten soldiers stand in the dark cellar with their rifles pointed at the family. Terror and panic are frozen on the faces of the children. The father holds his wife like a mannequin holding another mannequin. In front of the firing squad, a cloud of smoke lingers in the air, not dissipating. Bullets from the rifles hang in space like a perfectly still swarm. One has already struck the tutor in the thigh. Another is about to enter Aleksey. It is poised no more than two inches from his shoulder.

She steps into the silent scene from a dark corner, from behind the clock—its hands frozen in time. The clacking of her shoes on the stone floor is the only sound. Her bracelet, black onyx, was handmade here in Russia, a gift from the czar—over there holding his wife—before this ugly revolution. She steps through the clutter of suspended bullets; some fall to the floor. She cannot save them all, the children she has raised as her own. Already she knows she'll have to begin again, somewhere else, as governess to other royals. In frustra-

tion she points one soldier's rifle toward another soldier standing off to the side. When time begins again, they will shoot each other, and have no idea how or why. All the same, she knows Aleksey will never be strong. Anastasia is clever, though. She adjusts the bodies of the horrified family, moving them like dummies. Anastasia will be shielded by her family, possibly even survive this firing squad. The blond woman sighs and walks to the stairs. As she enters the endless summer, she snaps her fingers, the rain begins to fall again, a clock ticks its own life away, and the sound of gunshots begins to hammer into the forgotten night.

~∞◯∞~

The house was as silent as a morgue. Any other house with five teens, even in New York City, would be a carnival at that time in the evening. But not the Faust house. No sounds of vacuums or microwaves, no conversations. No buzz of TV or cars outside. No animals, no mice in the walls, no birds perched on the eaves. No creak in the floorboards. No music. None of the noises of life were in that house, only cold silent stillness.

Bicé's room was musty and littered with the last of the sunflower seed shells and pastry wrappers she had stashed away. It was pitch-black. Bicé was in the corner, huddled with her books, holding a flashlight like a phone on her shoulder, mumbling things to herself, constantly frightened by the stillness of the dark all around her. Still, she was used to them, these long silences. In the house where all the children had ambitions, deadlines, and big plans, Bicé wandered aimless and alone. But in her books, she could talk to the faceless, ageless friends who loved her, friends who didn't find her strange.

Hiding, that's what Vileroy called this. The most special gift of all, the ability to hide in the creases of time, like the comforting folds of a mother's skirts.

A spider hung motionless in the door frame, as it had four minutes ago. She knew those four minutes hadn't gone anywhere. She knew everything had stopped because she had wanted it to. Now the whole house, maybe the whole world, was her silent cave where nothing was moving, not even time. She was terrified of bumping into someone, because she never knew where they'd been when she stopped them. They would be frozen like dead bodies found after a blizzard thaws, expressions of a moment carved into their faces, backs bent in uncomfortable positions. At first they had seemed funny, like rag dolls. She would stroll around the house, put food in Victoria's constantly open mouth, slide Valentin's finger in his ear. Then they began reminding her of city ruins like Pompeii. People covered permanently in ash while trying to escape the wrath of a volcano. Belle looked like a mother curled over one of her old dolls, trying to save it. Christian running in his room looked in the middle of running away. Time had stopped still, and Bicé was in a ruined world.

The last time she was alone like this, she had spent what seemed like hours watching the frozen Belle. She had examined her new face, her new body, and wondered, *Is this my Belle? Is she in there somewhere?* She had touched her face and wondered if she could rub past this mask and find her sister. She had felt Belle's blond hair and closed her eyes, trying to remember all those times she had brushed it when they were little. It didn't feel the same. She felt her own hair to compare, keeping her eyes closed. For a moment, the old Belle had come back in Bicé's imagination, and then she was gone, leaving Bicé feeling like half of her had died.

Bicé cradled her empty stomach. She hadn't eaten in what seemed like days. If she were to faint, she didn't know what would happen. If she was conscious, she could let the world begin again. If she hit her head, maybe everything would remain lifeless — except for her body, incapable of healing itself, slowly but surely decaying in the constant flow of time. Maybe a spray of air freshener would last longer than she would. The droplets would stay like glass beads draped across the air above her as she lay unconscious — her cells screaming at breakneck speed toward oblivion.

She opened another textbook, a volume of Persian poetry. Her hair was ratty, her fingernails dirty and jagged. But no one was around to see her, and no one could hear her — except for the Singer, the elderly Persian poet in her book. He could hear her, but only when she spoke Farsi. That's what she was learning with the book, while talking to the void. She could hear him too, a gentle voice to fill the lonely hours. "Hello, my friend," said Bicé in Farsi. She turned the page.

The Singer said something back. Bicé squinted. The Singer leaned in, just to the border of the light, where Bicé only got a glance of his beard. He whispered, "A bird stole my pen."

Bicé grabbed another book, a dictionary. As the Bs flipped past, she wondered what thought Belle was having, which thought she was never finishing, all this time. "How will you write your letter to the king?" she asked the black room in beginners' Farsi. She saw a dull twinkle like a plaque-encrusted smile.

The Singer said in a sad, gravelly voice, "She doesn't want me to write my letters."

"But she's only a bird," Bicé practiced, her pronunciation near perfect.

"No," said the dark, mumbling some more in the old tongue.

And then, the Singer's voice changed. Gone was the grand-fatherly poet she knew.

Something else whispered her name. "Is someone there?" she asked.

"Yesss," said the dark. Bicé recoiled.

A flash in the blackness. Bicé looked at the silhouette of the old man, his kind smile wicked now, his eye suddenly changed. It was the burned and branded eye.

"Stop."

But the void continued to taunt her, its voice higher. "No place here for a little girl. No place to linger."

"Stop, Vileroy, stop!"

The house began to speak again. Appliances resumed their cricket hum. Outside her door, someone as heavy as Christian lumbered past. Bicé gasped for new air, starving for food, terrified that she could never fully escape the governess. The bodies were alive again. She was still afraid to turn the light on, afraid of all the noise. But she was relieved. Even though every squeak from a door hinge, every rustle of a skirt, jolted her, at least she wasn't alone anymore — alone with the dark. She'd have to clean herself up before she went out. She'd have to face the motion of time again, but that wouldn't be so horrible. Because at least the world of the living was a devil she knew.

When she opened the door, Madame Vileroy was waiting. Bicé didn't say anything. Madame Vileroy held out a glass vial. Bicé snatched it from her hand and swallowed the deep green sludge that slowly crawled out when she tipped the bottle. She looked at the governess, annoyed that she'd stood there to watch her drink it all.

"Well?" she said.

And Madame Vileroy said, "Good," and walked away.

~⤜☷☷⤏~

At the breakfast table, the four others looked tired, as if the night had gone too fast. Christian felt as if he'd closed his eyes to sleep and opened them a second later for his alarm. Belle was staring into a hand mirror, looking for bags under her eyes. Victoria took pills to keep her alert since she had stayed up studying or filling out scholarship forms.

"You slept late," said Valentin when Bicé walked in.

"Very," said Bicé. She grabbed at the bacon, eggs, and pancakes. She spoke to herself in Farsi as she chewed some smoked sausage.

"Great," said Victoria. "Now we can go to school with a mumbling cab driver."

Belle hit Victoria in the arm and mouthed, "Stop it!" *Leave her alone or else,* she thought, in case Vic might be cheating.

"Hey, Bicé, let's go to one of those Korean nail salons, and you can tell us what they're saying behind our backs!" said Belle.

"I think she's speaking Arabic," said Valentin. He slipped a hand into his pocket.

"All right, fine, let's go to an *Arabic* salon."

Suddenly Valentin broke out into hysterical laughter. Belle, Victoria, and Christian looked at him like he was crazy. "That was hilarious!"

"What?" said Belle.

"Oh, man, sometimes I'm too nice to you guys."

"You little rat!" Victoria whispered to him, grabbing his collar. "I know what you did."

"No, you don't," he whispered back.

"Uh, yeah, I do. I just heard you play it over in your head."

"What, what is it?" said Belle, trying to hear what Vic and Val were talking about.

"Don't do that again, Val. I'm serious," whispered Victoria, crossing her arms.

"Oh, come on, it was just a joke." Valentin leaned close and touched Victoria's chin, trying to win her over. Valentin was convinced that Victoria was the most sexually repressed girl in the world and that given the right circumstances, he could change her point of view on a lot of things. But she pushed his hand aside.

"If you keep playing like that, Bicé will know. And if she knows, she could ruin things. Is that what you want?" Victoria said through clenched teeth.

Christian looked up from his food. He'd been eating the whole time, content to stay out of another fight. But Victoria and Valentin looked very suspicious just now.

Valentin scoffed at the false memory of what could have happened in a thousand possibilities for a future that only he could see — and Victoria could cheat off.

"I only wanted to know what Bicé would do if she knew our secret. I went back and changed it."

"Maybe so, but it's dangerous." said Victoria, "Remember, she can play with time too."

"Hiding is different." Valentin seemed insulted. "She can only make things stop. It's not the same. Besides, don't you want to know how she reacted?"

"I saw it . . . in your head."

Belle touched her cheek. For some reason, her flesh was raw — where she may have been slapped by her sister in a past that never happened. She looked over at Bicé, who smiled lazily at her.

"Stop whispering, you two," said Belle.

"Stupid Val's playing God again!" Victoria yelled.

"Vic," said Christian, trying to calm her down. "Whatever he did is no big deal. Can we just have some peace?"

"It *is* a big deal!" shouted Victoria. "You don't know anything. He could rewind and do anything he wanted."

Valentin couldn't help smiling.

Belle said, "He wouldn't do *anything.*"

"He would," said Victoria. Then she turned to Valentin. "Just remember that I know everything you do, you stupid punk. You're too arrogant not to tell yourself all about it later."

Valentin was still smiling. Victoria's comments had barely affected him. She just glared at him, crossed her arms, and lowered her voice to a whisper again.

"You just do whatever you want. You don't care who it hurts. I guess that sort of thing runs in your family."

Valentin's face turned white. Victoria could see the hurt in his eyes when she referred to his family, and somehow his reaction calmed her, made her feel better. When he spoke, his voice was different, a bit strained. "Wow, Vic. You're a real piece of work."

Suddenly Belle started to sob. "I hate this house," she said softly, somehow emotional from a slap that never happened, a betrayal that was never discovered. "Why can't we just live in the guest house permanently?"

"That's so like you, Belle, thinking that a prettier house would make you happy," said Victoria. "I would never live in that house. It's not real."

"Neither is this!"

"Yes, it is!"

"No, it's not!"

Suddenly the entire kitchen table lifted into the air, turned on its side, and crashed to the floor. The plates and glasses shattered on the ground in a splatter of food and juice. Belle let out a little yip. The four of them sat, dazed, in their seats, in a circle. Christian stood in the middle, his chest heaving, his eyes on the floor. He didn't say anything, only stood in the center of the circle after his sudden splurge of violence. After a long pause, he said in a soft, regretful tone, "Stop fighting."

Then he bent down and picked up a bagel from the floor. He walked out.

"Happy family we have here," said Valentin.

"Shut up," said the other three, almost in unison.

Valentin just shrugged, grabbed a piece of toast, and got up to leave. As he walked down the hall, he noticed Vileroy walking beside him, as if she had been there all along. He leaned in and whispered in her ear, "I still need help." He crept close to her, letting his cheek touch hers as he spoke, his stray hairs mingling with hers.

Madame Vileroy glanced at Valentin's hand, which darted into his pocket and emerged with a folded white cloth napkin that seemed to be pulsing in his hand. Valentin always carried it with him.

"Have you been practicing?" she asked, encouraging his ever-flirtatious manner.

"All the time." Valentin opened the napkin instinctively. Inside was an old-fashioned stopwatch. It looked worn, beaten up, and weary with overuse. It beat with an unsteady rhythm. Like a defective metal heart.

"Let's see," Madame Vileroy whispered in his ear. Her breath made him shiver.

He began reciting her a poem. A love sonnet he had not fully memorized. Each time he messed up, he went back, trying to make it as seamless as possible. For her, he wanted to make it perfect. He was always willing to put on a show for his beautiful governess, the one who had given him so much.

"Why can't I get it right?" he asked when she informed him that the tic was still there.

She sighed. "You're not patient enough, Valentin." She put a long finger to her lips. "You don't go all the way back. You don't dare to grab that perfect moment, and so you flounder, grasping at the moments around it. And then what happens? It always seems like a stutter." She leaned toward him. "Choose an object to focus on. You need some small movement that you can track *constantly.*"

"But it's impossible to know what time I want to return to beforehand. Once I know I've messed up, that moment's already passed."

"Yes," said Madame Vileroy with a satisfied grin. "That's why you have to track something *all* the time. You can't suddenly remember that you need it after you mess up. By then it's too late."

"That's really hard," said Valentin.

"It's a tricky business, Valentin. That's why it's called *lying*. You have to remember a lot of details to pull it off."

"But is it really lying? I mean, the things I change technically never happen, right? I go back in time and change them."

"Well, in a way. You see, Valentin, there is no such thing as time. It's just a road, a path that people travel on. But most people can't go back and forth on this path. Most of the world is on a train, traveling forward all the time, speeding toward death, with a set schedule and someone else in charge. You, my dear, are the only one who gets to be on foot. You can go back and forth and experience things again and again. Sometimes you can do things to reroute the train. But people still feel how it should have been. They somehow sense the lie. That's why you have to be careful, or else they'll know, and hate you for it."

"I've been using this old watch," Valentin said as he ran his finger over the worn timepiece. "It's always lagging, and the rhythm keeps changing. I try to memorize the missed beats."

"That's a start," said Madame Vileroy.

Valentin inched toward her. "Wanna practice together?"

"No," said the beautiful governess, and walked away.

Valentin looked down at the watch perched in the palm of his hand. Even with all that power, the smallest rebuff weakened him, made him feel like a little kid. He hated that feeling the most — that he was disposable, unloved, nothing special. Nothing special to *her*. Slowly he closed his hand around the fitful old watch. It snapped in his hand and stopped beating. He heaved a long sigh and walked back to the empty breakfast table. He sat down in a chair soaked with juice, surveyed the food covering the floor, the crushed gears in his hand. He closed his eyes and brought it all back — to the way it should have been, to a moment when he was having fun.

"Yes, it is!"

"No, it's not!"

Suddenly, and again, the entire kitchen table lifted into the air — and even the milk from the pitcher followed the same arc as last time, Valentin noted—turned on its side, and crashed to the floor. Then Christian said, "Stop fighting."

And this time, in the pause right after, Valentin leaned back and said, "Who else thinks that Vileroy's kinda hot?"

"Shut up," said the other three, almost in unison.

~∞∞∞

Christian went to his room. On the way, he walked past Madame Vileroy, leaning against the wall. He didn't stop. "You are a good boy, Christian," she said as he passed.

But Christian didn't want anything to do with her right now. He ran to his room. When he opened the door, he saw that she'd changed things. "I have a present for you. You deserve a present." He couldn't feel her breath on his neck, but she was close enough that he should have. At the center of the room was an isolation tank. He had been lying down in that coffin for years now, staring up as the lid closed over him, letting the blood-thick water lap around his sides. The darkness would pour into every inch of space. The glittering liquid, teeming with tiny crystals, would press itself into the pores of his skin, knifing through the holes and into his bloodstream—little stones squeezing through every vein and capillary. His breath would quicken, every muscle contract, relax, and contract again. But then he would come out rejuvenated, stronger than an ox, supercharged like a dynamo. If he stayed in there long enough, Christian might have been able to leap tall buildings or stop a train.

And someday he would. That was the governess's plan all along. He would become a hero. The next big thing. Olympic medals, World Cup trophies, Super Bowl rings, and all the worship of fans, all the money from endorsements. What loving mother wouldn't want that? He would turn the world's attention to what he could do athletically — famous forever, rich, and not hungry. Not hungry or poor. That was the ambition Vileroy had preyed upon. Though it wasn't so much an ambition as a fear. And she would use it to make him a hero. Or maybe he'd be strong enough to crush a tall building or crash a train. He'd be powerful, able to shape public opinion with an iron fist — tyrannical, infamous, and starving for more.

In the corner of the room stood a young man, or that's what Christian thought, because it was impossible to tell. His face was ageless, with no lines or expressions, no sign of having laughed or cried or lived beyond today. He was very strongly built and was wearing a pair of white pants, like Christian's martial arts pants, and no shirt. He had a blank expression on his face and stood without moving, like a dummy or a toy soldier ready for his orders. That was what had caught Christian's attention, because he'd never seen this stranger before.

"Who's this?" Christian asked Madame Vileroy.

"Don't you want more practice?" The look of alarm on Christian's face seemed to amuse Madame Vileroy. "Even Valentin is improving. Your sisters are naturals at it. But you, you've been queasy."

"The others don't have to hurt people."

"You don't want to be weak, do you, Christian? Victoria cheats, because she has to. Bicé hides. Valentin lies. Belle tricks. They do what they do because that's what's best for them. Stealing is no different."

She said everything in a dead tone, a plain, assured, terrifying tone. Christian looked like he was about to cry. He couldn't ever seem to figure out what it would take to get him what he wanted. Quite frankly, Christian was starting to get distracted. His ravenous desire to be free from ever worrying about money was still there. But Vileroy knew he was spending more and more time writing instead of practicing. Now she'd make sure he got plenty of practice, in sports, in stealing, and most of all, in cruelty.

Suddenly, the dummy in the corner began to move. First its shoulder shrugged a bit. Then it looked up at Christian. It went into a fighting stance.

"He's not real," said Vileroy. "Trust me."

The dummy hopped from one stance to another, closing the distance between it and Christian. Christian knew it was simulating a Thai kick boxer. It would attack soon.

"I'd rather spend a whole day in the chamber," said Christian.

"It doesn't take nearly as long as you'd think to recover. He's very resilient."

The dummy lunged at Christian with a rising knee. Christian evaded, but just barely. It turned and struck Christian with an elbow. It seemed like it was made of something hard that gave a little but hurt a lot. Still, somehow, it felt like human flesh.

"Go away. I'm not doing this."

"Yes, you are," said Vileroy. "It's what you want."

It grabbed Christian behind the head. Christian knew the match would be over soon if he didn't do something.

"This is not what I want," said Christian.

He tried to look at Vileroy as he said it, but before he could even finish his sentence, the dummy wrenched his head down and thrust its knee into Christian's stomach. All the air left his body at once. The dummy had to hold him up. Christian tried to regain his breath to say something, but his chest and neck were getting battered by the dummy's knees. Finally, it took one step back, pulled Christian's head down farther, and rammed its knee into Christian's nose. Christian felt a warm liquid beginning to pool behind his eyes. Another smash was coming. Then he heard, "I couldn't do this if you didn't want it, Christian."

Christian reached out his hand and touched the dummy. A second later, it collapsed to the ground, and Christian stood up with a surge of energy running through his own body. Nothing felt worse than the guilt of how good it felt. He was perfectly fine now. His bloody nose was gone, his entire body recharged. Madame Vileroy didn't bother to congratulate him.

"You should name him. How about Connor? Like your new friend."

"No."

She glanced at the dummy. "He's a very useful toy, Christian. And you haven't even thanked me."

Madame Vileroy looked at the figure lying almost lifeless on the ground. Letters began to sear themselves across his forehead until the word *Buddy* was clearly visible. *Buddy.* The dummy rubbed his forehead as if it burned.

"There, now he has a name. He can be your buddy." The letters disappeared. She laughed at her own joke. "He'll begin making friends with you. After a while, he'll anticipate your stealing and will try to fight back. After that, he'll grovel. . . ."

Christian whispered, "No," but no sound came out.

Madame Vileroy smiled. "You're weak, Christian. That's why you have to steal. These children around you are not your friends, and neither is Buddy. Learn this quickly."

She walked out. Christian stood in the middle of the room with enough energy to run a marathon. His fists clenched and shook. He looked down at the dummy named Buddy and felt helpless and sorry for all the things he'd have to do.

~⊗◊⊙~

"You think Christian had a breakdown or something?" asked Belle as they sat around the messed-up room, the table still overturned next to them. None of them really cared enough to clean anything up. They'd just leave when they were done, and the next time they came back, it would be clean. It could have been maids, robots, elves, or slaves — to be honest, they never really thought about it.

"He just snapped," said Victoria.

"It's always the quiet ones," said Valentin, "the quiet ones with three black belts."

"We should see if he's all right," said Bicé.

They sat together looking at strawberry jam slopping down a pancake, egg yolks torn open on a saltshaker. Victoria finally stood up. "I don't have time to hang out with losers who can't control themselves. I have to prep a debate and figure out how to get out of gym."

"I'm working on a poem," said Valentin. "Maybe I can use all this."

"I'll be in my room looking for a potion to remove this," said Belle, fingering a tiny red mark on her shoulder.

"You don't need a potion to remove that," said Victoria, "just a zit cream."

"I don't want Thomas to see it . . ." Belle mused, her mind wandering again. "I should find out more about Lucy. How could he like her more than me?"

"Belle, no one will notice a dot," said Bicé in her most maternal tone. "And you can't spy on Lucy."

"Not spy, sis. Just research. Besides, she's probably spreading rumors already."

"Childish ones like, 'You smell,'" said Valentin.

"Cute, Valentin."

"That Charlotte girl thinks I'm cute. I should probably spend some time with her. She could be useful."

"Well, Miss Priss here might be above it, but I'm going to *spy* on Lucy," said Victoria. "See what she's up to for her Student Council campaign."

They all nodded. These were important things to put on their agenda. They each had so much that they wanted. Madame Vileroy would help them keep track, letting them know what they could have if they just did this or that. She'd be there to help them if they ever really wanted something, but otherwise, the house was like a clubhouse, or an island, where they ruled themselves. They were left to their own ambition to get ahead. They could achieve as much or as little as they dared. Victoria, Belle, and Valentin then turned to Bicé, waiting to hear from her. Bicé looked back at them, not getting it.

"What are *you* going to do?" asked Victoria.

Bicé didn't think it'd be hard to guess. "Me? I'm going to check on *Christian.*"

Then Valentin's faced jerked. His hand flew out of his pocket. He had stuttered half a word. His face blushed, and he wouldn't look in Bicé's direction. She couldn't tell whether she'd heard it in his stutter or just had a sense of it for some reason, but she knew the word he'd tried to keep himself from saying was "Why?"

Chapter 6

Water Mark

"My dear Monsieur Bodin, help me to better understand these theories of yours."

"No, please, madame. Let me go."

"You've said quite a deal on the subject of the witch mark. You had a wonderful closing statement on the poor young man you sentenced to death not long ago."

"It's only theory. I never —"

"You did. It's a matter of public record. August 3, 1585. The Inquisitorial trial court of Laon, France. Don't you remember? Just weeks ago. The boy on trial would have been a glorious dancer, you know — best the world has ever seen."

"I didn't know."

"You said to beware a witch mark on a person's body, for they are servants of the devil. But he had no mark, did he?"

"No. It was gone. I saw it in the baths, but then it was —"

"And so your clever answer was that the court must be more wary of those without the mark, because the devil doesn't need to mark them. They've gained his trust."

"Yes, but—"

"So whether he did or didn't have a mark—all that talent, my work, sentenced to death."

"Please stop this. Please let me go."

"Just two more questions, Monsieur Bodin. What makes you think the devil is a he? And why is it that there are no marks on you?"

~ⲟⲟⲟ~

That morning, like the morning before, Belle had woken up with parched lips and eyes sealed shut with dried tears. Since the Christmas party, Belle had felt the stench of herself more than ever. It was so much more palpable now that she had hope that it might go away, now that she had someone she wanted, someone who hadn't stayed. That morning, the morning after the school play, she had stumbled to the bathroom, splashed scalding water on her face again and again until finally she could open her eyes. When she did, she saw her perfect eyes—two crystalline oceans, wracked from a storm, now silent and infinitely sad.

At breakfast she scooped wedges of grapefruit. She no longer noticed that her breath fermented the bitter juice into rotten wine, or that in the morning, her milk curdled in her cereal bowl. She listened to the chatter, hoping not to catch Bicé looking at her. Then Valentin had laughed about something he had done. Every part of her felt afraid of it. Then Christian overturned the table and for some reason she felt safe afterward.

She walked to her room with her stomach churning—like after every meal. In the center of the house, she could look in any direction and see down a hall, branching to separate rooms. From above, the house might look like the sun, rays thrusting in every direction. Belle turned toward her hall and saw Madame Vileroy coming down the one next to it—from Christian's room. Belle said, "Where's my part of the deal?"

"Did you do what I asked?"

"Almost. The guy's coming, and I've got the snack ready."

"I know," said Madame Vileroy.

Madame Vileroy led Belle down a different hall, one she'd never been down before. Vileroy opened the door to a bathroom that looked more like a fiery lagoon. Its walls were white, but Belle could hardly tell through the eerie red light of the flames. The only light in the room came from the candles sticking out in all directions from the walls—fingers reaching out and on fire. The sharp edges of the cobblestone floor pricked Belle's feet. In the corner stood an ancient tub on strange legs. Everything here seemed wet, as if the room itself were sweating.

On the left was a wooden vanity and mirror. Behind it, the wood from the vanity had melded with the walls and seemed to have grown there. It stretched all the way up to the ceiling, making the entire wall behind the vanity look like mahogany. A thousand square cubbies were dug into the wood, and in them were all kinds of glass bottles and jars filled with different-colored powders, elixirs, and stones. She recognized them, all the tonics and pomades that she used every day. Vileroy had added more ingredients. Some of them seemed to be moving in their jars.

"So you put my stuff in here? That's it?" said Belle.

She took a step inside. The air was warm and dewy, like a rain forest.

"If you stand in the steam," said Vileroy, touching her face, "it'll make your skin as soft as mine."

"Will it put on my makeup too?" asked Belle.

"Would you like that?"

"Not enough to ask." Belle eyed the tepid water.

Madame Vileroy walked over to the vanity. She took a glass bottle from a cubby high up on the wall. Belle looked at the label.

Gray chalk.

Dried lemons.

Iridescent scales from a black asp.

Shards of stained glass from a fallen temple.

"This isn't what you promised," said Belle. "You said I could control it."

Vileroy mused, "The unfortunate disconnect of how very pretty you are on the outside . . ."

"Yes, now give it."

"Look behind you."

Belle turned around. She eyed the bathtub standing on the ossified legs of four different creatures—a leopard's paw, a goat's hoof, a monkey's hand, and a claw she couldn't recognize.

"A bath? That's not funny."

"How else?"

Vileroy walked to the tub. Belle thought she saw the legs shrink away from her. Vileroy held the bottle over the water and poured out the contents. The glass plopped to the bottom while the scales, chalk, and lemons floated up. Belle stepped closer. She noticed that the bottle in Madame Vileroy's hand had IRRESISTIBLE written on the side.

"Bathe in here."

"The smell will go away?"

"Go away? That smell is you, darling. No, it'll change how people smell it. Their mood, you might say."

"So that bottle will make me irresistible to Thomas?"

"To anyone. There's a bottle for everything — *fascinated, jealous, angry.*"

"Why would I want someone mad at me?"

"Not *at* you, *around* you. You'll still have to direct their emotions to whatever you want."

"I want to be attractive," said Belle, dabbing a moss-covered stone with her toe.

"Then get in," said Madame Vileroy.

Belle put one foot in. As soon as she put her weight on the foot to lift the other leg over, she felt a shard of glass pierce her skin. Belle jumped out. The ball of her foot was beginning to bleed. She winced, suddenly realizing that the pain was growing to a screech. The water infused with sour chalk, lemon juice, and snake oil wet the cut, shooting pincers through her leg. Belle almost collapsed but caught herself on Madame Vileroy's shoulder. "It's horrible," she said.

"It has to get inside, dear, where your ugliness is."

Belle remembered clearly that only a few years ago she had been identical to Bicé. She knew that her best features weren't really hers. They were Madame Vileroy's, modeled after her own youth centuries ago. But with these changes Madame Vileroy had given Belle the thing she wanted most desperately: a beautiful outside.

Belle gathered herself. She knew this was the deal she had made. She couldn't do anything but take it. Vileroy began to walk out to let her bathe in the horrible cauldron alone. She turned at the door. "If you didn't like that one," said Madame Vileroy, "be careful of *hope*. It'll boil you alive."

～❧～

A few hallways down, Valentin read over the newest poem that he was sure would top all others. "Wow," he said to himself as he stared at the parchment. "It's perfect." He lifted his pen to put the initials *VF* at the bottom of the page, as he did with all the poems. Before he got up to leave, he stuffed a few notes and random papers into a drawer and folded the finished poem in half. He put it into his pocket and set off to find Christian. Reading his poems to Christian was a guilty pleasure for Valentin. He knew how much it hurt Christian to listen, and the awe on Christian's face did wonders for Valentin's ego.

～❧～

"How did you get in here?" said Christian. He was sitting up in his coffin, holding the lid with one strong arm.

"Door was open," said Bicé, shrugging. "Just checking to see if you're OK. What's wrong with the little man over there?"

"He's not real."

"What were you doing?"

"Golfing."

"Funny."

Christian had just been lying there, in his coffin, losing track of the hours. He closed his eyes, opened them — there was no difference in the blackness. The gelatinous liquid rose slowly, burying him, forcing itself through his nose with every breath. At first he would always be panic-stricken for fear of drowning. He clawed at the lid, but it wouldn't move. Finally, he gagged and swallowed the same gulp over and over again, in and out of his throat. He gasped for air, got only water, vomited the water only to gasp again, and again only water. At the end, his reflexes surrendered. Every time he did this, he thought he was about to die, but then the liquid would suddenly start flowing in and out of his mouth like air. His lungs inflated and deflated, heavy in his chest like water balloons. He thought his eyes were floating in his head, the tiny charged stones in the water scraping them from behind. Christian would lie there, becoming super, thinking about how lucky Valentin was.

More than anything, Christian wanted to write. But Christian knew he wasn't good enough to make any money as a writer. Valentin was. His heartbreaking prose was already getting him attention from publishers. In his journal, Christian described listening to Val's readings like a cripple watching the Olympics. He'd be so jealous, he'd feel like his heart was gripping the bars of his rib cage, clutching so hard, wanting to get out and be in somebody else, almost tearing his chest apart. It was an Olympic amount of pain. So Christian wrote in secret and won every sport he tried, because actually there *was* one thing more important than writing — Christian could never be poor. He'd never sleep in a shanty or wear cast-off clothes. He'd never eat old stolen food. He didn't know why these things seemed so scary. He had no memory of living that way. But somehow, the fear was inside him. He was born with it. He'd rather be bored to death while smacking homers in the World Series if he had to. But he wouldn't ever worry about money. He didn't want to buy generic cereal. He didn't want to say no just because he couldn't afford it. Christian didn't want to be poor so bad that he had to be rich. That's what he'd been brooding over — and how much he wished he could write a single poem as good as Val's — when Bicé had walked in.

"What's wrong, Christian?"

"Nothing."

"I've got maple syrup on my shoe that says there is."

"I'm just tired of Vic's attitude, and Val — that idiot."

"That's it?" said Bicé, coming over and sitting down on the lip of the tank. Christian's hair was still soaked with the liquid. Gobs of it stuck to his temples like hair gel.

"You ever wonder why a woman like Vileroy would adopt all five of us?" asked Christian. He was playing with the drawstrings of his trunks.

"That's a pretty random question."

"I've been thinking about it. I mean, why us five?"

"I know it's hard to think about, Christian. Our real parents probably had some reason —"

"They didn't want us."

"Maybe they couldn't keep a baby."

"To hell with 'em if they couldn't."

"Christian."

"But why would Vileroy want us?"

Bicé sighed. She was concerned for Christian, but didn't have any answers to offer.

"Do you ever even think about how screwed up this is?" said Christian. "The things she does?"

"To be honest," said Bicé, "all I ever think about is being alone."

"You mean alone with your books," said Christian.

"I just meant I don't think about her all that much."

"If I won the lottery, I'd buy a ton of land and never worry about anything again."

"You'd get tired. You need goals, like that athletic award at Marlowe and then a Division One college."

"*You* don't have any goals," said Christian.

"And I'm dead tired."

Christian laughed at her dark humor. He lifted himself out of the tank and walked over to the sink. The thick liquid dropped on the floor and looked like beached jellyfish. Christian grabbed a towel and held it under the faucet. "Thanks, B. I'm sorry about breakfast."

Bicé was about to say something, but she stopped when she saw Christian wipe his wet towel over his bare chest. A faint black mark blotted the skin over his heart. It was just dark enough to be visible. She wasn't even sure it was there. Christian caught her stare.

"What?" he said.

"That spot," she said, "on your chest."

"It's a birthmark," he said.

"Yeah, I know. Belle has the same one, only much darker than that."

Christian stopped wiping. He looked at Bicé, not knowing quite what this meant. "She has the same mark?"

"And it only shows up when she gets wet."

"But we're not—I mean, she's not *really* my sister . . . you know, by blood."

"That doesn't matter. Birthmarks aren't genetic."

Just then the door to Christian's room swung open and Valentin stepped in holding a sheet of paper. "Hey, Christian, I finished my poem. Wanna hear?"

"No," said Christian, annoyed that his conversation with Bicé had been interrupted.

Valentin's face made a sudden twitch; his hand reached in his pocket. His smile looked like it had been jerked by a fishing hook. "Thanks," he said, "I'm really excited about this one." He unfolded the piece of paper to begin.

"Wait, I didn't say I wanted to hear it," said Christian.

"Yeah, you did," said Valentin. He was always confusing real memories with events that he had never allowed to happen. Memories only he would have. Sometimes, he got confused even when something had *just* happened or when he hadn't yet changed something and it was only an imagined future.

"No, I didn't," said Christian.

"Oh," said Valentin, and began to search for something that would interest Christian.

"But it's about chi—" Valentin's face twitched again. "Monst—" It twitched again. "Trains on a track, very poetic."

Christian perked up at the subject. "You've never mentioned that before," he said.

"It just came to me," said Valentin with pride.

As Valentin read his poem to him, Christian felt it washing over him. When Valentin finished, he looked up for Christian's response.

"It's really good. You're really good," he said with a faint smile. He rubbed the painful spot on his chest, the painful birthmark that Bicé had just noticed.

"Thanks," said Valentin. "I've been working on it all day."

~≪∞≫~

A few hours later, long after Bicé and Valentin had left to change clothes, Christian woke from a nap. Buddy was conscious now, sitting in the corner, tossing a racquetball against the wall. In a few minutes, they would flip houses and Belle's guest would arrive. Without warning anyone, she had invited some old man from the school play to their house. Christian turned around and noticed something sitting on the nightstand next to his bed. On a tray, next to a glass of orange juice, was a large plate of burgers with a note tucked underneath.

Hey, Christian,
Thought you could use a snack.
Love, Belle

It was a nice gesture, and he was hungry. He lifted the bun from one of the burgers. *What's this?* Instead of a hamburger patty, Belle had cut up hot dogs and spread out the pieces all across the bread. The hot dogs looked uncooked. It was as if she had thrown together scraps from the fridge and tossed it at him like he was a dog or some poor homeless mongrel orphan. He stared at the hot dog burgers for a while, feeling nothing at all. And then something inside him moved, and he felt anger rise up through his body and grab him by the throat.

At first, Christian pushed the feeling back, laughing at himself for reacting this way. After all, Belle was just trying to be nice. No one asked her to bring him a snack. So why criticize? Just throw it away and move on. But then, each time he looked at the plate, he felt his rage and sadness grow stronger and the plate began to look different. Like a last meal. Like a hopeless, homeless Sunday evening. Like the grief-stricken scavenging of a hungry boy who's just buried his mother. Like a fall to a different life. If he took a bite, he would be a different person. He would be someone with no options.

As he sat there, heaving with unexplainable fury, he felt a burning in his eyes. He looked up and saw the blinding blue light take over his room and shoot past his eyes. He closed them, but nothing helped. A moment later, he was sitting on the unused bed in the fake bedroom that he supposedly shared with Valentin, complete with its pristine furniture and unwrapped hockey sticks.

~⚬⚬⚬~

Victoria and Belle were waiting in the magazine-cover living room with Madame Vileroy when there was a knock on the door. Victoria jumped up from the plush creamy couch.

"What's the matter with *you?*" Belle asked with a raised eyebrow.

"Nothing. Just get the door."

"Why are you even here, Victoria? This is *my* guest. Madame Vileroy, can you tell her to leave?"

"No, dear, Victoria can stay."

"Then can you tell me why you made me invite this guy? I had to tell him I have a medical condition and I need him for a consultation. And he's so"—Belle shuddered from head to toe at the thought—"sleazy."

"Be patient, my dear," said Madame Vileroy. "I hear it's a virtue."

"OK, then what do I have to do? Can you tell me that much?"

"Get the door."

Belle opened the door to find the doctor she had met at the party, waiting with his hands behind his back. She let him in and invited him to sit down, all the while wondering what she was supposed to do, whether her first bath would work. After a few minutes of pleasantries, which grew more and more strange as the doctor became more accustomed to and infatuated with Belle's tricks, there was another knock on the door.

"That's her," said Victoria.

"Who?" said Belle.

But Victoria was already up and answering the door. Belle turned to find Ms. LeMieux being led into the house by a very happy Victoria. Thirty seconds into the counselor's arrival and Victoria was already chatting her up with the contents of her own mind. Belle heard Ms. LeMieux snort with delight. "What a self-assured girl you are."

Victoria demurred. "Thanks. I'm trying my best. It's just so hard, because even though I want to try for the Marlowe Prize, my grades will get killed in gym. I have a lot of . . . physical impairments."

"Oh." Ms. LeMieux put a hand to her mouth.

"I really shouldn't have to take that class. But it's a world ruled by jocks, you know."

Ms. LeMieux knew. She knew all too well. And Victoria just stood back and listened as Ms. LeMieux remembered all her own teenage injustices. The counselor's face grew softer as she thought of all that she had in common with this girl. *What ambition. What go-gettitude. Truly inspiring.* She allowed Victoria to lead her inside.

"My brother Christian's a jock," said Victoria. Then in a whisper, "I'm not saying 'roid rage, exactly, but carbo-loading doesn't make you flip tables, you know?"

Ms. LeMieux put a hand on Victoria's shoulder.

Madame Vileroy got up to greet the counselor, which was more than she had done for the doctor. Ms. LeMieux shook the governess's icy hand. "I'm sorry to have to make this house call, Madame Vileroy. But some of the things Victoria said on the phone this morning were rather alarming — and quite difficult to believe. I can't approve anything without seeing for myself."

"Of course. We understand," Madame Vileroy said smoothly.

At that moment, Christian burst into the room, red-faced, with tears knifing down his cheeks. He was screaming something incoherent, knocking over anything that would break. Madame Vileroy knew that even *he* couldn't say why he'd become so enraged. Seeing the hot dog burgers was like an accusation, and he'd just gone off. Now he was blabbering out profanities, crying like a baby, and smashing like a beast. Finally, as the heaving in his chest subsided, he noticed the guests, wide-eyed on the couch. He didn't say anything more, just turned and headed for the kitchen. From the living room, the stunned guests could hear Christian slamming doors and storming about.

"Girls, come with me, please," Madame Vileroy said, standing up, as if she were going to handle the situation. She put a motherly arm around Belle, who looked confused, wholly unaware of what had been done. These were the moments the governess lived for—the first moments of a giant rift to come, seedlings of mistrust that were surely now planted between Belle and Christian. "If you'll excuse us."

The two guests sat silently for a few minutes. The doctor spoke first.

"Schizophrenic rage. Rare at this age, but rather interesting . . ." he mumbled.

"Are you familiar with the family?"

"No, I'm a child psychologist," he said with contempt. "It's really quite sad to see a broken family. I'm going to request a one-on-one consultation with each of them immediately, especially the daughters. They seem the most in need."

"Really? A broken family?" asked Ms. LeMieux, taken back to her own damaged childhood and how hard she had had to work and how no one ever gave her a break.

"Absolutely. A classic case," said the doctor, stroking his beard. "The very fact that they're orphans makes them susceptible to all sorts of emotional scarring."

"But Victoria seems so above average. So concerned with her schoolwork, going after the Marlowe Prize. . . . I just think—"

"An elaborate facade. In my *professional* opinion, she's weeping on the inside," he said, clicking his tongue and shaking his head at the shame of it all. "They all are," he added.

"Poor dears," said Ms. LeMieux, sitting back in her chair. She felt such an immediate sympathy for Victoria and her physical and emotional handicaps, all the obstacles pushing her down as she tried to pull herself out of her unfortunate circumstances.

～◈◈◇

The next day, Victoria received a messengered letter from the Marlowe School, informing her that in regard to the phone call about her phobias and "weak constitution," she would be exempt from health and physical education classes from then on — and wishing her the best of luck in her pursuit of the Marlowe Prize at the end of the upcoming semester.

Chapter 7

The Moths

"You have had much success, Nicola. More than any other in the legion."

"I enjoy my work."

"Princes, philosophers, men and women of power. Your influence is great."

"I am a keen observer of the mark. I know when they are willing to bargain."

"You track it at an astonishing rate. It's as if you smell a weak soul."

"My winged friends watch for me. They tell me when a heart calls for us."

"You and your insects . . . I wonder if those little spies are the ones responsible for all your prosperity as a governess."

"Or maybe I'm responsible for theirs. They're everywhere. It's hardly a challenge."

"Are you bored, my friend?"

"I've exhausted my skills. I'm looking for an unattainable soul . . .
a soul that's not for sale. I want someone without the mark."

"You know that's not allowed, Nicola."

"I think I've found a way."

~ⱰⱰⱰ~

Victoria was happy — ever since Madame Vileroy had all but assured
that her future would be as bright as a morning star. She would go
down in history forever. Now *that* was a Christmas present.

Wrapped in towels, Victoria looked at herself in the mirror. She
eyed the black spot, still visible on the moist skin of her chest. Suddenly she was startled by a noise in the room. Victoria whipped
around to see Madame Vileroy sitting in the corner like a coiled
snake, so silent you'd think she wasn't paying attention— a smile on
her face like a demon trying to be demure. She looked like the picture of the perfect mother.

Then she spoke: "Put some clothes on. I want to show you
something."

As they made their way down the hall, Victoria grew more
excited and frightened. The candles had flickered out, and she was
beginning to feel something crawling on her arms and face. She
didn't know what it was, but somehow she didn't feel alone. Victoria
heard a buzzing noise, growing louder as they moved down the cold,
dark hall. It wasn't like the buzzing of bees or hornets. It was light
and fluttery, like millions of tiny wings flapping all over the place,
enclosed in a tiny space. Victoria closed her eyes, scared to see what

kind of horror Madame Vileroy had in store for her. They walked into a room. The buzzing had grown so loud that it was almost impossible to hear anything else. She felt Madame Vileroy's icy hand on her shoulder, compelling her to take a look.

Victoria opened her eyes to a sight that left her breathless. Moths, hundreds and thousands and millions of them. They filled the tiny room like a massive cloud of dust. They flew around in unison, flapping their wings in such harmony that the sound began to take on a sort of rhythm. In the thick fog of moths, Victoria was afraid to open her mouth to speak, since she might get a mouthful of bugs.

"Don't worry," Madame Vileroy read her mind. "You can talk. They won't harm you . . . much."

"W-what are they?" Victoria stammered.

"Meet your new family, Victoria. Your closest confidants. These creatures will become your eyes and ears throughout the city."

"How?"

"Did you ever wish you could be a fly on the wall in other people's lives?" Madame Vileroy smiled with malice.

"Well, yes, it's like that when I . . . you know . . ."

"Yes, but there's only one of you and thousands of *them* . . ."

Victoria was beginning to understand. These moths would spy for her. She wouldn't have to do the work anymore. In fact, she didn't even have to be in the room in order to do it.

"Take a few steps forward."

"What?" Victoria was shocked and scared. "You want me to go in? They're all over the place."

Madame Vileroy didn't respond. Victoria took a small step inside, then another, and soon she was standing in the middle of the cloud.

She couldn't see Madame Vileroy, or the door, or the walls — only moths flying around faster and faster. When they sensed her presence, they began to converge around her head, whipping around and around like flies drawn to a flame. Victoria had never been so scared in her life. She couldn't see anything except the mist of insects; she couldn't hear anything else either. All she could do was stand there and hope that they wouldn't hurt her. She became aware of the unnerving feeling of wings against her face. Then she reached out her hand and allowed a few of them to hover above and below her outstretched arm. Their wings felt soft, like a giant feather boa, and Victoria's fear began to subside. Still, she was far from comfortable. The moths were everywhere. Suddenly she wished she had put on more clothes.

Then she noticed something. The buzzing was not all that she could hear in this noisy whirl of insects. She could hear something else. Victoria's eyes fixed on a moth that was flying toward her. As it whizzed by her face, she heard a word whispered amid the flapping.

Rrrrrrrr. "Spencer." *Rrrrrrrrr.*

Then another moth came buzzing past. It too whispered something.

Rrrrrrr. "Divorce." *Rrrrrr.*

Then, as she turned around in a circle, she noticed that all of the little creatures were saying something. Words were flying at her, in a giant jumble, intermixed with buzzing and flapping. *Rrrrr.* "Thomas." *Rrrrr.*

Rrrrrrr. "Party." *Rrrrr.*

Rrrr. "School." *Rrrrr.*

Rrrr. "Election." *Rrrrrrr.*

Rrrrrr. "Suspicion." *Rrrrr.*

Victoria grabbed her head. There was no way she could piece together what all of these creatures were saying. They were all speaking at once, throwing words here and there. She called out for Madame Vileroy.

Madame Vileroy's voice came to her calmly, yet magnified, as if carried by the moths. "Don't try to listen, Victoria. Just close your eyes and remove yourself from the moment. Let them do the work. When they are finished, you will know."

Victoria reluctantly obeyed. She stopped trying to listen. She simply closed her eyes and tried to shut off her brain. She just stood there, almost in a trance. After a few minutes, she opened her eyes in shock and ecstasy.

"They put the information in my brain! I can see what happened for the last three days at Thomas's house. And Lucy's house. And at the neighbors' upstairs."

"All you have to do is stand there and let them whisper to your unconscious mind. There are enough of them to cover every house in the city, but you must be careful. They interpret information just as you would. They do make mistakes."

"Are you sure it's OK for me to know all this?"

"Knowledge is power — and power is good. Anyone who tries to tell you that you shouldn't know something is just afraid that you'll become powerful."

Victoria squealed with delight.

~⚬⚬⚬

"Well, that was petty," Belle spat as soon as she found her governess alone.

"Do you think so, dear? Tell me why."

"Because!" Belle raised her voice. "You knew he'd go nuts! And for what? You traded me the bath, only to set up Victoria's little plan. Since when is a nice deed enough of a reward for you?"

Madame Vileroy shrugged. Belle persisted.

"What's in it for you? Why help Vic? All the rest of us have to make deals . . ."

The governess looked at Belle with the kind of pity you would feel for the slowest kid in the class. "Did you really think I did it out of the kindness of my heart?"

"Vic got her way. . . . She must be your favorite, then." Belle stopped short, angry at herself for having just said that — having shown the governess that she cared. She whispered, "If you'd have me do all that for *her*. . . . The doctor and the snack were all for *her* sake."

Madame Vileroy looked at Belle with interest, with that look on her face that appeared only when she was studying someone or something. When she was deigning to find the children fascinating.

"I thought that the current wisdom among you children was that Valentin's my favorite."

"I just don't get why you couldn't do it all yourself. I mean why would you need me?"

"Well, dear, if you took a moment to think, you might realize that things aren't quite that simple and that it *had* to be you for a reason. If you were cleverer or savvier, you might even come to think that you, not Victoria, could be my favorite."

Belle looked confused.

"I don't care who wins that prize, Victoria or the poor fool who really deserves it. And I don't care about what ridiculous item triggers Christian's rage," said the governess, careful not to mention that Belle could be the new object of that rage. Instead she sat back and spun her web around Belle. Her naive charge. Her favorite. "This entire bargain only matters because of what *you* can learn from it. The way you use it. The ripples you produce."

"Ripples?" Belle asked.

Madame Vileroy waved away the question.

"I did it to teach *you* a lesson. I had to make you do it, so you would learn — for your future. This was all for you, Belle."

"That makes no sense. What can I learn from Christian going nuts over a snack?"

"Simply how difficult it is to predict people's reactions. How difficult and how useful. I want you to learn that no matter what your intentions are, other people will always interpret things in their own way, based on their own past. I want you to realize that if you knew in advance, if you could read people well enough, you would have more power than the bath could ever give you. Learn that, and you won't *need* to be my favorite. You can be anyone's favorite."

Belle spent a few moments thinking, wondering how much to trust Vileroy. Her heart beat fast, and the black mark above it lay dark and dormant, hidden beneath her dry skin. *Learn that, and you can be anyone's favorite.*

"I'm pretty good at reading people . . ."

"Darling, you managed even to misread my intentions. First you thought I was doing something nice for Christian. Then for Victoria. And all the time, you knew enough to figure it out. You must dig deeper."

Suddenly Belle felt utterly stupid. The governess went on: "People act and react based on things that go far deeper than what you expect. You have to dig and then dig deeper . . . always deeper."

"What happened to Christian? Why did he act like that?"

"He learned a lesson too," said Vileroy, her eyes fixed on Belle in such a way that she could hardly miss how intricately woven it all had been. She could hardly miss how, like a simple girl, she had missed it completely. "Christian got a taste of what it was like before. A tiny reminder of his old life — what it's like to be poor. So now he can focus on why he's here and not be distracted with this poet fantasy. We all know *that* has to die."

"Great. So he learns his lesson and hates me in the process."

Vileroy smiled at the many lasting effects of one small action.

"Well, if you can't read him well enough to make him love you again, you can always use the bath."

Even though she knew better, that last comment made Belle feel good.

"So you see, dear? Are you convinced? I've never bothered to teach lessons before. Never wasted a bargain. But you, my Belle. You could be special. You could go so far and do so well."

With that, the governess walked toward Belle and held her face in her hands. Those long, icy fingers around Belle's chin felt like falling into a pool of stagnant water, her face wrapped in slithering water snakes.

"You could be my favorite. Just like a daughter of my own . . . that is, if you don't disappoint me."

Just like a daughter.

Those words swam through Belle's heart and mind and landed

hard in her stomach, so that all day long she had to hold herself together, her arms wrapped around herself, warming her body against sudden chills — those frantic bursts of cold when the words left the back of her mind and splashed to the surface.

~∞∞∞

Victoria stood outside the cloud of moths alone, watching the moths circling the room, forming various shapes, speeding up and slowing down as if they too were thinking about something. She stepped back into the gray cloud, ignoring the fact that the hairs on her arms were standing on end. When she was in the middle, she shut off her mind and let the words buzz past her, melding into coherent thoughts. After a while, she knew that the neighbor upstairs was getting a divorce, the neighbor downstairs was having an affair with the door-man, and the mailman on Forty-second Street was stealing birthday cards for the cash. With this kind of power, Victoria could easily become the most successful student at Marlowe. *Harvard? Forget it. That's nothing. President of a small country? Try the United States!* She didn't ask to be liked; she didn't care if she hurt anyone, and she didn't feel too queasy about using the ideas Madame Vileroy whispered in her ear. She just wanted to win. Plain and simple.

The probing insects were hard to get used to, though, constantly touching her, barely letting her breathe. It was like being buried alive. She focused on Thomas, whom she knew to be her top competition in debate. She asked for more information about him, and the moths responded like obedient angels. *Thomas has been holed up in his room all day. His father came to him twice to see if he wanted to play a round of golf. His father kept saying not to put pressure on himself.*

Thomas has been practicing for the State Debate and Drama Tournament for months now. He has over a thousand pieces of evidence and a box full of data. His room is filled with debate trophies and certificates. He is a front-runner for the Marlowe Prize, the most prestigious merit-based award at the school — usually given to the top student. Thomas said to his dad that he has a great idea for winning the big tournament. Didn't hear the idea.

Victoria felt the beginning of a headache. It felt like the moths were getting heavier and heavier over her head. She wanted to swat them away. She still didn't know Thomas's idea. None of it helped. It was all just pointless gossip. What she needed was a way to cheat off Thomas — a way to go deep into his mind without interference, without being detected.

What was Lucy doing now? She asked the moths to spy for her, and without hesitation, a handful of them flew out the window. Victoria was surprised at their speed. They brought back information in almost no time, as if they were connected to each other, like a line of children playing telephone all the way from her house to Lucy's. She could hear Lucy now.

"They're such freaks! One of them tried to flirt with Thomas right there under my nose! She wasn't even polite enough to assume we were together."

"But, Lucy, you're *not* together. You weren't even together that much at the play." The moths carried Charlotte's voice now.

"But *she* didn't know that. And he kissed me, so we're as good as together."

"Really?" gushed Charlotte. "After the party? I *knew* it."

"There was some mistletoe." Lucy giggled, then she went on: "Anyway, that Victoria girl freaks me out. This is going to sound weird. You have to promise not to laugh."

"OK," said Charlotte with hesitation.

"I think she's psychic or something. I swear she was reading my mind."

"Oh, Lucy . . ."

"No, I'm serious! I tried to be nice. She was asking a million questions about grades and stuff. My mom says they're all trying to worm their way to the top."

"Everyone at Marlowe is competitive."

"Are you taking their side?"

"They're not all bad. What about Valentin? He's pretty cute, no?"

"Oh, right, you mean the one with Tourette's?"

"He doesn't have Tourette's. I think he's hot, and very poetic."

"You're just desperate to find another bleeding-heart poet."

"No, I'm not."

"Don't be such a spaz, Charlotte."

"So, Char," Lucy started after a few more minutes of random gossip. "Are you going to help me with my campaign?"

"Sure," Charlotte said in a bored tone.

"No, seriously! This is important. I *have* to be class president! My mom was class president!"

"Fine. I said I'd help."

"How about, 'Vote Lucy, She'll keep Marlowe free of mind-reading, grade-grubbing, boyfriend-pawing orphan freaks'? Can you put that on a hundred posters?"

"Yeah . . . maybe that's a little too specific, Luce," Charlotte said, laughing. "I'll write you a couple of good slogans."

〜❀〜

Victoria stumbled out of the fog with a raging migraine. She put a finger to her upper lip and found a drop of blood from her nose. She had taken in too much. Using the moths was definitely not easy. It hurt. It made her feel ashamed. But still, the room exhilarated Victoria — like the feeling of new friends. Thousands of friends that would always have time for her. Millions of sisters that would help her when she asked. For the first time, Victoria felt her heart filling with love. The others could keep their little clique and exclude her. They could laugh and it wouldn't matter. Victoria's new family would always do what she told them, say what she wanted. Victoria could open and shut the door at will. She could control the slightest flap of the smallest creature. And so for the first time, Victoria also felt loved.

〜❀〜

Down the hall, a lonely moth flew in zigzags through Madame Vileroy's cold, unwelcoming home. It followed Valentin into a small bedroom and watched as he tried to entice Christian into conversation. When that failed, it followed Valentin into Belle's room, where he thought he could catch her changing. He found the room empty, and so he loitered around the living room looking for Victoria — maybe he could bait her into driving herself crazy trying to cheat off of his thousand-version memories. That would be fun. But no luck. He decided to go back to hanging out with Christian. He grabbed his notebook and bounded into the room. But when he opened the door, he found Madame Vileroy waiting there, alone.

She was reclining on a chair, giving him a sidelong glance as though he amused her. She motioned for him to shut the door and said, "It must be fun toying with your brother like that." She nodded toward the notebook in Valentin's hand. "Reading to him every day. Making him listen, when you know he's secretly wishing he were you."

Valentin didn't answer. He clutched his notebook, with its perfectly printed poems, the initials *VF* on every page, and held it to his chest.

"I must remind Christian not to waste his time," she mused, almost to herself.

"What do you mean?" asked Valentin.

"Writing . . . listening to poems. He is here to become strong. To win at sports. That's what he wanted. Writing is a waste."

"You should let him do what he wants," said Valentin, averting his gaze, playing with the spine of his notebook. The sardonic look on Madame Vileroy's face, the gently mocking purse of her lips, made him falter, but he went on: "He likes to write. Just let him do what he likes."

Chapter 8

Queen Bee

The young pharaoh surveyed her kingdom, its fertile soil, its mountains of riches, the endless Nile. Only a girl, yet she had managed to become a god-queen, feared and loved at the same time. She had supreme power, complete control. Yet barely a day passed when someone, some traitorous soul, wasn't put to death for questioning her reign. In those days, she demanded more time alone. When her servants and handmaids left her chambers, satisfied that the pharaoh had retired for the day, she made her way to her hidden pyramid, the secret hiding place that her mother had built. Here, she knelt like a common pauper and dug her hidden treasures out of the ground, dozens of vials of colorful liquid. Here, in this dark, damp pyramid, in a hole dug in the dirt, she mixed together a bubbling, writhing bath the color of blood. She lowered herself into this pit without ceremony, forgetting that she was royalty, that she was wallowing in dirt and excrement like a street urchin. This dark world required no fanfare. And so she closed her eyes, determined to bear the pain of the bath, a

solution whose cleansing sting she craved daily now. A potion that
blinded and mesmerized her people, bound them to her like opium,
and made them forget their most fervent objections.

~⚬⚬⚬~

On the first day of school, Victoria got up early to print out her to-do list, review the activities she planned to join, reread her Harvard Business School catalog, and spend some time with the moths.

Valentin and the girls were driven to school in Madame Vileroy's sleek black Town Car. When they arrived, they split up without speaking. They didn't use a map or stop to ask anyone for directions. They knew exactly where to go, as if they had attended Marlowe for years. They didn't look around in a curious way; they didn't even wander around looking for their new lockers. Madame Vileroy had shown it all to them before, in the weeks before school started, when they were just watching. Their casual attitude made them more of a target for gaping eyes and gossip than if they had behaved like new kids are supposed to. Still, it made little difference to them since they were anticipating much worse. At the moment, they were only a strange family that had just moved into town. In a few weeks, they would be the strange family that had taken over the school.

Christian had left for school two hours earlier than everyone else to check out the swim team's morning practice and talk to the coach about joining late. Buddy had woken him up with a series of reluctant pulls and nudges. He shoved Christian's shoulder, pushing him to get going. Christian reached out as he shook off the groggy first light of waking up and dropped Buddy to the ground. Then he rolled out of bed and got dressed.

Christian had decided that he would join the golf, swimming, tennis, and martial arts teams this year. Since those were all individual sports for the most part, he wouldn't have to sort out any complications of teamwork. He could just win and leave it at that. But after a few solitary days of practicing, he thought that maybe one team sport wouldn't hurt, and he decided to play a bit of basketball too. Five sports in one semester—Christian would have to pick up the slack next year with a few more, but it was better to start off slow. He didn't really need the physical training, and he was stealing to make things certain. As for handling objections from coaches, well, Madame Vileroy was an expert at that. The martial arts team was an informal club that met on weekends, and she had arranged for Christian to simply show up for the tennis and golf matches. That left swimming, which practiced before school, and basketball, which met after.

From then on, Christian spent his nights locked away in his restoration chamber. More and more, he was absent from meals—so often that the others wondered if he was becoming addicted to it, the way some athletes became addicted to painkillers. Though he never talked about it, it had become obvious that he spent a lot of time practicing and learning to break Buddy by stealing at the right times. Since his arrival over Christmas break, Buddy had started becoming more animated, at first smiling or reacting to pain while they practiced and then perking up with excitement every time Christian walked into his room. Though Christian still found it incredibly hard to use Buddy for practice, his desperation to win left him little choice.

Instead, he looked for clever ways to avoid hurting Buddy when he didn't have to.

Meanwhile, as the children adjusted to Marlowe, Madame Vileroy crept into the lives of Mrs. Wirth and her fellow Marlowe parents. Somehow, no matter what strange things happened, Mrs. Wirth was always ready with an explanation of her own. "The door hit her in the head—hard." "The mothballs must be getting old." "That boy just needs a good speech therapist." None of the children mentioned to their new classmates that they had spent Christmas Day alone in their home. Victoria, Valentin, and Belle, who remembered once celebrating Christmas, were too focused to care. Bicé and Christian, the ones that didn't remember . . . well, they didn't remember.

⤬⬳⬰⬲⬱

One afternoon, only a few days after the start of school, Belle sat in the constant dark of Madame Vileroy's living room, mixing several strange-looking liquids. She was lost in her own world, measuring, diluting, wiping, and stirring, oblivious to anyone around her. She was in the process of pouring a crackling, fizzing yellow substance into a wooden beaker when Victoria walked in.

"You're not supposed to do that in here," Victoria said.

"Needed a change of scenery," said Belle.

Victoria was about to ask what Belle was smiling about when she felt a twitch in her nose. She wrinkled her face, not knowing where the itch was coming from. Then, as she sat down next to Belle, she felt a strange sensation washing over her.

"What are you—" She couldn't describe what she was feeling.

"Yes?" said Belle.

"I don't know . . . I . . . well . . ." Victoria stammered, her eyes darting back and forth. She looked around for a bit and then began hugging herself with both arms and lightly rocking back and forth. "D-d-do you hear something outside?"

"Yes," said Belle, "I think I do. Like a scratching at the window."

"Yeah, a scratching," said Victoria. "It's dark in here."

"Very dark. Are you scared?" said Belle.

"What? Me? Don't be ridiculous," Victoria said with disdain. "But . . ." she hedged, and suddenly whipped her head around. "What was that?"

"I heard it too!" said Belle. "Oh, my gosh, look!" Belle suddenly leaped up and pointed at the window. Victoria raised her hands above her head and screamed like a startled chicken. She jumped up from her seat to run away, but then rethought the idea and came right back down. She missed the seat and crashed to the ground. She scrambled up, threw her arms around Belle's neck, and buried her face in her shoulder. She didn't notice that Belle was laughing softly. The bath was working like a charm. This morning, she had poured in a bottle of *hallucination* mixed with a little *irrational fear.* After a little while, Victoria looked up cautiously.

"What's going on?" she said with a broken voice. "Why are you laughing?"

"I'm sorry, Vic. I didn't mean to trick you. You were just the first person who came in, and I was testing out the bath. It's amazing, isn't it?" Belle couldn't hide the ecstasy in her voice.

"What?" Victoria was very angry. "What did you do to me? Fix it, now!"

"Don't worry. It won't hurt you." Belle tried to calm Victoria down. Victoria continued to whimper, but it was wonderful. Victoria obviously didn't feel repulsed by her. She just felt scared. She felt exactly the way Belle wanted her to feel.

"So there's nothing at the window?" Victoria asked.

Belle shook her head. "Nothing," she said. "Here, take this. Just keep smelling it." Belle gave Victoria a cup full of coffee beans. As soon as Victoria put her nose in the cup, she seemed to calm down. She realized that she was still clinging to Belle and immediately pushed her away.

Just then, Bicé walked past them as if they weren't there. As usual, she was mumbling something. She looked weak and listless. She walked over to a cupboard and grabbed some cookies. As Victoria continued to sniff the coffee, Belle watched Bicé with interest. Was she sleepy? Was she stupid? She usually wasn't so out of it to just walk by like that. Just then, Belle saw Bicé jump three inches to the right. It was as if she just disappeared and appeared to the right of where she was standing before. But Belle knew better. It hadn't been just a split second at all. For all she knew, Bicé had stopped time for long enough to learn Navajo and Belle had been frozen for weeks. It was pretty impressive that Bicé managed to find her old spot within three inches.

~∞∞∞

Half an hour later, Belle was bathed (again), clothed in her trendiest designer outfit, and ready to head out. She had already taken several strolls around the city over the past few weeks. She knew where to go to find every type of New Yorker — burned-out twenty-something bankers, unwashed starving artists, models looking for father figures, and, of course, teen queens with their high-school entourages.

It was still early in the afternoon, so Belle made her way to a café near Marlowe. In the crowded streets, people stared at her because she was uncommonly beautiful. As she walked, she gazed at the frosty tree limbs in Central Park and the leftover Christmas decorations in the store windows. Patches of snow crunched under her feet, and she darted across town blithely, relishing the glances of the passersby. She passed a street lined with brownstones, warm lights spilling out of random windows, and she quickened her step, trying not to think of her own cold home.

The café was dark and decorated with big couches and pillows and a few tables here and there. Belle walked straight to one of the couches and sat down. She looked around. Teenagers were standing in groups, many of them wearing the gray-and-navy Marlowe School uniform. She recognized two of them right away: Charlotte Hill and Connor Wirth. They were standing with a third girl from Marlowe. They had just bought their drinks and were making their way to the empty couch next to Belle's. Belle turned her back so they wouldn't recognize her too soon.

The tiny blonde in the tennis outfit felt it first. Something sweet and fruity that made her think of spring and outdoor parties. It felt nice, like a tequila sunrise with lots of cherries. Instinctively, she turned around. There was Belle, sitting alone, reading a magazine, paying no attention to this girl or her group.

"Hi there," the girl said to Belle. Charlotte and Connor exchanged confused glances. Connor recognized Belle but didn't say anything, trying to play it cool. The girl turned to her friends with a big smile on her face and then bounced out of her seat and sat on the couch next to Belle. "I'm Maggie."

Her friends followed her to the couch, half because they were curious and half because they too felt a bit happier than usual — somehow drawn to the next couch. Belle didn't respond until all three of them were sitting next to her. She raised an eyebrow, as if annoyed by this unwelcome disturbance. In fact, she stayed silent throughout Maggie's introduction and Connor's and Charlotte's confused *hello*s. *This is working so well,* she thought.

"Hi," she finally said to Maggie, "I'm Belle." They smiled, except for Charlotte, who looked a bit uncomfortable. She kept rubbing her arm and looking around.

"Do you go to Marlowe too?" asked Maggie.

"Um . . . yeah, she does . . ." Connor answered for Belle. He kept smiling but was fidgeting in his chair. There was something strange about the Faust girl. Stranger than last time. Something uncomfortable. *She's so pretty. Like a celebrity. But not like the way they look on camera. She's like a celebrity in those candid shots. There was something unhealthy about her. Sickly white, like a starlet without makeup. I like her, though,* he thought. *She's so pretty.*

⌒⊗⊙⊙

An hour later, Belle had the unfortunate threesome in the palm of her hand. They had told her all the Marlowe gossip, all the best places to eat and shop and hang out, and they had even invited her to sit with them at lunch for the rest of the year. As soon as Charlotte found out she was talking to Valentin's sister, she inched a bit closer, inhaling even more of Belle's intoxicating air. She didn't care that

Lucy, her best friend, hated this girl and her upstart family. She just wanted to know more about her — and Valentin.

Connor, having completely forgotten his first impression of her at the party, asked Belle to the spring dance, but she laughed, saying that it was too early to pick a date.

"Connor?" she asked, still unsure of her own power. "Can I ask you something?"

"Sure . . . yeah . . . definitely." He stumbled over his words. He didn't know the question, but he wanted to answer it more than anything.

"How many girls has Thomas Goodman-Brown dated?" she asked shyly.

Connor thought for a second. Then he said, "If I find out for you, will you let me take you out?" He didn't bother to think too much about why Belle wanted to know about Thomas. He just wanted to be with her and make her happy.

"I promise to think about it."

"OK, I'll find out tonight."

"Hey, I know about one girl," Maggie said cheerfully as she played with her ponytail.

"Oh?" Belle said approvingly. "Tell me."

"Lucy Spencer. I've heard some talk about them."

A tiny pang of guilt kept Charlotte from saying anything for a split second. For a moment, she sat there fidgeting, trying to decide if she should betray her friend. But she quashed that feeling and volunteered everything she knew, saying, "They kissed at the party."

Belle flared with jealousy at the thought. A bead of sweat appeared on her forehead, and with it the smell of sewage. The stench passed quickly, making the others flinch. Belle smiled and wiped her brow, and the three went back to their half-witted admiration.

"She kissed him or he kissed her? Find out for me?" Belle asked sweetly.

"OK," Maggie said. She took out a pen and put it on her to-do list.

Belle now had her own throng of followers, as obedient as Victoria's insects, ready to do whatever she wanted.

"Charlotte, you wouldn't mind finding out all the places Lucy might see Thomas in the next couple of weeks, would you? You know, activities, parents' parties, stuff like that."

"Um . . . sure, Belle." Charlotte reasoned that the information was easily available to anyone. It wasn't *best friend* information. Besides, she *really* liked Belle.

〜☙◯◯◯

That night, the Faust home was silent. Victoria was sealed away, all alone in a sea of moths. Valentin spent the evening memorizing each errant tick of a rusty old watch. Christian was locked in a coffin, making his body and his habit stronger with each passing hour. Bicé slept. And Belle had dinner alone with Madame Vileroy.

Despite everything, Belle still didn't feel right. She had noticed that throughout the afternoon, her new friends were fidgety, sometimes hanging on her every word, telling her everything she wanted to know, and other times writhing around in their seats like tortured animals. When they were around her, it seemed that something happened to their adrenaline. It ebbed and flowed, starting and stopping, like soft whimpers after hard sobs. She didn't like this side effect. And she wasn't sure how long she could hold them.

She and Vileroy ate in silence, except for the sound of Belle's phone every few minutes, signaling the arrival of a text message.

Connor: **T only dated 2 grlz. Neither @ Mrlo. Never sees them.**

Belle: **Sure?**

Connor: **Ya, both dating other guys.**

Belle: **Kewl, thx.**

Connor: **Dinner?**

Before Belle had a chance to respond, Madame Vileroy looked up from her plate and said, "Becoming quite the queen bee, aren't you?"

"So?"

"So, you're wasting it." The governess ran her long fingers through her shiny hair.

"What do you mean?"

"Always dig deeper, Belle. Always look for the weak points. For instance, you could ask Connor to do so much more. He'll do it. Men always do. Look carefully and you'll see much more than just what's at the surface. Like the fact that Lucy and Connor aren't that close. You should be able to observe things like that by now."

Belle thought about that for a minute, then picked up her phone.

"And sending written messages seems a bit foolish," said the governess.

"What do you mean?" asked Belle.

"How can you read what he's thinking? How can you charm anyone using that hideous shorthand? It's so . . . frank. A waste, in my opinion . . ."

Belle shrugged and dialed Connor's number.

When he picked up, she got right to the point. "Know any good gossip about Lucy?" she asked.

"Like?" said Connor, obviously excited that she had called. Vileroy had been right — again.

"Like what?" Belle asked Madame Vileroy, putting her hand over the phone.

The governess waved a hand in the air dismissively. "Indiscretions, cheating, embarrassing medical conditions . . . whatever you like."

Belle said to Connor, "Like stuff she's done. Embarrassing things."

"I could find out."

"If you do, tell Thomas."

"What if there's nothing to find out?"

"It doesn't have to be true. You think she's not doing the same thing to me right now? Besides, she called you a dumb jock at your parents' party."

~⊕⊙⊙⊙

Just as they were finishing dinner, Belle heard the sound of a text message from Maggie.

Maggie: **Tru about kiss. Lucy has big crush. Been wrkng on him 4 dance.**

Belle: **Tell T that. Tell him L's dying 2 go out w/ him.**

Maggie: **Y?**

Belle: **Looks desperate.**

Just then, Madame Vileroy approached her from behind, whispering as usual. "It would be a lot more effective if you turn them against each other."

"Why?"

"Because then they would cling to you more." Creating a gulf between people — that was Madame Vileroy's favorite pastime. Every cold moment between Christian and Belle Madame Vileroy prized as her own recent accomplishment.

"Good idea," said Belle, feeling a bit stupid for not having thought of this herself.

"If you practice," said Vileroy as she slinked away, "you can come up with your own good ideas."

Belle: **Thx Mags. UR sweet. CW is just being a jerk btw.**

Maggie: **Huh?**

Belle: **He said UR really nasty to freshmen and hobos.**

Just then, Belle's phone rang. It was Maggie, tired of texting. Without saying hello, she screamed, "It was April Fool's! And he's done way worse!"

"I know. Will you just do that one thing for me, then? Please?"

"OK, sure."

Belle giggled at the extent of her own power. *This stuff isn't even because of the bath! I did that on my own.* For some reason, that made her proud. It had been so long since anything she'd done was her own work. And after what happened with Christian, after that talk with Madame Vileroy when the governess had told her how much she could do without the help of any baths or potions, after that, something about manipulating a bunch of unsuspecting classmates made her feel good. Each time she used some tidbit of information to predict exactly how they would react, a small part of her rejoiced.

As if she was learning.

As if she could do so much on her own.

Just like a daughter.

Later that night, when Belle was working on her laptop, she got an instant message from Charlotte.

> **CharChizzle:** They have debate together every day. Spencers are friends with G-Bs. They go to his golf games. Oh, and they hang out when Connor is around. C & T are friends.
>
> **Bellissima62:** Thx, babe.
>
> **CharChizzle:** No biggie. It's all public info anyway.
>
> **Bellissima62:** Will you do me one more little favor?
>
> **CharChizzle:** Sure. What is it?
>
> **Bellissima62:** Just keep watching her for me. Connor says she's a crazy witch. You never know what she'll do next.
>
> **CharChizzle:** She's not that bad.
>
> **Bellissima62:** Do it for me?
>
> **CharChizzle:** OK, but there isn't that much to tell.
>
> **Bellissima62:** You're a doll. Maggie was completely wrong about you.

Belle turned around in her chair just in time to see Bicé standing there, her arms crossed, having just read Belle's conversation over her shoulder.

"Belle, how can you be so nasty to them?"

Belle blanched and shrugged. "Just trying to find out more. . . ."

Bicé sat down next to Belle and looked her in the eyes, trying to find something of the old Belle, the one who looked like her, deep inside this beautiful girl. "You . . . the old Belle never would've played these games."

"They're not games. You don't understand, Bicé. You don't know how I feel about Thomas."

"Maybe not. But it's not worth losing your soul to win a guy."

Belle gasped at the word "soul." Did Bicé know? But the soft, sweet expression on Bicé's face suggested that she was only using it rhetorically. And so Belle kissed her sister good night — her heart pounding hard — and promised to be good.

Chapter 9

Picture Perfect

Too high for common selfishness, he could
At times resign his own for others' good,
But not in pity, not because he ought,
But in some strange perversity of thought,
That sway'd him onward with a secret pride
To do what few or none would do beside;
And this same impulse would, in tempting time,
Mislead his spirit equally to crime.

— Lord Byron, from *Lara*

After the initial excitement of starting school had died down, Valentin settled into a routine of people-watching, occasional writing of poetry that his teachers called "superb" and "exceptional," and frequent toying with the lives of his classmates. In the afternoons he managed to avoid every class, every obligation, and every family member by finding strings of flawless ten-minute increments and playing them over and over again so that he could just lounge, observing from all the various angles. Or he wandered around Marlowe, adding his signature here and there, sometimes undetected, writing the scene without appearing in it, sometimes placing himself at the center of it all, in the lead role.

One day, Valentin was slumped next to a row of lockers, legs extended into the busy hall, head back against a heavy metal door, as if he were so bored he could barely contain the urge to give up and fling his body in all directions, limb by limb succumbing to gravity. He didn't seem to care when people looked at him as if he were strange, or when girls giggled as he tapped his head against the locker and hummed tunes that may or may not have yet been written. To be fair, not all the girls thought he was weird. In fact, none of them did. In groups, they giggled and rolled their eyes, but each one, individually, found his indifference intoxicating. Each one thought she was the only one who saw how cool it was to be different, that she was the only visionary in the history of womankind to be attracted to the boy who simply didn't care. And so Valentin had plenty of friends, not in the mob-scene, competitive way that Belle had friends, or the tightly packed, five-on-five way that boys like Connor Wirth had friends. He was friends with everyone privately, individually — secretly. When he was alone, he wasn't truly, completely alone like Bicé. He was every girl's secret boyfriend. And a good number of guys gave him a nod and a slap on the back when the halls were empty enough. And for him, this was the ideal way to live. People didn't run from him, as they did from Victoria. Their giggles didn't come from deep down, as they did with Bicé. Secretly, everyone was in love with Valentin.

Valentin rolled his head lazily to the side. His eyes settled on a lanky stranger fumbling with a nearby locker. He was uncomfortably tall and skinny, like a boy on stilts. He wore a large pair of old brown loafers — the kind with the giant tassels and protruding outer rim that goes all the way around, making big feet look like boats. Above the shoes were two inches of scrunched-up athletic socks, another inch of dry, patchy skin, and then the shockingly tapered cuffs of a pair of worn-out jeans. He looked stretched. Like the recipe for a normal person that's been poured into the wrong mold, without enough mass to fill it completely. Valentin recognized him. He was a sophomore: Dustin McGuiness. Better known as Douchey McGee. You couldn't go five minutes in Marlowe without hearing the name Douchey McGee followed by fits of laughter.

Just then, something made Dustin go white in the face. He dropped all his books and scampered to pick them up. When Valentin saw what had caught Dustin's attention, his eyes lit up with all the possibilities — a nice long scene that could go on for hours.

Standing two lockers down from Dustin and Valentin was Missy Patterson, the head of the Pom Squad. Missy Patterson was the best-looking of them all. She wasn't classic like Belle. She was average height, perfectly proportioned, with long, thick brown hair, full lips, big blue eyes, and creamy, pale porcelain skin. Missy Patterson walked as if she was on a runway, her clothes always a little tight. A fantasy in an ill-fitting uniform.

Valentin got up and walked over to Dustin. "So you have a thing for Missy, huh? Well, you'd make a good pair. Neither one of you fits in your clothes."

"I gotta go," Dustin said, and turned to leave. But Valentin grabbed his arm and pulled him back.

"Now, now, Dusty, don't run off. Go and talk to her!"

"Are you nuts?" Dustin looked down at Valentin. "If I get within ten feet of her, that whole dance team will make sure I never hear the end of it."

But there was no stopping Valentin now. The gears in his head were going full speed, and he had no intention of missing out on this much fun. He slapped Dustin on the shoulder (which was a strange upward motion because of their height difference) and started pulling him toward Missy.

"I give you my personal guarantee that she will never bug you about this. I promise. Now come with me."

"Hey, let me go. I'm not talking to her." Dustin kept trying to pull free of Valentin's grip on his arm. But he was too bony and frail to pull it off. And his height was working against him, all that momentum making him stumble forward, right into Missy's locker.

"Hey!" she yelled as a pile of pencils fell out of their case. "What do *you* want?"

"Hi, Missy. I'm Valentin. And this is Dustin. Dustin McGuiness of the Belfast McGuinesses."

"Whatever." Missy rolled her eyes and pursed her lips, so that Dustin gave an involuntary sigh, which made Missy snicker disdainfully.

"Well." Valentin jumped right to the point. "We just want to know one little thing, Missy. What would it take for you to go on one date with our friend Dustin here?"

"Cute," Missy said, slamming her locker shut. "But I would never go out with him."

Dustin started to sweat and turned to walk away, whispering, "I'm sorry," almost to himself. Valentin grabbed his arm again.

"Your skirt is torn," Valentin said, catching Missy off guard.

"What?"

"Your skirt. The hem is coming loose."

Valentin was looking down at the lower half of Missy's Pom Squad uniform, a tiny, pleated skirt that hung well above her knees and bounced even higher with every step. Around the edge, half an inch of hemline was coming loose, as though her skirt was mortified of its current position around her upper thighs and was desperately reaching for lower ground. "It came undone in morning practice," Missy shot back. "Who knew there were so many freaking helpful people in this school?"

"OK, so tell me what it would take. Hypothetically . . ." Valentin kept pushing, putting on his most charming face. "Come on now, Missy. There must be some secret thing you'd want . . . a little fetish?"

Missy gave an involuntary "Hah!" and blushed. Dustin turned to go again. Val didn't even look back, just grabbed his arm.

"Look, even if he didn't look like a giant earthworm," said Missy, "I still don't go for the twitchy weakling type."

"Ouch," Valentin said, rubbing his chin, deep in thought. "OK, so the lady likes confidence. Let's see . . ."

Before Missy had a chance to say "Huh?" Valentin had grabbed her around the waist and kissed her right on the mouth.

She pulled away and slapped him across the face.

"OK, not that — something else. Take notes, Dusty."

"What?" At this point, Dustin was covered in sweat and clearly panicking.

"Never mind," Valentin said. He thrust his hands into his pockets and rewound, shaking his head at the confused, pathetic look that was frozen on Dustin's face. He stopped right before the kiss, when Missy was looking at him expectantly.

He reached over and caressed her on the cheek.

She pushed him away.

And so he rewound.

He grabbed her butt.

She kneed him in the stomach.

He rewound.

He read her a poem.

She yawned and walked away.

He rewound yet again.

Finally, after about a dozen tries, Valentin noticed the three Advanced Calculus books in her locker.

"Aren't you only a junior?" he asked her, eyeing the college-level books.

"Yeah, so?" she asked. He glanced at the books.

"Oh, right," she said. "I'm pretty, so I have to be stupid, right? And a total witch too. You know what I'd like? If someone for once assumed that I was nice!"

"OK." Valentin chuckled, because she was yelling about how nice she was, and then he caught her eye and picked a tiny piece of lint off her sweater. And then another.

She smiled and said, "Thanks."

Valentin pulled Dustin in the other direction.

"We have all we need, Dusty-boy. All we need."

"What are you talking about? She didn't even notice me there. Can I just go? It's time for class."

"Hey! It'll be time for class when I say it's time for class!" Valentin said, and threw his hands into his pockets yet again. This time, he went all the way back to when he was sitting by the locker, just before he had spotted Dustin.

He sat by the locker waiting, waiting. Maybe he had gone back a bit too far. Over his shoulder, a few moths hovered and waited. He slapped them away, but they somehow found their way again — just above his shoulder. Before long, he saw Madame Vileroy gliding down the hall in his direction. What was she doing here? Had he gone back too far? But then again, the governess had a way of appearing in the scenes that he replayed, even if she had never been in any of their previous permutations. She sometimes just showed up in one version or another. No warning. Nothing.

Valentin leaned on his elbow and sat up. But when he looked down the hall again, she was gone. The moths too had vanished from their perch above his shoulder. The hall filled with students rushing this way and that, and no matter how hard he looked, he couldn't find the governess.

To the kids loitering in the hall, the next moment was like a worn-out piece of the fabric of time, as if that particular second had been mutilated beyond recognition, ground down to a few wisps of itself, like a piece of an old movie reel that had been badly damaged, thinned out from overuse. Valentin must have replayed it a hundred times, trying to get things to work out just right with Dustin — to get him to do something so big, so antithetical to his nature. Something that, to someone like him, would seem drastic. Each time, Valentin refined his words to Dustin, his demeanor and tone, a little more. Finally, the poor, pathetic kid would do anything he wanted — because Valentin knew his psyche better than his parents, his psychologist, better than even he knew himself.

Valentin approached carefully.

"Hi, Dustin," he said, not tapping him on the back (since that had startled him once), not putting his hands behind his back (since that had made him suspicious), not slipping in front of him (since that had caused a near-collision). Instead, Valentin said the greeting in a low, soft tone and waited for Dustin to turn.

"Yeah."

"Dustin, you remember in that episode of *Stargate* where they go into some parallel universe and they can't explain how things work and so they just have to trust people sometimes?"

"They're all like that," Dustin said, laughing. "Who are you?"

"I'm Val," Valentin said with a smile, but not too big a smile (because that had made Dustin think this was a prank). "And you just have to trust me when I ask you to do something."

"Right." Dustin chuckled and started to leave when Valentin put something in his hand.

"What's that?"

"That's my wallet. With all my IDs and money and everything."

"Why're you giving it to me?"

"If this is a prank, you can keep it or burn it or whatever. But if it works out for you, you'll give it back to me later on."

Dustin just stared blankly at Valentin.

"OK, see Missy over there?"

"Yeah."

"I want you to go and talk to her."

"Uhh . . . right. OK, I'll just do that right after my lunch with Thomas Goodman-Brown and his chick brigade."

But Valentin went on. "I'll go over first, OK? Right after I talk to her, you go over, and do exactly as I say."

Valentin explained to Dustin what to do, sprinkling in all the positive triggers he had picked up from talking to Missy over and over again. He patted him on the back reassuringly. He made molecular biology jokes. He even threw in a couple of inspirational lines from Isaac Asimov. Finally Valentin presented Dustin with some random objects from his backpack: a calculus book ("I don't need that. I took that class last year."), a few safety pins ("Those are not as safe as they look!"), and a graphing calculator. After another round of encouragement and some more rousing speeches about "pressing on" and "keeping courage" from *Star Trek, I, Robot,* and other classics he'd never heard of, Valentin walked toward Missy's locker just as she was about to leave.

"Nice skirt," he said as he walked past. He reached over and flipped the loose hem of her skirt. "The Salvation Army run out of hand-me-downs?"

Missy was raging. But before she could respond, Valentin was out of sight. She dropped her book to try to fix her skirt, her face red, looking around to see if anyone heard. She fumbled with the hem, frustrated, as if that extra half an inch of covered thigh would be her social undoing. At that moment, she certainly didn't expect to look up to see Dustin McGuiness standing over her.

"Hi," he said, his voice a bit shaky but keeping a smile on his face. "Let me help you with that," he said, and bent to pick up her book.

Then he stood there, waiting.

There was a long, awkward pause as she accepted the book and waited for him to go away. But he didn't.

"Well, what do you want?" she said.

"Um . . . oh, right. I came over because my calculator broke." He showed her the graphing calculator Valentin had given him. "And I know you're in the advanced class, so I thought yours would definitely be programmed with all the . . . um . . . formulas and stuff . . ."

She kept staring at him.

"I know it's too much to ask . . . um . . . but, my friend said you were really nice . . . and . . . smart . . . um . . . and, I'll bring it back after class . . ."

Missy, who was still preoccupied with her skirt, just rolled her eyes and said, "OK." She handed him the calculator. "Don't program anything new."

"OK," Dustin said, a bit too loudly and excitedly, so that Missy almost jumped.

He started to walk away. Then he stopped and turned.

"Um . . . Missy?"

"Yeah, what is it?"

"Why don't you try these?" He took four safety pins out of his pocket and held them out for her. "These could hold the hem in place until you have a chance to . . . you know . . . Go to the tailor or whatever . . ."

Missy, who was still bent over her skirt, looked up into Dustin's nervous, smiling face.

"It happened in practice," she blurted out.

"Yeah, you guys are really good," he said. "All that twirling and stuff . . . Wardrobe malfunction . . . happens all the time on TV . . . sometimes even on purpose. . . ."

Missy let out a tiny laugh just then, and then she stopped herself and fixed her face into a frown again, taking the pins out of Dustin's hand. She pinned the hem in the front half of her tiny skirt, casually flipping the edges inside out, so that almost all of her legs were visible. Dustin grew more nervous.

"Um . . . I wish that sort of thing would happen to me," he said, drying the back of his neck with his hand. "Everything I have is always too short."

Missy who, in her bent position, had a perfect view of the inch of skin below Dustin's cuff, laughed again and tried putting in the last pin.

"OK, well, I should go. Thanks for the calculator," Dustin said. Then, feeling braver, he leaned over and picked the lint off Missy's shoulder. "Bye." He turned and walked away.

But before he had taken half a dozen steps, he heard Missy call his name. "Dustin, is it?"

"Yeah."

"Would you mind helping me with this last pin?"

It was unfathomable.

It was a true spectacle.

It was a good thing Valentin had a camera phone.

Because right there, in front of the entire school, Douchey McGee was down on one knee, pinning into place the skirt of the sexiest girl in school, his hands fumbling around under her skirt, flipping the hem back and forth, with Missy just standing there, looking over her shoulder, waiting for him to finish.

It was a moment for the yearbook. The very last day anyone called him anything but "Dustin."

As he gathered his books and said good-bye to Missy, Dustin turned around and spotted Valentin. It was hard to be inconspicuous at that moment, with the tall, geeky giant waving and pointing to the calculator, then tossing Valentin his wallet so clumsily that all the coins scattered on the floor.

Valentin was having so much fun watching Dustin walk away (a bit taller still), half the Pom Squad whisper in disbelief, and a few guys from the swim team look on with absolute confusion, that he barely noticed that the moths were back, hovering over his shoulder. He tapped the buttons on his phone to zoom in on the photo. A picture of Dustin kneeling beside Missy's skirt. "Perfect."

He scrolled through a dozen other photos, pictures from other versions of the same event, when Missy had slapped Dustin, or laughed at him until he'd run off. They'd disappear soon, these alternate versions of the past. They'd get lost or the images would scramble. They would all go away somehow. All except the one of Dustin kneeling next to Missy, fixing her skirt. The one picture that told the truth. Because those other versions never happened, and pictures never lie.

Then Valentin spotted Madame Vileroy walking toward him once more. The moths, invisible over Valentin's shoulder only a moment before, were now flying loosely around the governess, as if energized by her presence.

"Having fun?" the governess asked.

"Always," said Valentin with a bit of extra confidence.

She leaned over his shoulder, just in time to see the false photos disappear. "Well, dear. Are you going to undo this little . . . spectacle?"

"Undo it? Why would I undo it?"

Valentin's eyes were still on the one true photo. He looked up to see the governess raise the perfect arch of her left eyebrow, as if to emphasize that beautiful, broken eye. He held her gaze for only a moment. He couldn't hide anything from her. She knew. She knew what he loved about this freak show. The impossibility of it. Creating something hideous and grotesque and simply ridiculous. A two-headed monster. But what Valentin hoped she didn't know was that he couldn't help being the tiniest bit happy for Dustin too.

"It's sick . . ." Valentin shook his head as he put the phone in his pocket.

He turned his back to Madame Vileroy and thought he felt her go away. After a solitary moment, he pulled out the phone again and flipped to the photo. A smile spread across his face. But then, before he could put the phone away, there was a movement, a cold breath on his neck that made the whitish-yellow hairs stand on end, an enveloping presence creeping from behind. And then a whisper, delivered softly in his ear: "Don't worry, darling. You can keep your little trophy."

Chapter 10
Crush

At midnight — the witching hour — the wind howled in fear, the shut-
ters of the houses slapped hysterically at their hinges, and the village
lay in bed asleep. A murder of crows cast shadows by the fattened
moon like dark angels in the village square. Dogs and fathers snored
on their pillows — even the baker rolled over unaware, and the grave
digger nodded standing up with his chin resting on the butt of his
shovel. Earlier, the mothers had huddled their children around them
like nervous hens, intent on standing guard with garlic and wolf's
bane around their necks, boules and baubles, chanting the old protec-
tive words to keep them safe, to protect them from the aftermath of the
night's events — but they'd fallen asleep.

Outside, black riders now flew about. The tattered cloth flapped
across their bare rheumatic skin, unchilled by the air. Only the little
boy in the house up the hill was awake to see them, circling through
the clouds outside his window, calling to the crows in their banshee
voices. The boy knew he wouldn't be able to wake his mother or
father, the handmaid, or even his cat — they were all asleep as if dead.

He clutched his blanket and watched as one figure flew in smaller and smaller circles toward him.

She sat on a branch, her blond hair brilliant and strictly governed into a bun. She looked exactly as she had looked that afternoon, when she had been burned on a stake, her bun perfectly intact, her face calm. He had thought she was gone, that she would not answer now. But she had heard. She knew what he wanted so desperately that his heart burned with longing for it. Now that she had come, he wanted to run and close the curtains. He watched her watching him and wished for his mother. But she lay asleep. The whole village lay asleep well past the midnight when the little boy in the house up the hill disappeared.

~⌒∞⌒~

With the semester well under way, Belle spent her spare hours bathing and visiting coffee shops, clubs, restaurants — wherever Marlowe kids hung out — and creating more and more followers. She had avoided Thomas and Lucy, who were together more and more these days. Belle wanted him to hear about her from his friends, to hear them gushing and being in love with her. She wanted him to wonder why they acted that way — what Belle had that Lucy didn't. Then she would — accidentally — run into him one day. Thank God for Connor. Well, thank *Madame Vileroy* for Connor. Because once again, Vileroy had been right: the more Belle planted suspicion and jealousy among Connor and his two chirping little birds, Charlotte and Maggie, the more all of them loved her.

One day, Belle spotted Thomas and Connor hanging out in the Marlowe dining hall after school. With Lucy still in line for a veggie wrap and a smoothie, it was the perfect time to bump into him.

"Hi, Connor." She waved, winked, and walked right past them. Connor choked on his chocolate smoothie.

"Hey, you mind waiting here a minute?" he said to Thomas. "I'll be just a sec."

"You're going to talk to *her*? How well do you know each other?"

"Not as well as I'd like. . . ."

"She seemed weird at that play," said Thomas.

"She's a total Hottie Hotterson."

"Why are you talking like that?"

"Like what?" said Connor. He seemed confused, distracted.

"Like some tool on MTV."

"Gotta roll, hombre. Lady needs a refill."

"See? What is *that*?"

"What's what?" asked Connor with an innocent look.

"I didn't realize you'd moved to the . . . hood, or wherever it is they talk like that."

"West Side . . . bro."

"West Side?" Thomas raised both eyebrows. "Like Lincoln Center? Where they have the New York City Ballet?"

"Westchester, bi-atch!"

Thomas just shook his head and sat there while Connor bounced over to Belle, who was sitting alone at one of the round tables near the window. He watched as Connor sat down next to Belle, tried to put his arm around her, and smelled her neck as if she were made of

163

peppermint cream. *What's his deal?* Thomas watched as Connor grabbed Belle's hand and invited her back to their table. He swallowed the last bite of his sandwich. *She is gorgeous, though,* he admitted to himself. As Belle glided up to his table, Thomas wondered why he had been so judgmental before—about the smell. *It could be a foreign thing, or some feminine mystery.* Connor was reintroducing them, but Thomas couldn't hear anything. Something strange was happening to him. He felt relaxed and anxious at the same time. He could smell something new in the air, something indescribable but intoxicating, something that made him uncomfortably happy. He thought he heard Belle say something like "We've met." He just nodded. It was a nice smell. But somehow, on the inside, it felt the same as the way Belle had made him feel before: intoxicated, drugged. He heard Connor saying his name a couple of times, and then he snapped out of it. "Oh, sorry, Belle. I was just thinking of something else. Are you all settled in?"

Normally, Belle would have thought that was the lamest question ever. But for some reason, she began to scour her brain for the perfect answer. Out of the corner of her eye, she spotted Lucy, who had just come out of the smoothie line and was glaring in their direction. Fortunately, a teacher pulled her away. To Belle, Thomas was more than just a prize now. She really liked him. And she had to stand there long enough. So she started to describe everything she loved and hated about New York, comparing it to Rome and Paris, while Thomas and Connor listened, not missing a word while missing the whole story.

"Well, I should run," said Belle after half an hour of talking about nothing. She looked over at Thomas to see what he would say.

"Why?" the boys said in unison. Belle laughed.

"You could stay a little longer," said Thomas. "I mean, I think Connor has plans, but I was just gonna hang out here."

"I don't have plans," said Connor.

"Sure you do. Your dad's in town."

"I'll catch him later."

"Oh, Connor. It's so mean of you to blow off your own dad," said Belle with a disappointed look. It was all she could do not to push Connor out the door herself.

"Fine." Connor slumped in his chair, before finally getting up to leave.

Belle and Thomas talked for hours, long after the dining hall staff had gone home and the kitchen had been closed. Every time Belle pretended to leave, Thomas grabbed her hand (making all of the blood rush from her brain) or stole her keys or made up some reason why she couldn't go. When she asked about Lucy, he evaded, not wanting to ruin the moment. It hurt being near her, but he couldn't get enough. It was like eating peanut brittle after your teeth have cracked, like licking spray paint because the colors are so beautiful. Thomas was falling under her spell, and Belle could hardly believe her luck. Finally, though, Belle grabbed her purse and headed out the door, leaving Thomas with her number and a migraine.

❧✿☙

Belle came home to find Madame Vileroy sitting in the dark center space, doing something with needles.

"Since when do you knit?"

Madame Vileroy smiled. "You've been gone for a while."

"I saw Thomas. Everything is going perfectly," Belle sang.

"Not really."

"What do you mean?"

"I mean, you're not playing the game right, Belle. If you spend four hours talking to someone, then where's the mystery? Men like mystery . . . and suspense . . . and games."

"No, they don't."

"Yes, they do. They think they don't, but they do. They always go for the fickle brats — the ones that play games. And you're acting like a stupid girl with a crush."

"Maybe I *am* a stupid girl with a crush! Besides, Thomas already likes me."

"For now . . ."

"You think he'll stop?" Belle asked desperately.

"Not if you do what I say."

Belle waited. The ball of yarn by Vileroy's side rolled around itself like an endless boulder.

"You should ignore him for a few days. Let Lucy have him. Let him get a little bored. Then let him hear the rumors about her. Maybe give Connor some hope."

"I thought you said hope will boil me alive."

"Yes," she said, bemused, pleased, looking down at her material. The yarn twisted its last few yards and ended in a fuchsia ball, like a withered stomach.

Belle's phone vibrated in her purse. "I'm getting a text. Good night." Belle hurried down the hallway to her bathroom and took out the first bottle that would put her to sleep.

The next day, Victoria visited Ms. LeMieux in her office. The Marlowe administrative offices were large and sunny, and there were several students sitting in the waiting area. A plump woman of about fifty greeted Victoria and directed her to have a seat while Ms. LeMieux finished with her last appointment. Victoria sat next to a pretty blonde in a cheerleader outfit.

"Hi. I'm Maggie," the blonde said, extending her hand.

"Victoria Faust," Victoria said without looking at her.

"Oh, you're Belle's sister! Belle is just the nicest girl. I'm so happy I met her. I think we're going to be friends forever. . . ."

Her speech grew quicker as she spoke about Belle. She talked like someone on speed or the way you'd imagine a dog with rabies would talk. Victoria thought she saw her eyes grow glassy. Somewhere to the left, someone dropped a stapler. Maggie's head whipped around like a paranoid criminal.

The chubby secretary lumbered toward Victoria. "She's ready to see you now."

As Victoria got up, she saw an angry mother storm out of Ms. LeMieux's office.

"Honestly, I don't see what the problem is. My son is far more qualified than the ones you recommended for Yale last year. It was one small indiscretion."

"Good-bye, Mrs. Marcus," Ms. LeMieux said impatiently. "Ah, Victoria. Come on in."

Victoria adjusted her glasses and got up from her seat. She had made sure that she wore her biggest pair today, even though she hated the way they looked and felt. Ms. LeMieux led Victoria into her office and closed the door.

Just as the door was closing, Victoria saw Lucy enter the waiting area. She caught Lucy's gaze and waved mockingly with the tips of her fingers. When the counselor turned to refill her coffee, Victoria reached over and reopened the door, leaving it just barely ajar. Lucy sat outside the office, craning to hear. Victoria knew she would listen. She could *hear* her listening. Lucy scooted her chair toward the door just in time to overhear Victoria buttering up Ms. LeMieux with suspiciously familiar ploys.

"How did your first day go?" asked Ms. LeMieux. "Do you like your new classes?"

"I'm enjoying the challenge. I have seven advanced classes, you know." Victoria beamed, expecting Ms. LeMieux to be pleased.

Outside, Lucy was chewing on her lip. *Seven advanced classes? How's that possible?*

"Yes, well, I've been meaning to speak to you about that," said Ms. LeMieux. "It seems that a few parents think it's a bit unfair that one student has been allowed to take all five-point classes, while everyone else is required to take at least two four-point classes."

"Was it Mrs. Spencer? Did you tell her about my special needs?"

"I did, and we think we came to an ideal solution. Since you are exempt from the physical courses, we think you should consider replacing them with equivalent four-point courses. How about vocal chorus or home ec?"

Way to go, Mom! thought Lucy.

Victoria's nostrils flared. "How many *home economists* do you know in the White House, Ms. LeMieux?"

Ms. LeMieux blanched. "Nonetheless, we must be fair."

"Was it fair that I was stricken with all these ailments? Do you even know the kind of breakdown I would have onstage in a choral gown?" Ms. LeMieux could imagine, since she had hated her own choral gown as a girl.

"But you go onstage for debate."

Little cheater, thought Lucy.

"That's different. Please don't make me explain the intricacies of my condition. I'm not a doctor," said Victoria, her hands at her temples, mimicking the way the moths had shown Ms. LeMieux sitting, in her most frustrated moments. "All I want is to be *fairly* compensated for the course load I'm handling right now."

"Hmm." Ms. LeMieux sat silently for a few minutes. "I see your point. But still . . ."

What? thought Lucy. *LeMieux CANNOT be buying that!*

"And technically," continued Victoria, "even though the school has rules for exemption, it has no rule saying it can dictate student schedules or restrict their classes."

"Well, that's true. . . ." Ms. LeMieux had made that exact argument to Mrs. Spencer. Of course, it made perfect sense. Even a child could see it. "I'll speak to some people."

"It's only fair," said Victoria.

Lucy was about to storm into the office. Victoria could feel it. Now that the issue of classes was settled, she had to deal with Lucy — show her a little of what she was messing with . . .

"Ms. LeMieux," Victoria said, "did I tell you that I'm writing a paper on the effectiveness of UN peacekeeping tactics?"

Lucy almost choked on her Diet Snapple. That was *her* idea.

"Really?" said the counselor as she rifled through some papers. "Victoria, that is *such* a wonderful coincidence. I wrote my senior thesis at Yale on that topic!"

It had taken Lucy a month and a half to find that out—and Victoria only a moment at the party to cheat off her thoughts.

"I'm surprised that you're writing papers already," said Ms. LeMieux. "Have they given out assignments yet?"

Victoria smugly replied, "Learning is an assignment you give yourself."

Ms. LeMieux ate it up with her silver spoon.

Lucy was livid. *What just happened? How did she know? It's OK. Calm down. LeMieux will still write me a letter when I'm elected class president.*

"I'm going to be elected class president," said Victoria unprompted.

Lucy actually did choke that time. Victoria immediately regretted responding to one of Lucy's thoughts so directly. She'd have to be more careful next time.

"Good for you," said Ms. LeMieux as she turned to get more coffee. Victoria reached over with her foot and shut the door. That was enough eavesdropping for Lucy. When the counselor turned back to her, Victoria made a show of adjusting her thick glasses.

"About the election," said Victoria. "I wanted to tell you about my eye condition."

Ms. LeMieux gave a curious tilt of her head.

"Chronic Retinal Akinetic Paroxysms," said Victoria.

She rubbed her eyes with her fists like a little girl. "I was hoping you could do me a small favor." She opened her eyes wider and puffed out her cheeks, and then she rubbed her eyes again till they watered. A wave of shame and pity washed over Ms. LeMieux as she listened to Victoria explain about her special needs. *What an unfeeling world,* she thought. She took out her notepad and began to write.

On her way out, Ms. LeMieux's note in hand, Victoria saw Christian leaving the office. He was there signing up for another sports team. Victoria noticed that, before he left, he pocketed the sign-up pen, a handful of paper clips, and the little frog paperweight that was sitting by the clipboard. *Pathetic,* she thought.

~⟨∞⟩~

After another fairly uneventful day, Valentin was gathering his things to go home when Charlotte finally found him.

"Hi, Valentin. You didn't call me after the play. You forgot about me?" she said with a pouty face.

"Of course I didn't." Valentin put on his charming smile and grabbed her hand. "Have a good day?"

Charlotte beamed and started to tell him about her day, her activities, her friends, and anything else that came to mind. Valentin was such a good listener; Charlotte didn't notice she was doing all the talking. Finally she stopped and asked what he was up to.

Valentin stopped as well. His eyes darted to the wall clock, then back to her. A pause, and suddenly he lunged at her, threaded his arms around her waist, and kissed her deep on the lips. She wouldn't slap him like Missy had done. "Young man!" interrupted a teacher who had just that second turned the corner. Valentin pulled back; Charlotte blushed and touched her mouth. Valentin nodded to the teacher. He winked at Charlotte and thrust his hand in his pocket.

Then everything went in reverse—the shout, the teacher, the kiss. Charlotte was back in the hall, never having been kissed. She said again, "Enough about me. What're you up to?"

Valentin glanced at the clock, her lips, the teacher coming around the corner. Charlotte wondered what he was smiling about. "I'm going home. I want to work on my poetry book," Valentin said.

"Really? Did you know that I won the school prize last year for my short stories?"

"Well, I'm sure you're better than me."

Charlotte blushed and started to tell him about a story she was working on from the perspective of a vegetarian Venus flytrap. It made parallels to her parents' first divorce and also the Taliban.

"You know, you can enter your own original composition into the State Debate and Drama Tournament that's coming up. That's the best way to get started," she suggested.

Valentin, who already knew this, pretended to be thankful for the information. After a few more minutes of listening to Charlotte talk, he said, "Maybe we could get together one day and, you know, have a private reading."

"I would really like that," said Charlotte.

"And if you want, I could take a look at the prize-winning short story," Valentin said in his most buttery tone.

So they set a date to meet after school, and Valentin convinced Charlotte to bring her journal. They walked together to where their cars were waiting. Charlotte looked down, wanting to reach out and take Valentin's hand again, but it was in his pocket.

Valentin jogged to the black Town Car waiting for him in front of the school and hopped in. His sisters were already waiting there. Belle was complaining to Bicé about Lucy Spencer, and Victoria was pretending to read an Oxford brochure.

"They're dating. He's actually *dating* Lucy," Belle wailed, having just heard the news from her blond spy network. "And she told everyone we're *orphans.*"

"So what? We *were* adopted," said Bicé. "At least you and I are still together."

Victoria and Belle exchanged a glance. Belle changed the subject. "She told Thomas that I had plastic surgery."

Bicé laughed a bit and started picking a loose thread on the seat cushion. Again, the memory of when her sister looked just like her was like a painful ball of lead in her heart. "You did more than that, Belle. Be thankful that's all she thinks."

"I hope he doesn't believe her," said Belle.

"Haven't you talked to him?" asked Bicé.

"Not since a few days ago in the dining hall." Belle smiled coyly. "He's with Lucy, and I'm going to play the Connor angle until he breaks up with her."

"What do you mean?"

"I spent the day letting Connor show me around. I ignored Thomas. It was so hard."

"That's immature," said Bicé.

"Right, like you're the one to give relationship advice." Belle immediately felt sorry for that remark. "I'm sorry, Bicé, but I'll stop ignoring him after he's in love with me."

"What if he never falls in love with you?" Victoria said without looking up from her brochure. She had been "reading" the page on housing options for the last twenty minutes.

"He will."

"Boys are such a waste of time. Today at lunch, I was standing behind one of them in the cafeteria line. And he was thinking that if the girl in front of him got the turkey, he would ask her to the spring dance. Then when she did get the turkey, he thought, *If she gets ice cream, I'll ask her.* Then when she got ice cream too, he thought, *I'll ask her if she pays with exact change.* And it went on and on like that till she went to her table and he slumped off. It was pathetic. Why waste your time on losers, Belle?"

"Thomas wasn't a loser when you found out his dad owns half the city. And when we're married, we're not inviting you to any of our parties."

"Oh, no!" said Victoria in a mocking tone. "How will I sleep tonight? Please, *please,* Belle. Say you'll invite me to your parties."

The door flung open and Christian jumped in.

"I won all the sprints in swim practice today," he said excitedly.

"Big surprise," Victoria said. "How can you be excited knowing that you've done about two percent of everything you wanted to do this year?"

Christian shrugged and went on. "I talked to Connor again today. Nice guy. We're playing golf so he can teach me some stuff."

"Why would you practice with him?" said Victoria. "You could go pro. He's some random—"

"Yeah, I know," Christian interrupted. "But it'd be nice to make some friends—" Christian stopped himself. "He plays tennis too. He's won a lot of trophies. I just want to watch my back."

"How strategic," said Valentin.

"But, Christian, you knew all that already," said Bicé.

"I'm a bit worried now, I guess. After seeing all his records. We're teammates in basketball too—I just want to keep an eye on him."

"Devious. Positively devilish," said Valentin.

"You know the Scholar-Athlete Prize at the end of the year? Everyone thinks Connor will win it."

"Don't worry," said Bicé, patting his arm. "They've barely seen *you* yet."

"It's not that easy. It's a yearly award. Being the best in one semester won't be enough for all the time he's been here. I'd have to win at everything, steal from everybody, basically demolish the guy."

"That's the beauty of it," said Victoria. "You have everything you need to get it done. What's the problem?"

"I was hoping I could do it without that."

"That's pathetic," Victoria said in a disgusted tone, and went back to reading.

Chapter 11

Election

"Why do you care about all this? Why would someone like you bother helping someone like me?"

"Because some things that seem unimportant now can change the course of human history—and I am a student of human history."

"Well, I've only ever been a failure. I sign here?"

"Lots of big accomplishments begin with failures."

"Like what?"

"There was a man who owned a clothing store that went bankrupt."

"Let me guess. He learned from his failure and started over as Giorgio Armani."

"No. He left the clothing business. He became president and dropped a bomb on Hiroshima."

The Faust children spent the next few weeks in their own individual worlds. Bicé managed to stay below the radar of most of the dozens of kids who were jealous of her. Belle finally stopped ignoring Thomas and started showing up to all of his activities. And Thomas was showing more than a little interest. He would joke and flirt with Belle, even when Lucy was around. At first, it was just a few friendly conversations, or a few inside jokes from that day in the dining hall. Then, as Thomas spent more time with Belle, it became harder and harder for him to notice Lucy. Sometimes (on the days of the *irresistible* baths), he was so distracted, he forgot his manners altogether. After a while, Belle and Thomas started to meet after school and between classes. When they were alone, Thomas would bring her little presents and call her "princess." Lucy found their friendship more than infuriating, though she still thought of Thomas as her boyfriend, completely unaware that he was secretly meeting with Belle. Belle was tempted to use a big dose of anything lethal on Lucy, since she'd started to become such a pest, clinging to Thomas as if she had picked him up at a sample sale and constantly trying to ruin her reputation. It took weeks for Belle to prove that the dirty Internet pictures were Photoshopped.

Christian made it onto all of the sports teams he wanted to join and wasn't around most of the time. No one asked if he was still practicing on Buddy. They all secretly knew that he was, because he was fast becoming friends with Connor — and Christian liked losing to friends even less than he liked losing to strangers. Valentin was starting to hit his stride, too. He had written some of his best poetry in the past few weeks and was finally ready to submit his work in the State Debate and Drama Tournament.

Of all the children, the only one who truly hated Marlowe was Victoria. Her obsession with Lucy's presidential campaign was taking over. Lucy had put up posters all over campus with slogans like "Vote Lucy. She's been with you all along" and "Lucy Spencer, the *only* candidate who stands against all forms of cosmetic enhancement." Valentin's personal favorite read, "If you need a governess to run your life, can you really run a school?" He brought the poster home one day, and he and Madame Vileroy had a laugh at Victoria's expense. The moths didn't tell Victoria about the posters until two days before they were hung, and she was powerless to do anything about it.

As if Lucy wasn't enough, Thomas was everywhere related to debate. But for now, Victoria was too busy with the election to worry about Thomas. She couldn't force anyone to vote for her, so she had to win the old-fashioned way: meeting as many classmates as possible and reading their minds to find their weaknesses. This process took an annoyingly long time, but thankfully, she didn't have to be a sweet-talking politician with all her classmates. Some people had juicy secrets irresponsibly stored in accessible parts of their brain. Others were more difficult. But inevitably, everyone had something they loved or hated or wished for or feared that Victoria could share or emulate or avoid or exploit. Still, she secretly hated Belle for having it so easy. Every time she saw her surrounded by a group of fidgeting, fawning admirers, she thought that Belle didn't deserve it. Madame Vileroy had confirmed it. She too thought Victoria was the most deserving. *Then why is Belle getting all her attention?*

By the week of the election in early March, Victoria had dazzled or terrified at least half the class. Meanwhile, Lucy's games became more and more vicious and desperate. It was going to be close. When the posters got old, she began following Victoria to capture incriminating or embarrassing moments on film. Lurking outside the Fausts' apartment building one night, she thought she saw a huge mass of flies shoot out of one of the windows. But she didn't have time to take a picture. On another night, she saw some strange lights flashing on the inside and snapped a pretty good photo, but the next day, the picture showed nothing more than an ordinary building surrounded by the black of night. After a few days of finding nothing, Lucy switched to a less discreet strategy. She went to Ms. LeMieux to try to accuse Victoria of cheating on a test. Unfortunately for Lucy, Ms. LeMieux had become Victoria's biggest fan since their meeting a few weeks before. Lucy didn't know it, but when she walked into Ms. LeMieux's office to accuse Victoria, she was walking into enemy territory.

"Hello, Ms. LeMieux. Thank you for seeing me," she said as she sat down.

"That's all right, Lucy, but please be brief. I have a packed day."

"I'm here to see you about Victoria Faust," she said, stupidly missing the fact that Ms. LeMieux had perked up at the mention of Victoria's name. "I'm here to report her for cheating," Lucy continued.

"Excuse me?"

"Cheating. She's been cheating in European history. I know because I found this under her desk after the last test." Lucy pulled out a card, a cheat sheet with dates, names, and facts printed in tiny script.

"Lucy—" Ms. LeMieux began.

"I know you like her, Ms. LeMieux," Lucy interrupted, "but she's been manipulating you. She's a cheater."

"Lucy, stop right there. Now, let me ask you something. When was this test?"

"Two days ago." Lucy sat up.

"The test on the Franco-Prussian War?"

"Yes."

"Lucy, Victoria was absent from that test. She asked that I proctor her makeup test this morning. She took the test here, in my office, alone." Lucy's mind was racing. *How can that be true? I found the cheat sheet right under her desk.* Then again, Lucy wasn't exactly sure if Victoria had been in class that day. She missed so many of them with one excuse after another (foreign ailments, undocumented phobias, chronic this or that).

Ms. LeMieux remembered how enjoyable it had been giving Victoria that test. Victoria had asked her to read the questions out loud, because of her vision problem. Ms. LeMieux remembered thinking about each answer to herself and watching as Victoria got every one of them right. What a bright girl she was.

Lucy was speechless. Once again, Victoria was one step ahead of her. It was as if she knew that Lucy was planning this. That little witch. How was she always on top of everything?

"Lucy, let me warn you," Ms. LeMieux said, rising from her chair. "Unfounded accusations will not be tolerated here. I don't know where you got that cheat sheet, but for your sake, I'm going to pretend you were never here. Now leave."

~⊚∞⊚~

The night before the election, Victoria stayed up late. She sat cross-legged, weathering a storm of insects, her eyes closed, almost as if she were meditating on some cosmic truth. In reality, she was spying on Lucy again. Now an expert with the moths, Victoria could see the scene in Lucy's house as easily as if she were there, a fly on the wall. She shamelessly watched Lucy and Mrs. Spencer in a private mother-daughter moment, the likes of which was rarely seen in public. Victoria watched Mrs. Spencer bring her daughter a cup of tea. She watched the aging socialite stack boxes of cupcakes one on top of another, ready for the next day. And she watched as the two spent four solid hours putting fake diamond pendants on hundreds of necklaces for Lucy to give away.

"Darling, this is *such* a brilliant campaign. I'm so proud of you."

"Thanks, Mom! I think I could really win! Charlotte took an informal poll at lunch."

"Well, you've certainly worked hard enough."

"Yeah, and diamonds are so classic. The whole theme is a winner."

Victoria laughed. So self-righteous, that Lucy. As if using her parents' money was fair. As if she weren't cheating just by being herself.

"Mom?" Victoria heard Lucy say.

"Yes, dear." Mrs. Spencer was having trouble with a particularly tricky pendant hook.

"It's really fun working on this with you."

Mrs. Spencer stroked her daughter's cheek. "Well, you know,

darling. I was president of my class in high school. It's family tradition, though I never had a campaign this creative."

On the day of the election, Victoria was confident. She walked in two hours before school, with forty posters under one arm and a bag full of buttons in another. As she strolled toward Marlowe, her head full of plans and to-do lists, Victoria noticed Madame Vileroy walking beside her.

She jumped and dropped a few posters. "What are you doing here?"

"This is my job. To watch over you," Madame Vileroy whispered. "See who's coming?"

Victoria noticed Lucy and her mother, each carrying trays full of Magnolia cupcakes.

"Don't worry. I know about her campaign."

Madame Vileroy rolled her eyes, a move that was disconcerting to Victoria, who couldn't help but gaze into the governess's strange left eye. "Yes, the election. But you can't think of a single fun thing to do besides? With all that information?"

"What do you mean?" asked Victoria.

"You watched her for four hours last night."

Victoria waited.

"Where's the clever Victoria I used to know?" Vileroy goaded. "The girl that used to be my most talented, the one that could always give us a good laugh."

Victoria picked up her pace and approached Lucy and her mother.

"Hi, Mrs. Spencer. How are you?" Victoria said with concern. "I'm so sorry to hear about the divorce settlement."

Mrs. Spencer went white. "Excuse me?" She looked nothing like the tender mother of the night before.

"Oh, I'm sorry. Lucy told me. She said you only got half the house and two hundred grand a year for half the term of your marriage. I think it's totally unfair, but what can you do? It's a man's world." With that Victoria walked away. Her heart was beating fast; she could almost hear Madame Vileroy's approving laugh.

"Lucy!" Mrs. Spencer was livid. She dropped her tray of cupcakes and stared in shock at her daughter. A few boys who were running to swim practice slowed down to watch.

"Mom, she is lying. I swear, I would never—"

"Lucy! How could you betray me like this?"

"Mom, I swear I didn't—"

"You expect me to believe that?" Mrs. Spencer's hands shook as she shuffled through her purse for her keys. She then left her daughter, who stood alone in the middle of a pile of ruined cupcakes. Victoria looked on.

~◦◦◦◦~

For the rest of the day, Lucy distracted herself by putting up her campaign posters and spying on Victoria, who had ordered a constant stream of sushi and smoothies for everyone at Marlowe. Lucy and Charlotte countered with a hot new campaign that looked exactly like the De Beers diamonds ads. Her slogan was "Diamonds may be forever, but Lucy is a girl's best friend." She had faux diamond necklaces with *LS* pendants that she handed out to all the girls. For the guys, Lucy had designed her own version of a Super Bowl ring. Of course, both girls had gone over the Marlowe School limit on election spending.

In the early afternoon, Charlotte and Lucy were in the front lobby, handing out bling to everyone entering the school, when they noticed some noise coming from outside. On the front lawn, Victoria was making an impromptu speech with a loudspeaker.

"As president, I promise to take on important issues that affect our lives. Look at little Kweku here." Next to her stood a little black boy, about eight, wearing a tattered shirt and jeans. Victoria had found him that weekend playing Frisbee in Central Park and had paid him five hundred bucks to play along. His name was Colin. She put her hand on the boy's head. "His family was uprooted from their home in Africa. Their entire village was ransacked by diamond smugglers. His father lost his hand because he stole a diamond from the smugglers — just so his family could eat. The only reason he's here is because he stowed away on a ship carrying conflict diamonds to America. As president, I'm going to wage war against conflict diamonds!"

The growing crowd erupted in cheers. *Nothing like the liberal, guilt-ridden children of wealthy New Yorkers,* Victoria thought. She took out her bag of buttons. "If you want to support this little boy and his family, wear one of these buttons supporting Victoria for president. Show your stance against conflict diamonds!"

Lucy just stood there, holding a handful of faux diamond necklaces, wearing a button saying, "Diamonds are forever."

"Checkmate," Charlotte whispered, completely in shock.

"How did she find out?" Lucy couldn't even think straight. Then she turned on Charlotte. "You told her! You traitor!"

"I didn't!" Charlotte said. "I kept the whole campaign a secret. I swear."

"Oh, please! Everyone knows you have a crush on that Tourette's boy, Valentin!"

"He doesn't have Tourette's!"

Victoria, who had finished passing out buttons and was now hanging posters all over the school, walked past Lucy and Charlotte. "Here you go, girls," she said as she tossed them a couple of buttons. "Show the world you're against slavery and oppression."

~∞∞∞

A few hours later, the voting booths opened. Charlotte and Lucy stayed close by, making final efforts to win people to Lucy's side. It wasn't hard. Despite a better campaign, nobody liked Victoria. A sophomore girl who shouted slogans for Victoria's anti-diamond campaign one minute still preferred to have Lucy's love and approval in the next. A junior boy with no leanings, a self-proclaimed "man of the issues," still thought Victoria was creepy. Victoria could only stand to the side and watch. Before one boy walked into the voting booth, she grabbed his arm. "Make the right decision, Theo. You don't wanna be *Ted-wet-the-bed* again." The boy nodded fearfully.

Lucy looked up from her booth, glancing at the droves of kids she had been cultivating since primary school. This was a landslide, and it was sweet enough to take away all of today's stings. Then Lucy saw Belle and Thomas handing out buttons for Victoria's campaign. He whispered something in her ear, and she laughed. Lucy thought she saw Belle playing with Thomas's hair. Without taking her eyes off Thomas, Lucy asked Charlotte, "What's going on?"

Charlotte looked down and shrugged. "How should I know?"

Lucy shot up from her seat and marched toward the two.

"Thomas, are you handing out buttons for *her*?" She pointed an accusing finger at Victoria.

"Belle asked me to help," said Thomas.

Belle had asked Thomas, not because she cared who won, but because they'd be together in front of Lucy. A part of Belle felt bad for her, but it had all gone on long enough. It was time that this thing with Lucy was over.

"And if Belle asks you to betray your girlfr—"

Lucy stopped short. She wasn't so sure Thomas was her boyfriend anymore, or ever had been. The way Belle wrapped her arm around his, Lucy felt like a fool.

Thomas tried to explain. "I'm sorry, Luce. I never wanted to lead you on or anything. It's just that Belle and I . . . well, we've been . . ." He couldn't finish his sentence, because he wasn't sure what they were doing. Neither was Belle, for that matter. She had sat up at night, complaining to Bicé about the fact that he hadn't even kissed her yet. And now he wasn't using any of the right words, like *girlfriend* or *together*.

Lucy turned to leave. "Whatever. I'm still going to win." She didn't want his pity. And she didn't want Belle to see her cry. But instead of feeling satisfied, all Belle could think about were the words Thomas hadn't used.

Lucy sat back down at her table, and Charlotte put an arm around her.

"Don't worry, Luce. At least you're winning the election!"

Before Lucy had time to wipe her tears, she saw Ms. LeMieux walking toward her.

"Lucy Spencer, we need to talk," she said sternly.

Victoria watched as Ms. LeMieux began speaking with Lucy, who was gesticulating wildly to what seemed like a series of head shakes from Ms. LeMieux. Over Victoria's shoulder, two moths lingered, swaying up and down as if held there by a string, listening to every word. Between gestures, Lucy glared at Victoria, who waved and took a bite of Lucy's last Magnolia cupcake. Victoria watched with a satisfied grin as Lucy's diamond stand was dissembled and carried out of the school. Lucy stomped toward her with murder in her eyes.

"What's wrong with you?" she screamed at Victoria. "Didn't they teach you how to play fair in the orphanage?"

"Fair? Lucy, you were over the spending limit. Is that fair?" Victoria said calmly.

"You went over, too. Where did you get that boy, anyway?"

"Doesn't matter. I had permission." Victoria waved a note in Lucy's face. It was written on Ms. LeMieux's stationery. Lucy grabbed it from her and began to read.

Due to Ms. Faust's Chronic Retinal Akinetic Paroxysms, she will be excused from the budget limitation included in the election rules, which makes it impossible for her to employ the help of her private eye therapist on her campaign. Given the cost of the therapist, the budget constraint would put her at a severe disadvantage to the other students. Therefore, she is granted an unlimited budget in the interest of fairness and in keeping with the school's disability policies.

"This says *due to a disability.* None of the stuff you bought was for a disability. You're perfectly healthy. I've *seen* you at Pilates!"

"Doesn't matter. The note doesn't say what I can spend the money on. It just says *unlimited budget.* So you broke the rule and I didn't."

"And you're the one that turned me in!"

"I didn't say that," Victoria said, but her eyes told a different story. "Diamonds are a bit overmuch, don't you think? I mean, can you buy everyone's love?"

"You heinous little witch!" Lucy screamed, and lunged at Victoria. She grabbed a chunk of hair and pulled hard. Victoria let out a yelp and tried to fight back, but frankly, Victoria's powers were limited to manipulation and scheming. As Lucy continued to pull Victoria by the hair, a small crowd rushed around the girls. Christian and Connor, who were walking from a class together, came running up to the scene.

"What's going on?" Connor asked.

"That's Vic!" said Christian.

He pushed away the crowd to get to the girls, and Connor followed. They each grabbed one of the girls and pulled. When they were apart, Christian stepped in the center to keep them from attacking again. Lucy lunged at Victoria. Christian grabbed her arm to hold her back. Lucy was now seething with anger. It was all just too much, the way they had come in, so cocky, like they didn't need any friends. Through clenched teeth she spat out every vile, hateful thing she could think of. "You know what? Your whole family is a bunch of freaks. I should be thanking God that I don't have a bunch of orphan hatchling mutants for brothers and sisters. I—"

In a split second, Lucy had collapsed to the floor. She had been spewing her venom, then Christian had made a barely noticeable frown, and suddenly Christian was kneeling in the middle of the crowd, holding her limp arm. She was down.

Christian didn't waste any time taking Lucy to the school nurse. He picked her up and ran to the office with a throng of people running behind him. In the end, only Christian, Connor, and Victoria were allowed to stay, since the nurse needed someone to explain.

"She's unconscious," said the nurse. "Connor, call an ambulance."

"We don't know what happened to her. She just collapsed on her own. It must be a diabetic episode or something," said Victoria, eager to draw attention away from herself and always ready with an ailment when the need arose.

"So there wasn't a fight?" the nurse asked, eyeing the small red spot on Victoria's forehead.

"Lucy attacked me. I have about a hundred witnesses. And she must have overstrained herself, because she just collapsed."

"And you had nothing to do with it?"

"She collapsed *after* we'd been separated."

Connor was walking back into the room just as Victoria was finishing that last explanation.

"The ambulance is coming. Christian, you were holding her arm." Connor looked at Christian as if he didn't trust him anymore. Christian couldn't even open his mouth.

"No," said the nurse, "you can't make someone faint by squeezing their arm. If this didn't happen during the fight, then it must be a preexisting condition. All right, I've heard enough. Everyone out."

As they filed out, Christian breathed a sigh of relief and Victoria shot him a warning glance. He had almost given away the game, and that's the one thing Victoria feared most. Connor too was casting Christian sideways glances.

~∞⊙⊙

Despite every attempt to show herself as the victim, Lucy was disqualified for overspending and unsportsmanlike behavior. The election went on as planned, with Victoria as the default winner. Of course, that still didn't mean that anyone liked her. Rumors had already turned the situation into an all-out catfight. Even though Lucy and Victoria had barely touched, people were saying that Victoria had put Lucy into a coma, that she had punched her in the face, or pulled out all her hair, or had knocked her out with a ninja kick in midair.

Lucy spent the day in bed, crying and calling all her friends to whine. When she called Connor, Mrs. Wirth, who had heard the whole story, picked up the phone and gave her usual blind justifications. "Oh, you probably just fainted, dear. You girls and your crash diets! You really should be more careful." When Lucy tried to tell her about Victoria's wealth of information, Mrs. Wirth said, "Oh, she's just observant." And when Lucy told her about the moths or the smell, two things that Mrs. Wirth herself had noticed, she simply said, "You know the French: *toujours au naturel.*"

It wasn't a total win. Lucy did get a position on the Student Council. To Victoria, anything but total annihilation of her opponent was a loss. At least that's what Madame Vileroy said later. Besides, Christian had almost given away their secrets.

"Think of all the wonderful things you've done for him, Victoria.

All he's ever done is cause you trouble. Christian doesn't deserve your forgiveness."

It didn't matter how much Christian apologized. Victoria knew that apologies don't matter when you're constantly doing things wrong. It felt as if she'd had to forgive him seven hundred times. "The devil's in the details," she said to Christian one day, "and you always screw up the details." Even though Christian had saved her, she didn't speak to him for a week.

~~∞∞∞~~

Through the damp New York streets, two moths fluttered toward the dark home of the Fausts. Through an open window and past a candle-lit hallway, they found their way to the east wing. As the two moths danced across the room, Madame Vileroy was reading something particularly compelling in her book. She sat reclined in a chaise, propping the large skin-bound volume on her knees. Her black dress enfolded her. Without looking away from the book, she raised a long thin finger near her ear, where the moths perched and told their tale of children, of parents, of small crimes. The governess nodded, musing on the ways the world turns, and turns on itself. She delighted in all the tiny imperfections, how rust and dust slowly take everything, how even good hearts grow weary, and the lives of little moths decay into unsung deaths — just another little badness that the world is too busy limping along to notice. Madame Vileroy wiped her hand in a fold of her dress and thought of how well everything was going. *Just give them a little power, and watch a human burn down the world.* Like a Watchmaker Devil, she just introduced one little turn then sat back and watched the turning and turning of eternal gears come to a sudden crash.

Madame Vileroy smoothed her golden hair with a delicate ivory hand. The next bestowal was for Valentin—the writer. A writer believes anything, living a life of lies. For him, she had an old and precious gift. One that a desperate soul would surely embrace. A great lie for one who has yet to become a great liar.

Chapter 12
The Ideas of March

The Book of Julius

Prid. Id. Mart.
The year of the consulship of Publius Cornelius Lentulus Spinther
and Quintus Caecilius Metellus Nepos

It has been three years hence I began this miserable campaign against the Gauls — for money, though in my writings I have told the people of Rome it is for their glory. For I am the hand of Rome, but I am afraid I will never be its Caesar. While making camp at the river Sambre, we suffered a surprise attack on our rear guard. They drove into our shields with such might, I think perhaps my expedition may have been foolhardy. I may be forced to join the battle. I do not fear for my life. I fear for my name.

Id. Mart.
The year of the consulship of Publius Cornelius Lentulus Spinther
and Quintus Caecilius Metellus Nepos

I have met a woman.

March was a dying and dreary month, full of nothing but aborted promises. The New York weather was wet and unblooming. Madame Vileroy was ever-present, and for the most part, the Fausts were still not very welcome at Marlowe. Belle was undisputed queen bee, but nobody likes queen bees. Her baths were so painful that she'd need days to recover. Though she could control how others felt, her own moods would swing wildly out of control. She'd leave her bathroom broken, her nails dug into her forearm. She'd become irritated after initial recovery, then angry at the world. Those were the times she'd make mistakes, when the pain had made her bitter. And even if she was set to make you love her, she couldn't make herself play the part, even a little. One day she made a teacher cry. His big blubbering face looked ghoulish as he wailed in the middle of class, saying he loved Belle, calling his wife on his cell phone right there in front of them all to tell her he wanted out. It was such a ridiculous scene, a grown man on his knees, so desperate and lustful that the other students were grossed out. And the indecency of it made Belle look ugly.

Victoria's hatred for Marlowe had eased after she had won class president, joined the debate team, and settled into a calendar full of other activities. She found plenty to hate, though, like the frog-ugly ladies of the counselors' office who thought about ice cream a shocking amount of the time, the winning streak Thomas was on in debate, the wannabe gangsta rappers in the Investment Banking Club—and of course, there was an unhealthy dose of hate for Lucy Spencer.

Still, no Faust was more depressed during the endless March than Christian, who had lost his only friend after the hallway incident with Lucy. Connor had kept his distance after that. He didn't offer to play golf or to show Christian around school. Christian went on with his life, but he didn't handle friendlessness as well as Bicé. Once Bicé walked into his room with everything stopped and she saw Christian frozen in the middle of an awkward high five. Buddy's plasticine smile, after a nice shot, was the only human contact he had. Christian was leaning out to make the maneuver work since Buddy didn't know what a high five was and Christian seemed to be slapping his wave good-bye.

Bicé kept a low profile. Kids would laugh, saying she was retarded, the way she'd forget things you'd just told her, the way she'd almost screech if you touched her, the way she talked to herself in the middle of class while the teacher was talking. Even in public, Bicé acted like she'd been shipwrecked on a deserted island. She could have been insane or schizophrenic, until suddenly she'd translate Cicero's Latin as if it were Seuss's English, catch the Asian kids making fun of her in Cantonese and correct their grammar, or spend a whole hour explaining the inside jokes in *Finnegans Wake*. In those moments, she'd be magnanimous, and then she'd see the eyes staring at her and shrink. It was like being "in the monkey cage," she said, which was an idiom in Swahili. She had become famous. Teaching her was like excavating the library of Alexandria — you didn't have anything to add, only hoped to discover what was already there, hidden under a sea.

The attention made her unpopular, so much that she'd become infamous. If she had ridden the bus, she would have been the girl huddling in the seat directly behind the bus driver. Her brothers and sisters were busy with their hectic lives, so she spent more lunches and break periods by herself, reading and eating alone. While her siblings struggled for their prizes, as they drove toward their certain dreams, Bicé struggled to find a friend—anywhere, even in books. She kept thinking that if she could just learn more and more languages, maybe she'd even find one somewhere on the planet.

Most days, the other kids teased her, knowing that she wouldn't fight back. Somehow, they couldn't dig all the way down to that part of themselves that understood a girl like Bicé. And so, they found ways to use her as a toy, a raven-headed plaything that would keep her head bowed, except for those rare and delicious moments when she would respond so cleverly that they could laugh at her even more. Sometimes, Valentin would say, Bicé was so careless that it was like she was asking for it, setting herself up. Like the time she was caught reading the *Kama Sutra* in the original Sanskrit in the hallway between classes, right out in the open, lurid cover facing the hall traffic, pages flipping loudly. The way she furrowed her brows, trying to understand every word on the page—such concentration. Valentin said she had it coming.

In truth, Bicé had no choice but to concentrate like that. Because she was doing so much more than just learning languages. She was deciphering them. Undoing them, and putting them back together from scratch. She would spend hours poring over syntax and origin, using one language to learn another. That's why most of the international kids didn't like her. "So arrogant," they would call her. Like the incident with Pamposh Koul and his band of gorgeous South Asian imports—girls who had transferred to Marlowe from top Indian and Pakistani schools, most of whom were in training to compete for Miss Universe and packed themselves tightly by Pamposh's side. That was the day that Pamposh had asked her if she spoke Kashmiri and she said no, because she didn't. A few hours later, he and three of his girlfriends had sat around one of the tables at the library, a few feet away from Bicé, whispering cruel remarks in Kashmiri, making sure to emphasize the fact that, yes, they were making fun of her, and no, she could not understand for once.

Then, one of them had walked over to her table waving a piece of paper.

"Hey, you're that language girl, right?"

Bicé didn't say anything.

"We thought you'd like to learn Kashmiri. We wrote down some words. Here, have a look."

She showed Bicé her list, handwritten in pretty girlish loops. "Come and sit with us, and we'll teach you how to say it."

Bicé, who was looking at the paper with deep concentration, barely looked up as she allowed the girl to lead her to their table. She sat silently as they coaxed her to say a few phrases, as they told her to repeat this or to enunciate that. "This is the word for *hello.*" "This is how you ask for a nearby restaurant." "This is how you introduce your family."

Finally, after about ten minutes, Bicé looked up.

"This word doesn't mean *restaurant.*"

"Yeah, it does," Pamposh said innocently.

"Well, if it does, then I bet Urdu-speaking tourists don't eat out in Kashmir too often . . ."

"What?"

"And that part there, that doesn't mean 'It's a pleasure to meet you.' It's really gross." Bicé kept reading. "And I'm not saying any of that stuff about a big ape—that's obviously about Christian."

Pamposh, who, instead of feeling embarrassed, had decided to focus on the injustice of Bicé's apparent deception, crossed his arms and sat back. He watched as Bicé kept poring over his hilarious Kashmiri insults, deciphering each one slowly, sometimes writing notes. She was like an archeologist digging through petrified excrement (which he had inadvertently provided). He didn't exactly cherish the position.

"What, so you picked up Kashmiri in the last three hours?"

At times like this, when Bicé thought that her classmates really wanted an explanation, when she assumed that a reasonable answer would make her loved, these were the moments when she felt happy—and then, afterward, the most alone. The applause-winning defense argument just before the guilty verdict. But no matter how often it happened, she never saw it coming.

She folded the paper, a bit too excitedly.

"No, no! See, once you know seven or eight languages in the same family, the ninth one comes easy. You don't need a class or anything. Just a good conversation and an hour with a dictionary . . ."

They weren't impressed. Bicé went on.

"You can use the other languages—the syntax and roots and common words . . ."

When no one answered, Bicé faltered, thinking that they didn't understand.

"There are families of languages, see? Spanish, Italian, Portuguese." She counted on her fingers. "Those are Romance languages."

Still no response.

"Well, you have yours, right? The Indo-Aryan languages? Punjabi, Gujarati, Kashmiri? You see?"

After a moment, she saw that they didn't care. That they weren't looking for a lesson. That she had once again misread the moment. So she cleared her throat and whispered in a faint, singsong voice, "Klingon, Wookie, Elvish . . ."

No one got the joke.

~⊙⊙⊙~

At lunchtime, Marlowe's halls filled with popped collars, hot-pink cell phones, and *bento* boxes full of *unagi*. Bicé stood aimlessly outside the library, surveying the chatting teenagers in their Marlowe uniforms, their gray-and-navy blazers, slacks and skirts, and crisp white shirts. She was tempted to turn around and go home. Or to stop everything and explore the school alone. Or to just hide right there for a few more minutes. More than anything, Bicé hated crowds. She thought she'd return to the library, spend the lunch hour reading or deciphering another family of languages, maybe some Native American ones. But then from the corner of her eye, she spotted Belle walking urgently toward the girls' room. Forgetting about her pathetically short list of lunch options, Bicé got an overwhelming desire to look out for her sister. She followed her into the bathroom, shrinking back into the corner as Belle entered a stall. The door to the bathroom suddenly opened again, and Bicé had to duck behind it as a bouncy blonde with a ponytail walked in and started knocking on each stall.

"I'm in here, Mags," Bicé heard her sister's hoarse voice coming out of the stall. "Don't worry. There's no one else in here."

Bicé wondered what they were doing lingering in a bathroom.

Shouldn't Belle be off making her lunchtime entrance? Belle's dining hall entrances were never discreet. When she drifted through the heavy double doors, the whole school turned to watch, dropping their half-eaten sandwiches, abandoning their candy bars and conversations. When she approached a table, people made room, desperate to be closer to her. She was Marlowe's collective addiction, permeating the heart of the school with every gust of wind.

Maggie tried to step inside, but there was very little room in the stall. They let the door swing open carelessly. Inside, Bicé saw the two of them hovering over Belle's handbag. In turn, each of them reached into Belle's bag and popped a handful of pills. Maggie almost had a fit of giggles, and Belle had to put a hand over her mouth to silence her. Bicé, feeling sad and shocked, found the first opportunity to leave her hiding place and duck into an empty classroom.

～☜☉☉

Ever since that fateful day in late July, "fugly Friday," as she called it, Mrs. Wirth would not come near the Health and Racquet Club in Rockefeller Center, where all the ladies congregated after a long afternoon of "shopping till *they* drop!" ("they" being the servants.) The ladies would sit around the fitness lagoon discussing how tacky the phrase "bargain hunting" was, how wacky a kiwi–amino acid smoothie tasted, and how delectable the physical trainers looked when they demonstrated the ellipticals. So now on Friday afternoons, Mrs. Wirth avoided the health club like last season's thigh-highs. In fact, on this particular day, she couldn't be further from the "ladies who lunch 'n crunch." She stepped into Payard Patisserie and pointed to the fruit tarts on the third shelf, the hazelnut mousse on the fourth, the majority of the macaroons on shelf number one, and just about all that she could carry from shelves two, five, and six (except the banana pudding, which she heard was made with buttercream, which was a "don't" on her No Buttercream Diet). Mrs. Wirth ordered her nonfat cappuccino along with the tasties, taking a cannoli "for the road" to her table. She was trying to scoop out the cream with her tongue, smashing her shopping bags into other patrons' faces, when she noticed Nicola Vileroy sitting in a corner alcove, all by herself. She waved a hand in the air. "Yoo hoo! Nicola, dear!"

Vileroy didn't turn to look.

Mrs. Wirth pouted and went right over. "Nicola? Nicola!"

Madame Vileroy was seated at an empty table, staring—she seemed mindless—straight into a blank patch of wall. She wasn't blinking, and her chest, under her handwoven lace-trimmed, form-fitting black dress, didn't seem to rise and fall with breaths in the familiar human way. She was catatonic. Mrs. Wirth sat directly in front of her. If Madame Vileroy noticed her presence, or if she noticed anything, she didn't let on.

"Nicola, dear. Aren't you going to say hello?" Mrs. Wirth waved a hand in front of her face. "Would you like half my cannoli?"

Nothing. Mrs. Wirth reached out and touched Vileroy's hand. It was cold like an empty basement. Mrs. Wirth pinched her slightly, then pinched her as hard as she could. She dug her nails into the skin she had folded up on the back of Vileroy's hand, but nothing. It was as though Madame Vileroy felt nothing, heard, saw, smelled, tasted nothing. She lacked all senses—all good and bad sensations of the world.

Madame Vileroy awoke to see Mrs. Wirth poking her hand with a fork.

"Oh!" said Mrs. Wirth, retracting the silver. "Are you OK? I was about to call an ambulance."

"No need," said Madame Vileroy, forcing a smile, obviously flustered for the first time since Mrs. Wirth had known her. Vileroy put one hand to the bun in her hair, looked around as though wondering where she was, grabbed Mrs. Wirth's steaming-hot nonfat cappuccino, and drank it in one gulp.

"Nicola, darling, how are you? You scared me half to death," said Mrs. Wirth.

Madame Vileroy's face slowly melted into an oozing honey-soaked smile. "Care for a little indulgence?" she invited her new friend. Slowly, Mrs. Wirth forgot about her shock and became mesmerized by the magic of this woman's presence.

"Well, I really shouldn't. They're wrapping up my pastries now. Though it's tempting . . ."

"Who says you shouldn't give into temptation once in a while? As we say in Paris, *Tout en modération, même modération.* Everything in moderation, even moderation."

"Oooh," said Mrs. Wirth. "Yes, well, in that case . . ."

Mrs. Wirth tried to hail a waiter, but none of them noticed her. Madame Vileroy coughed gently into her hand. Suddenly a handsome young waiter brought a cup of Darjeeling tea and Mrs. Wirth's favorite dessert, a piece of devil's food cake — strange, since the restaurant didn't serve devil's food cake. Mrs. Wirth just sat, dumbfounded, as the waiter brought Madame Vileroy a red apple tart and a cup of Earl Grey. Madame Vileroy picked up her fork. She looked at the tart for a moment, then shot the waiter a glance, which was enough to cause him to quickly remove the raspberry from the top. As Mrs. Wirth tried to work out what had just happened in her head, as she tried to cook up some explanation or another, Madame Vileroy patiently ate her tart, took a long, thoughtful sip of her tea, and thought of all the casual sins that might liven up a lazy afternoon.

"What are you doing here?" Mrs. Wirth asked.

"Just putting together a present for Valentin."

"Oh! Is it his birthday?"

"No."

Mrs. Wirth waited, but no more information was forthcoming.

"Genevieve, dear," said Madame Vileroy after a brief pause, "I hear your son is competing in the golf tournament."

"Oh, yes!" Mrs. Wirth beamed. "My Connor always wins. He's very good."

"I know," said Madame Vileroy sweetly. "I was at practice the other day. To watch Christian."

"Wonderful." Mrs. Wirth took a bite of cake.

"I was concerned. Connor looked a bit . . . listless."

Mrs. Wirth looked up from her cake. "What do you mean?"

Madame Vileroy shrugged. "It just looked like someone had sucked the energy right out of him. . . ."

Mrs. Wirth was worried now. "Should I call his doctor?"

"Oh, I'm sure it's not as serious as that," said Madame Vileroy. "Teenagers are always tired. I just hope he doesn't have a sudden bout of adolescent lethargy at the tournament."

Mrs. Wirth gave an uneasy smile.

Madame Vileroy waited. She loved uncomfortable silences.

"Good cake," said Mrs. Wirth, fidgeting.

"Mmmm." Madame Vileroy waited. No need to strain oneself with unnecessary digging. Mrs. Wirth would soon volunteer any useful tidbits herself.

Suddenly, Mrs. Wirth thought of something to say. "Thomas is playing too, you know. And his father, Charles, is coming."

"Oh?"

"Yes. He's a lovely man. And such a good heart. He's working on a business deal to bring money to poor families in Turkey. Working with one of those formerly rich foreign philanthropists. Yamin, he's called. A Turk. They say he drove himself into debt trying to build some humanitarian finance organization. Charles is helping now."

"Hmm," said Madame Vileroy. "Well, this has been lovely, Genevieve, but I must run."

Mrs. Wirth was in the middle of a sip of tea. She swallowed hard and said, "Oh!" as though she were very disappointed.

"I have a gift to arrange." Madame Vileroy winked at her new friend.

"That's right, Valentin's gift," said Mrs. Wirth. "What are you giving him?"

Nicola Vileroy tilted her head, squinted thoughtfully at the vapid old socialite, and simply said, "Something to mesmerize and delight him. Something absolutely ethereal that would capture his imagination and not let go."

"Ooh, Nintendo, how lovely!" Mrs. Wirth squeaked as Madame Vileroy rubbed her aching head and silently called the waiter for a double espresso—to go.

~◦◦◦~

Nicola Vileroy enjoyed her evenings alone. While the children slept, she walked through the house and kept watch. She was unseen, unheard, her steps making no noise, her breath producing no heat. She simply slid through their rooms, like a vigilant mother guarding her young, and planned for the day ahead. Usually, the children were already asleep, and the governess remained in her own world. She didn't have to stand tall, keeping her posture regal. She stooped just a little. Her blond bun was far from tidy, tentacles of straggly hair escaping from all sides. Her branded eye did not shine blue, as in the light of day, but glowed dark and terrible by the harsh half-light of this house of eternal night. In the black of the house, there was no noise, except for the flutter of a few moths and the breathing of sleeping children. But tonight, as the governess made her rounds, as her long fingers hovered over Belle's beautiful body, coming just short of touching her, she heard a new sound, something she had not heard before, coming from across the room.

Madame Vileroy turned to look in the direction of Bicé's bed, where she heard the girl whispering to herself, her head covered by her gray bedsheets. Ordinarily, the sound of children talking in their sleep, the vibrant soundtrack of their nightmares, barely moved the governess. But tonight, something was different. She moved toward Bicé's bed. First she caught a word, and then another. Whispers in another tongue. *She is close. She is far too close.* Vileroy's hands shook as she leaned over the tiny lump of gray that was Bicé's frail body. She came to touch her, her bony hand shivering only inches from her back. But then, without a word, she pulled her hand back and glided out of the room, her back straight, her posture regal, her mind set on the day ahead. She had Valentin's new gift to think about. As for Bicé, she had no more gifts for her, because as any good governess knows, too many presents spoil a child, and who wants a child that's so out of one's control?

Chapter 13

White Window

"No, William, we are not puckish. We do not steal for sport. We are not deformed and lonely misanthropes, or else you'd never have had me—the dark lady for your sonnets—so kind to you. Am I not, William? I've been no villain. We build them, you see. Entire civilizations on the shoulders of a few. Like the first mother, we are mothers to the first among us—the great ones. A sisterhood to keep order. Weird perhaps—that would be better put, I think—a guild of weird sisters."

"Weird sisters . . . that was only a dream."

"No, William. It was no dream. No fit of delirium. You must believe that this is so. A mirage would not have been so real. It could not have inspired you to write your famous plays—the plays that made you great, and not merely the butcher's son."

"What are you doing there?" said Valentin, biting into an unripe peach and joining Bicé at the table in the center space of their home.

"Just reading," said Bicé. She was surrounded by a pile of scribbled pages full of indecipherable letters. "Trying to figure out this text."

He peeked over her shoulder and sank into a chair. "Don't you ever get bored with all that reading?"

"Don't you ever get bored writing?"

"Yeah, but at least that has a purpose. What are you doing exactly? I mean, listen, sis, you should find something to work toward. You're way smarter than Victoria."

"Thanks."

"Seriously. Why not?"

Bicé wanted to tell him all that she felt, how much she hated this place, how she had nowhere else to go except in her own mind. That being adopted isn't so great if you wind up all alone in the end. Maybe he'd understand that she just needed someplace to go. But he would never understand. He was having fun. He didn't know what it was like to be a twin and then suddenly not to be. But she didn't tell him any of these things. She just smiled and said "thanks" again.

"Why not go do something with Belle and her friends? She knows practically everyone now," Valentin persisted.

Bicé shrugged. "No, she doesn't want me around."

Valentin, seeing the pained look on Bicé's face, tried a bit harder. "OK, so I understand if Belle's too busy and you don't want to hang with Vic, but it can't be good to be alone *all* the time."

"OK, maybe later," Bicé said, and went back to her reading.

For a few moments, Val just chewed and stared at Bicé. "Notice anything about Vileroy lately?" said Valentin.

"Hmm?"

"She's just so . . . mysterious . . . so hard to figure out." He sighed loudly.

"Seems the same to me."

He watched her as she continued to read. "Yeah, I guess," he said. Then his face fell and he started poking at his peach. "Bicé, do you want to hear a really good story?"

Bicé looked up.

He leaned close.

"I have a story that's much better than anything in that book," Valentin whispered.

She looked at him but kept silent. Something inside her felt as though she had been waiting for this story all day. Or maybe she had heard it before. Maybe she had heard it over and over again in a hundred different ways, in some parallel reality that was never allowed to remain in her memory. Maybe this, too, would be only a momentary answer to all her questions.

"Do you want to hear it?" he asked, his eyes sad. "Should I tell it to you?"

She nodded.

"Once upon a time," he began, with all the usual Valentin drama, "there was a beautiful mother with five children . . ."

Bicé giggled a little. Valentin went on.

". . . five sad, unloved, unhappy kids."

Bicé stopped laughing. Valentin wasn't trying to be entertaining anymore. She had never seen him look so sad. She squirmed in her seat.

"There was a favorite, of course. One that she had promised to love. . . . *He* was the most unloved of all of them."

"Valentin . . ." Bicé reached for his hand. She didn't care much about the story anymore. "Don't say these things."

"Ever notice that she doesn't treat me the same . . . as before?"

As far as Bicé could remember, Vileroy had always treated Valentin the same way—with a mildly encouraging, inappropriately flirtatious disdain.

Valentin toyed with the idea of telling her all about the Vileroy he used to know. The Vileroy that had come to his home in France. The beautiful woman who had met him secretly and had promised to take the place of his own disloyal mother. He could tell Bicé all these things and then just turn back the clock. But he was too tired now. He wanted to have a conversation that someone would remember. He wanted to say something that wouldn't be lost inside some fold in time. Something inside him wanted Bicé to hold whatever he said next with her, at least for a few days.

"She doesn't love me anymore."

Bicé just patted Valentin's hand. "I doubt that's true," she said, lying without skill but with enough conviction to make Valentin smile.

~⊶⊙⊙⊙~

A few days earlier, Madame Vileroy had given a gift to Valentin—a new room, just as she had given to the others. At first Valentin thought she would make a deal for it, as she always did. But she hadn't. This room was a gift—a simple gift with no strings attached. Valentin thought this was strange, but he didn't like to think about Madame Vileroy's motivations. It was too difficult. She told him that the room would let him take his powers to the next level but that he would have to be careful. It could also wind up disassembling his organs from the inside out. Or it could leave him stranded in the ocean. She had told him all this with an unusual level of dramatic flair, her eyes glowing as she put her arm around his shoulder and whispered about the seriousness of this gift.

Using the room would feel surreal sometimes—even unreal, like a dream. But regardless of all this, he must press on because the room was a gift for the most talented of the children. And he must never ever question what it could do for him. Until now, Valentin had been scared to use it.

The room had blank white walls like snow-drowned fields. Valentin walked into it, the intensely nothing room—so true and untrue. The only thing in it was a window directly in the center of the back wall—a perfect white wooden-framed window, segmented into four with the same white boards crossing at its center. The window, quartered like that, the only source of light in a vast expanse of nothingness, reminded him of Vileroy's branded eye. But different. More soothing. It looked like the window to the perfect pastoral home, and if you squinted hard enough, through the fog would appear a patch of sunflowers and a picket fence behind them. The house would have been a wonderful place to grow up, a wonderful place to explore.

Valentin stood staring out the window—no place to rest an elbow—at the wholesome trees, the tire-swing dangling from a branch, a rolling hill. You could almost hear the rocks singing. Valentin knew a lie when he saw one. This wasn't that. At least he didn't think so, even though his head hurt when he stood in the room. It wasn't a lie, he said to himself. But it certainly wasn't the street outside their house in New York.

Valentin put his finger on the window. The fog began to stir and seep through the glass. Behind the fog, Valentin could see walls made of mud bricks. He could see the scene outside changing. As he looked around, the room he was in had become wooded; the floor beneath his feet had turned to grass. Now he was on the outside of the window, looking into a hut, someplace very different. A moment ago he had stood inside a white room in New York. A moment from now, he could be standing in front of any window in the world, because *this* was the window to the world, every window that had ever been, now or in years past. He closed his eyes, clenched his fists. When he opened them again, the room was white again, exactly as it had been. He was back on the inside of the window of their New York apartment, looking out onto the illusory sunflowers and picket fence.

Valentin turned and walked out, fully believing with his whole heart and soul that this room could help him bend time and space in ways that his old gift never could. The minute his feet left the room, Valentin felt as if he'd been hit in the face with a load of bricks. It was as if he had been asleep and was now jolted awake or as if he had walked out of a fog. Somehow, things felt different outside of that room. He shook off the strange feeling and kept going. The test had worked. Going into the test, Valentin had been a little afraid — even though Madame Vileroy had told him exactly how the room worked. She had told him what to do, what to bring, what to expect.

But it never hurt to be suspicious. Now, to do anything for real, he knew he'd need believable clothes.

Valentin almost ran through the center space, where Victoria was reading. He rushed into his bedroom, reached under his bed, and took out a pair of male ballet tights he'd stolen from the Marlowe dance room. "I can't believe I'm doing this," he said. He squeezed into the tights, then grabbed a white dress shirt from the closet. He pulled off the buttons, wrapped it around his body over the tights, and tied a beige pashmina scarf he had taken out of Belle's room around his waist. He took a quick look in the mirror. He looked ridiculous. He'd just have to pretend he was a vagabond or the village idiot. On the way back to the room with the window, he was so distracted with the constant shifting of the scarf that he didn't notice Victoria lurking in the hallway.

"Where are you going?" she asked. "And what are you wearing?"

"I don't have time to talk, Vic. I have things to do."

Victoria turned and followed him, picking up her pace when he started to walk faster.

Valentin kept looking behind. He could feel her cheating as he tried to get away.

"You're going back," she said. Then she was silent for a few seconds more. Valentin tried to shut off his thoughts, but she was too quick. "The room she gave you — that's what it does, doesn't it? How do you know it'll work? When are you coming back? Does she know that you're doing this?"

He reached the door with Victoria on his tail.

"Take me with you!" she cried. "I want to go too, Valentin. Take me too."

"What?" Valentin whipped around.

"I know what you're doing, Valentin. That ridiculous costume is supposed to be from the Middle Ages or the Renaissance, right? First of all, there are about ten things wrong with it. Second of all, you can't fool me. There's only one person I can imagine you'd want to visit during that time."

"Actually, there are about a million."

"You think you can meet Shakespeare. And I bet you were stupid enough to pick a time when he's already famous."

"I had to. I'm dying to know if it's true—if he actually got credit for Marlowe's work."

"Why's that matter?"

"It matters to me, OK? Just go away."

"No, I want to go too."

"Why?"

"We're not the only ones who've had a governess, you know. Lots of people have—famous people."

"How do you know?"

"I know lots of things you don't."

"Name five."

"The Grand Unification Theory, tax law, binary, the capital of Azerbaijan, and how tractors work."

"All right, fine, who else had a governess like ours?"

"The queen had one."

"Really?"

Victoria nodded excitedly.

"Even if she did, how would you meet her? She's the queen."

"I don't want to meet her, stupid. I want to meet the governess."

"Why would she tell you anything?"

"Because I'll have something on her. I know her future."

"Wouldn't she know her own future?"

"No one can travel to the future, Valentin."

Valentin laughed. "Too bad," he said, "because now I know something you don't."

"Like what?"

"Like you're not coming with me."

Victoria continued to talk, but Valentin ignored her. He closed his eyes again. Her voice suddenly cut out. When he opened his eyes, he was alone in front of the door. Victoria was still in the center room, reading. He'd gone back to just before he had run out there and caught her attention. For a second, Valentin allowed himself to reflect on the fact that when he used his original gift of lying to go back, it felt very different than when he used the room — and it wasn't just a matter of scale. It was a different experience altogether. Valentin suppressed that thought, turned around, and walked into the room. Valentin never considered the possibility that the room might be a trick, a way for Vileroy to corrupt his mind — a dream or a hallucination. A foggy feeling came back over him the second he stepped inside, and a little part of him fell back asleep again.

He went to the window and felt the watch in his shirt pocket. The white room became the forest again. The other side of the window became the inside of a hut. Valentin reached out and gracefully unlatched the window. The room filled with fresh air and smells from a different era. Roast boar. Dried anise and orange peel. A wet leather cloak drying from the rain. Valentin put his foot on the sill and lifted himself through. When he was inside, he turned around and looked through the window. He could see outside. It was a perfectly natural wood — a squirrel danced from a branch; a leaf glided gently down.

Valentin walked through the house. A black pot hung above the fireplace, filled with some kind of stew. A wooden chair sat next to a small desk, on which Valentin saw some unfinished letters. At the top of one, he read, "June 15, 1599." He reached into his pocket and lifted out his rusted watch. "Time to commune with some genius." Valentin walked out of the house, down the brick path along the tulips, toward the inn at Stratford-upon-Avon.

For a moment, Valentin felt a strange awareness of Victoria. Back in New York, she was sitting in the center room, wondering what Valentin had been up to all day. He knew this. He could see it, the way a person in a dream can see others outside an immediate scene. He questioned this strange omniscience — he had never experienced it before. But he ignored it, assuming it was a part of the room's power. This gift was too wonderful. And it *had* to be real. Valentin knew it, because Valentin knew about lies, and Madame Vileroy had told him that a good liar never falls for a lie.

Victoria had picked a book from the bookshelf lined with leather-bound volumes — some that could be found in all the world's libraries and some that could not. She was reading *The History of the World: A Work in Progress*, a fairly thick book that Valentin had seen Madame Vileroy reading from time to time. Valentin found the book too exhaustive in some places, but worth looking into for colorful anecdotes. Maybe Victoria was using them for her debates.

The passage she was reading went like this:

That day proved uneventful for Mr. Shakespeare. A bit of light reading in the morning over sausage and candied ham was followed by his daily walk through the glen. In the early afternoon, William paid a visit at the inn to James Stafford, whose daughter, Melissa, was recently sequestered in her room for allowing John Harding to hold her hand. The father Stafford's long feud with John's father was the cause of the forced separation of the young lovers. Upon the suggestion of a young acquaintance, William hurried home to begin his next play, The Innkeeper's Pretty Daughter and the Boy Who Fell in Love with Her (Despite a Questionable Personality).

Immediately after leaning over William's shoulder and whispering, "What a good story that would make," Valentin realized that he might have somehow changed the course of history. Just after he spoke, a little part of him, the part that was watching Victoria in the room's dream, caught a glimpse of what she had read and knew that he was responsible for it. He just wanted to start a conversation. He'd been sitting at the bar, eavesdropping on the portly old man's rant about Harding encroaching on his daughter. Valentin just wanted to introduce himself. But as soon as he did, Will excused himself and rushed off.

At that exact moment, Valentin felt a sudden pang near his rib cage, like his heart had stopped and diverted the rhythm of the cosmos in an instant. He immediately closed his eyes. The inn began to rewind. William was back at the bar, alternately spitting beer back into his mug and unrolling his eyes at the old man. Valentin opened his eyes, and the man began to shout again, something about "that rake Harding." Valentin didn't say anything this time.

In New York, Victoria didn't notice that between the time she blinked and the time she opened her eyes, the text in her book had completely changed. All of history had been altered and then altered again, and Shakespeare never ended up writing that long-winded play. Across time and space, Valentin could see all this happening somehow, but he didn't ask himself why.

Valentin stayed at the inn — without ever introducing himself — until he was sure Will had made it home. He decided he'd just pay him a visit and pretend he was a landowner from the Orkneys. It was midafternoon when he went strolling back up the path, along the tulips. He picked one of them to give to that dainty housekeeper he had seen up the way. He picked up a stone and skipped it along the pond. And when he got to the door, just as he knocked for the third time, he heard, "I'm coming, I'm coming," and was almost struck down by the force that hit his chest.

He closed his eyes immediately and walked backward down the path. Was it the flower? The pond? The third knock? Whatever it was, it had altered something. A thread from the fabric of the world had been ripped out. Any little thing could have set into motion a series of events that would eventually change the future of the past. Valentin would have to go back and try again. He would have to keep trying it till he could avoid whatever it was that had sent ripples into the timescape.

Victoria looked up from her book, and the bookcase caught her eye. It looked as if one of the volumes was getting thinner, as though a biography was getting shorter. Another book was becoming less worn, less important to literature perhaps. Then it happened in the corner of her eye. A whole book seemed to disappear. She shook her head. Too much reading was going to her head. She went back to her book.

Valentine cursed and kicked the head off of every tulip in the garden.

Behind Victoria's bent head, four more books faded and disappeared.

Valentin had been doing and undoing the same stupid walk up to the house more than a dozen times. He had tried every way he could think of, skipping up the path, sneaking around back, shouting from a hundred yards away. "Screw this," he said. "He's not that good." He closed his eyes and clenched his fist. He opened his eyes, his fist. The watch was in pieces in his sweaty palm. Valentin sighed. He closed his eyes until everything was back. Will was still at the inn. Valentin had just come through the window. He went over to the pot of stew, snorted up every glob of mucus in his nasal cavity, and spit it right in. He paused, waited to see if that might have given the greatest writer of all time some kind of flu or something. Nothing happened. Valentin smiled. "*Bon appétit,* jerkface."

Victoria hadn't been reading for more than a few minutes when she looked up to see Valentin storming through the hall looking like a cash-strapped geek from a preschool Renaissance Fair.

"How was it? Did you find out if he's a fraud?" Victoria said. Valentin stopped for a moment. He thought he had returned to the moment *before* he had told Victoria where he was going. He must have picked the wrong moment when he was coming back.

"You saw what happened!" he said.

"I did?"

"With the history book . . . the plays that didn't get written . . ."

"What are you talking about? What plays?"

Valentin looked down to see that Victoria was reading an ordinary textbook. Victoria gave him a confused stare. Valentin looked around, rubbed his eyes, and kept walking. He stomped into his bedroom and slammed the door. Behind him, a voice said from the shadows, "The best-laid scams . . . huh, Valentin?"

Valentin snapped around. "What do you want?" he said.

Madame Vileroy stepped out. She was so pretty in the half-light, like a centerfold. Valentin looked away. He was too tired to entertain his usual thoughts. He placed the watch on his nightstand. "Aren't you curious?" she asked, slinking across the room.

"About what?"

"About what went wrong."

"Time went wrong," said Valentin.

"There's time for everything you want, Valentin."

Madame Vileroy stared hard at Valentin. He had believed what the room had shown him. The room of lies — of hallucinations.

Madame Vileroy hid a smile behind her pretty hand. In fact, she knew, Valentin had not gone anywhere at all. He had spoken to Victoria. He had put on a makeshift costume. Then he had entered the room. He had breathed the fog, fallen asleep, and dreamed a beautiful scene. His mind had created all of it: the tulips, William, even Victoria with Vileroy's book. He had woken to find Victoria sitting there, only ten minutes after what seemed like a long adventure.

Valentin was convinced of what she had given him to dream. And this room, it would continue to deceive him, with all the fantastical experiences he could imagine, and slowly change him to the core, leaving him nothing but a shell of himself: a dummy. He had believed the lie with his very soul — because he wanted to.

And so Madame Vileroy confirmed something about human nature that she already knew. Even the best liars will believe anything — if they want to badly enough. "Hmph," she said under her breath, and then she licked her lips. Yes, the observation was interesting. But more than that, there was a satisfaction to it. Because this is why she had chosen Valentin, for his weaknesses — the weaknesses she specialized in, the weaknesses that allowed her to manipulate him — and so she could watch him slowly change, become entangled in a web of false beliefs. There was a satisfaction to it, watching him degenerate. The way his eyes darted or his hands smashed the pocket watch. Like the way Belle tortured herself in the bath, or how Christian suffered from a wavering heart, or the way Victoria justified everything in her mind. Or the challenge of Bicé.

Valentin sat on his bed, deep in thought. "So what was it?"

"Hmmm?"

"What was it that I missed? What was it that altered everything?"

"Oh . . . it was . . . the stone, dear."

"How?" Valentin was intrigued, never suspecting the lie, because after all, he wasn't the *most* talented of liars. In that, *she* had many more years of experience.

"Without the stone in the pathway, the maid would never trip and fall. William would never have put aside his writing to tend to her. Yes, he always remembered the gentle look she gave him as he helped her up — the meek and vulnerable eyes that would later inspire the sad state of . . . of Miranda . . . in *The Tempest*."

Valentin's eyes glimmered with recognition and excitement. "Of course! It's so obvious! Why didn't I see that?" He was like a child, to whom the tooth fairy sounds so logical.

She shrugged. "You must come to the room often . . . and practice."

"It'll take forever to get good at this," said Valentin, his chin resting on his fist. He was already thinking of the next time.

"There's time enough for all of it," she repeated, sitting next to him. "Don't worry, Valentin."

Chapter 14

Steal

In the Highlands, a woman with hair as red as the fires of hell stumbled across the grass on a rain-soaked night, terrified and ecstatic and aching. She sprinted across the pitch in her long dress, the hemline dragging in the puddles of mud. She looked back. Something was chasing her. The tresses of her curls flung themselves around like dancing flames. She fell. Her hands and knees splashed on the green. Behind her a figure loomed upward. A bodice like black death, her skin like a pale horse, her hair yellow like a jaundice plague. She stood above the fallen woman. The sign staked into the ground read: GENTLEMEN ONLY; LADIES FORBIDDEN. The woman's cheeks were flushed with blood just beneath her supple skin. It would take so little to puncture. The figure knelt beside the woman, hungry. She scrambled away. The figure clutched her foot. The woman fell, sapped of energy, her hair already less vibrant. The figure was on top of her. Teeth, sharp like nails. A laugh, chilling like rain. A scream, lost like children.

"And here we are at the prestigious Hampshire Country Club for the thirteenth annual Mid-Atlantic Regional High School Golf Benefit for Muscular Dystrophy and Attention Deficit Disorder Research, or MARHSGBMDADDR for short. I'm Charlotte Hill, vice president of the Journalism Club at Marlowe, and with me is the handsome Valentin Faust, an honorary member until next year."

"Thanks, Char. You're not so bad yourself. As you know, three Marlowe boys will be competing in this match-play tourney, and as always, the Marlowe coach will be using this unofficial opener to the season to choose this year's captain. Connor Wirth has to be a favorite as last year's champ and captain. But newcomer Christian Faust is the dark horse, and rumors of international glory have everyone abuzz with what Marlowe's newest prospect is capable of. To round out the threesome, Thomas Goodman-Brown should have another solid performance."

Charlotte giggled as she pressed the stop button on her digital voice recorder. At the same time as providing live commentary for the match, she and Valentin were recording their banter for the Journalism Club podcast. "That was great! We sounded so professional!"

"Yeah, it's fun," said Valentin. "And Coach K will be glad we mentioned his name."

"Wait. We didn't mention Coach K."

Valentin adjusted the wireless mike on his collar. "Right, my bad." He blinked as though the light was too bright for him, fidgeted as if he had too much caffeine in his system.

"Well, it was hot," said Charlotte. "Where'd you learn to do color commentary like that?"

Valentin smiled his dimpled smile. "Practice, I guess. You're good too." He touched her on the inside of her elbow, a place she thought incredibly intimate. "Practice and repetition."

Charlotte actually swooned. She made a droopy look with her eyes and a whiny noise with her throat. Her knees kind of buckled. It was pathetic to see, even from the clubhouse terrace.

⚬⚬⚬

Victoria stood on the clubhouse terrace, by the railing, watching Valentin twist Charlotte around his finger. She rolled her eyes. Behind her came a voice: "You ready, or what?" It was Lucy Spencer, standing by the doorway with her arms crossed. The two of them were assigned in Student Council to decorate the clubhouse for the banquet after the tournament. Since Victoria was class president now, she couldn't say no—though she certainly tried. Thankless chores were not Victoria's strong suit. They'd be spending the entire afternoon hanging banners. Victoria turned around and walked back toward the all-purpose room, grabbing a step stool on the way. She said in a snarky voice, "Coming, Your Majesty."

Lucy raised an eyebrow in disgust.

"Oh, I wouldn't dream of it," said Victoria as she passed her.

"Dream of what?" said Lucy.

"Pulling the ladder out from under you. You must think I'm some kind of monster."

"You have no idea what I think."

"You'd be surprised," said Victoria.

⚬⚬⚬

"I'm surprised to see you here, Mrs. Wirth," said Belle. "Connor is starting at a different hole." Belle was waiting with a large group of spectators at the hole where Thomas would be starting the match.

225 ❧

"Well, dear, I wouldn't want to be one of those *overbearing* mothers, now, would I?" said Mrs. Wirth, adjusting the many items in her purse. "Besides, I have our maid, Martha, sending me updates on the walkie-talkie."

"Hmm," breathed Madame Vileroy. She was standing right beside them, but no one had noticed. Madame Vileroy had a way of going back and forth between being the center of a conversation and being almost invisible, lurking around a conversation without distracting any of the participants.

~⧯⧯~

"Connor Wirth isn't distracted by anything this afternoon as he gets ready to tee off on the second hole." Valentin had twitched a couple times before the last few sentences. But Charlotte knew that love conquered all things. And she knew she was in love. And her mother knew a great speech pathologist.

"That's right, Val, he took the first hole easily off of a strong player from Rhode Island."

"And speaking of strong players, Christian Faust is also making a case for himself. Lucky for us, both of the Marlowe standouts are in the same four-man group."

"And of course, we'll be in the golf cart just behind them, bringing you the play-by-play."

"Isn't 'play-by-play' just for sports that *have* plays, Char?"

Charlotte pressed the stop button on her recorder.

"I dunno, I just thought it sounded good. But you're not supposed to mention that kind of thing while we're recording."

"No problem, just go back and record over it," said Valentin.

"All right, fine," said Charlotte. She rewound a bit and pressed

RECORD again. "And of course, we'll be *on course* just behind the Marlowe supersquad."

"'Supersquad'? Really?"

Charlotte let out a sigh and clicked the stop button again.

"What, what's wrong with *supersquad*?"

"Just sounds a bit *Cosmo Girl* is all," said Valentin. "For a writer, I just thought you'd be better at, you know, talking."

Charlotte looked like the air had been let out of her. "That's mean," she said, looking down. "I'm the best writer at Marlowe — and I might win State. You're just mean."

"It's not mean," said Valentin, oblivious to the fact that Charlotte's eyes were welling up. "I'd think you'd be used to criticism. Try it again."

"I don't want to. If you're so good, you do it."

"Are you kidding?"

"No."

"That's ridiculous. Just do it again. That's why there's a rewind button on the stupid thing. See?" He pointed to the digital recorder as if demonstrating to a four-year-old. "So you can do it again and again till you get it right. It's not a big deal."

"Hey," said Christian, looking back from his ready position over a ball resting tentatively on his tee, "can you two keep it down?"

"Yeah," said Connor, "this takes a little more concentration than recording yourself gab."

"Shut the hell up, Connor."

"What did you say, Valentin?"

Valentin didn't even bother answering. He just slammed his foot on the gas pedal of his golf cart and started barreling toward Connor on the green. Christian yelled and dived out of the way. Charlotte screamed, but Valentin pushed her and sent her flying out of the cart. The look on Connor's face froze just before he got pounded by the cart — the cart started going backward, Charlotte flew back in. Everything went back until Charlotte was saying, ". . . golf cart just behind them, bringing you the play-by-play."

She looked at him with a big faux smile, as though the listeners could see her as well. Valentin had a distant look on his face, a thousand-mile gaze, as if he were depressed. He looked up at her, squeezed out a grin, and said, "Sure will, Charlotte! We'll be here with real-time box scores."

"That was great!" said Charlotte.

Valentin shrugged. *The best in the state. It's almost depressing.*

Christian swung the club and snapped the ball into the air. Valentin looked up into the blue sky — so bright it was hazy — to find it, but he couldn't. He couldn't track the course of the ball.

~⧸⊚⊚⧹~

Mrs. Wirth tracked the entire course of Connor's play, even though she wasn't one of those overbearing mothers. Between bouts of yelling at Martha through her walkie-talkie, she quizzed Bicé about her plans for her future. "What are you planning to do with all those brains, anyway?"

"I don't know. Maybe I'll translate all the garbage on the Internet for foreign countries."

"Is that really a good use of your talent?" said Mrs. Wirth, in a very serious voice.

Bicé shrugged. "I'd say helping the Uzbeks get on Facebook is a noble cause. . . ." Bicé just trailed off, as if she were speaking to herself.

"Beg your pardon?" said Mrs. Wirth.

". . . get those Papua New Guineans on the blogosphere . . ."

Mrs. Wirth just looked at her and started blinking. Faster and faster. As if she were trying to start the motor in her brain.

". . . age-old question . . ." Bicé was saying.

Mrs. Wirth turned her attention to Thomas, who was joking with his opponent. Thomas's dad was in the group, walking with Belle. He was in his forties and still handsome. With that salt-and-pepper hair and massive fortune, he was the most eligible bachelor in town. But despite Mrs. Wirth's constant gossip-mongering, he wasn't looking for anyone new. Behind that natural tan, he was a romantic, still married to his dead wife. And the way he said "sweetheart" to Belle made him seem like a much older man — like somebody's grandpa or Santa Claus.

~⁙⊙⊙⊙⁙~

Thomas wasn't so good at golf, but he knew how to charm people. His dad always said that it was smart of him to have taken up the sport. Future bank presidents don't play golf to win. Thomas was letting his opponent take a practice swing with his favorite club. Mrs. Wirth said to Thomas's dad, "He's certainly friendly, isn't he, Charles?" But he was too busy talking to Belle and inadvertently ignored her. Mrs. Wirth looked back at Bicé, who was still talking to herself. She shook her head and barked into her walkie-talkie, "Martha. Martha! *Dondé está* my son?"

"Thomas looks nervous, doesn't he?" Thomas's dad said to

Belle. "I've told him it's only a game. . . . Oh, there he goes. Off to the fifth."

"Fifth what?"

"Fifth hole. You know why I think he's nervous?"

"Why?" asked Belle.

"Because golf is one thing he's not great at. His friend Connor, he's the best. And Thomas isn't used to that. He likes to play, though. He plays with me and my friends."

Belle knew about Mr. Goodman-Brown's friends. They were on the cover of *Fortune* every other week. Charles Goodman-Brown was the CEO of one of the largest private banks in New York. Everyone, especially Belle, knew who his friends were.

All this time, Belle could feel Madame Vileroy's presence behind her.

~⚬⚬⚬~

Outside the cluster of buzzing parents, friends, and disqualified competitors, Madame Vileroy looked for a place to interject. She came to speak to a pair of mothers from another school, but they were busily conversing about the newest diet craze. She turned to Mrs. Wirth only to find that she was now engrossed in an attempt to wrangle a donation for Marlowe. Once again, Madame Vileroy found herself on the outside of every cluster, every conversation. And so she sat back and watched.

~⚬⚬⚬~

Behind Madame Vileroy, Maggie followed Belle like a droid. She had an undead look to her, compelled by the light of Belle, addicted to her, but afraid to get too close. Mrs. Wirth, who had an explanation for everything, shook her head and thought, *Poor girl. Sooner or later, she is bound to get ahold of her mother's stash of Valium.*

~∞∞∞

"I don't know what high school from whatever backwater part of Asia you came from, but there's a specific way of decorating for banquets. So just do as I say and we'll be fine," said Lucy.

Victoria thought about breaking the punch bowl over her head.

~∞∞∞

"And here we are at the end of the first round of play. Connor Wirth and Christian Faust ate their opponents for breakfast."

~∞∞∞

"You should invite Thomas over," whispered Madame Vileroy to Belle. She lingered just behind Belle's shoulders, so close that Belle could hear her breathe. She could almost feel the governess's deep-blue eyes on Thomas — the way that one scary eye focused right in on whatever Vileroy wanted. Thomas's dad was still holding Belle's arm, talking about the intricacies of the grain in the putting green. He somehow couldn't hear their conversation.

Belle said, "Why?"

"Because I'd like that."

"Why do *you* care so much what these people do, anyway? Why are you always trying to get close to them?"

"Because their actions have the widest ripples."

"What?" said Belle, remembering another time when her governess had mentioned ripples. When she had taught her a lesson in reading people. In spotting reactions and consequences. Vileroy had taught her because she was the favorite.

Just like a daughter.

"Think, my dear. What can I possibly accomplish with an average person? If I worked my hardest, if I used my best tricks, what is the worst he would do?"

"I don't know." Belle shrugged. "Kill someone?"

"And then what would happen?"

"He'd go to jail, I guess."

"And the total damage?" Vileroy sounded like she was instructing a remedial math class.

"Huh?"

She gave an exasperated sigh. "A few people would be dead, a few would be hurt, and then the fool would be put away. But these people — they make huge ripples," she said.

"Like what?" asked Belle.

Madame Vileroy pointed to a balding executive with his hands in his pockets. "Take that one over there. He'd think big, like an entrepreneur. He'd channel money away from starving economies, maybe pump some of the profits into the pockets of politicians, maybe use some of it to erase some dirty dealings, buy some drugs, sell some drugs, fund an illegal gambling ring, separate a few hundred families from their life savings, and pour it all into some shoddy product made by starving children. He would have a good ten years of momentum before he ever got caught. How many people do you think that would affect? Ripples, my dear Belle. That's what I like. That's what I look for. Never make the mistake of counting all lives as equal. Never."

Thomas hooked the ball right into the water. Belle cringed.

"We won't hold his golf skills against him," Madame Vileroy said.

"I don't want him in our house."

"Don't worry, dear. He won't know your secrets."

"What does *that* mean?" said Belle. Thomas's dad was starting to finish up his conversation with himself. His voice seemed far-off, as if Vileroy had lowered its volume.

"It means secrets have a way of getting out, and you have plenty."

"You wouldn't."

"Not on purpose, dear; they just have a way of getting out."

Thomas's dad seemed to have said something. Belle glanced at him, and then back at Madame Vileroy. Her gaze fell on the freckle on the back of Vileroy's hand, and then the one on her wrist, and the three freckles forming a triangle by her elbow. Then she glanced at her own arm, where little brown spots formed the exact same formations — a reminder of their unbreakable connection, formed the moment Belle had accepted Vileroy's beautiful exterior. Thomas's dad repeated what he'd said. It was a question addressed to Belle. She turned, enraged, from Vileroy. "Hmm?"

"I was just asking if you saw him whack that out of the sand trap."

"No, I didn't. You know, Mr. Goodman-Brown, I was wondering if you'd let Thomas come to our house for dinner next Sunday night. I know it's a school night, but he'd get to know my family better . . . and Madame Vileroy."

"Call me Charles. And of course he can go to your house."

~◦◦◦

"Go to hell, you jealous troll. Hand me those balloons."

"Slut."

"Wench."

~◦◦◦

"You'd need a winch to get out of those woods. Christian Faust has gotten himself in a doozy of a pickle with a drive that sliced well into the forest."

"Shut up, Val!" Christian shouted to the golf cart from the green.

"Whoa there, captain. Not my fault you shanked it."

"Your brother seems really mad," said Charlotte.

"Yeah, he's one of those 'born winners.' Isn't that right, Christian?"

Christian had to stop himself from throwing his club at Valentin. It was only one hole, one hole for the entire tournament so far, but he was fuming about it. For Christian, this tournament was a test. He had practiced with Buddy for a solid week, spent every night in his chamber recuperating. He had actually become better at golf. All that practice had paid off. Now he was sending drives double the distance he used to, sinking putts he never would have. All so he wouldn't have to steal from Connor. Christian wanted to win on his own.

Maybe the coffin was cheating, fine, but at least he wasn't hurting people. That's why Vileroy had given him the coffin in the first place the first time he told her about how awful it felt to steal— when she learned that he was not a natural thief. She had given him the coffin, so that he could have another tool. Something else to satisfy his need to win, to get the big contracts and endorsements. Something else to draw him in. Something to serve as a starting point for his hunger.

So far, Connor had been a nice guy. He'd been more distant after the Lucy fiasco, but still nice. Even after Connor had been hurt by Belle and Thomas getting together, he hadn't held it against Christian. He'd patted Christian on the back when he made a good drive.

Christian had shied away. The contact made him hungry to use his gift. He felt tired, thirsty, clumsy. He could steal all of it. Just a little touch, Connor would barely feel it, and he'd be unstoppable. No, for Christian, this whole thing was to prove to himself that he didn't need to. All the sports coming up—he didn't have to leech from other kids to win them. That's why he overreacted at one dropped hole. When he had such a delicious power at his disposal, Christian knew he'd have to work twice as hard as everyone else not to be tempted.

"You should really have that facial tic checked out."

Valentin looked over at Charlotte. He had been looking over at Christian and grinning.

"Don't worry about it," said Valentin. He didn't make sense sometimes. His moods were so erratic. He seemed antsy, cynical, like he didn't ever care what happened. It was charming at first, as though he were carefree. Now he seemed careless, reckless, and maybe a little rude. For some reason, that made him even more appealing.

"I didn't mean anything by it," said Charlotte.

"What, the tic?"

"Yeah, I'm sorry. Don't be mad at me."

"I'm not."

"Good, 'cause I'd take it back if I could."

"Wouldn't that be something."

Charlotte was charmed. Almost nothing he said made any sense, but he said it all with such flair.

"Are you entering the State creative writing thing?" she asked.

"Maybe," he said in a suddenly sullen voice.

"What's wrong?" she asked, almost afraid.

"I just feel a little torn that's all. Not sure what to do—"

235 ⊙~

Charlotte had no idea what it was, but it seemed like it was really hurting him. His eyebrows were brooding. *He looks like he should be in a music video.*

"What is it, Valentin?"

"It's nothing. Don't worry —" He looked away at just the right moment.

"You can tell me anything," she said, really believing that he was struggling.

"It's just that, well, if I enter the writing contest, I'd have to enter against you. . . ."

"You mean . . ."

"I just . . . I don't want anything to come between us." It took Valentin three tries to make that comment with a straight face. The twitches just made Charlotte think he was nervous. She burst into a breathless, watery-eyed laugh.

Does this girl cry for everything?

She wrapped her arms around Valentin. (He tried desperately not to pull away.) He was so romantic. The idea of it was so romantic. *This must be what it's like,* thought Charlotte, *to be in love for real.* He said everything that she'd ever wanted to hear.

"I don't have to enter," she said, still holding him. "I won't enter, and we can be together forever." She was completely his.

~◦◦◦~

"You are completely hysterical, moron."

"No, I'm not!" yelled Lucy. "You just said something I was thinking. What do you have, some kind of wavelength reader or brain projector or something?"

"I don't have anything like that. Now, calm down," said Victoria, looking around the banquet hall to make sure no one was around. "You're just so predictable. I can read you like a book."

"Oh? You can read?"

"Well, you'd be one of those cardboard books they use for idiots and three-year-olds. Like *Goodnight Moon,* except the pictures would be of ho-bags."

"I know you're doing something. I've been reading about electro-magnetic pulses. You're doing something with my head. I can feel it."

"How many times do I have to tell you? I'm not doing anything to your head. You must have some kind of syphilis-related brain damage or something."

"Why would I have syphilis?"

"I don't know, 'cause you're paranoid. And you're a skank."

Lucy just rolled her eyes and went back to the table settings. That was close. Victoria kicked herself for letting it go so far. Victoria just wanted to put Lucy in her place, but Lucy could tell when she was cheating in her mind. It felt like a sudden headache. Victoria knew she couldn't read minds too deeply, not while they were awake. She went back to setting forks and knives around each plate. She'd need a way to cheat without the person finding out, especially with debate coming up.

~☙☙☙~

"It's a good thing the State Debate Tournament is coming up, ladies and gentlemen."

"Why is that, Valentin?"

"Because we've just gotten word that young Goodman-Brown

has been eliminated from the tournament, and I hear he's much better at debate."

∽⊙⊙⊙

Thomas came off the field laughing it up with the guy who had just beaten him. His dad gave him a high five as if nothing mattered. Belle watched them interact. It was as if they actually loved each other. She wondered what Thomas would think of her if she'd just been the girl she once was. Would he still glance over at her every chance he got while he hugged his dad? Would he come over for dinner?

"He's a good kid," said Bicé.

"Yeah, I'm starting to notice that," said Belle.

"Let's go," said Mrs. Wirth. "Connor is up against the Faust boy for the last match."

∽⊙⊙⊙

"Coach K is already celebrating, now that the finals of the tournament are being played by two Marlowe boys, Wirth and Faust."

"That's right, Valentin. Everyone is wondering who's going to win — which one will be the new star of the team. Connor Wirth is a little more familiar with the course. And earlier, he hit a two-hundred-fifty-yard drive, which is the longest drive he's ever had! But he has to come up big here on the twelfth hole if he wants to keep it neck and neck. He steadies his swing, hits, and that one is sailing . . . Wow, Valentin! Look at that! That has got to be two hundred eighty yards out, a personal best and record for the day's competition!"

∽⊙⊙⊙

Mrs. Wirth jumped up and down, patting Bicé on the head every time she landed.

"Wow!" said Mr. Goodman-Brown. "That's about two hundred seventy yards, I'd say."

"It's two hundred eighty-three," corrected Mrs. Wirth. She was pointing a laser measure at where the ball had landed in the distance.

"It's time for Christian Faust to see if he can match it," said Valentin.

⌒⊚⊚⊚

Christian was nervous. He'd never lost before. Would this be the first time? He looked at the plush clubhouse and his classmates in their polo shirts and slacks. Then he glanced over at his sweat-soaked caddy, picking dirt from under his nails. He felt embarrassed for the poor guy. What a life. Spending your weekends picking up balls for more fortunate kids. And then he felt only one thing: that he wanted to win. Christian saw Connor approaching, making his way to the sidelines after his brilliant shot. He looked at his friend-turned-rival and smiled.

"Good job, man," he said, and he patted Connor on the arm in a friendly gesture.

Connor smiled back and said, "Thanks." No one noticed Christian's hand shaking as he touched Connor's arm. Even Connor didn't notice, because Christian was not stealing his energy, just a little hand-eye coordination.

Christian approached the twelfth hole. He lifted his club and swung hard. The ball flew into the air and took off. Mrs. Wirth almost dropped her laser pointer trying to keep track of its distance. Valentin and Charlotte jumped up from the golf cart.

"I'm having a hard time seeing the ball from here . . . but it looks like . . . it's passed the three-hundred-yard mark . . . and the three hundred twenty . . . but it's slowing down. . . . He's made a three-hundred-seventy-yard drive!"

"That breaks the tournament record, doesn't it?"

"Actually, it's a new record for high-school golf overall."

"Well, I think we've got a pro on our hands," said Mr. Goodman-Brown, patting Thomas on the back as he spoke.

The moment the ball touched the ground, the crowd went wild. Connor made his way back to the green, while Christian, hanging his head lower than usual, walked into the collective embrace of the adoring crowd. Of course, Connor fumbled the next shot, and the one after that, and the one after that. The twelfth hole took him seven strokes to complete. It took Christian three.

"What a debacle for Connor Wirth," said Valentin. "It looks like he's just lost his mental edge."

Over the next few holes, Connor didn't just lose to Christian; he was humiliated. His balls caught every sand trap, hit every tree, fell into every puddle. Every putt took four or fives tries. On several occasions, he didn't even finish a hole, since Christian had already won. Once, he actually missed the ball with his club, sending a huge chunk of grass and dirt into the air. In the end, Christian won the game with three holes left unplayed, and Connor was thankful to be done with the day.

Mrs. Wirth was speechless. "What the hell just happened to my boy?" she said.

"No big deal, Genevieve," Mr. Goodman-Brown said. "You win some; you lose some."

"He *was* looking listless at practice," said Madame Vileroy, appearing out of nowhere. "Maybe you should see a doctor after all."

"But he was doing so well! Why did he suddenly choke like that? I just can't figure it out," said Mrs. Wirth, in a rare moment without an explanation.

"Now, don't say that, Genevieve. The boy will feel bad."

～⋙⊚⊚⊙

"Don't feel bad," whispered Madame Vileroy as Christian walked off the green.

"I feel bad," said Christian.

"Don't," said Vileroy. "You deserve it."

"I stole it."

"If you don't get caught, you deserve everything you steal."

～⋙⊚⊚⊙

Though Christian had stolen the show at the Hampshire Club, the biggest surprise came when the crowd walked into the clubhouse, expecting a beautifully arranged banquet. Instead they found tables turned over with plates broken on the floor, streamers hanging sadly, tufts of hair, and what looked like a torn drape speckled with blood. It looked as if someone had taken a perfectly decorated room and blown it up. No one ever got a straight story out of the Student Council as to why the room had been destroyed. If anyone ever mentioned it, Lucy would just mumble something about brain surgery, and Victoria would only say "ho-bag."

Chapter 15

Favorite

A Governess's Wish Fulfilled: A Soul Beyond Redemption
New York, 2062

"OK, we're ready in New York. Is the president on the line?"

"Everyone's here, Jack. Let's get started."

"Excellent. I'm here with the other executives of Kaffa Genetics Corporation. Also sitting in on this call is my assistant, Nicola. She will be taking notes."

(Just get to the point, Jack.)

"Let me get right to the point. Mr. President. I'm proud to report that we've done it. We have developed a genetic agent so powerful, it can end decades of biological warfare. Not since 2035 has such an important discovery—"

"What exactly are the capabilities of this weapon?"

"Sir, it's a pathogen that can discern subtle hereditary differences among ethnicities."

"So you're telling me that we can release it in a population, and only certain people will be harmed?"

"That's what I'm saying, Mr. President. The old profiling methods are obsolete now."

"How much will this cost?"

(No more than half a billion, Jack.)

"No more than half a billion, Mr. President."

"And you're sure that it's completely harmless to groups that aren't its target?"

(Only mention the short-term effects.)

"Short-term effects only. Otherwise, no harm whatsoever."

~∽⚬⚬∽~

Victoria practically power walked her way through the halls of Marlowe, carrying a pile of books, her backpack strapped tightly to her back.

"Where are you going so fast, ghoul girl?" a random boy yelled out as some cheerleaders around him burst into laughter.

Usually Victoria would have just walked on, too focused on her own plans to care. But today, she was in no mood. She whipped around and lunged at the boy, boring into his thoughts so deeply, cheating with such force and speed, that before she was two feet away from him, he turned and threw up all over his girlfriend.

"Ugh . . ."

"Yuck!"

"Gross!"

The girls started to scatter like a bunch of scared chickens, and the boy stood there, wiping his mouth and shrinking from Victoria's gaze.

"Well, you're lucky they weren't at your house two days ago, Scott. I'm sure this is nothing compared to *that* embarrassment."

Victoria turned and kept walking, even though half the school was looking at her as if she had just committed murder. Of course, she hadn't touched Scott, so no one could say anything. But somehow everyone knew. Most of them had experienced it, Victoria's cheating. They all knew she was strange. And she couldn't care less.

Just as she was making her way to the class officer meeting, Victoria spotted something dark moving in one of the side corridors. She stopped and peeked, half knowing what she would find. Madame Vileroy stepped out, tall and statuesque as always, walking with so much confidence you'd think she'd erected the school with one flip of her hair. Victoria wasn't surprised. Lately, Madame Vileroy showed up to a lot of her activities, and Victoria liked it. It was as if she were the favorite now. It wasn't Belle that got all the attention. It wasn't Valentin that got all her love. It was Victoria, and that made her more than satisfied. Someday, Victoria would show Madame Vileroy what she was worth. Someday, she would prove herself the very best. And then maybe the governess would share all her secrets. When Victoria was powerful in the world's eyes, she would be worthy of following in her governess's footsteps.

"Where to so fast, my dear?"

"Officer meeting."

"Hmm . . ." said Vileroy in a bored, uninterested tone.

"Well, I have to. I'm class president, remember?"

"Yes, I suppose the reason one becomes a high-school class president is for all that unmitigated power. Now, tell me, dear, how goes the fight against vending machine price inflation?"

"Hey, we all have to start somewhere."

"Yes, but the most you can get out of being president is already gotten. Understand?"

"Yes."

"Good girl. Now, I have something far more important for you to do."

Victoria leaned in, ignoring all the gawking, eavesdropping students passing by. "OK."

"I heard Bicé whispering again last night."

Victoria shrugged.

"When she hides . . . I need to know what she does. I need her to stop."

"What do you want me to do about that?"

"Nothing much. Just talk to her. Find out a few things." Madame Vileroy seemed thoughtful, as if she were trying to puzzle out some annoying riddle.

"Why not ask Belle?" Victoria tested. "Belle's her sister." She wanted to hear Madame Vileroy say that she was better, that Belle would screw it up. She wanted her to say that Belle was nothing to her. That Victoria was the most talented, that Victoria had the most potential, that Victoria would do great things.

"Because Belle's busy."

Victoria's shoulders slumped.

"And because you can handle more responsibility."

Victoria took the bait like a starved guppy. She was about to ask what she was to find out when Madame Vileroy spoke again.

"Try to find out how many languages she can speak now."

"I thought you knew stuff like that."

"Just get me the number."

~∞∞∞~

Sometimes Madame Vileroy would walk through the city alone. She would sit in dressing rooms and listen to the girls in the surrounding stalls, planting feelings of self-loathing and vanity into their heads. Sometimes she would walk through the dangerous city streets, leaving a stream of petty theft, violence, and resentment in her wake. Or she would linger in residential neighborhoods and send a handful of moths through every window, using them to plant suspicion between spouses, jealousy between sisters, hatred between siblings. One day, just after she had sent six moths into each of six different windows, she saw Mrs. Spencer walking out of the glitzy apartment building that dominated the street.

"Nicola, is that you?"

Vileroy smiled, and Mrs. Spencer gave her a cold embrace. Her daughter had regaled her with tales of Belle's and Victoria's wretchedness, and she was in no mood to befriend the woman she considered responsible for her daughter's misery.

"What are you doing in this neighborhood?"

"Visiting a friend," Madame Vileroy replied.

"Anyone I know?"

"Probably not."

"Well, Nicola. I see you're settling into life in the big city." Mrs. Spencer gave a half smile. "Far cry from the French country, no?"

Madame Vileroy, who had no need to rise to this challenge, simply nodded.

"How are those daughters of yours? I hear Belle is dating our own Thomas Goodman-Brown."

"Is she? I hardly keep track."

"You don't keep track of your own daughter?"

"Too much supervision is detrimental to a young woman's development. I'm sure you know this."

"Well, that's not how I raise my daughter."

"Perhaps if you let her have a bit of freedom . . ."

"To do what? Grow armpit hair and have sex with hooligans?"

"Hmm . . . No, but I understand that Thomas had asked her out first."

"That's not true."

"It is. Poor girl. So little experience. She let him slip right through her fingers."

Mrs. Spencer let out a chortle. "What exactly are you suggesting?"

"Darling, I just think you should spend a bit more time on yourself. You look so very tired. And all this worrying and chasing after your daughter can't be good for you. What she needs now is space. Lots of space to work out her own little high-school problems. You've taken care of the important things. She doesn't date waiters now. She knows what she wants and how to get it. Any more attention from you and she will be a stifled, frustrated old maid all tied up in her mother's skirts."

Mrs. Spencer's hand flew to her chest. "Well, I never!" she gasped.

"Oh, come on, darling," said Madame Vileroy with a smirk, "we both know you have."

Mrs. Spencer was shocked—partly from the fact that Madame Vileroy had the nerve to say such things, and partly from the image she had planted in her head. She was about to respond, but something about Nicola Vileroy made her stop, something about the way she looked at her, the bored and contemptuous look on her face that somehow still left room to desire her company. Something made Mrs. Spencer not want to retaliate. Instead, she cowered, said a quick good-bye, and ran off, holding Madame Vileroy's words close to her, clinging to them tightly so that they could slither under her skin like microscopic bugs and corrupt and ruin her.

On Tuesday after the golf tournament, Belle took another painful bath. Madame Vileroy didn't have many house rules. She could go out anytime she wanted. No curfew. No restrictions. That night, she was going out on a date with Thomas, who'd had to negotiate with his dad for an hour before *he* could get permission to go out on a weeknight. Thomas's dad didn't become the city's top banker by losing negotiations to fifteen-year-olds. By the time it was over, Thomas had given up next summer to intern in his dad's office, sat through a lecture on modern finance, and enrolled in a Japanese for Business class.

On her way out, Belle ran into Madame Vileroy, sitting in the center space of the house. "Be careful . . ." she said sweetly. "Don't get too attached to the boy. And don't forget Sunday."

"Everything's great with Thomas. He loves me."

"No. He thinks you're beautiful."

"Right. Whatever."

"But not really, since that's not your face. He thinks *I'm* beautiful."

"Yes, I know." Belle was annoyed at the constant reminder.

Christian walked in with Bicé just in time to hear that. "Her own looks aren't so bad. Belle and Bicé have a very nice-looking face." Bicé smiled and patted Christian's hand.

Madame Vileroy ignored her and said, "Maybe Christian's on to something. How about we stop the treatments and see how Thomas likes the real Belle?"

Belle shuddered. She knew the others thought she was incredibly vain and that Bicé saw her reaction and was insulted, but she couldn't help it. She needed Madame Vileroy. And she couldn't give up now. Last time they were together, Thomas had stood so close. He had played with her hair and held her hand, as he always did. But why did he never try to kiss her? Could he still smell it? Was the bath not enough? Was he afraid to get close to her? He seemed to have passed all the usual phases. He seemed so addicted . . .

"You're a good girl, Belle. You'll bring him here next Sunday, and then we'll all have a lovely time together."

"OK," Belle whispered.

"Don't be so sad. The other girls don't rely on what they're born with either. They all have some tricks up their sleeves. Yours are just better."

Belle walked out and slammed the door shut. She might as well enjoy this night with Thomas, because after Sunday, she wasn't sure anything would be the same. Belle had spent the last two days feeling guilty, clinging to Thomas like a schoolgirl. She had stopped playing coy games because she'd realized that Thomas didn't play games. He liked Belle, and sometimes Belle thought it wasn't because of the baths. She had switched from *irresistible* to *indifferent,* hoping that the effect of her bath could be a mild one that they could overcome with something real between them. But she couldn't keep him from acting paranoid and jumpy like the rest of her friends.

For her part, Belle did all she could to be close to Thomas, and to Madame Vileroy's disgust, she was having a harder and harder time playing the vixen. At Marlowe, everyone knew that Thomas and Belle were together now. They loved to gossip about the beautiful new girl who had swooped in and stolen Thomas from right under Lucy Spencer's nose. Lucy was in a state of denial, preferring to think of Belle as a flavor-of-the-month. She was focusing her hatred of the whole family on Victoria — for the time being.

Belle arrived at the SoHo bistro, where Thomas was already sitting at a table by a window. The days were getting longer now, and it was just beginning to get dark. Spring had always been Belle's favorite time of year. But there was something about New York that made her like it a lot less than before. It wasn't flowery and fresh and full of new things. It was more like the last dregs of winter. The melted yellow ice. The chilly air. But somehow, Thomas had managed to pick the one street that didn't depress Belle. There were little pots of flowers in the windows. A couple of the shops had old-fashioned signs hanging off the awnings; one of them had a picture of a bird. The cafés and restaurants had a charm that made every meal feel like Sunday brunch. "This is a pretty restaurant," Belle said as she looked around. She waved away a moth that was flying around her face as she sat down.

"I didn't think Madame Vileroy would let you come out. She looks really strict."

"Yeah . . ." Belle said vaguely. She blushed as Thomas reached for her hand.

"Well, anyway, she did let you come out. And she let you invite me over for dinner on Sunday," said Thomas. Belle felt a giant lump in her throat. She took a drink of water and smiled faintly.

Thomas went on. "So what's she like?" he asked, leaning forward as if she would tell him a secret.

"You know . . . just the typical governess."

"Ah, yes of course . . . typical governess." Thomas switched to a snooty British accent that was so right on, Belle remembered the way Victoria used to speak before losing her accent. "And your man-servant? Is he typical?"

Belle laughed and made a face.

"You have a cute laugh," said Thomas in his normal voice. Belle's smile faded as she thought of Sunday again.

"Is this bug bothering you?" Thomas asked, waving his hand at a moth nearby. "Maybe we should move."

"I'm OK," she said, not wanting him to let go of her hand.

"What's wrong?" Thomas asked, looking at her sad face.

"Oh, just Vileroy . . . It's stupid. . . . I hate her."

"I'm sorry. You said she adopted you, right?" Thomas said carefully. "I mean, you look a lot like her . . ."

"Yeah, we were . . . um . . . orphans. Madame Vileroy found us when we were babies."

"What happened to your parents?" asked Thomas with obvious interest, his eyes growing wider.

"We're not sure. But could we talk about something else?"

"Sure." Thomas couldn't help but ask one more question. "But how can you all be the same age?"

Suddenly Belle noticed the nervous tapping of his feet, and her stomach dropped.

"Well, we're not all really related. She adopted us . . . um . . . separately." Just then, Belle got the urge to tell Thomas something true. "Bicé and I are twins."

"No way! I thought Bicé was teasing when she said that at the play. She's nothing like—"

Thomas caught himself because Belle looked a little insulted.

"We're fraternal," she said shortly.

"Yeah." Thomas cleared his throat. "I just meant that . . . she looks different from you."

"We have the same eyes," Belle said.

"You know, I did notice that."

"Really?" Belle asked, her face full of skepticism.

"Yeah, they're my favorite part of you," Thomas mumbled.

"Thanks," Belle said slowly. Thomas had no idea that this was the first compliment he had actually paid to her. All the other compliments—they weren't really for her.

⌒✷⊚⊚

For the rest of the night, Belle kept the conversation on Thomas, who could have talked for hours as he unconsciously played with Belle's fingers. She barely interrupted him, for fear that he might stop. But as much as Belle wanted to avoid talking about her own family, Thomas mentioned Victoria.

"You know your sister's really hard-core. She's taking this debate tournament really seriously."

Belle didn't want to talk about the tournament. But she gave a small nod.

"I'm not worried." Thomas smiled.

"Why's that?" Belle asked playfully.

"Because . . . I have a secret weapon."

Thomas sat up in his chair. He leaned in closer, though his chair was already pulled up next to hers. Suddenly the romantic tone in his voice was gone, and Thomas's mind was elsewhere.

"The topic is intellectual property rights versus the right to life. Whether it's ethical for small companies in India to reverse-engineer patented drugs and then sell them cheaply to patients that can't afford the prices of the large drug companies."

Belle was so taken off guard, she chuckled.

"What's so funny?" asked Thomas, letting go of her fingers. *Oh man*, Belle thought, her fingers suddenly feeling cold.

"Just that you're so excited by such a boring topic! I barely understood half of what you said."

"It's not boring! It's about life and death."

"OK, sorry, go on. I'm all ears."

"Well, my dad works in finance, right?"

"Yeah, I think I've heard of him," Belle said jokingly.

"He put me in touch with his friend who specializes in this type of law. He's really well known. I got some great quotes and data from him on both sides of the issue. Some of his arguments are actually pretty new and impressive. So I'm in great shape."

"Why's that?"

"Because! Most people prepare for debate by clipping quotes from articles. Since those are public sources, anyone who's up against me can just find the same sources and prepare the opposite case. But if I have private quotes and data, and if I make points that are not as obvious, it would be harder for them to tear down my arguments."

"I'm impressed."

"Thanks."

Thomas beamed. "I'm trying to prepare like a real lawyer . . . for practice."

"What do you mean, *practice*?"

"Don't tell anyone. I mean, I haven't told my dad yet, but I think I want to become a lawyer."

"Doesn't he want to you work with him in finance or something?"

"Yeah, he's got his heart set on it. And maybe I will, eventually. But I want to do some human rights stuff first, like my dad's friend Mr. Yamin does in Turkey. And I just want to find the right time to tell him."

"Wow."

"Wow, what?"

"You're actually a good person, aren't you? Like, you actually care about all that stuff, and how your dad feels, and doing good for people."

Thomas blushed and rolled his eyes. "Yeah, I'm a saint."

~⚬⚭⚬~

As the evening passed, Thomas and Belle grew more and more engrossed in their conversation. They moved on to other topics and hardly noticed the hours pass, the people leave the restaurant, even the bustling scene outside. Belle felt as if she had known Thomas for years — that she had loved him all her life. And still, after so many weeks, he made no attempt to kiss her. As the pair chatted, a moth circled the solitary candle on their table. Halfway through their conversation, as if summoned by an outside force, the moth rose up from the table, zigzagged in the air, and flew out the French doors.

~⊗⊚⊚

Victoria was barely visible in the cloud of insects that circled her like a dust devil. She was no longer afraid of them. They were her friends now. Just as Madame Vileroy had predicted, they had become like family to her. More than family — they were her eyes and ears. Still, somehow, each time she visited them, their touch became harsher, more intrusive. Somehow, each time, the experience degenerated to something worse, so that it was always as scary as the first time. A few times, when Victoria looked up, she thought she saw other insects mingled with the moths. Was that a bee she saw? Were those flies? In any case, something felt a lot harsher than the soft feathery moths she had felt before. From the scratches on her face and neck, it was obvious that she had been waiting for hours, listening, but never getting enough.

At a glance, the scene surrounding Victoria might be familiar — like a perverse version of something ordinary. Standing there, in the cloud, with her arms in the air, eyes closed, twirling, she looked like a little girl dancing in a flurry of flower petals or a rain shower. She spun her arms, creating waves in the sea of insects. They moved with her, parting to make way yet never losing their enveloping hold on her body. At times, as she stood on her toes, it seemed as though they would lift her up and carry her around the room on their tiny wings. How pretty it would be if it weren't quite so gray, so thick . . . so unsettling. It would be a beautiful sight, if it were possible to forget what it actually was.

Victoria's mind was shut off. She was in a state of complete relaxation as she took in all that the moths had to say. She didn't see the three tiny ones flying in through the window to join their millions of brothers and sisters. Like a drop of blue ink released into a cup of clean water, their information disseminated through the maze of insects in seconds. It rapidly made its way to Victoria's open mind, along with dozens of other tidbits from all over the city. Just then, Victoria stopped twirling. Her moment of relaxation was gone; she was now paying careful attention. She stood upright, muscles tensed, mind alert, taking in all that her spies had to say. Belle was on a date with Thomas. Thomas had a secret weapon. Thomas had a resource that she didn't know about. She listened carefully as the moths told her all that they knew from Thomas's conversation with Belle. "Say more. Say more," Victoria said out loud. But there was nothing else. Thomas hadn't told Belle the actual content of his conversation with the patent lawyer.

Victoria stood on her tiptoes, tense as a rock, arms stretched behind her like the Winged Victory, straining to hear more. A few more hours showed her nothing. Thomas didn't do any work on debate that night; he didn't have any more conversations with his dad about debate; he didn't even have his notes in plain sight. Victoria dropped to the floor, looking defeated. *Stupid Belle and her ridiculous crush. None of the others have to work this hard. Belle doesn't deserve so much of Vileroy's attention for doing nothing. It's*

OK, she thought. *I'm still the favorite. I'll get all the information I need out of Thomas on Sunday.* The moths followed her to the ground. She got up, put her hands on her ears as if she was about to scream, and ran out of the room. The moths continued to circle one another, creating a vortex where Victoria had stood a moment ago. The roar of their wings was deafening, and Victoria could still hear words flying back and forth as she ran down the hallway.

Chapter 16

Slipping

"*Growing up in Edmond, did you ever think you'd be a rock star?*"

"*You know, I don't actually remember much, but I couldn't have imagined something like this . . . I mean,* Rolling Stone, *that's a real— this is a real honor.*"

"*Thanks. What was it like starting out?*"

"*Awful. It was like, gig after gig, we were getting booed off stage . . . and sometimes there wasn't even a stage! We played dumps.*"

"*What happened?*"

"*Inspiration, I guess. I met this chick. Our first three hits were about her actually—*"

"*'Unmensch Wench,' 'You're So Hot I'm Buyin',' and 'Don't Leave Me Addicted'?*"

"*Exactly! Yeah, those were all about this crazy time we had.*"

"*You did a lot of drugs together?*"

"*Didn't need 'em.*"

"But you said you can't remember much."

"Yeah, weirdest thing . . ."

"Says here you used to tell people you were raised in Ontario."

~☾◌◯☽~

After the tournament, Bicé started to watch Christian more carefully. She knew what he had done to Connor. She knew he felt guilty about it. For some reason, she felt responsible toward him. She noticed that Connor wasn't himself at school. He'd started to skip classes and (according to Christian) even a few practices. One day at lunch, Bicé tried to tell him that no one else cared that he had lost the golf tournament, but Connor didn't see things the same way as everyone else. His life was all about sports, and he just thought Bicé was being weird again. Thankfully, Christian had found plenty of friends among his admirers. Even though Bicé herself didn't have any friends, this fact made her happy. Still, she knew that every time Connor missed a practice or bolted for the door at the end of the day, Christian felt a pang of guilt. Christian didn't linger long after school either. Like Connor, he preferred to be alone. Unlike Connor, Christian had something to rush home to. He spent a lot of time in the chamber over the next few weeks. He said it seemed right that it made him feel like he was lying in a coffin. He said that it felt like an atonement. Bicé tried her best to shake him out of it. But what could she do? The coffin made her nervous — the way he would lie there and pretend that he was dead and free from the guilt of what he'd done, of what he would do again.

Sometime in the middle of the week, Bicé went with Valentin and Belle to watch Christian's swim meet. On the way over, they were discussing Victoria's latest excuse for not joining them when Bicé noticed that Christian hadn't said anything since they left the house. "What's wrong?" she said. "You worried you'll get beaten?"

Christian gave a small, unconvincing laugh. "I don't want to do it."

"I know," said Bicé. She thought about all the times Christian had been forced to steal, about the guilt he felt after each slip. But then had he always felt this way? She remembered a time when he didn't feel so guilty. When he stole with abandon and laughed like a carefree kid. Something didn't feel right. "Remember that time when we were eight . . . or maybe seven . . . and we were playing in the park with the other kids?" Christian nodded.

Bicé's eyes darted toward Valentin and Belle. Valentin coughed. Neither of them said anything, but they looked more than uncomfortable.

Bicé turned to Christian again. "Remember how you stole from them like ten times in one game? You did it every time they tried to play with us."

"Yeah." Christian laughed. "I remember."

"Why was it so easy then?" asked Bicé.

"What do you mean?" Christian was suddenly alert.

"I mean, why were you so happy stealing then, and now it's so hard? What's changed?"

Bicé glanced at Valentin and Belle again. Their heads were down.

"I don't know." Christian shrugged. "I'm older now."

"No, that's not it. It just doesn't make sense. There's so much that doesn't make sense."

Finally, Valentin spoke up. "Bicé, Christian has enough to worry about," he said as he pulled her aside. Bicé felt Valentin's tight, unsteady grip and looked up into his eyes, glazed as usual, pupils dilated. He had obviously been in that room again—his gift from Madame Vileroy. Bicé worried about the room. Valentin had told her that it gave him power beyond imagination and that he was absolutely intoxicated by it. She wasn't allowed to go in, but she had seen it before. When Madame Vileroy had first given her the ability to hide, she had wandered into many of the rooms, exploring, with everything frozen. Somehow, she could never find Vileroy in a frozen state. Maybe she never was. But she did find that room—and five years ago, the person she found inside, gazing through the solitary white window, was someone that looked an awful lot like Buddy. Bicé pushed those thoughts out of her head and returned to the present conversation. "Well, aren't you curious?" she asked.

"It's just his nerves, sis," said Belle, putting an arm around her sister. "And maybe he won't have to steal." Bicé tried to stifle her frustration at Valentin and Belle, who were being so obtuse. As they passed a kiosk, she grabbed a Bulgarian newspaper and tossed a dollar to the vendor, with a curt *mersi*.

Valentin's hand brushed against Belle's. A sort of reassurance that they were in this together. Neither one of them had enjoyed it, but it was a hazard of their chosen game. It wasn't the worst thing they had to do, nor the most disagreeable. Just an everyday nuisance—having to listen to Bicé relive scenes from a life they had supposedly lived, being reminded of the false memories that Madame Vileroy had used to fill the gaps in Bicé's and Christian's minds—of a shared childhood that had never existed.

~～⁂～

On the way over, Christian made himself a promise. *I'm not going to steal today. Today, for once, I won't give in to this sick habit.* But Christian knew that he couldn't always trust himself. Sometimes he wondered if it wouldn't be better to just give in to sucking at whatever he did. *Sports are supposed to be fun,* he thought. But he always let thoughts like that die. He needed to win. There would be scouts for the national team there. And this was the only way Christian knew to protect himself from a life of poverty. Besides, if he were doing it for the fun, he'd just quit sports and write.

Once again, Christian would have to face Connor Wirth. As the swimmers were preparing for the 400-meter butterfly, standing and stretching next to their platforms, pulling on their swim caps, Christian approached Connor.

Connor looked up. "Hey. Congrats on the tennis thing. I heard you made it to State."

"Thanks," said Christian.

"You're just cleaning up this season, aren't you?"

Just then, the announcer came on the loudspeaker. ". . . and by platform five, Connor Wirth, the clear favorite to win the race, is preparing for another Marlowe victory." Connor smiled and waved at his parents.

Christian felt something in his chest. *The announcer didn't even mention me. Did the scouts hear?* He turned to leave, the weight of his fears pressing on his body and making him so sick with worry that he didn't hear the announcer finally read his stellar swimming stats.

As Connor was bent over, stretching his hamstrings, Christian gave him a friendly pat on the back, right behind his lungs, and wished him good luck.

~∞∞∞

Just as he was finishing the race, Christian realized what he had done. He was the first to reach the end, and as he pulled himself out of the water, he saw that no one was looking. A lifeguard was jumping into the water. Parents were running from the stands. The other swimmers reached the end and, one by one, realized what had happened. Connor Wirth had almost drowned. In his hurry, Christian had taken a bit too much of Connor's lung capacity. He had assumed that Connor would just swim slower. But Connor had passed out before he even realized he needed to breathe.

Connor's parents were so scared that they kept him home from school for several days. Mrs. Wirth was absolutely wrecked with worry. But still, she had her explanations. To Mrs. Wirth, the world was a very logical place, with a rational reason for everything. Nothing inexplicable could ever be acknowledged. And so she put her son through a series of medical tests to pinpoint the underlying condition that must have been the cause of his accident. Connor's friends went to his house to see him in groups of three or four, each bringing little presents, best wishes, and gossip from school.

The only person who didn't go was Christian, who chose instead to remain holed up with Buddy, his only real friend. A few hours after the swim meet, Christian sat cross-legged on top of the closed lid of his water coffin. Buddy sat next to him, trying to entice him into a game of thumb war. Christian just sat there, head hung, shoulders slumped forward, while Buddy played thumb war with his flaccid hand. He didn't notice Madame Vileroy come in. She was standing in the corner, watching, and after a few minutes, he knew without having to look up that she was there.

"I'm so sorry," he said.

"Don't be sorry, Christian. You're always sorry," she said.

"He almost died. And you're telling me that's OK?"

"No. Stealing is supposed to make you look good. It's not heroic to beat a dead fish."

"I didn't think it through," said Christian.

"Practice makes perfect, my dear," she said as she swept out of the room.

Buddy tossed a basketball to Christian, trying to get him to play. Christian looked at Buddy and felt grateful for the reminder. He did have something to look forward to. The basketball game on Friday would be better. He could play for fun for a change and let the others take care of winning. "Good idea, Buddy. Let's play basketball."

On Friday, Christian walked back from the basketball game feeling great. Marlowe had won. Having convinced his parents that he was well enough to play, Connor had ended his confinement by midday Friday and had come to the game. In fact, Connor had sunk the winning shot — he was a hero. Christian actually had fun, and he didn't have to steal even once. The other guys were being nice to him. They invited him for pizza after the game. "Great pass, Christian," one of the guys said as they walked toward Vinnie's Pizza. Even Connor was acting friendly toward him again. Everything felt normal for once. When he got home, Christian went straight to the rejuvenation room. He felt like writing in his journal. But Madame Vileroy was waiting there, doing something to Buddy.

"Hey, leave him alone."

"He's not human, Christian," Vileroy responded. Then she added, softly, almost to herself, "Not anymore." She eyed Christian up and down and said, "Don't be so queasy."

Buddy was crying as Madame Vileroy twisted his ear to see that his perception of pain hadn't dulled too much. Christian turned her words over in his head. *Not anymore.*

"How was your game?" she asked.

"Great, we won."

"We?"

"Marlowe. The basketball team."

"But did *you* win?"

"Huh?"

"You didn't do anything out of the ordinary."

"I didn't need to do anything because we had it in the bag! We were already much better than them! There was no need to steal from the other team."

"And the other Marlowe children?"

"The other . . . we were on the same side! If I stole from them, we'd lose."

"You're not part of a team, Christian. You're a leader. A true leader doesn't belong to the team. The team belongs to him."

"So I should have made us lose?"

"You did lose. You lost to Connor."

Christian sighed and sat on the edge of his coffin. He wondered why Madame Vileroy cared so much whether he won or lost. *What does she gain from it?* She always made it sound like she did it for him, like she had nothing to gain.

"What do you want?" Christian screamed at her. No one could answer that question about Madame Vileroy. What did she want? Why had she adopted them? Why had she given them these gifts? Why did she push them to do these things? Sometimes, Christian thought she just got some perverse enjoyment out of it. Maybe it was a big experiment for her. Maybe she loved torturing them. Or maybe they were a prize to her. Maybe there was something in their future that made it all worthwhile. Or maybe she was after something entirely different.

Christian leaned on one hand and looked her straight in the eyes, ignoring the flash of light in her angry left eye.

She spoke with an even voice. "I want you to take a long pause and think about what I've said. . . . Think about what it means to really win. Think about it until you fully understand. . . . Yes, that's what you need. Some time alone . . . to think."

Madame Vileroy barely nodded. Suddenly Christian's hand slipped, and he landed hard in the pool of water. Before he could lift his head, the lid slammed shut with a loud bang. Christian pushed with his hand to open it, but something was keeping the lid shut. He pushed again. Nothing. He felt a slight panic mingled with confusion. He was sealed in, his mind drifting from fear to anger to the lingering thoughts of what it means to win.

~⟨⟩∞⟩

In the twilight, in the evening, in the black and dark night, Christian struggled as the water filled his lungs. He was sealed in. He coughed and spat the water out. He scratched and kicked. His fingernails bent backward on the immovable lid. They splintered and bled. Every time he lowered his arms back into the filthy water, the urine he'd had to let go on the second day would burn the wounds on his fingers. He couldn't remember how long he had screamed, crying for someone to help him, cursing the others for not even checking on him all that time.

There in the filthy lake, Christian gnashed his teeth and learned how much he could hate something he had once loved — the coffin, winning, his life.

⌘

By the third day, Christian smelled nothing but ammonia and his own skin dying and floating to the top of the liquid like soggy wheat flakes. It was only water this time, none of the blue gel, the super drug. Just dirty water, shriveling his hands. His muscles starved and hung limp on his bones. His back was raw with sores.

⌘

On Sunday, sometime late in the day, the lid of the coffin shifted, and then slammed open. Bicé jumped back from her chair beside it. Christian surged up from the water, sitting up and gasping for fresh air. After the sudden rush, he slumped back down, unable to muster any more energy, squinting in the light. He was completely soiled, but his skin was pale as a ghost. The patch of sunlight coming in from the tiny window hurt his eyes, now almost nocturnal after three days. The blue gel that had once made him inexhaustible was gone, fully spent after such a long confinement. And it seemed that for all that time trapped in the coffin, it had also been keeping him alive.

"You look like a junkie on the F train," said Bicé.

"How long has it been?"

"Four days."

All of a sudden, Christian got a whiff of himself.

"Have you been here this whole time?"

"More or less. We couldn't open it. We all tried. We figured it would just take time. Today I just tried it and it opened right up."

"Could you hear me?"

Bicé didn't want to embarrass him. "No."

She didn't want to tell him she had heard everything. Christian tried to lift himself out of the tub, but his arms trembled under his weight. Bicé walked over to help. Christian recoiled, aware of his own smell.

"It's OK," she said. "I've been on farms before. And I've lived with Belle for a while."

They laughed at that for some reason. It was the way normal things are funny in horrible situations, like cancer patients with balloon animals. Bicé helped lift him by his underarms. His skin was pale and cold. He grabbed a towel that was lying on a chair nearby and walked away. As she went to help him, Bicé noticed something in the tank. She looked and saw, scrawled on the underside of the lid, chaotic lines in bloody circles. Bicé squinted to read them. As she moved her eyes down, the letters became less frantic, more calm, and what looked like the beginning stanzas to a beautiful epic rose out of the sedge like a saving grace.

"God, will you look at me?" said Christian out loud. Bicé turned around. He was at the mirror. "I look awful."

"You should take a shower," said Bicé. "I'll get some food."

She started to walk out. Even though Christian's body was weak and dirty, something inside him felt clean, as if he had been washed from the inside, as if something filthy had been lifted out. He suddenly felt aware of everything that was under his own control. He could decide where to walk, what to say, what to eat. He felt a freedom that he had never felt before. He imagined that this must be how prisoners feel the first time they walk out into the world. More than anything Christian felt a lightness in his heart. The things that had scared him before didn't seem so bad anymore. It wouldn't be so scary to be poor or hungry or to lose once in a while. Maybe it would be nice to try something new.

"Hey, B?"

"Yeah?"

"Thanks for staying."

"Hey, what're big sisters for?" she said with a wink.

"I mean it."

"I know you do. I know what it's like . . . to be alone like that." Bicé knew a lot more about what Christian had been through than he thought. She had heard him yell and scream obscenities for hours at first. She had tried to get him out of the coffin. But then, after everyone else had given up and left, Bicé had listened to Christian's tone change from desperation to resolve. And by the end, it sounded as if he had completely let go of everything he had wanted before, with no desire ever to steal again. And then, out of the blue, the coffin had opened — as if to say that it had no more power over him.

Christian turned to Bicé, wanting to tell her all about what had happened to him. "It was hell . . . I was . . ." But just then, Bicé interrupted, realizing that Christian's body was still wet and that something was missing.

"Christian, look. The mark on your chest is gone!"

Chapter 17

Black Heart, Broken Heart

We will stay in the shadows, answering only a seeking heart. The mark is the sign of the willing soul and shall guide us. It is a black shadow falling over the heart of those who seek our power, a mark that oceans cannot cleanse but that a drop doth reveal. Legion, thou shall NOT capture a heart without the mark. If the mark disappears, thou shall set that sinner free.

— The Book of Legion, "Commandments"

Bicé found Belle in the kitchen, pacing back and forth in front of the fridge. She was combing her fingers through her hair, reaching for the refrigerator handle, then pulling away. On the table were half-empty bottles of all kinds. Bicé didn't say anything as she opened the cupboard for a packet of noodles. There were so many questions coming up for Bicé—the meaning of the mark, how both she and Christian didn't have it now, and Belle did. Even though they were sisters by blood, she didn't think Belle was on her side anymore, which made her incredibly sad. But Belle probably hadn't even noticed. She was too busy seducing the entire school and most of the city.

In midstride, Belle said, "Hey, sis. You're ready for tonight, right? Want me to help you pick out an outfit?"

"No. What's going on tonight?"

"*What?* Thomas, remember? Supremely perfect Thomas? The love of my life Thomas?"

"Today's Sunday?"

"Yes! And he's coming! Let's get you changed!" Belle grabbed her sister's hand and tried to pull her to her room, but Bicé didn't budge.

"What's wrong with what I'm wearing?"

"Are you an immigrant?" Belle said, annoyed.

"Maybe. I don't know."

Bicé tore open the seal on a cup of noodles. As she was filling it with water, she turned to Belle and said, "Do you still have that birthmark? The water one?"

Belle reached up and rubbed the area above her heart. There was nothing there at the moment but her flawless skin. Still, the thought fueled her anxiety.

"Yeah, why?"

"Did you know Christian had one?"

"Oh?" Belle already knew, but this was the last thing she wanted to discuss now.

"It went away," Bicé said casually.

Belle stopped pacing. She tried to flush the surprise from her face before Bicé turned around from the microwave. She had no idea what that could mean.

"Hmm, I don't know," she said, matching Bicé's casual tone.

"Don't you think it's odd that you both had that same birthmark?"

"Bicé . . . please . . . I'm so nervous about tonight."

"Belle! Stop changing the subject! I always knew we were gifted and that we all paid for that. But you're scaring me lately. I researched all kinds of skin disorders. There's no such thing as a mark that only appears in water. And every time I mention something that doesn't make sense around here, you change the subject."

Belle tried to say something.

"This place scares me, Belle, and I don't want to be a part of any of this. So you can keep your secrets, but we can't be sisters if you're hiding something."

Belle plopped down on a chair, and for a moment, Bicé could see her sister's pain under this facade. "I'm not hiding anything. I know as much as you do, and I'm just nervous now. Can you understand that?"

Bicé felt bad for scolding her sister. She sat down next to her. "Don't be nervous. I'm sure he's desperately in love with you." She smoothed her sister's golden hair.

"He hasn't even tried to kiss me yet," Belle whined.

"So? You've only known each other for . . . how long has it been? A few months or weeks? Something like that . . ."

"Bicé! It's not a missile launch! How long does it take?"

"Maybe he's shy . . ."

"He kissed Lucy!"

"Oh, so that's it," said Bicé. "You just want to get past the Lucy benchmark—gain some sort of competitive advantage and establish yourself as the dominant player."

"*What* are you babbling about?" asked Belle, a confused smirk on her lips.

"Just working on my business talk," said Bicé defensively. "I'm widening my definition of *language:* shoptalk, sign language, clicking dialects of certain tribes . . ."

Belle raised an eyebrow.

"I'm *serious*," said Bicé. "It's a real language! It's what they speak on the 4/5 to Wall Street. Can we get back on the ball here? You're just trying to beat Lucy."

"No." Belle looked at her shoes. "What if things don't go well tonight?"

"They will. I promise not to say a word to ruin your night."

"Oh, Bicé. Don't say that!"

"I know I embarrass you."

Belle shook her head and reached out to hold her sister's hand. "Why are you so scared all the time? You used to be so good with people."

"Yeah . . ." Bicé dropped her gaze. "But now I spend most of my time alone."

"But why? Why do you hide so much?"

"I like it, Belle. I like to read my books and learn new languages. You have your goals and I have mine. And like I said, this place scares me."

Belle glanced at her watch. "Oh, look at the time. I have to get ready." Belle looked at her sister sweetly. "Bicé, *please* change your clothes."

Bicé ignored that. "I'm going to give this food to Christian now, and I'm not changing. I like this outfit, Belle. I may not be gorgeous, but that's not all there is in life. I hope you learn that."

Bicé walked out of the room. Belle stood in the center, not quite sure whether she was hurt, nervous, or ashamed. She wanted to say something to Bicé. Her vanity wanted her to have the last word, and her conscience wanted her to apologize. She was pretty sure she was ashamed of herself, and hurt that she'd lost Bicé's respect, but when she opened her mouth, all that came out was, "How about just the corduroys?"

~⚬⚬⚬⚬~

Lurking in a narrow hallway leading to the center of her house, the governess watched as Belle and Bicé talked. Bicé had come so far in the few weeks in this city. She knew so much. And yet she was wholly unaware of what she knew. Now she had fixated on the mark, the external manifestation of a heart so desperate and willing to be sold to darkness that it stained the skin above it. Bicé would soon know this. She would soon figure out what her sister had done, and why Christian no longer had the mark. The governess watched, her body as still as the walls, but not so, since the walls undulated with so much dripping wax and candlelight, dancing grotesquely around her. *It doesn't matter what Bicé knows about the mark,* the governess thought. *Soon Bicé too will be given a choice. Soon she will have to do what the others have done.* But how to ensure that? Over the past few nights, Victoria had come to Madame Vileroy and told her what she knew about Bicé's progress. So much progress. The governess ran her fingers across her cheek, contemplating what might come of this new disaster. Yes, something must be done. Something must certainly be done.

But not tonight. Tonight the children will learn a crucial lesson. Tonight Belle will learn about love. She will learn where to place her affection. To not throw it away like cheap trinkets and ornaments. She will learn that love makes you lose control and that control is more precious than a moment's affection. Love fades. Control remains and grows stronger with time, tightly weaving itself with power, dependence, and a lifetime of secrets. Tonight Victoria will learn that loyalty has its rewards and that success is hard-won—but only for the weak. Tonight Bicé will learn not to hang her hopes on an undeserving sister, and her heart may be too lonely and broken to reject any new offer of happiness.

Madame Vileroy swept out of the room with the swiftness of a gust of wind but without a single noise, without disturbing the tiniest particle. Like a flash of light, she was gone, and then she was outside, her high heels tapping a careful rhythm on the cobblestones, her coat floating elegantly behind her, a stylish hat tucked under her arm. Soon she found herself on Park Avenue, near the home of the Goodman-Browns. She hadn't walked for more than two minutes in that neighborhood when she heard a familiar voice.

"Nicola! How nice to see you here."

Madame Vileroy turned and smiled at Charles Goodman-Brown,

who had one foot in the back of his Bentley and one foot on the sidewalk.

"Charles, how are you?"

"Fine, fine. Where are you headed? Care for a lift?"

In the car, Charles leaned back, straightened his tie, and flashed Madame Vileroy a big, affectionate smile.

"Well, this is a nice surprise running into you, Nicola. Thomas will kill me for telling you this, but I can tell he's really nervous about coming to your place tonight."

"We're looking forward to having him over. He's a lovely boy," she said without much enthusiasm.

"Well, they're a lovely couple," Charles offered, as if making a wedding toast.

"Hmm." Madame Vileroy's lips turned up just slightly, not enough to give encouragement.

"You know, I've been a bit curious about Belle," Charles prodded. "Now that, well, they're getting so close, I wanted to . . . um . . . Where did she grow up?"

"Belle has been raised all over the world. She has had an impeccable education."

"Yes. She does strike me as very sophisticated . . . like you," he said sweetly, in that warm, genuine way some people give praise when they are used to their words falling on welcome, solicitous ears.

Madame Vileroy drummed her fingers on the armrest. "She is, of course, adopted."

Charles was taken aback at the timing of this comment. "Huh. You look so much alike."

"I supposed you think all blue-eyed blondes look the same?"

Mr. Goodman-Brown laughed and then, for the first time, noticed Nicola's left eye, the burned, yet beautiful eye, which gazed back at him with such confidence, as if to suggest that *his* eyes were the problem, that they were so very ordinary. He straightened his tie again, nervously.

"Thomas hasn't had much luck with girlfriends," he offered.

"No? He seems to have his share of admirers."

"None like Belle. And now that they're spending all their time together. . . ." He smiled at her teasingly. "I think it's love, Nicola," he said with a wink.

"We'll see."

Madame Vileroy knew it had gone too far. But this was enough. Belle was supposed to be thinking of her future. She was supposed to be thinking ten years ahead, to a time when Thomas would be worth having. She wasn't supposed to waste all the novelty of this relationship on the present.

As she was preparing to climb out of the car, Madame Vileroy noticed a file in Charles's hands. Thanks to the moths (and Mrs. Wirth), Madame Vileroy already knew about the deal he was working on today, on his Sunday off. It was a major investment in a Turkish humanitarian network—a financial scheme that would make low-cost credit available to the poor. She leaned over, kissed Charles Goodman-Brown on the cheek, and said, "Have a nice day, Charles. And watch out for that thief Yamin. I was his son's tutor in Turkey. You may be entering quite the house of cards."

✺

Bicé sat alone in her room and counted aloud. Afrikaans, Aghul, Algonquin, Arabic . . . 5 . . .10 . . . 21 . . . 23 . . . 33 . . .

She lost count and had to start over. *Concentrate,* she told herself. She had to do this. For the first time ever, she wasn't just doing this to get away from her own fears. She wasn't just trying to find a space to hide. Ever since she had confronted Belle in the kitchen, Bicé was acutely aware that she herself finally *did* have a goal. Something that she knew would make a difference. And now that Christian's mark had mysteriously disappeared (and Belle's hadn't), she had something important that she had to figure out. But lately, she had felt someone watching. Madame Vileroy had started coming to her in her dreams, when she was alone, when she was hiding. She had begun to interrupt Bicé's thoughts, her work. She had begun to infiltrate the sanctuary of her cave and force her to stop. It was as if the governess were afraid of something and trying to transfer that fear to Bicé, so that she wouldn't find her own real power. Even Victoria was snooping around, trying to figure out what she was doing. Bicé had seen the moths flying around. For once she had something on the governess, something that seemed to be worth her attention. And for all the tricks the governess had played on her, for all the sins Bicé had or hadn't committed, she had some possible redemption—for herself and her sister. For once, Bicé didn't feel like a pariah, not at all aimless or lost. For once, she had a glimmer of hope. Because she knew that one good trick deserves another—and her whole existence, her life so far, had been no choice, but a trick.

Chapter 18
Cheat

Jacob hadn't studied his arithmetic, but it wasn't his fault. It was harvest season, when the sun would hang low in the sky, like a dandy on a porch swing, while he and his brother did the threshing. They'd work the wheat, and Jake would stare wistfully across the panning land at the red schoolhouse. Their daddy valued schooling, so they went once a week, and Jake would stare at the new teacher — hair like a wheat field, scent like cinnamon. And Jacob wanted so bad to be good. And she was so good at teaching. And he was glancing at Laura's tablet . . . just a glance. Then that hand came down on his shoulder and he closed his eyes, knowing he was in for it. But she just ran her hand through his hair and moved on, turning to wink at him with that one bewitching eye.

~◦◦◦~

Each of them had a role in that night's dinner. Madame Vileroy had assigned each of them something special to do. No one was enthusiastic about it but Belle. Still, they had to keep up appearances. There wasn't any preparation involved. They would just switch to the blue-cube house a few minutes before Thomas arrived. The sights, sounds, and smells of a home-cooked Alsatian feast would be conjured up. And Thomas would leave with a great impression. Madame Vileroy playing a beautiful Parisian June Cleaver was just the image she wanted him to take home to his dad. It would do him good. After all, Madame Vileroy deduced, he was in need of an adviser. And who wouldn't trust someone as wholesome as she? What man wouldn't take her into his confidence?

The doorbell rang and Belle jumped up to get it. She realized right afterward that she was revealing way too much of herself to Madame Vileroy, and immediately slowed down. Thomas was at the door with a bouquet of lilies.

"Hi!" he said as he handed her the flowers and tried to kiss her on the cheek. But Belle was so aware of Madame Vileroy that she turned, and he kissed the back of her head instead.

"How festive," said Madame Vileroy as she approached the door.

"They're for everyone. To thank you for having me over," said Thomas after recovering from his fumble.

Christian took Thomas's coat. No one noticed him wobble a little as he walked to the closet, still not used to standing up. Bicé went to find a vase.

Thomas took a seat at the couch. Belle sat next to him, as if the two of them were on an interview. Vileroy was standing across the room, leaning with uncharacteristic casualness on a table that Valentin was sitting on. As usual, he was charming, a little shady, and too close to Vileroy. With her eyes, Belle told him to get off the table. But he just crossed his legs tighter and continued to sit cross-legged on top of the dining table.

"You have a lovely home, Madame Vileroy," said Thomas. He sat with his hands folded on his lap.

"Thank you, dear. We were lucky to find it on such short notice."

"So, Tommy," said Valentin with twinkling eyes, "how's your mommy?"

Belle gasped audibly and gave him a deadly look. That comment was a bit too much, even for Valentin.

Thomas tried to lighten up, laughed a little, and said, "Still dead."

Valentin seemed to enjoy Thomas's response, as if he were experimenting with how far he could go. He leaned close and opened his mouth to speak again, but Madame Vileroy put a loving hand on his shoulder and whispered something in his ear. He seemed to change tack.

"I'm sorry . . ." he said. Then he looked over at Vileroy as if he were about to do something reckless and quickly added, "I just assumed that was a lie to keep people from knowing she ran off or something."

Just then, Victoria walked in. She was wearing the sweats she wore when pulling all-nighters studying. "Hi, Thomas," she said as she walked across the room. "I'm glad you made it." Meanwhile, Belle was getting more and more incensed. She had specifically gotten Victoria's promise that she would dress nice. And Victoria usually dressed decently anyway. Why had she picked tonight to get the Bicé makeover?

"Thanks," said Thomas, standing up. When he sat back down, Victoria stayed where she was, towering over Belle and Thomas. "So you're here to court our pretty sister."

Thomas gave the courtesy laugh. "That's one way to put it." Belle shifted back on the couch and pushed the words *Stop being so rude. Sit down* to the front of her brain, where Victoria, who never stopped cheating, would be sure to hear. But Victoria ignored her.

"What's the other way?"

"Victoria!" said Belle out loud. She felt herself jump out of her seat.

"What? Calm down." Victoria seemed to be enjoying herself.

"Calm down, Belle," said Vileroy. Belle was confused now. Wasn't Vileroy the one who had wanted Thomas to come over? Wasn't she the one who had wanted to lure him and his powerful father into their net? Belle hadn't wanted him to come over. But Vileroy had forced her to invite him. So why was she letting Valentin and Victoria behave like this? Belle sat back on the couch and crossed her arms.

"So I hear you have some big plan for the debate tournament," said Victoria.

Thomas turned and looked at Belle. She shrugged nervously. "Sure, I guess," he said.

"Well?" said Victoria.

Belle sat up again. "What are you doing, Victoria? Just go away. Madame Vileroy —"

"So what's the plan?" said Victoria, still looming over the two of them.

Thomas tried to laugh it off.

"You should probably tell her," said Valentin, his eyes widening as though he were trying to scare Thomas but was obviously having fun. "She has a way of finding things out. . . ."

"It's just a debate tournament," said Thomas, still laughing.

But Victoria wasn't laughing. What seemed so petty and small to Thomas was Victoria's next prize. She would do anything. . . . "It'd be best for you if you told me what you're planning," she said.

Belle was on the verge of tears now. She seemed calmer, though, as if she knew what was going on.

"I think maybe I should leave," said Thomas.

"No," said Belle instinctively, then suddenly seemed to change her mind and said, "OK."

"You're not going anywhere," said Victoria. "I'm getting what I want if I have to break your head open and puzzle back the pieces of your brain."

Belle stood up. "Victoria, stop it right now."

"Relax," said Victoria. "Vileroy won't let him remember any of this. He'll go nuts if he stays awake another minute." Victoria gave Thomas a crazed look of pure satisfaction. Valentin was playing with that old pocket watch again. Madame Vileroy patted him on the leg and nodded to Victoria.

"Won't let him remember what?" said Belle.

"I'm going to read his mind. What do you think?" said Victoria. Then she turned to Thomas, who was looking horrified. "This wouldn't be a problem if you paid less attention in school. I keep trying to burrow into your thoughts, and you keep realizing something's going on. But we have our pretty little bait here, and you followed her right home. Now if you wouldn't mind just—"

Thomas stood up. "Get away from me."

"Don't do this," said Belle.

"Shhh . . . I want to see her do it. Go ahead, Vic, let's see some cheating," said Valentin.

"What's going on?" said Christian, stumbling back in.

"Belle, what's wrong?" said Bicé with a worried tone and her usual nervous scan as she followed Christian into the living room.

Everyone was standing in the living room, staring at one another. Belle was already shaking, the way she did before she wept.

Bicé sensed that something horrible had just happened. She resisted the urge to cower behind Christian and said, "We're going to redo all this, aren't we? Valentin, whatever just happened, fix it!" Her eyes darted from Belle to Victoria to Thomas.

But Valentin didn't have time to respond. Madame Vileroy suddenly lunged out toward Thomas. Her black dress flapped behind her like wings. For a second, Belle thought she saw her make a face like a gargoyle—she had seen it before, once. In that instant, Madame Vileroy almost enveloped Thomas, and Belle couldn't be sure of what she saw. She shrieked. Victoria was knocked out of the way. Bicé put down the vase and rushed to Belle's side.

Thomas stopped midexclamation. His entire body wilted and fell lifeless on the couch. Like a cub whose mother has just brought home a carcass, Victoria pounced. She arranged Thomas's legs so that he was sitting upright on the couch.

Belle was seething with anger and paralyzed with the fear that she had caused all this. After all that scheming from afar, all that research into what perfumes he liked best, what kind of hairstyles caught his attention — somehow — Belle had actually met the real Thomas Goodman-Brown and, believe it or not, she had begun to like him. Now she was staring as Victoria ran to the back of the couch and pulled him up by his sweater so he wouldn't slump.

Madame Vileroy moved back to the dining room table and poured herself a glass of wine. Valentin, who had finally lost his power of speech, was watching Victoria with awe.

"A glass of wine, my dear?" Madame Vileroy offered Valentin, as if nothing were going on in her living room.

"Sure," he said. They clinked their crystal glasses and drank. They almost seemed to disappear into the corner of the room.

"What are you going to do?" cried Belle. "You can't hurt him."

"Shh," said Victoria. She pulled up a chair across from the couch. She moved her face close to Thomas's, at first only reading the thoughts on the surface. There wasn't really much there since he was unconscious. She began boring deeper and deeper into his subconscious. It was invigorating to move so deeply into someone's mind without having them flail and fight and yell at her to stop. She didn't have to worry about Thomas feeling violated or losing his mind.

"No, tell me now," Belle interrupted.

Victoria couldn't keep her focus with Belle talking to her. She looked up. Belle looked like she was about to attack. Bicé had moved next to her for support. Christian was behind her in case she wanted to look away, or cry on a shoulder, or something like that.

"I'm getting the information I need," said Victoria. "Stay out of my way."

"I don't want to do this. I never agreed to this."

"Yes, you did. You agreed to bring him."

"But—but I was forced. I don't want to—"

Victoria hated that weak prissy debutante crap. She had hated Belle from the day they met—when all five children were only ten. She hated all her dainty airs covering her disgusting stench. She turned on Belle and began to shout.

"First of all, shut the hell up. Second of all, stop pretending. You agreed to all of this, just like me. You're not some pretty-pretty princess with all us ogres. You're one of us. You signed the deal Vileroy offered, you sold your soul, and now you owe the devil her due. So back up, let me search this idiot's head, and we'll all be back to pretending you're the good little prom queen you wish you were."

Christian groaned. Victoria whipped around and seemed to realize for the first time that Christian and Bicé were in the room. For a moment, she looked taken aback, as if she had let something valuable get away and didn't know what to do now. She whispered a curse to herself and then turned her back to finish what she had come to do.

Madame Vileroy and Valentin became visible in the room again. The air was sucked from the room. Bicé stood motionless. Suddenly she understood so much more. Belle began to swing her arm in a wild slap at Victoria, but Christian caught her by the wrist. She struggled to get free but felt a twinge of pain, a loss of strength so delicate that she just felt a little sleepy. She rested her tired head on Christian's shoulder. Christian just stood there, shaking a little, his mouth open, his shoulders aching, his mind bursting with questions.

~◦◦◦◦~

Later that night, after Victoria had learned more than she could ever find out from the moths, Vileroy adjusted Thomas's memories so that he thought he had had a wonderful time. Bicé sat in the chair in Christian's room. "Why don't we remember?" said Christian.

"What, selling our souls? Being adopted into the house of the devil? Charging into the world as agents of the fallen angel? I have no idea, Christian. I don't have a clue. Stop asking stupid questions," Bicé said hysterically.

"We have to figure out what to do."

"Are you crazy? This is the end. It's all over." Christian had never seen Bicé so agitated. She was darting back and forth, wringing her hands as if they had betrayed her, and throwing wild glances all over the room.

"No. You and I didn't know . . . We didn't . . ." Christian said, feeling almost certain.

"I don't know," said Bicé, wrinkling her brow, worried for the others and for herself. "I don't know what we did."

Bicé sat cross-legged on the floor and put her face in her hands. Christian came and sat at her feet. "We've known we have 'gifts.' We've known we're completely different than everyone at school. And we've even known we're not family."

"Yeah." For a moment Bicé got her hysteria under control and looked reflective, like someone looking for a hopeful sign. "We've known it, but it's never occurred to us. It's almost like we've been ignoring the truth, and it's been in our face the whole time."

Christian nodded.

"But why does Vic remember it and we don't?" Bicé asked.

"I think because we didn't do it."

"Then why are we here? Why are we living with her? And when did they find out who she is so they could make this deal? I mean, *we* never found out who she was, did we? Even though we've been living with her for fifteen years . . ."

Christian put his head in Bicé's lap like a child. She stroked his curly red hair. She didn't have a single hair on her head that color. Christian thought for a moment and then said, "Thomas went home thinking he had dinner with all of us."

Bicé stopped stroking his hair and put her hand over her mouth. "So, I guess Vileroy can give false memories. She could make us forget things . . . like selling our souls . . ."

She thought hard about this possibility. Somehow, it was easier to think that Vileroy had made her forget selling her soul than to even fathom the possibility that she had not always lived here, that she had forgotten something entirely different.

"But again, she didn't make Vic or Belle forget, so that can't be it," said Christian. "They must have found out who she was and made the deal . . . and we didn't."

"That doesn't make sense. Why would she adopt us all in the first place? Why would she tell them who she was and not us? Why would she give us these 'gifts'? Why keep us . . ."

"Nothing's keeping us here anymore. Let's just leave."

"No . . ." Bicé mumbled something to herself in a language Christian didn't understand.

"Why not? What else can she do?"

"I think anything somebody wants. Thomas wanted to have a great time with all of us."

Christian shook, like a terrified little boy, quivering under a mother's touch.

"What does she want with us?"

"I don't know, Christian. Maybe she wants a relationship. Maybe selling your soul is something you do every day."

"But my black mark is gone," protested Christian. "That means we're safe, right?"

"I don't know, Christian. I have no idea what it means."

They were silent for a while. Then Christian spoke.

"You really think we sold our souls and don't remember, Bicé?"

"Think hard. Did you ever want to?"

"If I did, I don't anymore."

Chapter 19
Rights

Simon sat at the windowsill of the plantation house and watched their heads bob up and down in the fields like umber lures on a green-and-white lake. It was busy season, and some of the house workers had had to go outside. Simon could see them having a harder time. Their hands had not yet calloused to the cotton spurs. They hummed to keep their minds off the heat. Simon felt nothing for them because, after all, they were property. And he had his rights. He turned back to his book, wondered about earnings and afternoon cake.

~∞∞~

Belle woke up with her eyes glued shut. She had never fully fallen asleep that night. Every time she came close, something jolted her awake. *What have I done?* She sat up in bed and noticed that Bicé was sitting at the foot of her bed.

"Sleep well?" Bicé asked with a ghostly look in her eye.

Belle pulled her covers up higher over herself. What was Bicé doing up? Bicé just watched her. She was waiting, as if she thought Belle would just come out and tell her everything; explain why she had done such an unforgivable thing. But Belle didn't say anything. So many thoughts flooded Bicé's mind. Belle's change, the deals, the mark. What did that mark mean? And how had they come to live here — with *her* — for fifteen years? The adoption story didn't make sense anymore. How had Belle come to find out who Madame Vileroy was? And when had she taken the deal? Was it when they were ten — when she started changing her face? That must have been it. Before that, in Bicé's false memories of their childhood, Madame Vileroy had never given Belle anything. But Madame Vileroy had never made such an offer to Bicé or Christian. Had she made the deal with Valentin? Belle didn't look like she was about to volunteer anything. She just got up and started to get ready. *What's happened to her?* Bicé said to herself. *Doesn't she realize what she's done?*

"You OK?" Belle asked. Bicé's face was white as a sheet. There were bags under her eyes and she was fidgeting more than usual.

"Belle, you have to tell me . . ."

"I'm tired now."

⚬᷼᷼᷼᷼᷼

The week before the Debate and Drama Tournament passed like a whirlwind. Christian and Bicé had spent the last week hidden away, talking in secret. Victoria continued with her life as if nothing were wrong. In fact, everything was going brilliantly for Victoria, who now had Thomas's entire strategy at her disposal and was building a solid countercase. After that Sunday night, Belle was sure that Thomas would never want to speak to her again. Or maybe he wouldn't even be the same person. Maybe he would lose his mind or have a melt-down or something. But nothing like that happened. Thomas was completely oblivious to what had happened, and he was happier than ever to be with Belle. He was still sweet, still awkwardly charm-ing, and still too shy to make a move. But he did ask her to the spring dance, which was the day after the Debate Tournament. She said yes, but Belle wasn't so sure anymore. Sometimes, when she saw him quiver around her or tap his feet involuntarily or count on his fingers as if he had OCD, the guilt of that Sunday night would wash over her. Being with Belle was changing him, and the more time Belle spent with Thomas, the less she wanted him to change.

~∽⊚⊚⊃

Belle walked into her bedroom to get ready for the tournament. She had promised Thomas she would come to watch. Christian and Bicé were already in there, looking around her room, whispering about something.

"I just don't get it. Why not just go . . ." Christian was saying.

"Just trust me, I need time . . ." Bicé whispered back.

They looked up when Belle walked in. Christian left without say-ing hello. Bicé glanced in Belle's direction, and then she left too. Belle tried to ignore them, but she felt sick to her stomach. She felt utterly alone. They had been ignoring her for a week, and Belle was so sorry that they knew what she had done. But they didn't know everything.

"Are you going like that?" It was Madame Vileroy. Belle turned around. "Not leaving much time for a bath . . ."

"I was going to take one." She sighed. She hadn't really planned on it.

"Guilt is a useless feeling. It's never enough to make you change direction — only enough to paralyze you and make you . . . well, useless."

"I don't feel guilty."

"But you aren't happy for Victoria. She's getting what she wanted. You're getting what you wanted. You should be happy."

"Maybe I want something different now," Belle muttered.

"That's a waste, after everything you gave up."

"The problem is, every time I give something up, you use it to benefit Victoria."

"No, dear. I do it for you. It's just like last time. It's to teach you a lesson, so you can do great things. So you don't waste your one chance with someone like Thomas at just the wrong time. So you take what is yours at precisely the most useful moment."

"He deserves a chance to win."

"It's too late. You can't ruin things for Victoria. She has great potential, like you used to have."

"Thomas has potential."

"You're not Thomas's keeper," Madame Vileroy snapped in a low voice. Belle stepped back. The governess slid around to face her. "Belle, dear, I have a proposition . . ."

"I don't want to hear it."

"I can help Thomas win . . . if you really want."

"What about Victoria?"

"Don't worry too much about her, dear."

"Well, I still don't want to hear it."

"I'll let you have Thomas. I'll let you do it your way. He can win, and you can be together . . . if you want it badly enough."

Even though she didn't want to, Belle had to listen. She looked Vileroy straight in the eyes and waited.

Vileroy spoke softly, her words carefully measured. "I want to know about your parents."

For a moment, Belle was stunned. Vileroy had never asked about their parents before. She had never mentioned them.

"I know that your mother told you . . . about a particular language. An ancient one . . ."

Belle couldn't move. Her hands were moist with sweat, her throat was dry.

"I know you know about it, Belle. About that old, forgotten tongue. The one your mother and her friends spent so many years researching?"

"So?" Belle managed to croak.

"I want to know what she told you. What she told you and Bicé," the governess crooned, softly, gently, her voice sweet and hoarse at the same time. "Try to remember, Belle. Try to remember what your mother said, all those years ago. What do you know? What does Bicé know?"

With each word, the governess moved, inching closer and closer to Belle, until she could feel her cold breath on her face, could see her shattered eye move with anticipation.

"No." Belle pulled away.

There was a moment. An angry beat.

A broken flash of a broken eye.

Belle recoiled. "Go away—I don't care if Thomas wins."

Madame Vileroy wasn't angry. She was calm and smiling. She cupped Belle's face in her cold hand. "I'll see you in the car, dear," she said, and shut the door behind her.

~∞∞∞∞∞

Half an hour later, Belle was dressed and ready to leave. She hadn't taken a bath since the day before. She felt tired and dirty and unattractive. She grabbed her purse and reached for the door, but it didn't open. She pulled and jiggled the doorknob. Nothing. She yanked harder. Still nothing. The door was locked. She banged on the door, yelling for someone to come and get her. But the house was empty. Thomas would think she had abandoned him. Lucy would spend the whole day by his side. Belle slumped on her bed and buried her pretty face in her hands.

What have I done? I really have become her daughter.

~∞∞∞∞∞

Bicé was searching around the house, looking for Christian. She was ready to leave for the tournament, but these days, she wouldn't go anywhere without Christian. He was the only one she trusted — though not with everything.

"Christian, are you in here?" She poked her head into his room — the room he used to rejuvenate and practice. Bicé noticed Buddy sitting alone in a corner, his back turned to the entrance. When he heard the door open, his broad shoulders rose in anticipation. She looked around, but Christian wasn't there. She wasn't sure what to do. Should she say hello? She turned to leave, but before she could go, Buddy had turned from what he was doing and spotted her.

Timidly, he nodded hello.

"Hi, Buddy. Remember me? I'm Bicé."

He had a blank look. She said her name again, slowly this time. "Bee . . . cheh."

Buddy stood up and something caught Bicé's eye. He was holding a piece of paper.

"What do you have there?" Bicé asked.

He hid the paper behind his back and shook his head.

Bicé stepped closer. "It's OK, Buddy. You can tell me. Christian and I are friends."

Buddy's eyes flicked toward the door, and Bicé knew why he was afraid.

"I won't tell her," she said. "You don't have to worry."

Buddy stepped back into his corner. "I promise I won't tell," said Bicé. "I know she makes people do things. But not me. You can trust me."

Buddy held up the paper for Bicé to see. It was a letter, a tattered old letter from a long time ago. She took it from him. The words were big and shaky, a child's handwriting. It was addressed to a guy named Phineas the Fence. She read it over. *To: Phineas the Fence, Celtic 31. From: Christian W.*

Christian W.? Bicé's heart raced. A clue to Christian's past. His name before it was Faust. Reading over the letter, Bicé felt the tears trickle down her face. She let them fall and drip onto the paper, smudging the ink. *What's the worst thing you've ever done?* Christian had done it too. *I'm gonna handle things. For the sake of him and me.* He was just a desperate kid who couldn't think of anything else.

Buddy looked on with his plasticine face, his expression just slightly pained, just slightly knowing, just slightly anxious.

"Where did you find this?" asked Bicé, pushing the letter back into his hands. "Did Christian give it to you?"

He shook his head.

"Does Christian know about this?"

He shook his head again. Bicé took a deep breath. "You took it from *her.*"

Buddy's nod was just barely perceptible.

"Oh, God," said Bicé. She paced the room, thinking of what to do. Christian would be desperate to see this. He was already itching to run away. But she couldn't leave just yet. She still had work to do.

Suddenly, Buddy looked scared, his gaze moving beyond Bicé. He pulled himself deeper into the corner and buried his face in the wall. A cool voice slithered in from behind the door. Whatever blood may have remained in Buddy's veins froze in that instant. There was only one thing Buddy feared.

Bicé turned around. Madame Vileroy was standing there.

"Bicé, I want you to give me that letter."

"No."

"Bicé. Remember what happens if you don't do what I say?"

Bicé shook with rage.

Madame Vileroy shot her a smile and held out her hand.

"I'm sorry, Buddy, but I have to take that," Bicé said.

Buddy shook his head.

"Buddy, just give it to me." Bicé leaned over and grabbed the letter from a whimpering Buddy. She whispered in his ear, "I'll tell him what he needs to know. Just give it to me."

Buddy let go of the letter. The governess tucked it into the pocket of her perfectly tailored jacket. "I see you've taken an interest in reading," she said to Buddy, though he never looked directly into her face. Bicé wondered if this mindless shell of a man saw the same image that the rest of the world saw when he looked the lovely Nicola Vileroy in the face. Maybe he was the only one who could look past the trappings, into the true face of his torturer, a face that was not beautiful, but dark and hungry.

Vileroy strolled into the room casually, turning over small items as she walked, a pillow here, a textbook there. "What's this?" she said when she came upon a notebook. She flipped through the pages. There was nothing but a few scribbled letters, shaky — not childlike — more timid, as if written by an aged, uncertain hand. An amnesiac relearning to write.

She turned to Buddy. "Tell me, what is it that you and Christian do with your time?"

He stood frozen. Bicé was confused. *Has Christian stopped using Buddy for practice?*

Madame Vileroy shut the book, tucked it under her arm, and left.

After a moment's waiting, Bicé too turned and ran out of the room.

~∙⊚⊚⊚∙~

Before his big debate with Victoria Faust, Thomas was pacing back and forth in the lobby, wondering where on earth Belle could be. *She'll come,* he thought, but looked at his watch and began pacing even faster.

"Hey, there," came a sweet voice behind him.

Thomas turned with a huge grin on his face. "You made it," he said, but stopped when he saw Lucy instead of Belle. She was dressed up a little too much for a debate tournament, but she looked good.

"Hi, Luce," said Thomas. "What are you doing here?"

"Just wanted to support you. We're still friends, right?"

"Of course," said Thomas, relieved that she'd stopped ignoring him after the election day fiasco. Besides, if Belle wasn't going to show, it would be nice to have a cheering section.

"They're starting. Let's go," he said, putting a friendly arm around Lucy. Lucy leaned into the embrace and walked with him back into the auditorium.

⸺◦⊗◦⸺

"Mr. Goodman-Brown. You will take the affirmative side. You will be defending the following statement: *It is ethical to disregard drug patents in order to provide affordable treatments to dying third-world patients.* Ms. Faust, you will take the negative side."

Awesome! Thomas said to himself. He looked around for Belle, but she still wasn't there. Lucy smiled at him from the front row.

"Perfect," Victoria said. "Negative is so much easier . . . right to property and all that . . ."

"Are you ready?" Madame Vileroy whispered.

"Please. I have a copy of all his arguments here." She waved a stack of papers. "*And* I have the negative case he would have given if he were assigned negative."

"You should probably go and pretend to take notes. He's about to start."

Victoria looked at the judge, eyeing her as she talked with Madame Vileroy. "Oh, right. I'll go sit down."

Thomas took the podium and started to speak. The timekeeper started his stopwatch. "This is not an issue of right to property but rather of the right to life. . . ."

~~∞∞∞~~

"We have to leave for good," Christian whispered to Bicé as they searched for Belle. After thirty minutes, Belle still hadn't shown up at the tournament.

"No, I have to stay. I have to find out some things."

"I don't get it. What could be that important . . . Argh. Not again." Christian kept getting text messages from Valentin to come hear the poem he was reading for the tournament. Finally, he decided to go back home to look for Belle. Something had to be wrong.

"Look, Bicé. I'm worried about leaving her there, in that house. You know the kind of stuff she has in that bathroom. I'm going to find her."

"I'll go with you." Bicé crossed herself several times as she ran after Christian down the corridor.

~~∞∞∞~~

As Christian fiddled with the lock on the main door of the apartment, Bicé heard Belle's door slamming against its hinges. They could barely make out Belle's screams through the rattling.

"Let me out!" Belle shouted as she yanked on the knob. "Somebody let me out! Bicé! Bicé! Are you out there?" This was not how things were supposed to work. She had given Madame Vileroy as much as Victoria had. Why was Vileroy helping her so much?

Bicé and Christian walked into the apartment just in time to see Belle smash through the door with a chair.

"What are you doing?" Christian said in shock.

"What are *you* doing? I've been calling for help for an hour."

Belle knew she had to get back before Victoria blindsided Thomas with all her stolen information. The tournament meant nothing to her. She just couldn't stand the thought of Thomas being used like that by Victoria. Christian and the girls made it back just as Victoria was taking the podium. They waited in the back while Victoria smoothed out her papers and smiled to Thomas and the judges. She actually took the first twenty seconds of her time to thank the judges. The judges may have bought the act, but to someone who knew her as well as Belle did, her smile looked like a leer.

"I will respond to each of Mr. Goodman-Brown's points in turn. Point one: Without the right to property, there would be no motive to work or innovate and we would fall into a state of communism. I would like to offer the following quotes from Adam Smith, George Washington, David Ricardo, Ronald Reagan, and the head of the WTO."

"Wow, a bit dramatic, even for Vic . . ." Bicé mumbled to herself.

"Shh . . ." Belle nudged her sister. She was intently focused on seeing Thomas's reaction.

～◎♋◎◎

As soon as Valentin finished reading, the crowd stood up and started clapping feverishly. *All those weepy mothers and unstable teenage girls,* Valentin thought. *I could have been reading random excerpts from Bicé's Kazak-English dictionary.*

Charlotte had tears in her eyes. *He's looking right at me. I can't believe he wrote that whole sonnet just for me.*

~∽⊚⊚⊚∼

"Point two: Contrary to my opponent's statement, drug companies *do* have incentive to do their part for the poor. It's good for public relations. I have here six consumer surveys indicating that customers are four times more likely to support a company that helps the poor . . ."

"PR? What about helping people?" said Bicé.

"I think she's foaming at the mouth," said Belle.

~∽⊚⊚⊚∼

"Valentin, that was amazing."

"Thanks."

Valentin was distracted. A crowd of five girls and three moms had just gathered around him. They pushed Charlotte to the back.

"Where did you get the inspiration for that poem?"

"How long did it take to write?"

"Was it for anyone special?"

Charlotte caught Valentin's eye, and her heart skipped a beat. Did he smile just then? *Yes, I knew it. It was for me.*

"No one in particular," Valentin said casually.

Valentin stood on his toes and looked past the crowd at the door. "Hey, it's Christian! Fantastic." He pushed through to the back and almost walked right by Charlotte. He wouldn't have stopped if she hadn't called his name.

"Oh . . . hi, Charlotte. Love that sweater." He started to walk off. Charlotte noticed the stack of papers, neatly folded in his hand. She could see his initials, *VF*, beautifully scripted at the bottom of each page. She wondered if any of those were written for her.

"So did you really mean what you said? That you didn't write that poem for anyone?"

"Oh . . . no, of course not," he said with a grin. "Gotta run now. Next round coming up and I'm starving."

"I'll get you something to eat if you want."

"Ahh, you're a doll." He kissed her on the cheek. "Can you be back in five minutes?"

Bicé was so absorbed in what Victoria was saying that she didn't notice Madame Vileroy standing behind her, putting a hand on her shoulder. "Bicé, did you help Belle get here?"

"Don't talk to me," Bicé whispered.

"I thought it best that she stay at home."

"She broke out on her own. Not that I have to explain . . ."

"Of course you do. You and I are friends, aren't we?" Vileroy crooned.

"You're not my friend."

"We've been together for so long, Bicé Faust. I *am* your friend."

Bicé shuddered at the sound of her own name. Somehow it sounded artificial now.

"You know so many languages," goaded the governess. "And now you know who I am. Can you figure out my name?"

Bicé turned it all over in her head. *I am your friend* . . .

"*I am Friend of Faust,*" Bicé whispered and began translating to herself until she arrived at something. *Me Fausto Philos*—Mephistopheles.

It only took a second to regain her resolve. "Look, Nicola. I want to leave. I want out of this whole thing. Just let me go."

"But you need me. I don't have to remind you—"

"I'm not making any deals with you."

"What's important is the deal you've already made. The one you make every day."

Bicé tried to look Nicola Vileroy in the eye. But she couldn't hold her gaze.

"You need me," said the demon-governess, "and we both know you'll never leave."

⚬━◉◉◉

"Point three: The fact that a higher percentage of the dead would be poor is irrelevant."

⚬━◉◉◉

Christian sat in the back of the room for Valentin's next reading. Charlotte had just run in with an iced coffee and three cakes from the coffee shop next door and was making her way to join Christian in the back. She looked flushed and sweaty.

"I can't wait to hear the next one. He's so talented. Did you know that he didn't want to enter? He didn't want anything to come between us . . ."

"Is that why you didn't enter?" Christian asked with a look of sympathy. As far as he knew, Valentin had planned to enter this competition for months.

"Yep. And it was worth it. You shouldn't have missed his first reading. It was amazing."

Christian listened as Valentin began reading. From the first moment, there was no question in his mind that Valentin would win. It was beautiful, heartfelt, and funny. It made him sad. Not just because he realized that he wasn't as good, but because all this time, he had been going about things all wrong. He had never written anything good. He had just spent all his energy brooding over Valentin's successes.

⤳⚬⚬⚬⤶

"In conclusion, patent infringement is stealing—even if it's to help the poor. Even if there are some negative consequences, we live in a society made up of rights and rules. . . ."

Thomas was in shock. He looked over at the Marlowe debate coach with an expression of disbelief. "How—where did she get—?" Victoria's rebuttals had been so on target, so perfectly tailored to what Thomas had said, that it was hard to believe it was just because she was a good debater. After all, there were only three minutes of prep time between their speeches. How could she have rewritten her speech to refute him point by point in three minutes? And all that data? How did she know?

Just as Thomas was mulling all this over, Victoria was smiling to the judges and leaving the podium. She walked past Thomas, leaned over, patted him on the back, and said, "So much for preparing like a lawyer, huh?" She held his gaze and waited for the words to sink in before she winked at Thomas and walked toward Madame Vileroy.

"Good job, my dear. You were brilliant," Madame Vileroy said.

"Thanks, and the best part is that now he thinks it's Belle's fault."

⤳⚬⚬⚬⤶

As soon as the round was over, Belle and Lucy both ran over to Thomas from opposite sides of the hall. He was listlessly shuffling papers on his desk.

"Hi. I'm so sorry I'm late. Don't worry, you can totally bounce back from that," said Belle.

"And you're going to help him?" spat Lucy.

"Of course I am," said Belle, looking at Thomas for support. He still hadn't looked up from his papers. She reached for his hand, but he pulled it away so fast, she let out a yelp.

"Like you helped Victoria?" he finally said.

Belle's heart stopped. Did he know? Did he finally feel what had happened to him that night?

"What are you talking about?"

"Belle, you told her my entire strategy. About the patent lawyer and all the arguments I was using. You're the one who told her."

"No . . ."

"Yeah, Thomas, I bet it was her," Lucy said, jumping in.

"What's worse is that you told her about my plans — about wanting to be a lawyer. No one else knew about that. You're the only one who could have said anything."

"No, Thomas. I didn't tell her that. I swear."

"I wish I could believe you."

~∞∞∞

Valentin's creative writing teacher pushed his way past the crowd to congratulate his student. Valentin's poems had just won first place in the original compositions category, and everyone wanted to talk to the gifted young artist. Charlotte had to claw and trample her way to the front, where Christian was already congratulating Valentin.

"Hey, Charlotte," Valentin said when she stumbled into him. "What did you think?

Christian felt sorry for Charlotte. Valentin had such a dismissive tone. But still, who could blame him? He didn't like her. And he had been nice to her for so long.

"It was great! What was your inspiration for that one?" Charlotte fished.

"Nothing. Just came to me."

Charlotte looked hurt, and upset, and generally confused. "OK, well, I have to go. What time are you going to pick me up tomorrow?"

"Tomorrow?"

"You know. The spring dance?"

"Uh . . . Charlotte, I asked someone . . ." Valentin racked his brain. *Did I ask Charlotte? No, no, definitely not.*

Charlotte's lip quivered. "But you asked *me*."

Oh, geez.

"I'm sorry, Charlotte. I promised to go . . . with my sister. . . . She doesn't have a date. And anyway . . . I'm sorry."

Charlotte burst into tears and ran off. Christian just stood there waiting.

"Aren't you going to go back . . . to fix that?" he asked Valentin.

"Fix what? There's nothing to fix. It's better not to lead her on."

～◦◎◦～

Belle was crying. "I didn't tell her that. I promise."

"Belle, can you leave him alone?" said Lucy.

"Yeah, please leave. I only get fifteen minutes to prepare my comeback."

Belle wiped her face on her sleeve. Thomas was fidgeting again, and his voice grew louder as he spoke to her. He was already nervous, but sitting near Belle, he felt as if he were being pricked all over with pins and needles that sent an unpleasant tingling through his hands and feet.

"Well, that's why I came. I want to help," said Belle slowly, noticing his nervousness.

"I don't cheat. And I don't want to talk to you."

"Thomas, just trust me. Yes, Vic cheated. Yes, she got a look at your strategy in advance. But I promise that I had nothing to do with it." Lucy snorted. Belle went on, "And what I have here is a speech that evens the playing field. It's all based on the stuff you found on your own, but she hasn't seen this speech. It's fair."

"OK, let me see and then I'll decide."

"No. You have to promise that you won't look at it until you're about to give the speech."

"Are you kidding?" said Lucy. "He'd be crazy to trust you now."

Belle glanced over at Victoria, who was intently watching the three of them, with a mean look. She was always cheating. Belle couldn't let Thomas read the speech now.

"You're serious?" said Thomas. "You want me to go up there and read something I've never seen?"

"If you read it now, she'll have time to— Never mind, just do it for me. What do you have to lose? I can't imagine you have much in that file box that'll help you win in less than"—Belle checked her watch—"ten minutes."

~⚬⚬⚬~

Christian and Valentin slipped into the classroom just as Belle was leaving Thomas and walking toward Bicé. She gave them a thumbs-up, completely ignoring Victoria, who was standing with Madame Vileroy and giving her the most hateful glare she could conjure. Thomas approached the podium feeling as if someone were holding him by the throat, thinking, *I'm such a pushover.* But something about the way Belle had pleaded with him had made him want to listen. It wasn't the way he'd felt before. He didn't feel groggy and happy and totally in love. Something about the way she looked at him made him trust her. It was her eyes. She had honest eyes. Thomas opened the paper that Belle had given him and began to read.

"What is stealing? When is it excusable? When is it a crime?" Thomas looked uncomfortable as he read. Christian perked up. Belle saw Christian listening with interest and looked down at her shoes.

"An action becomes stealing when one of two conditions are met. First, when there is harm to the victim. Second, when the act is done for personal gain." Thomas looked up and smiled. He seemed happy with where the speech was going, and Belle breathed a sigh of relief. Christian's face had gone white. He stood frozen in his spot. Belle smiled as if to say that things were different with him. That stealing was different in their world. She was torn between excitement for Thomas and embarrassment for Christian.

"If both these criteria are met, there is no question where society stands. When one of the two criteria is in question, society begins to debate. For example, is it wrong when someone takes something that has been thrown away? Perhaps not, since there is no detriment to the victim. Is it wrong when someone takes a loaf of bread to feed a starving baby or taxes the rich to help the poor? Perhaps not, since the motive is unselfish."

Victoria wasn't even looking at Thomas anymore. She was glaring at Belle. She looked like she was about to lunge at her. Belle signaled to her that perhaps she should be taking notes. But Victoria wasn't used to preparing rebuttals without advance notice.

"When neither of the criteria is met, however, I propose that there is no crime against ethics. Is it wrong to take a syringe from a drug addict? Of course not. I think this issue can be resolved if we find a way to violate neither of these two rules. Then it may be easier for skeptics to say that the right to life trumps the right to intellectual property, since it will be hard to prove that any property has been taken at all." Thomas began to speak emphatically, like a politician. Belle looked proud. Victoria was livid.

"My plan involves a combination of safeguards including export restrictions and marketing measures to ensure that the pharmaceutical companies' profits are not affected. Meanwhile, I propose various distribution measures and profit caps to ensure that no one will stand to gain significantly from violating patents, thus removing incentive for selfish profiteers to enter this business."

Thomas went on to present a perfect twelve-point plan, ad-libbing along the way, and visibly winning over all the judges. In the next round, Victoria, who suddenly seemed at a loss for evidence or coherent arguments, resorted to poking a few holes in Thomas's plan and rereading pieces of her original speech. She finished with a minute left to spare and stormed out before the judges announced Thomas the winner.

Thomas threw his arms around Belle. He lifted her off the ground and kissed her . . . on the forehead.

"I'm so sorry. I—I thought you were the one that—" he stammered, embarrassed at himself but still holding on to her, "you know."

"That's OK," she whispered. "But you believe me now, right?"

Over Thomas's shoulder, Belle saw Lucy walking out, slamming the door behind her.

"Sure I do. If you were trying to sell me out to Victoria, you wouldn't have saved me like that. By the way, where did you get that speech?"

"I wrote it." Thomas's eyebrows shot up. "What? You thought I was just a dumb blonde?"

"No. But where did you get all the evidence and that plan . . ."

"I started with your arguments and researched the rest online. You don't need inside info to form opinions on stuff."

"That's the hottest thing I've ever heard," said Thomas, too happy to wonder how she had had the time.

After the tournament, Victoria was nowhere to be found. Valentin and Thomas went to the awards ceremony. Christian and Bicé were outside when Belle ran up and hugged Bicé.

"Thank you," she said. "He said I was brilliant."

Bicé awkwardly returned the hug, still conflicted about her prodigal sister. "Glad I could help."

"How did you help?" asked Christian.

"She stopped everything . . . to give me time to write that speech."

"You *stopped* everything?" asked Christian.

"Yeah," said Bicé, still visibly uncomfortable in her relationship with Belle.

"And she was there with you? What about everything that . . . ?"

"We're sisters," said Bicé, resigned. "I had to help."

Belle hugged her again. She seemed genuinely sorry for what had happened. They'd begin the precarious rebuilding of their relationship now, of the trust that had been lost. Belle held her sister and wished for forgiveness, and Bicé did her best to forgive.

When they separated, Belle ran back for the awards ceremony. She thought about that moment together, when they had held hands, and Belle had finally experienced a little of Bicé's world. There was an incredible feeling of loneliness, and it was a moment she would never forget, when she thought she could be lost to the dark, when she began to see why Bicé was the way she was — a pariah. Bicé and Christian walked off by themselves, whispering.

"All I know is that I'm never stealing again," said Christian. "Not after that speech. We have to get out of her house."

"Just a couple more days, Christian. I just need a few more days." She thought about his childhood letter, about the mark on Christian's chest that had now disappeared. She would get Christian out of there, she resolved. But not yet.

"OK, but I want to know what you're doing."

"Later."

"I need to figure out a way to get Buddy out, too."

"Buddy?" Bicé felt a wave of guilt. "He . . . he isn't human, right?"

"I'm not sure, Bicé. He learns. He feels pain. He processes information. Sometimes he does weird things . . . like he has a history, you know? What if he's a real person? What if she . . . ?" Christian was obviously distressed at that thought.

Bicé thought about the scribbled letters she had seen in the notebook, and Buddy at the white window. Suddenly, she stopped at the door of one of the classrooms.

"Hold on, Christian. Look who's in there. Shhh, I want to hear."

Victoria and Madame Vileroy were in the classroom. Victoria was raging as usual.

"You broke our deal!" she screamed.

"I didn't. I gave you all the tools. You lost because you didn't anticipate—"

"I lost because of Belle! And you didn't even warn me!"

"Well, I can't force Belle to do anything."

"Yes, you can. There are things you can do."

"Why would I want to?"

"For me. You owe me."

"Victoria, I believe I've made it clear that I've fulfilled my end of the bargain."

"You could have kept her at home, like you said you would. It was obvious she's been wimping out since Sunday."

"I locked her in. Anything more would be charity. You're not a charity case, are you, Victoria?"

"So you're just going to abandon me? You always pick Belle over me. I don't get it. She betrayed you."

"There is no betrayal, Victoria. No relationships—just simple bargains. She never broke her word to me. So what will I gain from punishing her? But if you want more, I *am* willing to make another trade. . . ."

"What do I have to do?" As always Victoria jumped at the bait.

"Victoria, darling, do you ever pray at night?"

Chapter 20
Trick

"You know what I think?"

"I don't care."

"I think the biggest lie the devil ever told was that beauty and goodness are the same."

"Great."

Belle was happy for the first time in a long time. Thomas loved her. Lucy was completely out of the picture. She was sure of that. She thought that maybe she would skip her bath tonight and see if Thomas would notice. But she knew that he would. Lately, they had more and more *real* moments between them. But in the end, no matter how she masked it, the air around her was always tainted, always addictive, always a distortion from the truth. She could still see him reacting to her, could still feel him changing. She pushed those thoughts out of her mind and grabbed the bottle marked *indifferent* again. This was the closest she would get to spending a few more real moments with Thomas.

Just then, her phone rang. It was Maggie. The second Belle picked up, Maggie started talking at top speed. She had Charlotte on three-way.

"Mags, I'm getting ready for the dance. Can we talk later?" said Belle.

"No, no, no." Belle could almost see her shaking her head. "It's about Lucy. She's planning something big. She's going to do something horrible to you tonight."

"Mags, slow down. I doubt she's planning anything—"

"No, no, I'm sure there's something." Maggie was panting. She was like this all the time now. She never slowed down these days. And she never stopped following Belle, her eyes glazed over, always frantic, always paranoid. Nowadays, she was like this when they were apart too. "I'm sure. Totally sure. Definitely totally sure. Char, tell her."

Charlotte was torn as usual. On the one hand, Lucy was her best friend. On the other hand, Belle was so interesting, so appealing — even if she *was* Valentin's sister. There was just something about her. And Lucy *had* been acting very suspicious lately. Charlotte had never realized it before she met Belle. She'd never noticed all the strange things about Lucy. Yes, being with Belle had definitely made her see things much more clearly. Something was wrong with Lucy. Something was unnatural about her. Lucy was strange. Lucy was twisted. It was *Lucy* who was giving her headaches every day now.

"She asked me a bunch of stuff about you and the dance — like what you're wearing, how you're getting there, stuff like that. I think she's going to —"

"Char, so what?" Belle cut in. "I asked you stuff about her too. I have to get ready."

"No, no, I think she's going to do something!"

"Like what?"

"I don't know. Tamper with your car, find a way to steal Thomas, cover you in pig's blood. I don't know. I just know it's something."

"Yeah, yeah, and I think I saw her talking to some teachers. I bet she's trying to get you in trouble," said Maggie.

"I think I saw her following Thomas after school," said Charlotte.

"And she was at my dad's office the other day. Why would she want a lawyer? I bet she's planning to sue!" Maggie was getting more and more excited.

"Maggie, her parents are getting a divorce," Belle said, sounding exhausted.

Maggie didn't let her finish. "We should do something. I can go over to her house and slash her dress so she can't go. Would you like me to do that? I could, you know. No, no, she has tons of dresses. I could put hair remover in her shampoo! But, no, that never works. You have to leave it on for like fifteen minutes. I could tell her mom about that tattoo! Then she'd be grounded. It would be the best thing for everyone."

Belle let out a deep sigh. She knew what this was. She wondered if the *indifferent* bath would make them less like this — less addicted, less paranoid. But she knew it wouldn't. They were well past that stage. "No, Maggie. Don't do anything. I'll watch out for her at the dance. But right now, I have to go."

~☙☙☙~

Victoria stood in a corner of the ballroom, sipping her drink. The spring dance was nothing short of a full-scale, over-the-top gala for kids who were used to big parties and were trained to notice imperfections. The venue was like a massive greenhouse with flowers and shrubs growing just outside and trees towering over the glass ceilings and walls. The lights were low, and there were big couches and round tables set up all around the dance floor. The sun was setting, and the room had an eerie glow, a strange mix of night and day, with the twilight streaming through the glass and mixing oddly with the nightclub atmosphere of the room. But Victoria wasn't paying much attention to the décor. She looked around again, eyeing the door and smoothing down her black dress.

Just then, she felt a tap on her shoulder. She turned around to find Ms. LeMieux smiling down at her. She put on her sweetest smile and said hello.

"Don't tell me a lovely young lady like you is here alone?" Ms. LeMieux said, sounding disappointed that the young version of herself was dateless.

Victoria said sweetly, "I haven't had much time to meet any boys."

"Well, you *are* a busy girl. I don't know how you find time for everything you do."

Victoria giggled, which she hated doing. But she remembered what Madame Vileroy had told her countless times, about being sweeter to people who matter, more likable, and she went on. "Yeah, it's mostly thanks to you, Ms. LeMieux. I mean, you're the only one who took my disability seriously. If you hadn't made all the teachers keep giving me extra time on the tests and homework and stuff . . ."

"Oh, don't you mention it. At Marlowe we try to have the utmost sensitivity to our students' needs."

"Thanks. But things still haven't been easy."

"What do you mean, dear?"

"Well, I'm class president, as you know, but I think Lucy may still be holding a grudge about the election. She doesn't pull her weight in Student Council and so I have double the work." Victoria rubbed her eyes. "I haven't had much time for homework."

Ms. LeMieux looked distraught. Victoria went on.

"I was wondering if it would be OK if I take more classes at home next semester, you know, with my own tutors? It would give me more time to handle this stuff. I have to deal with a lot of insensitivity about my condition."

"Well, of course, dear. Of course. I will talk to the principal about it on Monday. But hey, I do have some good news for you."

Victoria knew it. She didn't want to be too hasty and cheat unless she had to. But she knew it was the time of year to announce the Marlowe Prize. For weeks she had been padding her grades, persuading her teachers to give her the tests orally, getting the moths to bring her the best essays, even getting Jason Choi suspended afterward for plagiarizing "her" essay. With the help of her new class schedule, her GPA was a perfect and unattainable 5.0. Now, finally, she'd get the recognition she deserved.

"Well, it's a bit premature," said Ms. LeMieux. "I'm not supposed to tell you till Monday. But you are the cowinner of this year's Marlowe Prize! It goes to the person with the highest —"

"Yes, I know." Victoria lost her sweet tone. Ms. LeMieux was taken aback. "It's for the highest GPA and most meaningful activities in the class. But what do you mean 'cowinner'?"

Victoria glanced at all the cuts on her arms from her extended time with the moths. All that for a measly "cowinner"?

"Oh, well, yes. The committee decided that even though you have the highest GPA so far, you should share the prize with Jamie Mendez."

"What? Why?"

"Because, well, Jamie's GPA is very close to yours, dear. And she has spent all her free time over the last year raising money for hungry children in the Sudan. And since the prize is about both GPA and —"

"No. The prize has *always* been given to the person with the highest GPA. I know they say it's for activities too, but for the last ten years, the person with the highest GPA has always won!"

"Yes, dear, but the committee thought that given all the special privileges you've been —"

"But I have a *han-di-cap*!"

"Hmm . . . Well, I'm not sure if you're aware, but Ms. Mendez has asthma, and she has still followed the normal curriculum, including gym, and —"

"So? Asthma is irrelevant! You don't learn with your lungs! This is because she's Hispanic, isn't it? That's what this is all about!"

Ms. LeMieux gasped. She was about to respond when she saw

Valentin approaching from behind Victoria. Ever since the Christmas play, Ms. LeMieux had been wary of Valentin, finding him very odd. She edged away as he moved closer and shot her a smile bordering on sleazy. She quickly said good-bye and walked away. Valentin called after her, "It's OK, Trisha, sweetheart. It meant nothing."

"Who's Trisha?"

"Trisha LeMieux. That sweet thing walking away."

"Val, that's gross. She's like thirty."

"Forty. I thought I'd get in while it was still illegal. Another three years before I have to switch to nine-year-olds," Valentin said with a leer.

"Gross!"

"Kidding . . . Geez, I heard your little tantrum from across the room."

"There's always something. The stupid moths didn't—"

"Look, Vic. You know what your problem is?"

Victoria didn't want another lecture on being less catty or not thinking only about herself. She got enough of those from Bicé. "What?" she said in an exasperated tone.

"You're not subtle enough."

"Whatever."

"Fine, don't listen. I've got plenty of things to do. And then do again."

Valentin walked away from Victoria feeling utterly superior. He looked back and saw her chewing her nails, staring intently at Belle and Thomas, who had just walked in. She had a smile on her face, as if she was glad to see them together. Then he saw Christian standing with Bicé. They were whispering to each other conspiratorially and watching Belle with the same intentness as Victoria. Valentin reached into his pocket. He remembered that Christian had still not heard the first poem that he read at the tournament. He had been rescuing Belle and missed it.

"Hey, Christian," he said, a little too enthusiastically. Christian jumped. "Hey, I need a quick favor."

"Sure. What?"

"Would you just listen to me read this poem? It's the one I wrote for the tournament yesterday."

"Now? Val, are you nuts?"

Valentin looked like he had no idea what Christian was talking about. "OK, read it yourself, then. Here." He tried to force the page into Christian's hand. But Christian just looked at him, shocked.

"Valentin." Bicé jumped in with a suspicious look. "This is not the right time."

"OK. Maybe later tonight, then?"

"Why does it have to be tonight?" said Christian. "We have a lot to deal with right now, Valentin."

"OK, later tonight, then." Valentin licked his lips nervously. "Later . . . when we're home . . . when you're not overwhelmed. It'll only take a second." Valentin quickly walked away before Christian could object.

Bicé shot a glance at Christian and then looked at Belle again. Christian looked mad. "Why is he always rubbing it in my face?"

"Oh, that's not what he's doing. You're the only real friend he has."

"B, he's rubbing it in my face. Every chance he gets. I'm starting to get sick of it."

"Can we just get back to the clues? We know Vic made a deal with Vileroy. Obviously she wants to get back at Belle. Obviously it's got to have something to do with Thomas. She hates them both . . ."" Christian nodded as Bicé counted on her fingers.

~∞∞∞~

Belle laughed as Thomas whispered something in her ear. She seemed completely unaware of all the people around her, behaving more and more indifferently as they moved closer to her. She didn't mind. That's what she wanted, to be alone with Thomas. At first, when he had picked her up for the dance, it seemed that he was fighting with himself. Part of him wanted to be aloof. To ignore her. To act as if he didn't care. Another part of him didn't understand why he was acting that way. Hadn't he sprinted to her door only five minutes before? That part of him wanted to tell her how wonderful she looked. And in the end, he did. Belle was ecstatic to see that even though he twitched and fought with himself a few times, he was basically attentive and very interested in everything she did and said. Maybe tonight, he would finally get over his shyness and make a move. She wasn't hoping for much. Any kind of progress from his current comfort zone of cheeks and forehead would be welcome. *What's wrong here?* Belle asked herself. *Maybe he only likes to kiss at formal occasions. He kissed Lucy at the Christmas party.* It was something to cling to.

~∞∞∞~

From a distance, Victoria and Bicé were both watching Belle. But Belle didn't notice. She was having too much fun. Thomas seemed so proud of her for helping him at the tournament. He had always found her charming and beautiful. But to have such a smart girlfriend seemed to make him inflate. He tried to approach some of his friends with Belle on his arm, but they all recoiled. The only one even remotely interested in them was Lucy, who was hanging on to Connor Wirth's arm while never taking her eyes off Thomas. In the rare moments when Thomas looked over, she clung tighter to Connor and tried to pretend she was having the best time ever.

～☙☙☙

Across the room, Valentin was eyeing a group of girls sitting on one of the couches. He noticed the one in the middle — overweight, bad skin, tacky dress, and a mean look on her face as if she didn't need friends anyway. Wow, she could use some help. She was probably the type of girl who had to be forced by her mother to come to the dance. Valentin stuffed his poem back into his pocket. As he walked toward her, he became more and more aware of his own body — sleek, handsome; designer shirt tucked in, golden hair brushed back. He felt perfect. Looking at the poor, pathetic girls in front of him made him feel a rush. And that was a bigger turn-on than all the spritely beauties who were casually glancing in his direction.

"Hey, ladies. Who wants to dance?" he said as he eyed the wall-flowers with a hungry look. The fat one backed away. Valentin put on his saddest face.

"You're turning me down? Not even a 'maybe'?" He gave the sweetest look he could muster. Yes, that's the one he wanted. That's the one who would make him feel flawless. A girl like that would put up with anything. He wouldn't have to lie; wouldn't have to change anything. *Like throwing a party in a crack house. No need to clean up afterward.*

The girl looked at him with suspicion, but then smiled. There was a bit of fear in her smile. It made Valentin want to dance with her even more.

"Isn't that sweet?" a pretty young girl nearby said to her friend. "He's trying to make her feel better."

"Yeah, he's a really nice guy."

The night flew by quickly for the Faust children. All except Bicé, who spent the entire night thinking and being afraid. She knew something was coming. She had heard the conversation between Victoria and Vileroy, the deal being hatched. It was enough to distract her from all thoughts of Christian's childhood letter, his disappearing mark, or his plan to escape. For a moment, she looked at Belle. She saw the way Thomas looked at her. He laughed at something she said. But more than anything, he was mesmerized by her beauty. Suddenly Bicé felt a dreadful knowing feeling wash over her. She knew what was coming and dashed toward her sister.

"Belle. Belle, you have to listen to me."

"Bicé! Can't you see I'm busy? Sorry, Thomas, but my sister is in one of her moods."

Bicé cowered for a minute and then gathered herself. "Belle, you have to listen. Vileroy and Victoria, they're — well, I'm not sure what they're doing. I think you should go home."

"Oh, no. Not another insane conspiracy theory. I've had enough from Maggie."

"Huh? No, listen. You should go home now."

"OK, whatever. Can you please go away?"

Belle pushed her sister aside and walked with Thomas to another private corner.

Just as Bicé was about to follow them, she was overtaken by Maggie and Charlotte, who had just left Lucy's side and were making their way back to Belle. They were hysterical.

"Bicé, Bicé—we have to stop Lucy!"

Bicé had no patience for them. "I have to go. Belle needs me."

"Belle? Did you say Belle? Lucy did something, didn't she? Did she steal Thomas?"

They sounded concerned, but the look in their eyes wasn't a look of worry. They looked exhilarated and eager. Bicé tried to keep walking, all the while watching Belle from the corner of her eye, wanting desperately to get to her so she could take her away from here. Bicé made a beeline toward Belle, but before she could reach her—yet another distraction—she heard someone clearing her throat into the microphone.

"Welcome to the Marlowe School spring dance, everyone!"

Ms. LeMieux and Coach K were standing in the front of the room. Ms. LeMieux spoke first, looking at Coach K with big, condescending eyes every few minutes to make sure he was following.

"We hope you've had a lovely evening. As you all know, one of the biggest honors at Marlowe, the Scholar-Athlete Prize, is traditionally presented at the spring dance."

She waited a moment for applause. When none came, she went on. "Coach K and I represent the two fields in which this phenomenal student has excelled: athletics"—she nodded to Coach K—"and scholarship"—she stretched to her full height. "In a short time, this student has shown that great things can be achieved by someone very young. This student has been a role model to the class—"

Before she could finish, Coach K stepped in. There was a mild applause that died down quickly when she gave them a dirty glance. "Without further ado, we present this year's winner of the Marlowe Scholar-Athlete Prize . . ."

Christian couldn't help himself. He was curious. Even though his heart wasn't in it, he wanted to know if they had noticed him, if they thought he was the best. He still wanted to win, to get one step closer to an easy life, or rather one step further from a hard one.

"Connor Wirth."

Christian looked at his shoes. The class erupted. Connor started to jog toward the front, while all his friends patted him on the back.

"In his years at Marlowe, Connor Wirth has led the school to numerous championships in golf, swimming, and basketball, all the while setting a positive example for his fellow classmates. His integrity, sportsmanlike attitude, persistence in the face of adversity, and competitive drive are admirable, and the reason that he is this year's Scholar-Athlete."

Ms. LeMieux yanked the mic away from the coach. "Connor, you have shown us that unflinching diligence can be a recipe for a successful life. Congratulations."

Half the audience groaned at her sappy words. Christian tried to fight the feeling that was welling up in his chest. He tried to push it down deep inside his body. But a part of him still wanted to run up onto the podium and steal that happy smirk off Connor's face.

"Jealous?" a cool voice said. He turned around to see Madame Vileroy standing next to him, her hair in her signature low bun, wearing a beautiful white gown that made her stand out as the most striking woman in the room.

"No," Christian said flatly. "I'm happy for him."

"What's going on in there?" She tapped him gently on the chest. "Don't you want to be a winner? Rich? Not even now that you've lost? Did your heart stop crying black tears?"

Christian didn't answer.

"You know, it's not too late. You can still have it all. Now that you know the whole story, you and I can make another deal, Christian. I'm giving you another chance to be happy, to be a winner." She grabbed his arm and walked him away from the crowd cheering Connor. Christian was about to tell her where she could go when a lingering doubt overtook him. Was this the time to cash in? He had probably already sold his soul. What more could she ask for? Maybe this time he could focus on being a good writer. Forget about fame and fortune.

"Christian, dear." She bent over to whisper into his ear. "Would you like to be a writer?"

His ears perked up. "I saw that you're helping Buddy to remember."

She waited for a response. "We'll do great things. I promise," she prodded.

The lingering doubt in Christian's mind was gone. He pictured Buddy's personal hell. What if that happened to him?

"No. You can't make me stay. You obviously don't have my soul, or you wouldn't be trying to make deals."

Madame Vileroy straightened up. She remained as composed as ever, but her devil eye flickered with rage. "Very well, my dear. Have it your way."

Bicé looked over at Thomas and Belle, who were in their own world, oblivious to the excitement in front of them. Bicé started marching toward them. She was determined to take Belle home no matter what anyone said. After getting Belle safely home, she would have to figure out what's going on with Valentin. It wasn't entirely like him to rub his writing in Christian's face. Why had he been in such a rush to have Christian read the poem? He had never even acknowledged what Bicé and Christian had found out the night Victoria cheated Thomas at their house. He never brought it up, as if he wasn't sure it really happened. And they had never asked him about it, afraid of what he would say. But as soon as they got home tonight, Bicé would find out everything.

Bicé tried again to make her way through the crowd. She knew what was coming. And it was coming soon. She sped up to a run, bumping into couples along the way. "Belle," she heard herself saying, a little louder. "Belle!" Suddenly a hand reached out and grabbed her by the arm. She spun around. She didn't have time for this. It was Christian. He had finally worked up the courage to ask Charlotte to dance when Bicé had rushed past.

"What's going on?" said Christian.

"Belle!" said Bicé. "We have to help her. Let me go!"

The urgency in Bicé's voice made Christian let go. Bicé ran on. Christian grabbed Charlotte's hand and followed.

They finally reached Belle, just as Thomas was making his move, his face inches away from Belle's. Bicé reached her hand toward her sister. She could feel Madame Vileroy moving closer behind her. But in that instant, something made Bicé stop. Something made her step back. Something made Thomas stop in his tracks—his face barely touching Belle's—yell out, and push Belle so hard she almost hit the floor.

"Thomas? Why did you do that?" Belle said, shocked and flustered.

A room full of people stood around with their mouths hanging open, quiet as ghosts. Victoria was elated, overjoyed by the bargain she had made. She had a Cheshire-cat smile on her face. Lucy was stunned and quickly made her way to Thomas's side. In two seconds, she had pulled him away and was whispering consoling words in his ear, pretending she had known all along. Bicé was grabbing Belle's arm and making for the door before Belle could see for herself. But Belle already knew. In a flash, everything had changed. Her beautiful face had suddenly transformed into something else. Not her old face, but something worse. She was truly, unforgivably, indescribably ugly.

Chapter 21
Lie

Ladies and Gentlemen:

Tonight's performance by the incomparable magician Scorpius has been canceled due to the unexpected disappearance of the artist. It is well known that this magnificent talent has risen to world renown while struggling with the debilitating effects of seizures and Tourette's syndrome. As such, his exit from the world of magic is not wholly unexpected, as he often spoke of departing the stage to pursue a more substantial gift, one that would consume all of his time and effort. Let us wish him well, in whatever adventures await him and his lovely assistant, who is presumed to have gone with him.

Tickets will not be refunded.

— *The Management*

The tears rolling down her face were no help. The way the red-stained eyes, the bloated cheeks, and tousled hair of weeping starlets made them so irresistible—the way you'd want to comfort them, kiss the tears that cover them—that was not the way for Belle as she sat at her windowsill, crying ugly tears. She had gathered her crumpled dress around herself like a blanket, and now she had pressed her pimpled forehead against the glass, looking down to the street. She imagined her tears piercing the glass, falling to the curb like rain. It was as though the sky was sobbing for her. The clouds had retched in their anguish, the great unfairness of existence, the plague of consequences. She watched as Thomas Goodman-Brown—his collar unbuttoned, his flowers sagging—walked up to their door. From above, Belle scooted up, leaned even harder on the glass. Was it disappointment on his face? Rain?

Belle didn't notice that Bicé had walked in, maybe just appeared on the other side of the door. She was staring straight down at the globe of the boy's head. In the distance, she heard the doorbell ringing. It was muted by a thousand walls. Belle didn't move to get it. She never could, not with her face like this. But the bell kept shouting for her. Maybe Thomas was a good man. Maybe he wasn't disgusted with her. Maybe in the movie, she'd run out in the rain, fall into his open arms, and he'd say he loved her anyway—and the sky would be crying tears of joy. Maybe. But Belle couldn't do it. She couldn't stand it.

She imagined that after the happy ending, after the credits were finished, Thomas would put her down, breathe out, and do his best to look into her dull eyes. He'd be good enough to accept the promise he'd made. He'd take her home with people glancing at them.

They could get married in a courthouse, and he wouldn't ever tell her, but he'd always remember the way her hair had been as glossy as a magazine cover, her cheeks as smooth as melon flesh. She'd always know — in the unexcited way he'd take her to dinner, his secret requests to be seated in the corners — his self-sacrifice for a promise he made when he was just too young.

Belle caught a glimpse of her own profile in a shadow on the floor. She shuddered at the lumbering indelicacy of it, her nose growing bigger by the hour, her jaw losing its refined lines. After her face had changed for an instant at the dance, the rest of her had gradually gone back to what it should look like. Her height and stature were the same as Bicé's now; she was no longer a tall and willowy statuette. Her face, on the other hand, was a far far cry from Bicé's sweet face. Thomas probably didn't even want her. Maybe he just wanted to see, out of curiosity, and then leave. After all, this was no movie, no fairy tale.

Belle cried harder, listening as Thomas kept ringing. He was so determined. Her skin was as pockmarked as a melon rind. She had been masked all this time with Madame Vileroy's own face, that gorgeous face. And all that time she had been rotting on the inside, becoming rancid. She had imagined making the world addicted to her. In the end, she was the addict. She had imagined herself with an intoxicating presence, and even that was nothing more than the smell of the rotting Belle inside the mask. And now, with the mask removed, she was uglier than she had ever been. A perfect match to the heart she had made for herself. She'd never see him again.

"You should see him again."

Belle turned around. Bicé was standing behind her. Belle hadn't noticed Bicé's hand on her shoulder. "He wants to see you," she said.

"No."

"He likes you for the real you."

"This *is* the real me."

"I know."

Belle instinctively put her head on Bicé's shoulder. Bicé cradled it like a baby. Belle hadn't realized how much she missed her sister, ever since that night when Thomas had come over, and yesterday at the tournament, when Bicé had helped her. But now that Belle really needed her, Bicé wasn't so mad. Belle wet her shirt with her tears. Bicé hummed gently and rocked her back and forth. She tried to make jokes to cheer her up, but nothing worked. She said, "Don't worry, Belle. Vic and Lucy will get into another fight in a few days and everyone will forget this." Belle laughed for a second. After another wave of tears, Belle calmed, whimpering with her face still on Bicé's shoulder. Bicé said, "I know it seems important. I don't want to play it down. But do you remember when we were little? When we looked the same?"

Belle nodded, remembering how much she used to hate her face then, Bicé's face. And now she'd give anything to have it back.

"I don't remember who said this, but it was something I used to think about a lot. Maybe it was Vileroy. No, I don't think it was. It couldn't have been. But I remember thinking it a lot. It was something like, *Do you know what makes someone beautiful?*"

"I remember that," said Belle, her throat hoarse.

"Confidence. You don't have to have this shape eyes or that

shape lips. No one seems to be able to decide which shape is best anyway. You can have every kind of blemish. It's confidence that attracts people. That's what everybody's looking for. It's what no potion can really give you. And believe me, Belle, you've got it. You've got it if you want it."

Belle spoke up. "It's believing that somebody loves you already, unconditionally."

"Yeah, how'd you know what I was going to say?"

"Mom used to say that . . . whenever I felt ugly or you felt sad," said Belle, sounding resigned, as if she no longer had reason to keep secrets.

Bicé's eyes widened. Her mouth opened, but there was no sound.

The door slammed open. Bicé was trying to understand. Victoria came in. She was furious, like a thunderclap. She was always furious. "You idiot!"

Belle looked up. Bicé turned around. "You ruin everything, you stupid, stupid idiot."

The two of them weren't sure to whom she was talking.

"See what you've made me do? Do you have any idea how much work some of us did? We have to leave here now, you know that? We can't just have one of us stop showing up and pretend you never existed. We can't just erase you from the picture! Ughh!"

Bicé put her hands up to stop her ranting. "Calm down."

"I don't want to calm down. This was supposed to teach her a lesson. Now all my work is ruined, because we can't stay anymore. And it's all her fault!"

"You did a vicious, awful thing and just because you didn't think of the consequences for yourself, now you're trying to blame Belle?" said Bicé.

"You don't even know what I'm talking about, Bicé." Looking at Belle, Victoria went on: "But you know what you did. And now you look like a baboon and you deserve it. You weren't even strong enough to take what was given to you."

Belle couldn't find her voice. Bicé raised hers. "Calm down, Victoria."

"No! I hate all of you! I hate that I have to live with you! And you don't even know what she's done. You're here playing the fairy godmother, and you have no idea what she's done to you."

Belle suddenly woke up. "Don't, Victoria."

"How're you going to stop me? You don't have *her* helping you anymore. You're just another pilgrim."

"It'll hurt you too . . . if you tell," said Belle.

"How? We're leaving. I don't ever want to see you again."

"What're you two talking about?" said Bicé.

"You," said Victoria. "We're talking about you, and you don't know it. Just like you don't know how any of us got here. You don't know how we all made the deal with Vileroy, how she came to our real homes at midnight and told us we could have what we wanted. You don't know because you never had the heart. You would never have taken the deal. That's why you don't have the mark. You don't even know that we weren't adopted at birth. We did it when we were ten! Everything you remember before then is fake. Why do you think everything you remember doing is so unlike you? So uncreative?

None of it happened. You were a happy little twin in Italy till your sister here sold you out."

"Stop!" screamed Belle, but Victoria wasn't about to stop now.

"She wanted to be pretty so bad, she had you kidnapped and brainwashed in your sleep. Go ahead, ask her. And she didn't even have to. She just wanted to keep something from her past life. You were the teddy bear she dragged along. Face it, Belle, you've done some ugly things. You sold your own sister to the devil and then pretended all this time that you actually care about her. Just like you've pretended to be the pretty little queen. Well, you've done some ugly things. And now you have the face you deserve."

Belle was standing still, slow, silent tears rolling down her cheeks. Bicé stood next to her. Victoria was still fuming, her chest expanding and contracting as if she'd just lost a race.

In the aftershock, from the doorway, Christian — who had been standing there a while — said, "I don't get it," and Valentin — who had been lurking behind him — laughed.

~⊙⊙⊙

After Belle had fainted or pretended to faint (no one ever knew), and Valentin had disappeared to his room, Victoria stormed out toward the east wing of the house, where Madame Vileroy lived, because that was the only comfort she had. Christian and Bicé walked by themselves, and Bicé told him everything she'd heard. She told him about the letter she had seen — the desperate query of a boy with no options. It was all clear now. The four of them had made the deal when they were ten — even Christian. He must have changed his mind later on. Otherwise, why the fake memories?

"That's why my mark was so light," said Christian, rubbing his heart.

"That's why I don't have one and yours went away when you decided you didn't want to steal anymore," said Bicé. "And it explains why we remember you being so eager to steal when we were eight. The memories before we were ten are all fake. Oh, Christian. We had an entire life somewhere else."

"We have to get out of here," said Christian, stopping midstride. Bicé kept walking. "We have to leave," he said again.

"Maybe," said Bicé.

"That's the only way to make this right," he said. "We have to get out."

"Not yet."

"I don't understand. I thought you'd want to leave tonight. You've been the biggest victim."

Bicé stopped.

"I'm sorry," he said. "I didn't mean to bring it up. Belle probably—"

"There's still more to this than we know." They were in front of a door that Christian hadn't seen before. It was Victoria's.

"What're we doing?" asked Christian.

"Victoria has been spying on us."

Christian looked on. He felt a hiccup in his breathing. It looked to him as though Bicé was disappearing and appearing again, like a cut in a film. Then the door was open.

"How'd you open it?" said Christian. The knobs only opened for their owners.

"I froze everything and dragged her over here," Bicé said with a quick grin.

"You put her back so she wouldn't know?"

"Yeah, but I spit in her ear."

The image of the short Bicé dragging an inanimate Victoria like a mannequin to the door, using her hand to fool the doorknob, and dragging her back, probably by her ankles, made Christian smile.

The insects in the room were terrifying to Bicé, the ultimate invasion of privacy. Christian recognized them immediately. He had seen them all over the city, stealing information. He'd even caught a few as they floated through his window, around the tennis court, inside the locker room. He had wondered what their lives were like and let them go.

Now the two of them stared at the room, a plague of flies, moths, mosquitoes, beetles, and bees. They hovered and buzzed and droned around everything. Their wings clattered against one another. Larvae were falling from the undulating swarm onto the linoleum, dropping like candies onto a factory floor.

"This is grotesque," whispered Bicé.

"What?" said Christian.

"This is how she's been spying," said Bicé.

"I heard her talking about her moths . . . but this . . ." Christian kept his lips tight.

"They've evolved. The moths must not have been enough. She's so . . . so greedy."

"How does it work? They spell it out in the air or something?"

"Maybe they sting it in her ear."

The knowing cloud sparkled in Christian's eyes as he stepped forward. Bicé didn't stop him.

"How did you find out about this place?" asked Christian, walking curiously toward the swarm.

"When I stop things to study, I've started looking around. Vileroy doesn't want me to, but I've been trying to figure out the secrets of this place. I caught Victoria in here. She uses it all the time."

"Will they attack us?" asked Christian.

"They shouldn't, I don't think. They seem to be programmed. I think they'll obey whoever's got access to the room."

Bicé fingered the can of insecticide in her pocket. She had picked it up when she stopped everything to open the door, just in case anything went wrong.

As Christian stepped closer and closer to the center of the swarm, he thought about everything that had happened, everything he could possibly ask. He wanted to know how they had each gotten here to this miserable place. Was it one big decision or a thousand small ones? He wondered who their parents had been. How could Belle betray her sister the way she had or Victoria continue worshipping Madame Vileroy even after knowing who she was? And he wondered why Bicé seemed so reluctant to leave.

Deep in thought, Christian barely noticed how muffled Bicé's voice sounded as she gave out instructions. He looked over at her and saw her motioning to him. He tried to make out her words, but he couldn't. Dozens of little antennae were prodding inside his eardrums. He tried to fight the impulse to struggle. They were touching every inch of him. If he brought up his hand to swat them away from his face, he would only bring more insects. It was like trying to dry your face in a swimming pool. But Christian was used to being submerged. Instead of the crystals of his blue lagoon or the refuse of his watery grave, now he had tiny legs probing at every pore in his skin. He didn't know how to get the insects to speak to him.

Outside, Bicé yelled, "Tell them what to do!"

Christian shook his head but couldn't get any space. He said, "Bicé, help."

Suddenly Bicé's voice became magnified in his ear midscream. "What to do! They'll listen to what we say."

Hearing her voice was like being thrown a life preserver. And at the same time, with the bugs acting as his ears, it was as if they suddenly became one body. Christian calmed down a little. "What should we ask them?"

"All I know is what I've guessed so far."

"Show us the future," said Christian.

Bicé started to say, "I don't think they can do that," when they both heard the buzzing grow louder. At first it was just static, but soon they both began to catch words, here and there in the garbled hissing. The feeling was uncomfortable at first, as though each little sting was a hardwired cable being jacked into their ears. They weren't exactly hearing the words of the insects, more like their brains were having the information shoved into them. Soon, not only were they hearing, but they could also see visions forming behind their eyelids. The experience of every little bug, whatever it had seen and heard, was being forcefully uploaded into their heads. And soon, they didn't even notice the discomfort.

They saw Valentin alone in his room. He was playing a first-person shooter on his computer.

"What is this?" said Christian.

"It's happening right now, in the other room."

"But that's just Val, gaming. I asked for the future."

"Oh my," said Bicé, "look at his clock."

Christian saw the clock at the upper right-hand corner of Valentin's computer. It was six hours ahead.

"He's going *forward* in time?"

"I didn't think he could."

"How are we seeing this?"

"Look."

There was a tiny moth, sitting quietly like a porcelain statuette on the back of Valentin's chair. Val jumped up from his seat with his arms raised in victory. He strolled out of the room. The moth followed, apparently reporting back to the hive — now including Christian and Bicé — instantaneously. Bicé was about to say something, but neither she nor Christian could speak when they saw Valentin walk down the hall and into a room where *another* Christian and *another* Bicé were sitting. From the thick of the hive, Christian and Bicé watched as the moth hovered around Valentin. In the other room, Christian looked to Valentin and the scene played out like this:

Christian: *"Val, guess what?"*

Valentin: *"What?"*

Christian: *"I just wrote my first poem — well, the first one I'm proud of."*

Valentin *(with a sneer): "How cute."*

Bicé: *"You should be proud, Christian. It's good."*

Christian *(to Valentin, embarrassed):* *"It's not as good as yours. Would you mind looking at it? I could use the help."*

Valentin *(as though he doesn't care at all about keeping up appearances):* *"Oh, stop the humble routine. It's nauseating."*

> *(Christian looks confused, but then Valentin smiles as if he's joking and Christian laughs and moves on.)*

Valentin: *"Is that the final draft?"*

Christian: *"Yep. It's as good as it's gonna get."*

Valentin: *"Confident, aren't we?"* *(And then he leans against the wall, his arms crossed defensively, as he watches Christian like an experiment.)* *"Well, I know a Christian that's scared all he'll ever be is a thief and a leech. And I think somewhere deep inside, that Christian knows the truth, and he's too much of a coward to call me on it."*

The Christian who was watching, the one in the storm of insects, was surprised that Valentin was talking about him like that.

(In the other room, Bicé looks worried.)

Bicé: *"What are you talking about, Val?"*

Valentin: *"Anything I want. I can say whatever I want, see? And I can do whatever I want and no one will know but me. I've even shot everyone in the school for fun. Let me see that."*

> *(Christian hands Val the poem, staring blankly at him, wondering if this is all a joke.)*

Bicé: *"So then why are you confessing everything now?"*

Valentin *(palming the sheet of paper):* *"Confessing? I'm not confessing,* *because* this" *(waving the poem at them)* *"is just another lie, and you"* *(pointing at Christian)* *"aren't the only thief."*

(The Christian in the other room leaps at Valentin to get back his poem, but he stops in midair. His desperation at losing his first great poem, the arrogant grin on Valentin — both freeze for an instant on their faces. Then Christian leaps backward. His conversation with Bicé unwinds. He walks out of the room, sits at his desk, deletes the poem, unthinks the title, then suddenly is inspired, and just as suddenly forgets his favorite poem.)

The Christian who was watching, the one in the hive, said, "What's happening?"

"I don't know," said Bicé. She didn't even understand how they could see what they were seeing, let alone explain Valentin's strange behavior. Then she spotted the moth again and realized. The moth had gone with Valentin, like an appendage; it had traveled with him, carrying with it the hive's eye. And she was here now, because she was part of the hive, able to observe the future without being a passenger on Valentin's train. This was a room apart. A room unlike any other. The hive, with its one mind, was able to hold its connection through both space and time. It was able to travel with Valentin to the future and spy on a future Christian and a future Bicé. No wonder Victoria knew so much.

They watched Val, back in his room, back in the current time, in front of his computer with Gauss rifles blasting at him from the riverbank, his arms raised in ultimate victory. In his hand was the paper.

Val unfolded it and immediately began copying it into his journal. Then he got up and walked out the door, taking his journal but leaving the paper behind. "Where's he going?" said Christian. Then to the insects all around him, "Show me the paper."

"He's going to find you," said Bicé, "so he can read it to you."

Christian still didn't understand. He looked at the paper on the bed, the words in his own handwriting. As he read each sentence, it disappeared. At first the title, a phrase he had been thinking of lately. And then the lines, until he reached the end, and just before it disappeared, he saw the author's initials, *CF*, fade and become the letters *VF.*

The poem (at least the version in his handwriting) was gone — just like all those times that Valentin had made him listen — because now he thought it was Valentin's poem. He could never go on to write it in the future, because now Valentin had beaten him to it. And so no matter how much of a connection he felt to those words, however painful it was to wish he had written them, he would never actually come to write his poems now, because now they were Val's.

Bicé watched as Christian realized that he had always been the writer he wished to be, that everything had been stolen from him. She yelled over the buzzing of the insects that they should leave. Suddenly, every inch of Christian shuddered with the hunger to steal. He fumed into the violent halo of insects, their creepy touch making him angrier, more ravenous by the second. Then, every moth and bee and bug fell to the ground like a tree struck by lightning, dropping every leaf at once, leaving only the trunk. Christian, fists clenched, felt a thousand droplets of stolen energy enter him at once, so for a moment his whole body tingled like a foot that had fallen asleep.

"He's been stealing my stuff."

"I know."

"I'll break his face."

"Let's just leave."

"*Now* you want to leave?"

"No, I just mean here, this room."

"Let's run away."

"I can't. Not yet."

As they turned to leave, Victoria swooped into the room. She saw the insects twitching on the floor, a few of them flying in dazed circles. "What have you done?" she yelled. "What have you done to them?"

"We're leaving," said Christian.

"Get out!" said Victoria, wishing they had said something else so that she could scream at them.

The two of them stopped. They wanted to say they were sorry. Not for anything they had done, but for the fact that those bugs were the only friends Victoria knew. But they realized that if they stayed, they would only encourage her to fume at them.

"I hate you!" she yelled after them.

As they walked on, they heard Victoria ranting in a voice more bitter and enraged than they had ever heard before. It was as though Victoria was losing more of herself every day, becoming more and more the faceless generic villain, the kind of hobgoblin you'd be afraid of but just as soon forget, the gremlin you'd see in pictures of hell that symbolizes something else, serves something else, without any idea who it used to be.

～✦∞✦～

Victoria lay on the floor and nuzzled her poor babies. She alternately licked their wounds and, in angry fits, crushed their spines. Finally she gathered the few that had recovered in her hand and hissed into their faces, "Follow them."

Chapter 22
Wasted Time

"Johann my friend, I am doubly cursed—a failure whose friends have found fame."

"Stop your self-pity. You have money. Go and live your dreams."

"I'm afraid I don't have courage enough to match my dreams."

"Whatever you can do or dream you can do, begin it. Boldness has genius, power, and magic in it."

"Ah, very pretty, Johann, very pretty. Easy to say for a man who has already achieved greatness. You think the world exists to serve your purpose."

"It does not?"

"Not for me."

"Then I say, 'Make the world serve your purpose!'"

"What do you suggest? Shall I sell my soul to the devil?"

"I imagine the devil doesn't want such a puling soul. I imagine that the ones he wants most are the ones the least for sale."

I should have seen it, Bicé thought. It had been so obvious, for so long. Valentin had lost hold of reality. Day after day, she had seen him sneak off to his white room, that room that Vileroy had given him, the one that reminded Bicé of the whitewashed, padded rooms in insane asylums. He had gone from carefree and playful to lascivious, nervous . . . almost mad. He trembled, fidgeted, his eyes darted. Sometimes, he would stare at a demo of a video game playing on his computer, thinking he was controlling it. His fingers shook and tapped the keys out of sync with the character onscreen. He was saying things, having fragments of conversations over and over again in a hundred possibilities of pasts real only to him. In the past few weeks he had made so many jumps, backward and forward, that his senses had finally given up. He didn't know which crimes he'd committed, which lives he'd led. She should have seen it. It was obvious now — his gift wasn't meant to last him long. He was never supposed to get what he was promised. It would continue confusing him, perverting his mind until he became so full of memories that he would beg the governess to kill him.

But Vileroy already had the soul she wanted from him. Maybe, if it would help her plans, she'd give him what he wanted, erase the million voices in his head, make him into a mindless dummy. But that hadn't happened yet — not to Valentin. Bicé thought of Buddy, the other person she had seen at the white window. And finally, she understood. Buddy was Valentin's future. He was a shell. The remaining portion of a real person with a past, a family, a life corrupted many years ago. In the weeks he had spent with Christian, he had gained back a little of his old self, a little of his lost humanity. But bringing back a lost soul, in its complex and undamaged entirety, isn't a job for a few weeks. *Poor Buddy,* she thought.

Bicé and Christian ran out of Victoria's room and into the center space of the house.

"Where is he?" asked Christian in a voice too calm to mean anything good. He wasn't whipping around frantically, as Bicé had expected.

"Where's who?"

"Our *brother,* Valentin."

Bicé didn't know where to start. *He's not our brother. Do we even have a real family? Do they know we exist? Maybe we should focus on the evil incarnate that raised us.* But Christian didn't seem interested.

"Why would you want to see Val?" asked Bicé.

"Because," said Christian, still infuriated, it seemed — but calm, impressively calm.

"Because why?" said Bicé, trying to chuckle while she said it.

"Because I want to find him — and kill him." Bicé shook her head. Christian wasn't the only one bubbling with anger, she thought. Belle had taken so much from her. She had taken her childhood, her memories of their parents, her whole life, all for some petty desire to be beautiful. What made Bicé furious more than anything else was that she knew now that Belle remembered. Belle knew what their parents looked like. She knew if their mother had an infectious laugh or if their father had a beard.

"I'm going to my room," said Bicé as she checked her watch.

Christian seemed to snap out of it. "What? Now?"

"I have a headache. I need to think. You can find Valentin on your own."

"OK, but I wasn't going to *actually* kill him. I just . . . he's just . . . It's just a lot."

"I know. That's why I'm going to my room."

"We should get out of here."

Bicé didn't bother to respond. She just went to her room, the room she used to study, her soothing, secluded cave, where she had everything she needed. Bicé turned the corner of her hall, practically running the last few steps. She had lost track of the time. Real time. After everything that had happened tonight, she hadn't had a chance to be alone. She pushed the door open and ran inside. She looked around, her eyes darting, and went straight for the end table. It was a little wooden table with a single drawer, hardly worth noticing. When she saw the empty tabletop, Bicé froze. Hands shaking, she reached for the drawer and pulled it open. It was empty. Trembling from head to toe, Bicé managed to pull herself toward a chair. She put both hands under her legs, to keep them from shaking. But she couldn't stop her breathing from growing more desperate, more frantic, until her whole body was wracked by giant dry heaves.

No one knew how lonely Bicé felt when she hid in her timeless cave. The darkness of those moments haunted her — the hopeless-ness of a world no longer spinning to its inevitable conclusion. The day before, she had allowed Belle into this space — this sacred and terrible space — so that she could help her redeem herself with Thomas. After knowing that Belle had given herself to Vileroy, it was an act of forgiveness by Bicé. And it only added to the pain when she found out later that it was Belle who had betrayed her. None of the other children could guess how she felt after all that, and now she couldn't even find the green bottles.

~⚮~

Valentin popped his head into Belle's room. She was still crying. Valentin ignored it. "Is Christian in here?" he asked. "Whoa, Belle, you should stop crying. It's getting worse."

"I don't care," she sobbed. "I don't care"—hiccup—"how ugly I get. Bicé hates me. I've lost my sister"—hiccup—"forever. I"—hiccup—"sold"—hiccup—"her out."

"Ah, Belle, don't cry. Maybe she'll forgive you. Now, can you just tell me where Christian is?"

Belle calmed down a bit and gave Valentin a strange look. "I don't know. What's wrong with you? Can't you see everything's falling apart?"

"OK, but when was the last time you saw him? Did he say where he was?"

Belle got up from her seat by the window.

"Where are you going?" Valentin asked.

"To find Bicé."

Belle wiped the tears off her face as she ran toward Bicé's room. On her way over, she caught a glimpse of herself in a candlelit window. Her heart gave a lurch. When Belle finally made it all the way down Bicé's hall, she stopped abruptly. She had expected to have to knock, to have to beg for Bicé to open the door. But the door was ajar. It had been left open carelessly—so unlike Bicé. The silence gave her an eerie feeling, as if something was wrong. She felt the way she used to feel when she was little and something bad had happened to Bicé. Like the way her knees hurt when Bicé got a scrape or the way she got a lump in her throat when their mother yelled at Bicé.

She reached for the door and pushed it open. She opened her mouth to say something, but suddenly all the air was knocked out of her body. There, staring silently into a tiny hand mirror, was Bicé. But it wasn't Bicé. Her hair was longer, her body shapelier, her face thinner, like their mother's. Belle gave a silent gasp. Her twin sister was at least twenty-five years old.

Belle wanted to rush over to her sister, to find out what had happened, but her legs wouldn't move. "Bicé — Bicé, is that you?"

Bicé's hands were still shaking, but she managed to motion her sister over. Suddenly something inside Belle felt absolutely, utterly, irreversibly sorry. Through her tear-blurred eyes, the twenty-five-year-old Bicé looked exactly like their mother. Belle ran over and buried her ruined face in Bicé's lap.

"I'm so sorry. I'm so sorry, Bicé. Please forgive me."

Bicé stroked Belle's dull mousy hair lovingly. She hadn't expected her anger to melt away so quickly. But Belle was sorry, and these were extreme circumstances. Belle could feel Bicé's hands still trembling. She lifted her head.

"What happened to you? Why?"

"I'm old, Belle."

"What do you mean?"

"I wasted my life, sitting alone, reading my books."

"What are you talking about?"

"Remember when Nicola gave us these gifts? When she told me that I could hide anytime I wanted?"

Hearing Bicé call Madame Vileroy by her first name was jarring to Belle. "Yeah," she said. "It was just five years ago, when we all got our gifts. I'm so sorry she's made you think you've been here all your life. It was just five years . . . not fifteen."

"No. I *have* been here all my life. She tricked me, Belle."

"But . . ."

"It's been so many years. At first, it was great. I could read all the books I wanted. She gave me tons of them. I could learn languages. She pushed me to keep going. How long do you think it takes to learn so many?"

"I . . . I don't know."

"Not days . . . not months. It takes *years. Years.* Do you understand?"

"But if you stopped time, then it doesn't matter how long—"

"She didn't tell me that my body would keep growing old. Everyone else stopped, but I kept going."

Belle's eyes grew round with understanding. "Oh, no," she whispered.

"She's been keeping me the same age as the rest of you with a serum that she gave me every night—a serum that erases the time that I spend hiding, as long as I keep taking it for the rest of my life. At first, when I didn't know that I was still growing, she told me it was medicine . . . for my headaches. But then, after I had done it way too much, she finally told me. But by then, I couldn't stop. Without the serum, I would die."

"Die?"

"I'm past death, Belle. The time I spent hiding, it's been more than a hundred years."

Belle felt a wave of nausea. Bicé let out a small laugh and went on.

"I was already in my twenties when we got here. Remember when we went to that school play? I turned thirty in the library. I spent a big chunk of my seventies at some golf game. Without the serum, I'll grow to my natural age and die."

Belle looked confused. "But you've already taken the serum, right? So it's done its work. Those years didn't count."

"That's not how it works. Maybe *erase* is the wrong word. The serum doesn't erase those years. It masks them. It hides the years that I spent hidden. See? And it only works if I keep taking it. She designed it like that on purpose. Nicola wants me to be dependent on her." Then Bicé looked down, ashamed. "That's how she's been keeping me here. I need her."

"I . . . I don't understand. Why would she . . . ?"

"It wasn't really clear to me either until tonight. I always wondered why she would give me such a big gift, with no strings attached. But then again, before that night when you brought Thomas over, I didn't really know who she was, and I thought she gave me the gift for the same reason she gave it to all of you. That she was some sort of witch and she had adopted us. But then, when I found out what you guys did, I wondered why she would give me the ability to hide. Did I sell my soul, too? Did I sell something else? Tonight, I finally realized what happened. She kidnapped me at first because that was the only way she could have you."

"I'm so sorry . . ."

Bicé put up her hand to silence her. "But then, at some point after that, she started to want my soul, too."

Belle gasped.

"But I wouldn't give it to her. I guess that's why I didn't have that mark on my chest. I just wasn't willing. And she never actually asked me flat out, since I didn't know who she was, and my memory was gone. So she gave me the gift, because she knew that I was confused and scared, that I would find it attractive—the chance to hide away, to be alone with my books. She knew that I would become addicted to hiding, use it too much, and then become dependent on her forever—even be willing to barter for my soul. She didn't tell me about the aging until I was already too old. Up until then, I thought the serum was for my headaches and to keep me awake while I hid."

Belle hiccuped, remembering the time when she had shared her sister's loneliness.

Bicé went on. "Then, after I found out about who she was, she gave me some time to decide, to choose between my soul and the serum. My soul or my life. And so I began to hide more and more, to prolong my life, and also because . . ." Bicé stopped, reconsidering her words. "My time has run out, Belle."

"What happens now?"

Bicé's voice broke. "She didn't leave me any for tonight. She doesn't need me anymore. She knows she can't have me. And she can't trust me." Belle looked confused, and Bicé went on. "A little while ago, even before I knew about the trick she had played on me, I started to reach a goal she never thought I would reach. It all went wrong for her and her plan, and so she started trying to stop me from hiding. I was learning too much. She would do things to scare me, send Victoria to spy, torture me in my dreams, come to me while I was hiding . . ."

Belle didn't want to know any more of this horrible story, this curse that she had inflicted on her sister, but she asked anyway. "What were you trying to do?"

"You'll know in time," said Bicé.

Bicé's resolve made Belle feel two inches tall. The only reason Bicé had been worth keeping was that she was the key to keeping Belle. But now it seemed that Madame Vileroy didn't want Belle anymore — and so she didn't need Bicé. A fresh surge of guilt washed over her.

"I'm sorry, Bicé. It's my fault you got into this." Belle began to sob again on Bicé's lap. "You don't deserve this."

"Yeah, I do. You wanted to be pretty, but I accepted her gift too. I drank her serum. I was arrogant enough to think I could know everything there was to know in one lifetime. I can't believe it . . . I spent my whole life in a cave." Bicé gave an ironic laugh.

Belle knew now why her sister had been so fidgety, so scared of the world she spent so little time in, always looking for a place to hide away.

"I wish I'd just waited," Belle said, her head still in Bicé's lap.

"What do you mean?" Bicé asked.

"You look beautiful. *We* would have been beautiful. Now, because of me, neither of us gets a chance."

Belle couldn't stop the tears from racing down her rough, blotchy cheeks. Inside, she felt a torrential regret. At twenty-five, her twin sister was something out of a 1920s postcard — so classic, her eyes like an oasis, pools so blue you'd think they were a mirage in the pale desert, even in a black-and-white card. She could almost see Bicé, the traveler, a true beauty with her gorgeous raven hair and long olive legs, how she would have been in another life, standing in a train station with a fashionable hat, hair like feathers, posing for a picture, looking so timeless you'd think she might not be real. But it was too late. Bicé looked older now, the fresh-faced beauty hurtling slowly toward middle age, and the unthinkable beyond. She was changing by the minute, and Belle felt her heart jump up in her throat.

"Bicé, we have to find the rest of that serum."

"And what about you?" asked Bicé.

"We don't have time for that. I'm OK with myself now. I've been addicted to that stuff long enough. I just want to leave. I'll live with what I have."

Bicé smiled at her sister. She could smell her stench stronger than ever now, like a rotting corpse turned inside out. As sorry as she felt for her sister, and for herself, Bicé knew that Belle had given up on her obsession. And that made her want to forgive, to live the last few hours of her life in peace with her sister.

Just then, Christian burst into the room. At the sight of Bicé, he stopped.

"I'm growing old." Bicé looked back at him.

Christian just stood there, looking stupid.

"Christian. It's me," said Bicé, trying to snap him out of it.

He stopped staring and said, "What?"

"Let's get out of here."

"You didn't want to leave before."

"I had to think about some things."

"But now?"

"Now I want to leave."

Belle, Bicé, and Christian ran out of the room with a new determination. Along the way, Belle told Christian the story. Finally, after all this time, Christian understood why Bicé had been reluctant to leave — that it was a life-and-death decision for her.

Had a sister ever made such a sacrifice, or even fathomed doing what Bicé was willing to do just then? She had forgiven all that they had done to her and decided to leave, knowing that if she took them away from there, away from any chance of finding her green bottles, she'd die before they even made it downtown. Christian realized that whenever he pressured her to leave, he had been telling her to lay down her life for them. They were halfway to the front door when Christian stopped.

"We can't go."

"I'm not spending my last hours here," Bicé said, pulling his arm.

"No, we're not just going to let you die. What happens if we get back that serum? Will you be able to go back to normal?"

Bicé shrugged. She wasn't sure of anything now.

"No matter what we do, we have to hurry," said Belle, watching the two moths circling their heads. "If those things are around, it's only a matter of time before Vileroy finds out."

Christian said, "I have a plan."

~∽∰∾~

Victoria had spent the better part of the night trying to revive her dying hive. She picked them up, one by one, to see if they were dead

359 ⓒ

or just stunned. Finally she had lain down and fallen asleep with the creatures covering her, some dead, some moving like a fitful blanket. When she awoke, what seemed like hours later, several of them had begun to fly around on their own and the floor full of carcasses began to clear, giving way to a new gray buzzing cloud. Victoria stood to one side, watching. They weren't as strong as they used to be. They were slow, weak, disoriented. Sometimes, a few of them would knock into each other. She stepped into the middle of the cloud. She caught a word here, a phrase there. She was about to stomp away when she saw two giant hornets fly in through the door, past her head, and into the dwindling, emaciated hive. Her mind began to soak up what the hornets had seen, what some of their brothers were seeing now — Buddy running down the hall, looking back at the bugs while they chased him. *Stupid droid.* He kept looking back, as if expecting that they would catch up with him. Then Victoria saw him enter Christian's room, sit by Christian's side, and pick up a colored pencil.

Christian looked at Buddy and said, "Maybe it's worth it."

Buddy sat with his notebook on his lap as if he was trying to entice Christian into teaching him some more.

"You think she'll take me back?"

Buddy nodded, keeping his head bowed, his sad eyes fixed on the floor.

Victoria's heart was beating faster and faster. Was Christian changing his mind again? When he had come into the house all those years ago as a ten-year-old, he had taken one look at all of them, and it seemed like he knew immediately what Vileroy was. He had changed his mind, didn't want her deal anymore, and tried to run away. Of course, by then it was too late. And now, Victoria laughed at the inconsistency of his decisions. So typical. So weak. Now he was back to grabbing for the prize.

"Maybe I could use it for good somehow. I could try to help people once I got powerful," said Christian.

Poor naive Christian. He had no idea. But it didn't matter to Victoria. All that mattered was that he seemed willing. She knew how much Madame Vileroy wanted Christian, how important this was to her. If Victoria could somehow get the credit for this, then Madame Vileroy would see how useful she was. She could teach her new things. They would get rid of the twins together.

"I should have won that award tonight, not Connor," said Christian.

Buddy nodded, skimming his finger on a page as if he was trying to remember each word.

"Victoria was right. I should have destroyed all of them."

Buddy looked up with a sympathetic grin. "Take a look at my chest," said Christian. He unbuttoned his shirt a little to show what had suddenly stung him. Victoria saw his bare chest, the water bottle in his hand, and the black oozing mark over his heart that had seemed to appear with a tiny squirt. That was it. She ran out of her gaunt, withered cloud of insects and toward Christian's room.

"Christian!" she yelled, a little too excitedly.

"What do *you* want?" Christian whipped around, with the dumbfounded Buddy peeking from behind him. A hornet and some moths were still circling overhead. One was resting on the ceiling. Victoria looked up at them thankfully. Then she looked back at Christian and said, "I just overhead some of what you said."

"So?"

"So I can help you. We can figure out what to ask Madame Vileroy. I'll take you to her."

"Why would I need you?"

"Because I'm Vileroy's favorite now."

"I'm pretty sure she still likes Valentin more than you," said Christian.

Victoria tried not to cringe. "I can send the moths to get her for you . . . if you want. We can talk to her together."

Victoria was trying to sound sweet but managed to sound greedier than ever. All she knew was that she wanted a piece of this action.

Victoria reached out her hand and took the two moths in her palm. She held them close to her face, as if she were nuzzling them. She whispered something to them, and in an instant, they took off toward the east wing.

~~∞~~

Bicé was hiding in a tiny hallway, branching out from the main hall leading to the east wing. Belle was with her, cowering, waiting for Madame Vileroy to come out.

"You think this will work?" she asked Belle.

"I know one thing. The only way she spies on us is those moths. She's not omniscient. She's not God."

"Still . . ." Bicé stopped talking for a moment and dropped her head. She couldn't stop staring at her aging hands. She ran her hands through her hair, now silvery-gray and a bit thinner. She felt the lines on her face, which were the lines of a woman even older than she was a few minutes before. "We're running out of time," she said.

Chapter 23

The Devil's Due

"Sarah? Sarah, are you there?"

"No, Benjamin, it's just the two of us now."

"Where did you take my Sarah?"

"Nowhere, dear. She's at home. Safe."

"I want to go back!"

"You can't go back. You sold your soul. You gave it to me so that I would save her life. And now she's back in your home, alive, happy—until tomorrow, when she finds you gone."

"You promised she wouldn't suffer."

"She won't. I'll make her forget all about you, if you like. You, on the other hand, are mine."

"Where are we?"

"This is my home. For you, it is a sort of purgatory. You will stay here. You will serve my children. You will help me give them the desires of their heart. And thus you will repay your debt to me."

"And what if I refuse to help you?"

"You won't. Because in exchange, I will give you a gift."

"What gift?"

"See this room? The one with the white window? You remember the white window, don't you? It can take you anywhere. You can see your Sarah, long after she's dead."

~⌒∞⌒~

Belle and Bicé saw the moths racing back toward the center space of the house, Madame Vileroy trailing behind them, her long black dress flying behind her. From this dark angle, she looked like a giant moth, perhaps the mother of all moths, following them toward some juicy prey. As soon as she had passed, Bicé took a deep breath and bolted toward the east wing, with Belle just behind her. The hall was dark and cold. Along the way, candles flickered in shallow winds from every direction, as if a million little mouths were breathing on them. But Belle and Bicé didn't notice. They had to get into the east wing; they had to find that serum. Still, entering Madame Vileroy's personal sanctuary felt like setting foot in the deepest circle of hell.

After a couple of minutes of poking around the branching hallways, they saw doors everywhere, halfway up the walls, on the ceiling, lying on their backs on the floor like hospital patients. It was as if a thousand different paths and decisions would lead to the same place, like all the dead ends of a maze. Belle and Bicé noticed a huge mahogany door that looked much too big to even fit into the apartment. It towered over them, like an ever-vigilant guard.

"That has to be it," said Belle.

"Wait," said Bicé. "No, I don't have a good feeling about this."

"Well, of course you don't," said Belle as she moved toward the door. "It's Vileroy's wing. But we have to find—" But before Belle could finish, she jumped back and screamed. Bicé leaped toward her and slapped her hand over Belle's mouth. The door was moving. It was alive. Something was writhing and undulating under the wood. Giant wormlike shapes were swimming through the wood.

"I . . . I saw . . . a face."

"I think I know what it is," said Bicé, pulling her sister away. "That's not the one we want."

"How do you know?" said Belle, frightened, trying to figure out what the big door could possibly be.

"I've lived in this house for a lot of years."

Belle and Bicé ran toward the door. Belle was surprised that it was unlocked, but Bicé didn't seem to notice. Belle had expected to find something scary behind that door, something truly evil. She thought that maybe Madame Vileroy lived in a state of constant fire and agony. She thought maybe the room would be hot and rancid like her room or filled with creepy-crawly things like Victoria's or a cave like Bicé's or home to a lost and tortured soul like Christian's. But it was none of these things. It was cool and pleasant, decorated lavishly, like the blue house. There were couches and pillows and big plush chairs. There were antique dressers full of drawers. There was a coffee table decorated with flowers. Belle wanted to laugh, and then she wanted to cry, because she realized that, of course, Vileroy would not live in the same horror that she gave to them.

"Watch the door. And watch for bugs," said Bicé as she began to ransack the room.

~⚬⚬⚬~

Madame Vileroy swept into the room.

"Well, Victoria. What do you want?"

Victoria ran up to Madame Vileroy. Christian watched as Victoria kept glancing back at him, making sure he couldn't hear as she whispered something to the governess.

"Madame Vileroy, I made him change his mind."

"Oh?"

"He's ready now. He wants to sell his soul. He wants to be one of us."

"Darling, you are such a fool. He turned me down only hours ago."

"He's changed his mind. I swear. *I* changed his mind."

Madame Vileroy spoke up, eyeing the water bottle: "Christian, dear, let me see your chest."

"Not yet," said Christian.

"See, Victoria?" Vileroy crossed her arms. "He hasn't changed his mind."

"Yes, I have," said Christian. "I just don't think you should get to see anything until you tell me exactly what I'm getting out of this."

"What would you like, dear?"

"I want to be a famous athlete."

"All right."

"And rich."

"Of course."

"And I want Victoria gone."

"What?" Victoria jumped.

For the first time since Christian had known him, Buddy burst into a joyous laugh. He slapped Christian on the back.

"I want Victoria to be sent back home. To her family. To live an ordinary life and not get her hands on any more power."

Victoria began to laugh.

But then: "Done," said Madame Vileroy.

Victoria let out an indescribable guttural noise. "Christian. What do you think you're doing?"

"So you would do that? You'd get rid of Victoria to get me?"

"Victoria will do well on her own. She is very clever," Madame Vileroy answered coolly.

"Well," said Christian, throwing a meaningful look at Victoria, "I'm not totally sure that's what I want." He wanted her to read his mind at that moment, to hear him say, *See, Victoria? She doesn't love you. You can't trust her. Give this up.* But there was no sign of recognition on her face.

"All right, what else would you like?" Madame Vileroy asked.

"I want Buddy to be safe, and I want him cured of whatever it is that made him this way."

Victoria had moved into a corner now. She seemed to be talking to her fists again. She whirled around before Vileroy could answer and yelled out.

"Belle and Bicé are in the east wing!"

Madame Vileroy narrowed her eyes at Christian. He couldn't hide it anymore. Her eyes searched him. She turned and walked out of the room. As she strode out, Christian heard her honey-sweet voice drifting back into the room, whispering, "Good-bye, Benjamin."

Without thinking, Christian turned to Buddy. Looking into his face, Christian could tell that he was no longer a mindless droid. There was something very alive in his eyes, as if a lost part of him had come back.

"Buddy, what's wrong?" Christian asked. But Buddy could barely catch his breath.

"Christian," he spat out slowly, gurgling on the first word that Christian had ever heard him speak.

"What is it?" Christian grabbed hold of Buddy's arm.

But Buddy fell to the ground, lifeless.

Christian's eyes welled up with tears. He pulled aside his shirt for Victoria to see. The black mark on his chest had streaked down to his stomach. "It was ink."

When Christian had come up with the plan to fool the insects, Buddy had been scared. But he had pulled it off with all the loyalty of a true friend. He had played his part perfectly and tricked even the smartest. And Victoria had fallen for it and so had her disgusting swarm; Buddy had led them right to Christian. It was so easy for Victoria to believe that Buddy was stupid, that he was an empty dummy, that he would let Christian sell his soul. But even though so much of his mind had been erased or corrupted by Vileroy's tricks and tortures, Buddy had a good soul. He was a real person, as real as any of them. *Benjamin.* He had only wanted to help Christian, and the children before him. Buddy was dead now, but before that, he had been Christian's best friend.

~∽⊙⊙⊙

"Hurry up, hurry up!" said Belle from the other side of the small door.

"Are you sure there aren't any bugs here?" Bicé called back.

"Just move —"

But Belle didn't have time to finish her sentence. Because just then, she felt a hand on her shoulder.

"Having fun without me?" said Valentin, in that sort of slimy tone he'd taken on more and more lately.

"Valentin, what are you doing?"

"What are *you* doing? And where's Christian?"

"Christian's in the main room. Go find him. I'm sure he'll want to hear your poem or whatever."

"Who's in there?" Valentin glanced past Belle toward the door.

"Nobody. Just go, Valentin."

~∽⊙⊙⊙

Bicé could hear talking just outside the door. Someone was there. She had pulled the entire room apart and still no serum. There were bottles and boxes everywhere, but not a single one looked like the stuff she'd been drinking every night. She was so scared; she was losing her concentration. She kept opening the same drawers over and over, pulling the same pillows apart. Her hand was twitching visibly now. All that nervousness and paranoia that had built up inside her — the effect of years of solitary living, of slowly becoming a recluse — seemed to be coming out all at once.

"Where is that bottle? Where is it? Where is it?"

Bicé started to mumble nervously to herself. First in Greek, then Welsh, then Korean. Her mind seemed to be operating separately from her body, running at its own breakneck speed. She heard the voices outside again.

"Forget it, Belle. I'm going in." It was Valentin. Then she heard a noise, like a kick to the stomach, and a gasp.

Then she saw it, the drawer in the wall, painted the same color as the wallpaper.

"What's this?" she said to herself as she pulled it open. Her hands were now shaking so much that the drawer came crashing out, spilling all its contents to the floor. But there it was, the familiar bottle, full of the green liquid she had come to know so well. She grabbed it and tried to pull the top off, but it was stuck, and her arms were growing weak. Bicé pulled and pulled, every few moments turning toward the door, just waiting for someone to come bursting through.

Then she saw something else. A rolled-up piece of parchment was lying on the floor. Taking another look over her shoulder, she opened it up to read. The message was cryptic. Written in a scrawling script, it looked as if it was thousands of years old. Bicé had to squint to make it out. It was some sort of recipe. A set of instructions set in rhyme by Vileroy or maybe someone even older. *How long has Vileroy been doing this?* Bicé wondered. *Was she ever a child herself?* Maybe the recipe was written by Vileroy's own governess, or her governess's governess. Whatever the case, there it was—her way out, a recipe for a lifetime of potion to keep her alive:

A nightly sip to stay the hand of time,
A fount of youth to keep you in your prime,
But nothing in this world comes without cost:
For every gain, an equal treasure lost.

Youth in a jar, a witch's brew: ensnare
The beauty of a child whose blood you share.
One taste and your two fates forever tie,
A curse to use the other till you die.

A single pool of youth to share, some each;
An ugly death for one, and one a leech.
Escape this fate? You won't, though you might try,
Though you might weep, and cheat, and steal, and lie.

As Bicé read the message on the parchment, she finally understood, and she felt sad, for herself and her sister, whose lives had been ruined by each other. Bicé threw another glance at the door. Her hands were sweaty, and she felt cheated. *How can this be?* The antiaging serum was made by stealing someone's beauty. Someone with shared blood. Bicé didn't want to accept it, but it was hardly a question. Poor Belle. *That's the reason she became ugly — because all her beauty was used to make this potion so that Vileroy could trap me.* Vileroy must have slowly leached away Belle's true beauty — the beauty that was inherent in her before the governess gave her a new, mesmerizing face. Under that ravishing mask, no one would have noticed that she was getting worse and worse, her loveliness seeping away and replaced by vanity and pride, leaving her ugly inside and out. Then, finally, when Vileroy wanted it, years of deterioration appeared suddenly on the poor girl's face. Bicé felt a deep pain in her chest. She was complicit in her sister's ugliness — and in her extreme vanity — because she had spent years drinking away her sister's true beauty.

At the same time, a part of Bicé, the part that mourned the loss of her formative years, remembered that Belle was the one who had gotten them into this. *In a way, isn't this a fitting punishment for her? Wasn't she the one who traded me in so she could be beautiful? Wasn't she the one who saw my life as less valuable than her vanity?* But then Bicé chastised herself for thinking this way. She was far too old for pettiness now. Besides, there was something that bothered her even more. *A curse to use the other till you die.* Would she have to keep using Belle in order to stay alive? Make her uglier? Die when her beauty was fully spent?

For a terrible moment, Bicé just stood there, losing track of the seconds — not hiding, not grabbing hold of the fabric of time but letting it slip through her fingers as she stood motionless. *So this is how it's going to be, just like before, even if we escape? How appropriate.* For Bicé to stay alive, Belle would have to give up the one thing she had betrayed her sister for in the first place. She'd have to atone for handing Bicé's life over to the demon Vileroy by giving up the outer beauty that had seemed so much more important. Maybe this way, she'd regain some shred of integrity, or if not that, a little redemption. Someday, Bicé would be a shriveled old woman, tired of mind, back sore, and Belle would be a ghoul, deformed and undignified, but they could still be together, and they'd be as close as any twins could ever be.

∽⊗⊗⊙

"You'll be sorry for that!" hissed Valentin after Belle kicked him in the stomach.

"Sorry — so sorry, Valentin." Belle tried to help Valentin up, but Valentin pushed her away. She turned toward the room again.

"Belle, would you like to explain what you're doing in my wing?"

Belle froze when she heard Madame Vileroy's voice. She turned to see the governess standing behind a fallen Valentin, arms crossed, with Victoria lingering behind her. Christian was running down the hall after them, and came to a skid when he saw Valentin. Suddenly he felt sorry for Valentin, lying there, emaciated, eyes bloodshot from trying to remember his own lies, tangled in a web of his own creation, never sure which parts of his life had actually happened. For a moment, Christian thought that Valentin was the unluckiest of them all.

"Where's Bicé?" Madame Vileroy demanded.

No one spoke. But Belle's heart was audible. She closed her eyes and prayed hard that Madame Vileroy would not go into the room.

"Step aside."

Madame Vileroy moved past Belle and pushed the door open.

~⊗⊗⊙

Ignoring the recipe for the moment, forgetting all its ghastly implications, Bicé focused her strength on the task of pulling open the bottle, which was still firmly stuck. Finally, with a barely audible *pop*, the cork came loose in her hands. Bicé's hands shook as she moved it to her lips, making sure not to spill a drop. Could she really do this? Could she take a drink knowing that every sip came at the expense of her sister's soul? But then, before she could drink, she heard a noise, and the governess glided into the room like a raging storm. On seeing Madame Vileroy, a flood of desperation washed over Bicé. Her eyes darted, and her lips quivered. She couldn't die here. She couldn't surrender in the presence of so much evil. Bicé's frail body shook at the awful thing that she had to do, the thing she knew she *would* do for the very first time with full knowledge. In that instant, as she prepared to drink, Bicé felt her heart thump and her head spin. She gasped as Vileroy neared, and before she knew it, she had dropped the bottle to the floor, shattering it into a thousand pieces, spilling the liquid across Madame Vileroy's sanctuary.

"Ah, poor Bicé. It seems we're going to lose you, dear."

Bicé simply stood, not knowing what to say, what to do in this moment, the most important moment of her life. She had lost the liquid that would save her life. But no one could save her from Vileroy but herself. Before they could escape, they had to confront her. The children would finally have to face their governess.

The old demon tilted her head. "Why waste your last few hours trying to leave? Might as well stay here and die in comfort."

Bicé tried to say something, but all she could do was squeak out a tiny "no."

"What *are* you going to do without that bottle? Of course, dear, I'm always willing to make a deal."

Bicé hesitated, the fear of death so palpable and real in her heart that she almost choked on her own spit and tears. She felt the fear overtake her, make her weak, make everything else fade in comparison. And then she felt a wave of guilt and shame. Because there, in that instant, she had almost given in. She had asked herself the fateful question: *What is a soul, anyway? Can I sell something so intangible for something as precious as my life?*

But then, Bicé had another realization. *How can Vileroy give me my life? The potion is gone. What gives her this power to give and take life? To dangle death like a toy over my head?* Bicé's tears dried and she pulled herself to her full height.

"No!" she said loudly, without hesitation.

The demon governess raised an eyebrow. "Are you sure that's a wise choice?"

"I'm not talking about your deal, Nicola."

The governess's smile faded.

Everything that had happened over the years, everything she had done and not done showed itself clearly in Bicé's mind. She thought of all the deals the others had made. Had she made one? She thought of all the opportunities. All the times she had resisted. Why had she taken the potion? The first time, all those years ago, she didn't know she was aging. But now Bicé could see things much more clearly.

"I'm talking about this. This trick you've played on me. I'm saying no to *that*. I'm saying no to everything you did to me while my eyes were closed. And no to everything you took while my back was turned. You have no right!"

Vileroy laughed nervously.

"I never got anything for this," said Bicé. "I never asked you for anything. I have not once made a deal with you."

"You drank the potion."

"You tricked me! I accepted a cure for my headaches. Nothing more. I did *not* give you my life!"

At that, Nicola Vileroy recoiled and her face grew red with fury.

"There are rules, Nicola. You can't just take what you want."

"And what do *you* know about *that*? What do you know about *my* rules?"

"Because you don't spend so many decades in someone's house without knowing their game."

Belle and Christian moved toward the door, standing to one side and peering in fearfully, while Victoria and Valentin looked in from the other side of the door.

"Whoa . . ."

"Who's that?"

"What the . . ."

It seemed they all spotted it at once.

Inside the room stood two women. Both looked regal, proud, and in the prime of adulthood, though they were both much older. Both were beautiful, facing each other like hungry tigers. Bicé's silver mane was loose and shining, and her face had the steely resolve of a woman who had taken control. Was she still aging? None of them could tell. She was certainly not fifteen. Her eyes shone with the wisdom of her years. But her face and body were strong now, and to Belle, she looked more like their mother than ever. Bicé would never again be a teenager; she could never go back. She had spent far too much time living, had learned too much, gained too much knowledge about this world. But while the others were standing outside, something had happened to make Bicé stop dying.

Behind the two women, a giant hole had been blown into the wall. But it wasn't a hole, really — more like a tear. Somehow, Bicé had managed to tear through the crimson-cube house, revealing the empty space on the other side. The curtain that usually hung against that wall was torn in half, and the crimson wall behind it looked like shredded fabric. Behind that was the open air, leading straight down to the street. *The far wall must be beyond the actual apartment,* Belle thought. A strong night wind was blowing into the room through the tear, and a patch of moonlight was illuminating the two women, their fists clenched, their hair blowing. For the first time, they could see

Madame Vileroy with her blond hair wild and loose and her branded eye grotesque with fear. The room had been completely torn apart. All the beautiful things that had decorated it minutes before were destroyed, leaving nothing but a moonlit heap of garbage on the floor.

"Why is Bicé just standing there?" Belle whispered.

"I think she's done hiding," Christian whispered back.

"What happened to the wall?" Valentin asked no one in particular.

Belle yelled out, "Bicé, let's go!"

Madame Vileroy laughed. "And where will you go, my dear? With a face like that?"

Belle began to cry. But then she noticed that something was making Madame Vileroy look alarmed. Bicé was mumbling something under her breath, softly at first. It sounded like all those times when Bicé was trying to decipher languages. Using one to learn another. Figuring things out in her head. Completing families of tongues and dialects, and then connecting them with each other. Finding the links between entire groups of languages, not just one dialect with another.

She started with whispering . . . whispering . . . whispering.

What are these words? How do they fit together?

And then the realization of how much she knew. Building blocks falling together after that one crucial piece is found.

Bicé's words grew louder and louder as she continued, until everyone else could hear her too.

"What language is *that*?" Victoria said.

"Something Asian."

"No, that's just French."

"It's some kind of African."

"Shh," Belle said, listening intently to her twin sister. "It sounds like all of them."

Bicé was speaking louder and louder, saying something that made Madame Vileroy take a step back.

"You foolish girl," Vileroy said, and attempted to step forward again. But Bicé didn't stop. And Madame Vileroy couldn't move forward.

"Look!" Christian said, pointing behind Madame Vileroy. Another wall behind her was beginning to tear — big, thick pieces of it falling to the ground, singed. Behind it, they could see the white walls of their real Manhattan apartment, completely unharmed.

"What is she saying?" Victoria said as she clung to Valentin, who was trying to push her away.

"It's all of them," Belle whispered to Christian.

"What do you mean?"

"It's none of the languages, but it's all of them. The one people used to speak, before it was split into hundreds of different ones. It's a combination of every language on earth — some people say it's some kind of angelic language. Somehow otherworldly."

"How do you know?"

"That must have been Bicé's goal. To learn all the languages, so that she could learn the one lost language that links everyone. That's why Vileroy was trying to stop her. That's why she asked me about our parents."

"Belle, how the hell do you know that?" Valentin asked, skeptical.

"Because our mother told us about it. She told us about the theories that this language exists, that scholars have tried to decipher it, to put it back together. But none of them can speak enough languages to do it."

"Wow, I feel like an idiot," said Christian, his mouth hanging open.

"Why?"

"I told Bicé she needed more goals. . . ."

Madame Vileroy turned around to see her house tearing itself apart. Though her face looked as serene as ever, her fingers were twitching at her side. She turned to Bicé and said something back, something harsh and cacophonous, in a language none of them understood. The sound of her voice made Belle cringe. Christian's hands automatically flew to his ears. Every syllable coming out of her mouth was excruciating. As Madame Vileroy continued, Bicé's voice countered. For a moment, Belle thought that her sister was winning this war. But then, suddenly, Bicé spoke in a language Belle could understand.

"Nicola, I'm taking the children." Her voice was thunderous, like a lioness protecting her cubs.

"They're *my* children. They chose me. They sold themselves to me."

"I'm taking them back." Bicé signaled for Belle and Christian, and instinctively they ran to her. Victoria and Valentin followed but stood apart, close to Madame Vileroy.

Standing there, in the windy room, Belle felt like she was looking in a mirror. An old, yet ageless woman with her two children, her daughter a monster and her son a thief. That was the picture on both sides of the room.

Vileroy. The old demon. Breathtaking. Fearsome. Timeless.

And Bicé. Weary traveler. Sister. Mother. The girl who spoke every language in the world but never managed a conversation. How strange, thought Belle, what her sister had done. Bicé had failed to entice even one person to be her friend, yet she had learned to summon God and the angels in their own words.

"You can't—" Vileroy's voice thundered.

"You have done enough to me to buy back both of their lives. They can choose."

On hearing Bicé's words, Christian turned to Victoria and Valentin. "Come with us," he said. "Don't stay here."

Victoria laughed. She ran to Madame Vileroy and looked up at her, seeking some approval. Madame Vileroy, once more the loving mother, put her hand on Victoria's head. "Your parents would be proud, Victoria. They wanted you to be the best. And now you will be."

Victoria beamed with happiness. Madame Vileroy turned to Christian. "Victoria is smart enough to know that I'm her only family. Christian, are you going to give up everything now? Be mediocre? Poor?"

"I'm going," Christian said. "Valentin, come with us. Please. It doesn't matter what happened. She made you do those things. If we leave, we can start over. It'll be for real this time."

Valentin had his hands in his pockets, and he seemed to be writing something on the floor with his feet. For the first time since he had known Valentin, Christian saw him look ashamed. He looked as though he could cry for everything he had done, as though he were truly sorry. Christian smiled at him and said again, "Come with us, Val."

Valentin took his hands out of his pockets and ran them through his hair. "I'm sorry, Christian. For all the stuff I did. . . ."

"That's OK," said Christian. "Come on anyway. I know she made you do it."

But when Valentin finally moved from his spot, he didn't go toward Christian. He dropped his head and walked shamefully toward Madame Vileroy. "No. She didn't make me do anything."

A noise flew from Christian's mouth, as if he were trying to say something and laugh and cry and cough at the same time.

"Sorry, bro," said Valentin. "Ordinary just isn't enough for me."

"Let's go," said Bicé.

"You can't," said Madame Vileroy again, just as Bicé was making her way to the door. "I still have Belle's soul." Madame Vileroy glanced at the big mahogany door, across the hall. It began to move and writhe, as it had done before. A sick feeling swept through Belle's stomach. Is that what that was? Like a zombie, Belle began to walk toward the door. She could feel herself walking, but somehow she had no control over it. Bicé reached out and grabbed her hand.

"Belle, no!" she yelled. But Belle kept walking. Bicé ran around and stood in front of Belle. "Don't go through that door. Do you understand me?"

"Don't listen to her, Belle," Madame Vileroy said in a soothing voice. "You want it back, don't you? Go and get it. It's right there, beyond that door."

Belle's feet kept moving, as if on their own, toward the threshold. Christian, too, was mesmerized by the writhing, pulsating structure, watching the weird shapes trying to escape through the wood. Suddenly

Bicé whipped around. In one motion, she put one arm around Belle's waist and held out the other like a shield, toward Madame Vileroy. She said something else, loudly, furiously, in the language she had spoken before. Madame Vileroy was knocked backward, and another section of the crimson house fell away, revealing a tiny window and a fire escape. Bicé made a beeline for the fire escape. Christian followed, and Bicé dragged Belle, as she tried to resist and reach out for the mahogany door. "Stop it, Belle. Stop it!" Bicé yelled to her sister. "We're leaving; we're going to start over."

"But she'll come for us."

"No! She doesn't have any power over us. We've accepted our consequences. It's all a bluff."

"But look at that door!" Belle shrieked. "She has my—"

"It's an illusion, Belle. Selling your soul—it's not like that. It's something you keep doing every day. It's something you can stop doing now!"

Belle swallowed and waited, as if somehow someone would confirm this.

In that moment of indecision, when Bicé could see that Belle had no idea what she was supposed to do, Bicé felt an immense grief for her. Belle had gone along with the deals. She had given herself to evil so easily. She had done enough to fill her with a lifetime of guilt and agony. But she too had been tricked.

Taking hold of Belle's hand, trying to force her to leave this place, Bicé felt Belle's pain as her own. Much more than she ever did before. Much more than when they were small and Bicé winced at Belle's small wounds. Now the pain was coming from deep inside. It was a part of her own experience. Not like a twin. But like a daughter.

Just like a daughter.

Belle reached out toward the writhing door. The hands and faces trapped inside seemed to pull at the wood, as if trying to run through a curtain. But to her own surprise, Belle felt no fear. Her hand quivered as she finally touched it, inching past the surface of the wood. She reached inside and felt around, but there was nothing. Like a trick of the light, the faces disappeared as her hand moved through them. Belle turned and ran.

"But . . . are you going to die?" Christian asked Bicé, as they ran past the shredded wall and through the window.

"I found the cure," said Bicé.

"But you're not getting younger."

"I'm going to stay this way." Bicé gave Christian a smile that told him that this was better — that he should have courage.

Just as the three were making their way down the fire escape and onto one of the balconies below, Christian heard something.

"What's that?" he said, looking up through the window into their apartment. Madame Vileroy had receded into the shadows, but something was growing louder and louder, until it was deafening. Suddenly, a plague of insects shot out of the window like a cannon, covering them like a thick, revolting blanket. Belle screamed. Bicé turned to Christian. "Stop them like you did before." As the swarm hovered around Christian, touching every surface of his body, he closed his eyes and prepared to steal one last time. After a moment, he opened his eyes. No change.

"We should have known. We can't use her gifts now," said Bicé. "Just run."

They tried to ignore the insects as they climbed down the fire escape and ran down the street. Bicé glanced back and caught the frightened look on Christian's face. He tried to seem tough, but without his gift, he was unarmed for the first time in a long time. At a nearby intersection, the three stopped and looked at one another, confused, wondering which way to turn. They lingered there like little children running from home, aimless and scared and full of self-doubt. But then Bicé smiled and continued on and the other two followed. In the distance, they could hear a passing car on the avenue. But on that little street in New York, there was no one to notice the three fugitives running away in the night.

Postlude

Aftermath

It was over. But for three lost children, it was the beginning of something new. They could feel it already, in the cool night, not so terrifying anymore. The darkness was no longer hopeless, but full of the promise of daylight. Christian, Bicé, and Belle walked down the streets, everything awake around them — shops, bistros, delis. Had the whole world gone on without them? Had their battle with Vileroy changed a thing? No, it wouldn't make the morning news for Thomas's father to see. Mrs. Wirth and Mrs. Spencer wouldn't whisper about it to their so-called friends. They wouldn't care. They'd be too busy pushing their children, Lucy and Connor, too far, too much. Ms. LeMieux would keep capitalizing on their obsessions, and competition would get stiffer every year. But these three souls had escaped. They were out of it. After this, no evil would scale their walls and steal them in the night. Because somehow, inside their hearts, they knew something about their governess, something about Madame Vileroy, this *friend of Faust,* that they didn't know before.

Here's what they know: that *she* doesn't know everything. She has spies everywhere, maybe some on your shoulder, but she can't be in your heart— not if you don't want her to be. She's lived a long time, though. Stories, myths, and fables of her are all over history books. She's been around so long that she has a sense about people, knows what they're like. If you imagine someone watching you all the time, even when you think you're alone, hearing every word you whisper to yourself, seeing every time you make a face, that someone would know more about you than you think. She could even guess what you're thinking—and even though she wouldn't know for sure, she'd mostly be right.

Even though they were no longer afraid, the three runaways would never stop wondering about their other two siblings. They had tried to bring Victoria and Valentin with them. For Christian's part, he forgave Valentin what he'd done. Over the years, Christian took the time to voice his hopes for Valentin, many times over. *If he gets another chance, I hope he takes it.*

And maybe Victoria too. But somehow they all knew that what Victoria wanted most couldn't be had the way she'd chosen to get it.

As for the three of them, they had a whole world to discover. But the lesson was hard-won. They all lost something. Everything didn't go back to normal, and redemption didn't come with a do-over. Vileroy's house was behind them, but Bicé was exhausted after only a few miles. Belle bought a hooded sweatshirt to hide her face, even in the warm weather.

As they walked, Belle found the courage to tell her sister about that night—that frightful, lonely night when the thief Vileroy came to her and offered her the world she wanted. And though Bicé forgave her, Belle never mentioned that moment when Bicé first woke up in a strange bed of a dark house, her mind aching, and said, "Where are we?" and Belle looked at her, pretending not to get it and said, "We're at home, silly."

Where would you find five lost children after so many years gone by? Years after their escape, perhaps they would think back and reflect on the family they had made for themselves, the dark counterparts they had left behind. From that day on, Bicé took care of Belle and Christian, as if they were real adopted children. No, they didn't fit in anywhere they went, but for the most part, that was all right with them. They had each other. And they had more. Did Belle and Bicé ever find their parents? Did Christian become a writer? Did he conquer his fears? Perhaps. They may do so still. They may do so many things. For three lost children, this was no storybook ending, but it wasn't over. Maybe it was a storybook beginning.